THE BANYA

Previous titles by the author

NOVELS

Angels in the Snow
The Kites of War
For Infamous Conduct
The Red House
The Yermakov Transfer
Touch the Lion's Paw (filmed as Rough Cut)
Grand Slam
The Great Land
St Peter's Plot
I, Said the Spy
Trance
The Memory Man
The Red Dove
The Judas Code
The Golden Express
The Man Who Was Saturday
Vendetta
Chase
Triad
The Night and the City
The Gate of the Sun

AUTOBIOGRAPHIES

The Sheltered Days
Don't Quote Me But
And I Quote
Unquote

UNDER THE PSEUDONYM RICHARD FALKIRK

Blackstone
Blackstone's Fancy
Beau Blackstone
Blackstone and the Scourge of Europe
Blackstone Underground
Blackstone on Broadway
The Twisted Wire
The Chill Factor

THE BANYA

Derek Lambert

SINCLAIR-STEVENSON

First published in Great Britain by
Sinclair-Stevenson Limited
7/8 Kendrick Mews
London SW7 3HG, England

A CIP catalogue record for this book is
available from the British Library.
ISBN: 1 85619 044 7

Photoset by Rowland Phototypesetting Limited
Bury St Edmunds, Suffolk
Printed and bound in Great Britain by
Clays Limited, St Ives plc

FOR
DON RIDGE,
Informant and Friend

Acknowledgements

M Y thanks to my good friend Basil Cudlipp-Green, former pairs skating champion of the world, for his help in explaining the technicalities of skating. Although I once lived there, I have also read many books about Russia and I should like to single out *Soviet Union* by Martin Walker, one of the Collins Independent Travellers' Guides series, and one of the best of its kind. Also inevitably, *The Russians*, by Hedrick Smith, still the ultimate reference book about modern Russia.

'The land and the past are like the steadying sails of reassurance to the Russians. So often the emigré, who is deprived of them, finds himself at an odd disadvantage in the world outside. He finds it hard to set a safe course.' – Peter Ustinov

Part I

1

The little pickpocket, carrying a bottle of vodka stolen from a grave, sensed the unease in the bath-house the moment he entered the changing-room from the street.

The Kremlin chauffeur who usually smacked down the dominoes as though he despised them was parading them gently; the bodybuilder was flexing his biceps without the reverence he normally accorded them; the stallholder was chewing his salted fish abstractedly, splashing beer on the foothills of his belly.

The pickpocket handed the vodka – Golden Ring, the best – to the ancient attendant, gave him fifty kopeks to guard it and, in a voice as furtive as his fingers, asked the stallholder what was wrong.

The stallholder, pouring beer down his salt-thirsty throat, wiped his mouth with the back of his hand and nodded towards a corner of the room not favoured by the light from the chandelier.

The pickpocket understood. The man standing in the gloom was not merely a stranger – they were common enough in a Moscow banya – he was an alien. The pickpocket felt this as keenly as he felt the presence of a police decoy in the metro stations where he plied his trade.

The newcomer was embarking upon the ritual conventionally enough. Stripping, weighing himself, wrapping a sheet round his waist. . . . And yet. . . . Although his face had Slavonic angles to it, his black hair was too fashionably cut, athlete's body too competitive to be a run-of-the-mill visitor; more pertinently, he conducted himself with a wariness that the pickpocket instantly identified.

'Who is he?' the pickpocket asked.

3

'Why don't you find out?' replied the stallholder whose truculence might one day be his executioner. 'You're the one to do it.'

'How can I search the pockets of a naked man?'

'His clothes are over there.' The stallholder pointed at a row of disparate jackets and trousers, symbolising a classless society that existed only inside the banya, suspended from mangled wire hangers.

'I've given my word not to deprive patrons.' He rarely used the harsher terminology of his profession.

'Your word.' The stallholder nodded towards the attendant who was clutching the bottle of vodka as though it contained nitroglycerine. 'Where did you get that fire-water? From a corpse?'

The pickpocket, astonished at his perspicacity, said: 'From a grave as it happens. Left there as a bribe for a degenerate caretaker. But I didn't take the cakes,' added the pickpocket who set his own ethical standards.

'Ah, the food for the birds, the wings of the soul.' Despite his rough exterior the stallholder possessed a lyrical turn of phrase which he punctuated with oaths. 'By eating the cakes they will immortalise the spirit of the corpse. Shit, didn't it occur to you that they might take a nip of vodka as well.'

'In a sealed bottle?' The pickpocket examined his restless fingers, their nails painted with colourless lacquer.

'God, what people we are. Birds sustain the soul and yet if one flies into a room it means death.'

The stranger walked past, bare feet slapping the chipped, marble floor trodden in Tsarist times by the feet of the noble and the decadent.

The stallholder nudged the pickpocket. 'Now's your chance.'

'To do what?'

'Pick his brains instead of his pockets.'

'You know I can't stand the heat.'

'Why come to a banya then?'

'I like the company,' replied the pickpocket, mentally excluding the stallholder from the generalisation.

'He may be a spy. They will do anything to undermine us.'

The pickpocket, aware that *they* were the city planners who

4

wanted to pull down the bath-house, said: 'If he's a spy then I'm a people's court judge.'

'A double bluff? Who would suspect anyone so obvious? Now get in there.' The stallholder took a bite from the leathery fish and chewed aggressively.

The pickpocket undressed and, conscious of his apologetic body, swathed himself with a sheet and strode into the steam-room.

The heat was a wall.

Coughing, he made his way to the lowest tier of the seats where the heat was supposed to be less intense. 'Water!' some-one shouted. Dutifully the pickpocket, as the latest arrival, fetched a zinc bucket and tossed its contents onto the fire-bricks. Someone added eucalyptus. Not beer, thank God, which was sometimes favoured.

The pickpocket peered through the steam for the stranger, praying that he wouldn't be at the top of the tiers where the heat poached your eyes.

Around him patrons beat each other with bundles of birch twigs until their limbs and torsos were as pink as boiled prawns.

A growling voice which the pickpocket recognised as the property of a coal miner from Ukraine issued from the fog. 'More water on the bricks.'

Another voice, a little breathless: 'The heat will melt us.'

'Only Muscovites and members of the great Russian Republic. Why don't you all go and play games in the changing-room?'

'There are old people here,' said the breathless voice.

'So? Isn't that why we all came here, to suffer?'

'But not to die.'

'Very well,' the miner said. 'No more water. What hope is there for *perestroika* with Russians organising it? It should have been left to the Ukrainians.'

Here we go, thought the pickpocket, continuing to peruse the steam. He spotted the stranger two steps above the floor. He wore his sheet like a toga and the pickpocket felt that he wanted company. He closed in on him. 'Haven't seen you around here before, comrade.'

'My first visit.' The stranger, the alien, regarded the pick-pocket with grey, uncompromising eyes.

'Are you from Moscow?'

5

'I sometimes wonder where I am from.'

The accent eluded the pickpocket. He tried again. 'But you have a residential permit for Moscow?' He shifted uneasily on the hard ledge, aware that, although he was the scrutineer, it was he who was being scrutinised. 'You're visiting a relative?'

'Trying to trace one.'

'Ah. Perhaps I can help you. . . .'

'Perhaps.' The stranger stared at the pickpocket who had endured just such perusals in court.

On the tier above them two stalwarts smote each other with their twigs as though they were duelling.

'I come here most days,' the pickpocket said. 'Not necessarily in the steam-room. . . .'

'What do you do for a living?' the stranger asked.

'I'm a collector.'

'Of what?'

'Valuables.' The pickpocket shrugged his wet, chicken-bone shoulders.

'Then you must know many influential people in Moscow.' The stranger stretched and the muscles clasped to his ribs moved sinuously. 'And your parents. . . .?'

'What about them?'

'They must have been here during the Great Patriotic War.'

'One of them. My mother died when the Germans were at the gates of Moscow.'

'And your father is still alive?'

'Just.'

'Could I speak to him? He might be able to help me find out what happened to the relative.'

The pickpocket frowned: the accent was tantalising. 'What part of the Soviet Union do you come from, comrade?'

'I'm not Russian,' the stranger said. 'I'm American.'

Or was he? Michael Cooper had never been sure. Not even when he changed his name to try and exorcise the spirit of *Rodina*, Mother Russia.

After World War II, the Great Patriotic War, his parents, accused unjustly of collaborating with the Germans, had es-

caped from the Soviet Union to the United States. Michael –
Mikhail in those days – was born in 1948 in New York on the
fringe of the Lower East Side between Second Avenue and
Lafayette Street but he might just as well have been in the Arbat
in Moscow. His parents spoke only Russian in the cabbage-
smelling apartment house, the neighbours were Russian and
Ukrainian and his father, a man moulded to suffer, reminded
him continually of his birthright.

Even now, at the age of forty-two, whispers of those childhood sermons delivered to him in bed, reached him through
the years. His father pacing the creaking floorboards on nights
when the air was like soup and transporting him to a wooden
house in Vitebsk, west of Moscow.

'How those houses blazed when the German tanks rolled in.'
He stood at the window, sniffing the long-ago smoke. 'And do
you know who set fire to them?'

'The Germans?' ventured Mikhail, hearing the sound of
breaking glass and a woman's cackling laugh in the street
outside.

'We did. Burned our own homes so that the Germans couldn't
shelter in them in the winter. God, those winters, how I loved
them. Skates singing, snow like icing-sugar.' Two vodkas made
him lyrical, four wretched.

He retired to the living room where his mother, knitting
needles clicking, was listening to Jack Benny on the radio; she
didn't understand the jokes but, being a busily cheerful woman,
she enjoyed the laughter. Mikhail heard the click of bottle
against glass. When his father returned his emotions were
ranging freely.

'Gallant soldiers, the Fritzes. But in the end they were no
match for us.' Mikhail had vaguely heard that the Russian
winter had helped to defeat the Germans but he kept his
counsel. His father leaned over the bed and Mikhail, who knew
what was coming, turned his head to dodge the vodka breath
that smelled of a zoo. 'Never forget you're Russian, son. Never
forget that.'

As he grew older, as the children of the Jews, Russians,
Ukrainians, Poles and Armenians in the district became Americans, albeit with ethnic loyalties, Mikhail became increasingly
confused about his identity. Why was his father so passionately

devoted to the country from which he had fled? If he had stayed he would have been shot. And why did he always emphasise Russia and not the Soviet Union? The Russian Republic, admittedly the largest, was only one of fifteen republics in a land where more than one hundred languages were spoken.

Some of the answers, Mikhail felt, lay in the disappearance of the brother he had never met – in Moscow late in 1941 when the Germans were at the gates of the city. A photograph of him, hair glossy in studio lights, smiling fiercely at the challenge of life, stood on the sideboard. An avuncular Stalin stared back from the top of the second-hand radio.

Mikhail made his approach walking with his father down the Bowery on his tenth birthday. Snow from the steppe was blowing down that bleak thoroughfare dressing its wounds; the mood of the day was therefore propitious.

Cautiously, Mikhail said: 'Papa, why do I *have* to be Russian?' The ensuing silence was even more unnerving than the predictable anger or sorrow.

They walked past a man sitting in the doorway of a tenement, drinking from a bottle. Snowflakes alighted like moths on their faces. Mikhail glanced at his father. He was leaning into the wind, holding on to the peak of his black cap with one arthritic hand, and, for a moment, Mikhail sensed adult vulnerability; it frightened him.

Finally his father said: 'You shouldn't have to ask.'

'But you've never explained.' Mikhail hesitated. 'If Stalin drove you out of Russia why do you keep his picture on the radio?' When Stalin had died five years earlier his father had mourned for a week.

'Many mistakes were made after the war.'

'And during it? Isn't war itself a mistake?'

They reached Astor Place, bore right and stopped at a store that sold rotting fruit from the emporiums of mid-town Manhattan. His father fished in the pockets of his reefer jacket for coins. His hands shook and his face, grey eyes watering in the cold, was older than the faces of other fathers. He replaced the coins in his pocket and they rejoined the wind that, having lost direction, was confusing the snowflakes.

Mikhail, now committed, said: 'I really don't understand, Papa. I was born in America. I live in America. . . .'

'But you are Russian. It is a very precious possession and it has withstood many onslaughts. Sometimes, like a cross, it is a burden but it must always be held high. It is because it is so precious that we Russians endure so many hardships.'

'Like communism?'

'You've been listening to your mother.'

At night when he was supposed to be asleep in the apartment, so cramped that it did not sanction privacy, he heard her reproaching his father for his political obstinancy.

'She is a good woman, your mother.'

Mikhail, who had never doubted this, waited while his father, who apparently possessed enough coins to buy a bottle of vodka – cheaper presumably, than rotting fruit – went into a liquor store.

When he emerged, nipping from the bottle, he elaborated. 'A wonderful woman.' Mikhail stared at his boots; they were tipped with steel and sometimes scratched sparks on the side-walk. 'But she has suffered greatly.'

Had she? It was his father who wept, not his mother. 'Because she's Russian?' Mikhail asked.

'Partly.'

'And partly because of my brother, Vasily?' Mikhail asked craftily.

His father drank from the bottle which he held in a brown paper-bag. A pan-handler with a gooseberry chin came out of the liquor store and thrust a wooden bowl at them; Mikhail's father absent-mindedly pushed it aside. 'I think,' he said care-fully, 'that we should speak about your brother.'

And, pausing occasionally to tilt the bottle, he recalled the battle for Moscow when the Germans were at the threshold of the city. How Mikhail's brother had volunteered to fight with the Communist Battalions defending the capital. How he had disappeared in a skirmish on the outskirts. 'On the twenty-fourth anniversary of the Glorious Revolution.' His father licked his lips which, in the cold, turned mauve.

'So he *is* dead?' Mikhail had never been quite sure. There had always been evasion when Vasily's name was mentioned and his mother's knitting needles had always clicked a little faster.

'Your mother has never given up hoping.'

'But it was a long time ago, Papa.'

9

'Seventeen years. . . . But sometimes men were taken to camps.'

'Because they fought for Russia?'

'I told you, mistakes were made.'

'I think it's very hard being a Russian,' said Mikhail who by now was almost sure that he didn't want to be one.

'I said, perhaps we can do a deal.' The pickpocket stared anxiously at Michael Cooper. 'You seemed to have left me. . . .'

'I was in America,' Michael said. 'What sort of a deal?'

'Currency. I will give you many times the going rate for dollars. There are many things we can buy in the hard currency shops which we can't buy with roubles. Do you have any jeans, Comrade Cooper? I will give you good money.'

'If your father can help me find my brother I'll give you jeans. Dollars too.'

'Give?' The pickpocket pondered this heresy. He smoothed the fingers of his right hand, his dipping hand, as though he were pulling on tight gloves. 'Very well, I will talk to my father.'

'And anyone else in the bath-house who knew my family. They used to come here.'

'I will ask. Don't forget the women.' He pointed through the steam in the direction of their changing-room. 'The Fighting Comrades' Club perhaps. Women veterans of the Great Patriotic War who were awarded eight medals or more. Tough ladies.' He flapped his left hand. 'Forgive me, Comrade Cooper, but do you have a lady with you in Moscow? Your wife, perhaps?' *With a gold bracelet loosely clasped to her wrist. . . .*

Michael said: 'I *had* a wife,' and, adjusting the sheet round his waist, descended the two steps and made his way to the changing-room. The pickpocket followed gratefully.

Although Mikhail's father only worked as a caretaker no one had ever suggested that he wasn't smart; you didn't survive the Germany occupation and escape from Stalin's vengeance squads if you were dumb. And he passed on his quick wits to his son.

Armed with these, and funded by his mother who, having subsisted for part of the war on linseed-oil cake and potato skins, shopped thriftily, Mikhail set about improving himself.

And what profession most readily rewards quick wits? Mikhail never had any doubt that he was going to become a lawyer. A courtroom advocate who would charge the wealthy whopping fees and represent his own kind still living in the ghettos for peanuts.

He studied at night school, won a scholarship to Columbia University Law School and, before graduating, met a girl named Barbara Pickford. She was blonde and brisk and as smart as he was; she was also privileged, a legacy he was happy not to possess because it stunted ambition. Both she and her father, a widower and a respected broker on the New York Stock Exchange, enthused about the spirit with which he had surmounted his humble origins. Her father promised to help him find a job; Barbara took his parents a present – a jar of Beluga caviar. His father threw it across the room narrowly missing the photograph of Stalin.

When she joined an advertising agency on Madison Avenue, Barbara suggested that he should change his name. It would, she said, enhance his prospects. Since when, he demanded, had an exotic name been a handicap in the United States? But manifestly Miss Pickford did not want to become Mrs Vysotsky. Mikhail agonised for days, finally concluding that the change – Cooper from the Cooper Union near his birthplace – would help to establish an American identity. But his guilt was singularly Russian.

They were married in 1976 and three years later Barbara gave birth to a child, a boy, who was stillborn. She returned to the advertising agency and devoted herself to furthering both their careers. She understood his support for ethnic minorities in the courts of law but advised him that this shouldn't interfere with the mainstream of his practice. When a fashionable architect dismissed him from a case because he was too engrossed with a loan shark's persecution of a Russian Jew, she worried for him.

When Mikhail's mother died stoically in the renovated apartment in the East Village he had bought for her and his father, Barbara, who had a lunch meeting with an executive of a company trying to launch a new board game, considerately stayed away from the funeral because, as she explained, her presence would only agitate his father.

'And now,' said the pickpocket who had dispatched the attendant to buy a jug of Zhigulovsky beer, 'we can enjoy ourselves. Because, you see,' addressing Michael, 'that's what a banya is all about – the relief after the torture.'

'Perhaps that's what Soviet life is all about,' said the stallholder bringing his philosophy and his drum-belly to the plastic-topped table, one of several that obtruded into the majestic decay of the bath-house.

Some patrons lounged naked, steam-heated genitals hanging loosely, others wore underpants or the sheets which invested their oratory with a dignity it did not always deserve. They played dominoes and chess with battle-scarred pieces said to have been carved by prisoners in penal camps, the knights snarling like dogs, and debated football, women and *glasnost*.

'Please introduce me.' The bodybuilder stood at the table; he wore only a pouch and his oiled muscles moved like trapped animals. His black hair was slicked back; his profile was noble.

When the pickpocket had completed the introductions the bodybuilder shook Michael's hand, his powerful grip slippery with linament. 'So, Comrade Cooper, you are a tennis player.' He sat down. 'I can always tell from the play of the muscles.' He slapped the stallholder on his bare back. 'This man is a champion beer drinker.' He drank Narzan mineral water. 'So, what brings you to Moscow, comrade?'

The pickpocket who regarded Michael as his property – had he not been boiled alive because of him? – told him. 'And I think because of wife trouble. Isn't that so, Mikhail?' he asked shyly.

The marriage had come to an end neatly and predictably when his father died.

12

His father, who was eighty-five, sustained, he claimed, by regular administrations of vodka, suffered a heart attack after a surfeit of blinys and sour cream in a Great Patriotic War get-together in a restaurant near Bellevue Hospital.

'So, how are you feeling?' Michael asked in the rhetorical vernacular of hospitals. His father was sitting up in bed staring across the ward, eyes cloudy with cataracts, seeing, Michael conjectured, a wooden cottage with fretted eaves nestling in a copse of birch trees.

'Fine.' The old man's head turned woodenly like a marionette's. 'I'm going back, you see.'

'I know, Papa.'

'And I want you to go too. Not with me' – his mauve lips smiled – 'but soon while there's still plenty of life ahead of you. Find out what happened to your brother. . . .'

'Of course, Papa.'

Such a mission seemed to Michael to be futile because, since the advent of *glasnost*, he had, through the United States Embassy in Moscow and two American journalists based there, checked every record that could relate to the disappearance of Vasily who, if he were alive, would be sixty-eight.

'I want you to be proud of him,' his father said as the bubbles rose rhythmically in the bottle of his drip-feed.

'I am, Papa. He died for Russia,' because that's what the old man wanted to hear. Or had Vasily died in a penal camp, another victim of Stalin's paranoia? Or was he still alive?

'You promise?'

'I promise.'

'When you find him you will know that you, too, are Russian.'

'I know that already, Papa,' Michael lied.

'I wish I could have gone there a long time ago.'

'He understands that.'

'Never forget. . . .'

'I won't,' said Michael, placing his hand on his father's cold and polished knuckles.

After the funeral he told Barbara that he was going to Russia.

She didn't appear to be surprised. 'For how long?' She applied herself to a flower arrangement for a dinner party that night at their house in the Hamptons.

'I promised to try and trace Vasily.'

13

'The brother you never knew? Good luck.' She nodded as though, after a long debate, she had reached a decision; her soft fair hair moved busily. She was thirty-nine and yet she still reminded Michael of a model in one of her own advertisements – the girl stepping into a bath to lather herself with a brand soap. He had once suggested that the way the model was staring into the camera she might slip on it.

He said: 'You never liked my faher, did you?'

'He never liked me.'

'Beluga caviar, Jesus!'

'So I forgot the dry toast.'

'You didn't try to understand how he felt in a foreign country.'

'And you, Michael, are you in a foreign land?' She snipped the stem of a pink carnation. 'Other immigrant families integrate. Why not the Vysotskys?'

'I have integrated. I was born here, for Christ's sake. I am an American.'

'Then don't go to Russia.'

'I promised.'

'But you know there's no point.'

'Do I?' He sat at the head of the mahogany table and listened to the sea and the summery murmur of insects.

'He must be dead.'

'I have to find out.'

'And if he isn't what will you do? Bring him back here to share our house and our apartment with Mother Russia?'

Michael clasped his hands together and a great serenity settled on him. It had settled before when he had peered through a transparency in a witness's testimony and had suddenly known what line he had to take. He gazed benignly at his admirable wife and perceived no reason to regret their years together. August 1989 – they had been married fifteen years almost to the day.

'How would it be,' he said evenly, 'if I moved out and took Mother Russia with me?'

'If that's what you want.' She brushed pollen from the table.

'It's what you want too. I saw it just now.'

'I wish you'd seen it five years ago – when I still had good prospects.'

14

'You look twenty-five and you'll always have good prospects.'

He stood up, walked round the table and kissed her on the back of the neck. 'Will you get married again?'

'You bet – to an American.'

'I guess I'll skip the dinner party.'

'Goodbye, Michael,' she said.

'*Dasvidanya*,' he said.

The Kremlin chauffeur, narrowly built with shoulder blades like wings, whose job emboldened him with an inquisitorial manner, rid himself of his last domino. 'So what,' he asked, 'do you do for a living?'

Michael told him he was a lawyer.

Silence settled like dust in the changing-room. The stallholder leaned forward making a desk out of his belly. The pickpocket studied his anxious fingers. The bodybuilder massaged his glistening thighs.

Finally the stallholder spoke. 'Good,' he said. 'You can help us. You see we have a problem.'

2

The bath-house stood to the north of the Kremlin between the Kitay-Gorad, the ancient hub of the city that embraces Red Square, and the girdle of green avenues known as the Boulevard Ring Road.

And indeed from the retiring grey façade of the banya, shouldered by baronial institutions, you could see the golden husks of the most illustrious kremlin or fortress in the world and, at night, the illuminated red stars that had replaced the double-headed eagles of Tsarist days on some of its towers.

But somehow it was in the bath-house rather than this sixty-nine acre triangle of august contradiction – a divinity of cathedrals amid seats of applied atheism – that the past was most resonant. It was, perhaps, the aristocratic decay that did the trick. The decadent chandeliers, brass hand-rails polished tissue-thin by the passing trade, samovars and spittoons in unsteady attendance.

No one seemed to know how old the bath-house was but when senses reeled in the searing, eucalyptus heat ghosts marched. A Golden Horde of Tartars, a troop of pillaging Cossacks. . . . Ivan the Great, the first Tsar, Ivan the Terrible beating his son to death, Catherine the Great with lovers in tow, Kutuzov relaxing after he had dispatched Napoleon, Tsar Nicholas the Second facing his Bolshevik assassins, an avuncular Lenin, a brooding Stalin. . . .

There in their vaporous embrace lay the anguished history of Russia, an epic dictated by its massive insularity, its leaders' fear of attack along its infinite borders and latterly the belief of its rulers that 280 million people occupying a sixth of the world's land surface could be governed from one city.

But if the spectres of the past hovered in the steam-room then the changing-rooms were the preserve of the present which was debated as robustly as it had been since the first hot-breathed banya summoned a Russian to cleanse and purge himself. In particular *glasnost*, the new freedom that had capriciously brought new hardships to the land.

In the mens' room the debate raged around the closure of liquor shops and the shortage of vodka – how can you enjoy freedom unless you are fuelled by fire-water? – and the strikes and ethnic protest in the scattered lands that comprise the Soviet Union. Sparks flew from this particular anvil. Who the hell did the Russians – the inhabitants of the Russian Republic, that was – think they were? Wasn't Stalin a Georgian, Mikoyan an Armenian, Gromyko a Byelorussian? Where would Russia be if it wasn't for the Ukraine, its bread-basket?

In the womens' room husbands' shortcomings and the wayward habits of teenage children were still in the forefront of discourse but it was shortages that normally held sway. The dwindling supplies of flour and sugar in the markets, the dearth of large-cupped brassieres in the Moda clothing store. What sort of freedom was it that bred scarcity?

But in both forums one topic had of late dominated: the threat by the city planners to bulldoze the bath-house off the face of Moscow.

On the summer day that Michael Cooper infiltrated the mens' rooms seventeen-year-old Tanya Agursky, Jewish and suffering because of it, sat in the womens' changing-room cooling off, scanning the Soviet edition of the West German fashion magazine *Burda* and listening idly to the debate. As usual it was led by a founder member of the Fighting Comrades, who was provider for the banya.

She was a red-haired laundress, joint-owner of a laundrette co-operative, built like the Battleship Potemkin but a nimble forager. Armed with four *avoskas*, string bags, that could expand miraculously, she patrolled such stores as Gum, Tsum and Moskva, looking for queues. When she found one she pounced, establishing her place, moved to another, then another, returning to each as the customer keeping her place approached the counter.

She was also adept in defeating the three-line system – one line to order and price a purchase, two to pay the cashier, three to pick up the purchases; she knew the cost of all commodities and majestically bypassed the first by merely grabbing what she wanted. As a war veteran she should have been allowed to go to the head of the queues but she had so abused this privilege that in most stores she had to take her place with her juniors. Frequently she joined a queue without knowing what trough of gold lay at the end.

She employed informers to tell her when foreign luxuries would be released – British tights, Spanish shoes, Yugoslav sweaters – and her high-rise apartment to the north of the city near Sheremetievo Airport was a miniature warehouse.

Today, with negotiable mark-up, she was selling a remote-controlled toy tank from Children's World, a carton of Bulgarian toothpaste, curtaining from the House of Material, bologna sausages, a carpet-sweeper and a gross of American condoms which were at a premium because Soviet sheaths were so thick they were known as galoshes.

'How much?' asked another Fighting Comrade, a lively blue-rinse born to haggle, pointing at the contraceptives. She had put on her brown uniform prior to attending a reunion and as she spoke medals on her bosom jingled.

The laundress placed her hands on her sheet-clad hips.'Does it matter at your age?'

'Many a good tune played on an old fiddle,' the second veteran, a seamstress, said. 'But in any case they aren't for me.'

'Not unless you're deformed.'

'For my daughter and her husband. Didn't you get the leaflet about AIDS in your apartment?'

'And yet you haggle?'

'Barter,' the seamstress said. She had dug trenches with the laundress outside Moscow in 1941 and they knew each other well.

'Twenty roubles the lot,' the laundress said.

'You've increased your percentage.'

'Who can put a price on love?'

'Where did you get them, off the back of a lorry?'

'Perhaps she would like them,' said a sallow-faced mens' hairdresser from the Ukraina Hotel who could never quite forgive beauty in others and occasionally ventured her resentment on the hair she cut. She pointed to Tanya Agursky.

'Leave her out of it,' snapped the laundress. She still revered youth even though many young people were sexually promiscuous – a minority, she believed – and smoked *ganasha*, marijuana, at rock concerts in Gorky Park.

'I don't mind. I'm not a child. I know about these things.' Tanya thought about Yury, how delicately he had held her as they skated secretly on a lake in the countryside last winter. She shivered and turned a page of the magazine.

'Fifteen roubles,' said the seamstress.

'Done. In the interests of your daughter and her husband,' said the laundress who, during forty years of marriage, had born two children and undergone seven abortions.

The seamstress quietened her medals with one hand and, sipping tea from the samovar, said: 'When you have finished counting the last kopek we should talk about the banya. I'll have the toothpaste too,' she added.

'All in good time. I have news for you.' The laundress smiled at the seamstress and a gold tooth gleamed in a shaft of dusty sunlight.

They waited while she counted her notes and coins and dropped them into a worn leather bag. Tanya stopped turning the pages of *Burda*. Yury frequented the men's section of the bath-house and she was worried about its future. How could they stage chance meetings outside if it were destroyed?

The hairdresser combed her dank hair. 'Get on with it, woman, some of us have to work. Real work, that is.'

'So you don't have time to sample the chocolates?' The laundress had bought chocolate liqueurs that morning from a diplomat's maid who had received them as a present from her master who had bought them in a hard-currency *beriozka* shop; the laundress had bought them with roubles at quadruple their dollar value.

'What chocolates? I can't see any chocolates.' The hairdresser's voice was thick with saliva.

The laundress fetched them from a string bag under her tunic on the clothes' rack. She read the small shiny labels. 'Brandy, whisky, anis, vodka. . . .'

'What do you want in exchange?' asked the hairdresser because bartering always followed cash deals.

'Hair lacquer that doesn't set like cement,' said the laundress who favoured a bouffant hair-style.

'I only cut men's hair.'

'I know – I've seen them around without their ears. But you use lacquer, don't you?'

'Isn't that only for the fairies outside the Bolshoi?' the seamstress asked.

'You live in the Dark Ages,' the hairdresser said.

'Do you want the chocolates or not?' the laundress demanded. 'They're French. Bite one and the liqueur flows sweetly on your tongue.'

'Two cans of lacquer. Here tomorrow.'

'Three.'

'You're a hard bitch,' the hairdresser said. 'Very well, three. Now give me the chocolates.'

'Half today, half tomorrow.' The laundress removed half the little chocolate bottles from their nests in the box. 'And now to business. I have some news. . . .' She tightened the sheet around her bosom which, the seamstress claimed, could accommodate a row of books. 'We are agreed, are we not, that we should take the lead. They,' indicating the mens' section as though it contained a lurking enemy, 'are too immersed in themselves. Drink, food, football – '

'Fornicating,' the hairdresser said.

' – that they can't get to grips with *perestroika*, the application of freedom. They don't realise that we are now their equals. Lenin preached equality but never made it work. What equality was that?' She spread wide her muscular arms. 'One job for the man, two for the woman? Digging potatoes *and* housework,' she explained to Tanya. 'And what was our reward? A kiss and a bunch of flowers on Womens' Day, that's what. Now all that is changing.'

'In your home?' the hairdresser asked, smirking.

'He washed the dishes last night,' the laundress said.

'And broke a few on purpose?'

'I broke his head.'

The seamstress said: 'Olga Ivanovna, get off your platform. The future of Soviet women is assured, the future of the bath-house isn't.'

The laundress took up a position near the hanging clothes. 'The campaign has begun,' she said. 'We are planning a petition to the Kremlin, a march, interviews in the Press – *Moscow News, Ogonyok, Sovietskaya Rossiya* – and on radio and television. How dare they pull down the banya where Lenin meditated.'

'Did he?' Tanya asked.

'Does it matter? The point is that we, the people, want to keep our bath-house. Why should they, the bureaucrats, destroy it. Is that *glasnost*?'

'*They* say it's old and unsanitary,' the hairdresser remarked.

'Kiss my ass. How can it be unsanitary with all this cleansing inside?'

'There is talk of rats.'

'Are you with us or against us?'

'With you, of course. Where else would I obtain chocolate liqueurs?' She bit a chocolate, stemming a leak of whisky with the tip of her tongue. 'I'm merely repeating what they say.'

'We all know what they want. A site for a new store. As if we hadn't got enough empty shelves in the city.'

'Perhaps they will try and fill these.'

'You've been listening to Vilkin the Planner. A sheep in wolf's clothing. Every night he walks in Red Square sniffing the winds of change. Whichever way they blow he follows.'

Tanya said: 'You still haven't told us what the news is.' She went to the clothes' rack and took her watch, a present from Yury, from the breast pocket of her white blouse. 12.30. She was due to meet Yury accidentally at 12.45. She began to dress.

The laundress paused because timing was everything. Then she said: 'There is an American in the banya.' The silence quivered. 'He is a lawyer and he has come to Moscow to find a lost brother. I think he can be very useful to us.' She folded her arms and gazed conspiratorially at the other woman.

Behind her Tanya dressed distractedly, flustered by possibilities. As she pulled on her Wrangler jeans, obtained mysteriously by the laundress, she tried to discipline her thoughts. What they

21

amount to, she thought, is this: if the American can help us to save the banya then he can help me too.

She opened the door and stepped into the sunlight.

Outside she lingered warily, glancing surreptitiously at parked cars or loitering pedestrians. As far as she knew the KGB wasn't keeping her under surveillance but it was advisable to be cautious. A *kvas* van came to her aid and she bought a glass, savouring the taste of fermented bread and taking her time drinking it. Where was Yury? An airliner chalked a line across the blue sky; fleece from cottonwood poplars, Stalin's snow, stirred in the gutter. And, as she always did in times of stress, she blamed her father for her predicament.

If it hadn't been for his flamboyant Zionism, his campaign to emigrate to Israel, his attacks on the State, she would be training now for the Olympic winter sports.

She peered down the years. Felt the fuzz of his dark beard against her cheek and saw his lips moving within it. Heard again the fables of courage and faith that surfaced from the history of persecution. Remembered Passover and Rosh Hashanah in their communal, second-class apartment. Waited in her bed for the God of Abraham, Isaac and Jacob to appease her worries.

What she had never understood was why Jews were different to everyone else. Why they were despised by some. And she had never quite grasped her father's explanations. He blamed initially the purity of their religion, the One True God, that made lesser creeds vengeful; then, the guilt of individuals, communities or nations, looking for a scapegoat for their own failings.

Tanya felt truly that she was Jewish. How could it be otherwise in a small household where the Talmud prevailed? But she believed she was just as Russian as she was Jewish and she couldn't understand the desire of her father – not so much her mother – to journey to the Promised Land. Why couldn't they stay Jewish *and* Russian just as citizens of the United States could be Jewish *and* American?

She could have understood his obsession years ago in the

days of rampant anti-Semitism. But not now, not since *glasnost*. And if he wanted to emigrate so passionately why didn't he make his approach routinely and join the flow of Jews – 1,000 a month, it was said – who were leaving for Israel?

But such was the vehemence of his protest that he had become an enemy of the State which wouldn't let him go because it would be conceding defeat. And such was his towering obstinancy that she couldn't train with the Olympic Team. Because, an official from OVIR had told her, he might use her for publicity, might persuade her to defect during the winter Olympics in France. The official, a kindly woman and mother of a teenage girl, had quoted an imaginary headline in a Western newspaper – DAUGHTER OF JEWISH MARTYR SKATES TO FREEDOM. And the woman had gently suggested that she should try to persuade her father to climb down from his soap-box. Fat chance.

Tanya sipped her *kvas*. Had Yury been interrogated, warned not to consort with the daughter of a trouble-maker? Ah, they skated so beautifully together, scarcely thinking about their feet, just understanding each other.

A middle-aged man with a Black Sea tan sauntered past. He stared at her appreciatively. She had become accustomed to such looks in the past two years; men, she knew, liked the thrust of her skater's thighs, the swell of her breasts, the slither of her black hair – tight-combed for skating; most of all they were affected by her indifference, intimidated or cowed. This admirer looked away and hurried home to his wife.

She finished the *kvas*. No sign of Yury, only two children towing silver, hydrogen-filled balloons. Heat lay wet and trapped in the street; the pavements were stained with summer juices. Then she saw him, approaching from the direction of Petrovsky Boulevard instead of the banya. Why?

She walked towards him, love and apprehension fusing. He walked with a gliding, skater's stride but he looked vulnerable just the same; slight and taut, blond hair dishevelled above his pale features, a small scar that smiled at the corner of his mouth. When he took to the ice he grew in stature, greenish eyes glittering, scar smiling fiercely.

Did they have to be so furtive? she wondered. Would it really prejudice his future if it was known that he was courting the daughter of a Jewish dissident with an unruly tongue? She wanted to walk the way other couples did, arms round each other's waists, feeling each other's warmth.

'Why weren't you in the banya?' she asked, walking beside him.

'A late session at the rink. I'm glad you waited. . . .'

'You're looking very trendy,' she said, taking in his white training shoes, jeans, T-shirt bearing the Olympic motif.

'Part of the image. They want us to look modern. Rock, pop, Boris Grebenshikov, all that.'

'Boris Grebenshikov isn't young,' said Tanya. The *us* upset her.

'So? His sons are young. And he represents freedom. In the old days he didn't even get any royalties because he didn't conform. Now he records in Los Angeles.'

'If this freedom is so . . . so abundant,' said Tanya, choosing her words with care, 'why do we have to meet in secret?'

Yury frowned, walked a little quicker. They made their way along the Petrovsky stretch of the boulevard, passing close to the police headquarters on Petrovka. Still he didn't speak.

'I asked you a question,' she said as they crossed Gorky Street at the junction dominated by the offices of *Izvestia* and *Moscow News*.

Yury pointed at the Rossiya cinema. 'It all started behind there.'

'What started there?'

'*Glasnost*, Khrushchev style. In the offices of *Novy Mir*. They published Solzhenitsyn.'

'Shall I repeat my question?'

'You know the answer.'

'I'm not a degenerate,' she said. 'I'm not infectious.' She walked more quickly, parting the lazy, lunch-time crowds outside the theatres, the Malaya Bronnaya and the Pushkin, on Tverskoy.

He caught up with her. 'You know perfectly well I've been advised not to see you and you know why.'

'Because I'm Jewish?'

'Because your father is a trouble-maker. They, the selection committee, think he'll use you.'

'He won't,' Tanya said. 'You know that.'

24

'They can't take the risk. If you were in the Olympics the media would never stop asking questions. "Will you join your father if he goes to Israel?" That sort of thing.'

'And I would answer truthfully – I wouldn't join him. I'm Russian.'

'They'd make something of that, too.'

They stopped at a *shashlik* stall in the Arbat pedestrian precinct. It occurred to her as she ate the spicy, skewered meat that Yury was being uncharacteristically daring lingering here.

He answered the unspoken question. 'As a matter of fact someone suggested I had a word with you.'

'Belov?'

'He's a good trainer.'

'I didn't say he wasn't. He's also a brain-washed Party member of the Old Guard.'

'He doesn't want trouble,' said Yury who was a member of the Komsomol, the Young Communist League. 'You can't blame him for that.'

'And what does Comrade Belov want you to tell me?'

Yury chewed a morsel of meat. A strolling player, a guitarist, wandered past. A portrait artist sitting at his easel beside the *shashlik* stall began to sketch. But who? No one was sitting for him.

Yury said: 'It's about your father.'

'You want me to ask him to drop his campaign?' Sometimes it was beautiful the way they anticipated each other; not today.

'If he keeps his head down for a few months they'll let him go to Israel.'

'And you really think he'll listen to me?'

'You're the only one.'

'You don't know my father.'

'Everyone knows your father,' Yury said. 'That's the problem.'

'Don't you think I've tried?'

'Tell him that if he stops protesting you will be able to skate in the Olympics.'

'In the pairs?'

'Of course. How were your axels and salchows today?'

'Papa won't back down,' Tanya said. 'But I'll speak to him again.'

The portrait artist continued to sketch. A middle-aged man with a sad moustache began to sing melancholy songs from the steppe.

'Did Belov say anything else?' Tanya asked, anticipating again.

Yury spoke softly. 'He said that if your father refused to abandon his protest we mustn't see each other again. He seems to know that we do meet. . . .'

'And if we do see each other?'

'Then I won't be picked for the Olympics.'

'I see.' She sensed his strength; it was a different calibre to hers but it was there all right. He won't see me any more, she thought, and that in its way is strength. 'And will you be picked for the Olympics?'

'I shall continue to see you,' he said stiffly and there was a song inside her.

'You mustn't.'

'But we must be more careful.'

'Supposing you're followed?'

'I shall lead them to the steam-room in the banya and leave them there.' The little scar smiled.

'Where can we meet?'

'In the country, by the lake. The way we used to.'

'But not outside the banya?'

'Too risky. But perhaps your father. . . .'

'Like trying to convert the Pope to Judaism.'

'But you must try.'

'I promise,' she said, loving him.

'And maybe one day we can turn professional.'

'In the Soviet Union?'

'Abroad. If footballers can make money overseas so can skaters. But our chances would be better,' Yury said, 'if you took part in the Olympics.'

'Better still if we won.'

'Speak to your father.'

The portrait artist handed her his sketch. Around her neck hung a pair of skates.

'How did you know?' she asked.

'I have good hearing.'

'How much?'

26

'An Olympic gold medal,' he said. 'There's no hurry – I can wait.'

That afternoon Tanya trained for three hours on the rink at the Dynamo stadium on Leningradsky Prospect. Jumps and spins mostly – she practised figures early in the morning before the crowds began to circle the ice. She had taken her preliminary here when she was a child, and later her bronze, intersilver, silver, intergold and gold.

Then she went by metro to Komsomol Square emerging among the peasants heading for the three railway stations there – Leningrad in the old classical style, Kazan with its tower copied from a kremlin in the Tartar capital and Yaroslav, the terminal of the Trans-Siberian. Once in Kazan station, exhausted after a day's training, she had been mistaken for a prostitute.

She skirted Kazan and made her way down a side-street to the decaying apartment block where she had been born. If she had been in the Olympic Squad her parents would have been moved to one of the modern blocks between the sweeping motorway encircling the city twenty-five kilometres from its fulcrum and the first of the two inner ring roads, the eight-lane Sadovoye Koltso. As it was they shared a bathroom with two other families.

She opened the blistered brown door and climbed the stairs past the single word sprayed on the wall, *zhid*, accompanied by an arrow pointing to their apartment. It no longer bothered her; she felt sorry for anyone who had been taught prejudice; God knows they may have been unwilling pupils.

Her father opened the door of the apartment. He was, she thought, magnificently Jewish. The luxuriant fold of his beard, the suffering brown eyes, the bald patch in his hair doing service for a skull-cap.

Tanya went into the little home. It smelled of childhood and although the furniture was cheap, the colours were warm autumn reds and golds. Why did he want to leave?

Her mother served chopped liver. Like the laundress, she knew how to shop, plundering the market on Tsvetnoi Boulevard. Her face was set somewhere between strength and patience and her greying hair was combed placidly into a bun. She would have happily stayed in Moscow but would accompany her husband wherever he went.

27

Tanya's father, sitting at the head of the table, if such a modest item of furniture could have such a grand extremity, asked her about her skating. He always did so during the first course; he couldn't understand her passion and she never told him that it sprang, perhaps, from the wintry soul of Russia.

'But not tomorrow.'

'Of course not,' although she had in the past skated secretly on the Sabbath.

During the next course, chicken broth with matzo-meal dumplings, he moved majestically onto *perestroika*.

'We are privileged to be witnesses to a watershed in history; the break-up of the communist empire. What next? The Ukraine? If that turns against the Kremlin the Soviet Union is finished.' He wiped his lips with a pristine napkin. 'Strikes, shortages, bloodshed in Georgia, Azerbaijan. . . . It's taken the people seventy years but at last they've discovered the myth of communism.'

Tanya laid down her fork gently; it was difficult to oppose her father but there were times when it had to be done. 'But it isn't communism that has caused this unrest is it. It's enlightenment.'

He combed his beard with his fingers. 'And what made this enlightenment necessary?'

'Mistakes.' Courage, she told herself. 'Just as there have been mistakes in Israel.' The silence tautened and she hurried on. 'What we're witnessing is the result of one man's courage. That's why it's so ironic; freedom encouraging protest, that is.'

Her mother said: 'It was inevitable, wasn't it? Storms follow the changes of the seasons.' She gazed calmly at her husband.

With the arrival of the poppy-seed cake Tanya's father embarked on Zionism. Tanya waited her chance.

'So what,' he demanded, 'do you make of these new freedoms that still prevent a man from seeking his birthright?'

'Perhaps,' Tanya's mother said, licking her fingers, 'you make too much noise.'

Tanya struck.

'Mama's right. If you waited a few months, then applied in the normal way, you would get an exit visa.'

'Compromise?' He looked at her knowingly. Or was it her

28

imagination? 'Abandon a campaign that cost me two years of my life in a penal camp?'

'As it is you're the enemy: if they let you go they'd be admitting defeat.'

'And if I dropped my campaign I'd be admitting defeat.'

'What do you want?' Tanya's mother asked. 'To protest or to go to Israel?'

'I want to go to Israel through my protest. I want to force the authorities to prove that true democracy has come to Russia.'

Here goes, Tanya thought. She said: 'If you dropped your campaign for a while, went quietly to Israel, I might be asked to join the Olympic Squad.'

He looked at her sadly. 'Who's been getting at you, Tanya? Yury? Is skating more important than the plight of the Jews in Russia?'

'There isn't any plight,' Tanya's mother said crisply. 'Not any longer.'

'If you're right then I have to prove it to the world.'

'Or yourself?'

Tanya said: 'So you won't do it?'

Her father clasped his hands together; made a synagogue of them, she thought. 'You know I'd do anything else for you. But I can't submit to blackmail. Can I?' he said gently.

That left the American.

3

Summer can end abruptly in Moscow; one push of a celestial button and fog and rain descend, harbingers of aching winter, and it is not glimpsed again for six months or so.

On just such a day, when mist and powdered rain were washing away the scents of roses in the gardens and tanning oil on the river beaches, Robert Hanson decided to drive into Moscow from his modest dacha outside the city and visit the bath-house.

He had been going there for twenty years or more, but usually in the winter when the steam-heat thawed the frost in his joints and stupified his neuroses.

Certainly therapy was what he needed today because that morning he had stared into the mottled mirror in his bathroom and seen a stranger. Grey eyes like his own but winsome rather than devious, and hair less grey than his own theatrically rumpled. A statesman's nose, a politician's smile.

The face was familiar. I've known you all my life, Hanson thought. Admired you, envied you, despised you.

And he turned his back on the familiar stranger and gazed at the garden through a window already sealed against winter with strips of newspaper.

A bird sang in a silver birch and, although it was morning, its song evoked evenings in England. Bundles of gnats suspended over an ornamental pool, an antique aeroplane strumming the sky.

Soon, he reflected with anticipation not far removed from apprehension, he might return.

He sat on the edge of a stumpy-legged bath on which rust had eaten a stain shaped like Australia. An old-fashioned geyser bracketed to the wall hung over the taps waiting for take-off.

Still staring through the branches of the tree towards the cubes and domes of Moscow, he silently addressed the stranger. *'I know what you want.'*

'Tell me,' words part of the resonant silence.

'Why should I feed your ego?'

'There's a very good answer to that. . . .'

'Please enlighten me.' Hanson turned his head abruptly, twisting a small shock of pain in his neck, but the stranger had vanished.

He poured a measure of deep-frozen Stolichnaya vodka into a glass. It emerged as lazily as oil. He drank it in one gulp and went into the garden, making his way across the grass to the diminutive river where grey fish navigated tresses of weed. There had been goldfish in the ornamental pond in Surrey, one of them weary and white-blotched with disease.

Yellow and russet chrysanthemums bloomed stubbornly, their seed brought long ago by a visitor from London – his last as far as he could remember – who had also delivered kippers and Earl Grey tea.

He strolled along the bank of the river to a pool where the water lay quietly with spurious depth.

Fifteen years ago when he was a stripling of thirty-two he had dug a hole there and, for the benefit of a defector's son, fooled the river into filling it. The boy had placed plastic soldiers on its ice-tissued surface and when they sank had pummelled the hibernating grass in fury.

He knelt beside the pool and removed two floating leaves. The stranger returned among the ripples his fingers had left behind.

Why hadn't he accompanied him that day in 1950 outside the library?

The stranger seemed to broaden his electioneering smile but it could have been one of the ripples. A breeze shivered in the garden; soon it would snow; it had been starting to snow outside the library.

*

31

4.40 and his mother who had been lecturing on first-aid had said 4.30. Where was she? Her punctuality was a familiar joke in their placid grey house in North London. As predictable as the sea-and-shingle holidays in summer and the garden bonfires of winter and Sunday roast.

A few hesitant flakes of snow skipped among the traffic. At school they had been willing it to snow all day but now Robert, aged nine, wished it would stop because, in the dusk, the flakes were threatening.

4.45. Mothers with children left the library stealthily still cowed by injunctions to keep quiet and made their way home past the lighted shop-windows of Muswell Hill. And the snow was more confident now, hovering in the glow of the street lamps, taking its time to melt on the street. He tried to think of snow falling at Christmas while he was asleep; waking to find the garden hushed and white, the lawn daintily patterned with birds' claw prints. But the images were fanged with icicles.

He strolled up and down the pavement with exaggerated nonchalance. 4.47 according to his wrist watch. Obviously his mother was dead. But she's only seventeen minutes late, stupid. He began to shiver.

His mother rounded the corner, face flushed, wearing her Red Cross uniform. The breast of her starched apron crackled as she embraced him.

'Were you worried, dear?'

'Of course not.'

'There was a bad accident coming up the hill; I had to help.'

He noticed a bloodstain, bright and damp, on her apron. He wondered if it would freeze.

'Was anyone killed?' he asked carelessly.

'Badly injured. The brakes failed on a bus and it ran into a car.' She noticed the bloodstain and touched it with one finger. 'Arterial. I had to apply a tourniquet to the car driver.'

'Did it work?' He wished she wasn't quite so dramatic but then she did look like an actress, especially in the sepia photographs on the piano.

'Fairly well,' she said unsatisfactorily.

She took his arm and guided him through the snow which was now falling steadily. They took a roundabout route home

32

because, he guessed, the wrecked car was still on the hill and he knew the driver had died – tourniquets did not work 'fairly well'.

In the bathroom she took off her apron and soaked the bloodstain in the wash-basin.

A key turned in the front door. It was 5.35, his father as punctual as his mother usually was. He stared into the basin where the blood was flowing from the cloth into the water in wavering capillaries before fusing into a pink cloud.

Was that when the course was set? The first alarm in his safe life, as insidious as an envelope slid beneath a door? Or was it the cuts across the palm of his left hand for being stubbornly sinistral, or the revelations about the death of Max Weinreb's brother, killed in action, or the dischords that his lungs played on the playing fields?

Hanson thrashed the water in the pool with a twig and the stranger disappeared. He walked back to the wooden dacha, drank another vodka and a glass of Narzan and ate some dill pickle sliced on black bread.

Then he took his grey Zhiguli out of the leaning garage and drove along Volokolamsk, past a loop in the Moscva River where, in winter, he fished through a hole in the ice. As he made his way down Leningradsky he glanced in the driving mirror. No stranger there. Just the usual pouched features that had once had the set of minor nobility, their matrix subsequently confused by doubt.

He parked the little car and went into the banya.

He was greeted politely in the changing-room. The attitude of the patrons had never changed, he reflected, because they could not wholly accept anyone who had deserted his home-land. But he had been going there for so long that, like the mottled tears of the chandeliers, he was one of the fittings and he enjoyed the vicarious cameraderie. In fact he felt more at home with the regulars here than he did with the defectors in Moscow.

Not that he was a defector. Neither spy, nor traitor. Just an individual – son of a worthy accountant, scholar with an ear finely tuned to languages – who had refused to accept that, because he was born in England of British parents, he had to stay in a capitalist society. And now, after two decades, he was becalmed in a country that was bounding towards the democratic capitalism that he had rejected.

He wrapped a sheet round himself and made his way to the steam-room, passing the pickpocket and the bodybuilder and a stranger, tall and well-muscled, who was engaged in earnest conversation with them. In the steam-room an officer in the Red Army and a schoolmaster were swatting each other energetically with birch twigs. Hanson climbed the tiers to his usual perch.

The heat began to cook him. Time melted. He massaged the palm of his left hand with the thumb of his right, a habit of his.

The classroom of the private boarding school in the mannered countryside north of London smelled of carbolic and ancient dust. The master smelled of tweed and snuff and some of the latter had lodged in his ragged moustache – like fleas in a dog's fur, Robert Hanson, aged thirteen, thought. The master went for long walks with his red setter and, according to Max Weinreb who spied on him, switched furiously with his stick at the bracken in the woods.

For his part Robert cared little about the moods of Mr Fawcett, BA, because he was in love with one of the mistresses, Miss Holtby – 'Like Winifred,' she confided mysteriously – and glowed when she complimented him for some task ably performed.

He was not as intimidated by the countryside as he thought he might have been. Miss Holtby was there and the fields were mauve with clover and, in a meadow where the mud sucked at cows' hooves, there was stream making its way to London.

He also discovered that he could make people laugh, a practical substitute for athletic prowess which he did not possess. He felt sorry for boys who hid their unhappiness behind buffoonery and was thankful that he had been blessed with a sort of a wit that was later to be known as mordant. What puzzled him greatly at this time was the hostility that being different could attract.

Mr Fawcett put him right on that one.

'Your handwriting,' he said, stopping beside Robert's desk, 'is atrocious. Do you know why?'

'No, sir.'

'Because you write with the sinistral instead of the dextral. You write, sir, with the Unclean Hand.'

Robert examined his left hand; true it was not sensationally clean but then again it was not filthy.

'Place the pen in the other hand, sir.'

Robert did as he was told.

'Now write *I must not be cack-handed.*'

'Cack-handed, sir?'

'Write it.'

He tried but he found that he was no longer pushing the letters before him; instead they wandered disobediently behind his fingers. His arm was heavy as he reached for the ink-well on the right-hand side of the desk; two blots splashed on the lined paper.

Mr Fawcett, standing grimly beside him, tugged at the tatters of his moustache. Robert laid down his pen. Together they stared at the paper, Mr Fawcett in disbelief. Understandably, Robert conceded – the writing looked as though a spider had escaped from the ink-well and made good its escape.

'You're a comedian are you, Hanson?'

'No sir.'

'Then what is this aberration?' He held the exercise book aloft for the rest of the class to see and was rewarded by uneasy laughter. 'Try again, sir. With your dextral.'

The result was, if anything, worse because, sensing retribution, he was trembling.

'We shall have to teach that sinistral of yours a lesson, shan't we. Stand up and hold out your left hand.'

Mr Fawcett fetched a wooden ruler from his own magisterial desk. It was bladed on the edges with metal that was barely perceptible.

Mr Fawcett intoned: 'Say after me, I. . . .'

'I.'

The edge of the ruler struck the palm of his hand. The pain was cold and sharp.

'Must.'

'Must.'

The second blow struck the crease which was, according to his mother, his life-line.

'Write.'

He repeated it, waiting for the third stroke, thinking about the warm burrow of his bed at home, coals shifting in the grate in the living-room.

He heard the metal blade strike the bones at the base of his fingers, refused to cry because he knew that was what Mr Fawcett wanted.

He glanced at his hand. It was bleeding in three criss-cross lines but Mr Fawcett did not appear to have noticed them. He was, in fact, distressed, tongue lolling in his mouth.

'With.'

'With.'

The pain leaped up his arm.

'Sir!' Weinreb leaped to his feet, knocking over a chair.

Mr Fawcett took no notice. His hand, white-knuckled, was raised.

'Sir!' Again from Weinreb who had got between the ruler and Robert's hand.

The ruler stopped midway in its descent.

Mr Fawcett looked vague. Blinked, retracted his tongue, studied the ruler, noticed the blood on Robert's hand. 'Here, boy,' taking a handkerchief from the breast pocket of his jacket, replacing the ruler on the desk. And to the rest of the class: 'Now, where were we?'

Robert felt cold expanding in his skull.

'Are you all right?' Mr Fawcett asked.

'I feel a little. . . .' The cold flowed into his legs.

'Weinreb, look after your chum.'

Outside the classroom Robert clumsily thanked Max Weinreb and headed for the meadow bisected by the London-bound stream. There, lying in the wet grass and staring at the jigsaw pieces of sky between the leaves of a chestnut tree, he cradled his left hand in his right.

*

Hot-eyed and dry-nosed, Hanson tightened his sheet and strode into the changing-room. He sent the attendant out for a jug of beer and sat at a table where he was sometimes lucky enough to play a game of chess.

He looked fondly at his fellow patrons. The skinny chauffeur from the Kremlin, features tight with nebulous intrigue. The bodybuilder, a reformed thug from one of the keep-fit outfits in the suburb of Lyubertsi that spent their leisure beating up hippies and punks, who now trained wolf-dogs outside Moscow. The pickpocket willing his restless fingers to keep themselves to themselves. . . .

They all seemed to be making telling points to the black-haired stranger about the fight to save the banya from the bulldozers. Who was he?

The bodybuilder: 'We can use force. They, militia and KGB, daren't make a fight of it. They're trying to clean up their image. The head of the KGB giving press conferences would you believe.'

The pickpocket: 'Maybe I can lay my hands on some important documents. You know, evidence that they're acting outside the law.'

The stallholder: 'As if they care. . . .'

The chauffeur: 'Things have changed, comrade. There is such a thing as public opinion.' And to the stranger: 'Supposing you're a spy?'

The stranger: 'It was you who suggested I might be able to help.'

The door to the street opened and Yury, the skater, came in.

The chauffeur: 'But just the same. . . .'

The bodybuilder: 'What harm can he do? Keep your intrigues with you in the drivers' pool.'

The chauffeur: 'So you can help us? A lawyer. You must have some ideas.'

The stranger: 'I don't know anything about Soviet law.'

So he wasn't a Russian. And yet his grasp of the language, although slightly accented, was perfect.

Hanson said: 'I'm a foreigner too.' He folded a smile. 'Robert Hanson, English.'

'Michael Cooper, American.'

The chauffeur said: 'You might not know anything about

our law but you know how to draw up documents, protests, petitions.'

'I can try,' Michael Cooper said. 'We still have a deal?'

'Of course, we shook hands on it.'

What sort of deal? Hanson wondered. He laid out the venerable chess pieces. *Blat*, the swapping of benefits? Pass marks for your son at Moscow University in exchange for elevation in the waiting list for a car; *Playboy* for an under-the-counter record of the Rolling Stones. Or out-and-out *vzyatka*, bribery?

When he first settled in Moscow these practices had disappointed him. But he had found many excuses for them, notably the shortages that were the legacy of World War II in which the Soviet Union had lost twenty million lives, and for a long time he had kept a secret from himself: that the weakness of communism was that it didn't work. Seventy years on from the October Revolution and professional classes still patronised the workers!

Hanson moved the white king's pawn two squares, replied with the same move by black. Playing himself at chess. . . . Could there be a more apposite pasttime for a man who had never belonged?

The American sat down at the table. 'How about a game?' he said.

A Sunday afternoon in autumn. He and Weinreb, both sixteen, old hands at the school and superior with it, were loitering in the field beside the stream talking about girls. After a while the talk wandered back through the years to the day Mr Fawcett, BA, had assaulted Hanson's sinistral hand.

'I should have kicked him in the goolies,' Weinreb said.

'You were terrific; no one else lifted a finger.'

Robert wondered, as he had wondered before, how their friendship had endured. Weinreb was not, after all, everyone's cup of tea – on the small side, bespectacled and raw-nerved, inclined to defensive violence.

He knew little about the background of Weinreb's family, only that they were Jewish and that, long before Max had been born, before the war that was, they had left Germany and settled in North London.

They had both attended a preparatory school in Muswell Hill where they had learned about the glory of war, particularly when the British were the victors, as they had been in 1945. And Weinreb had talked sadly but with modest pride about his brother who had died in France in that glorious war.

'Well at least Fawcett got the boot,' Weinreb remarked as the cows converged at the gate staring at them incuriously. 'Should have been shot at dawn.'

Robert rubbed the palm of his left hand. He had at the time tried to conceal the wounds but finally, when the hand was bloated and leaking, the form-master had taken him to a doctor who favoured kaolin poultices, linctus codeine and Parish's Chemical Food. Robert, shivering and aching, imagined him delivering babies and taking away their corpses in his black bag.

His scalpel had cut red and yellow lines in the swollen flesh. 'Put your head between your knees,' the doctor had advised and given him tablets from a bowl where he kept free samples.

He and Weinreb began to walk towards the school, past the cottage where Miss Holtby, now married to the games master, lived. She waved from the window but they cut her dead.

'Don't you ever wonder why he went for you like that?' Weinreb asked.

'Because I was different, I suppose.'

'You aren't the only left-handed twit in the world.'

'Different to most then. Did you know the King was left-handed?'

Weinreb did not.

'And Nelson?'

Weinreb didn't know that either.

'Not much option: he lost his right arm at Santa Cruz.'

Robert felt a wave of laughter climbing but he had learned not to laugh at his own witticisms.

'And Marx, of course.'

'Karl?'

'Harpo.' He contained his laughter.

They walked on through the chilling evening air, yellow leaves of chestnuts spinning around them. When the gates

39

were in sight Weinreb said: 'Being different. . . . That's the reason for all the trouble in the world, isn't it?'

'I suppose so. We fought the Germans because they were different.'

Robert had been recently puzzling over the fact that the Russians who had been our allies in the war were now our enemies.

Weinreb said: 'Can I tell you a secret?'

'If you want to.'

'And you won't tell a soul?'

'Cut my throat if I tell a lie.'

'You remember me telling you about my brother? How he died in France.'

'He didn't?'

'Oh he died all right.' Weinreb caught a leaf and examined it minutely. 'Only he was fighting for the Germans.'

The American examined the board. 'You play a mean game.'

'Average. Most of the veterans in Gorky Park could lick the pants off me. Maybe we could have a game there one day.'

'I'd like that. I'm trying to get my visa extended.'

'I wish you luck. I'm trying to get out.'

'That's difficult?'

'If you're a citizen of the Soviet Union like me.'

The American stared at him acutely. Then he said: 'You're lucky. I don't know what the hell I am.' He stretched his hand over the board. 'A draw?'

They shook on it.

4

Michael Cooper left his one-hundred-rouble-a-night room in the old and gracious National Hotel at dawn. He ate a breakfast of boiled eggs, bread and butter and plum jam, and walked onto Marx Prospect. Tucking the three-dollar umbrella he had bought on an East Side street corner when the heavens had opened above New York under his arm, he charged the rain, skuttled into the metro station next door, paid his five kopeks and boarded a train.

It was packed but it was clean. No grafitti. No mugging, so he had been told. And such stations, the older ones like chapels or the foyers of theatres. Drop litter at your peril. Bonus points for socialism in the insoluble equation with capitalism. Full employment versus unemployment, cheap holidays and cheap consumer goods versus price hikes. Or, from the other camp, freedom versus oppression, plenty versus scarcity. Which had the edge? Neither in Michael Cooper's opinion.

He stood in the train wedged between close-packed, damp-smelling passengers trying to belong. Trying? No need, you *are* Russian.

As the train nosed south the passengers thinned out. A stout woman with a potato face barged on board dragging a little girl wearing the red scarf of the Young Pioneers. The girl looked away from him abruptly; the woman smiled at him, her smile like sunshine on a bare mountain.

He alighted at Varsavskaja and walked briskly along the main road that ultimately lead to Kursk. The high-rise development where the pickpocket lived had a high crime rate and, as he neared the purpose-built blocks, youths whistled at him and walked behind him imitating his stride.

A group followed him onto the first-floor communal balcony.

He waited till he reached the pickpocket's door, number twenty-one, then turned. The kids, three of them, grinned uneasily. One of them, his scalp shaven, brandished a baseball bat.

Shit, Michael thought, I've seen you before in the South Bronx. He walked towards them. 'I'm an officer from the 130th Precinct,' the police station he had noticed round the corner.

The kid with the shaven scalp, nicked blood-red in a couple of places, swung the bat. 'We thought you might like a game.'

'You look like a home-run hitter.'

The kid stared at him uncertainly. 'You've played?'

'A few years back.' .

'In Moscow?'

'In the Big Apple.'

'Huh?'

'In New York,' Michael said.

'Shit! You're American?'

'As apple pie,' Michael said in English.

They gazed at him in awe.

'I've got an appointment right now,' Michael said in Russian. 'When I'm through I'll see how good you are. Have you got somewhere to play?'

'Over there.' The kid with the polished scalp pointed at a grassed area outside the block. 'But we. . . . '

'Haven't got a ball and you use that thing,' pointing at the bat, 'to break heads?' And when the kid stared at the concrete floor: 'I'll tell you what I'll do. When I get back to New York I'll send you a real bat made of ash. And balls and leather mitts.'

'Who would we play?'

'Two bats, two sets of gloves. . . . Get a league started. Give me an address to send them to.'

'Sure you're not a cop?'

'Do I look like a cop?'

'Not a Russian cop.'

'I thought all cops looked the same.'

'Not on the 130th Precinct,' said a future second baseman. 'They look like British soccer hooligans.'

They laughed but this time the laughter was comfortable.

'So,' said shaven-scalp, 'you'd better keep your appointment.'

'An address first.'

'What's the point? You won't send the gear.'

'My word.'

'You really mean it?'

'The address.'

They found a chewed pencil and he handed them the document he had been given at the National in temporary exchange for his passport. The kid wrote an address on the back.

'On one condition,' Michael said.

'Shit, conditions.'

'That you get a haircut.'

He turned on his heel and knocked on the blue door of number twenty-one. The pickpocket opened it and peered out anxiously at the youths.

'Dangerous kids,' he said, shutting the door behind them.

'Just kids.'

'They beat up an old lady the other day.'

'Those kids?'

'I don't know which kids they were. There are a lot of delinquents round here.'

'With a baseball bat?'

'With their fists.'

'Not those kids,' Michael said.

He glanced round the small living room where the pickpocket relaxed and dined with his wife and son. The furniture was cheap but the white walls were clean and adorned with a couple of fake icons. A crystal decanter fielded small rainbows on the plastic-topped sideboard and the apples on the bowl on the table had been freshly polished.

'Where's your wife?' Michael asked.

'Working at the soap factory. Good currency these days, soap.'

'Your son?'

'At school. I've just got back from work,' the pickpocket said. He wore a white shirt and black trousers and looked like a waiter.

'On the metro?'

'Biblioteka Station. Good pickings there. All those absent-minded professors. . . . Did you know that the station was so badly tunnelled that the Lenin Library is beginning to fall into it?'

Michael thought: I'll remember that for the petition. The same planners who want to demolish the bath-house?

'Tea?'

Michael who yearned for a decent cup of coffee said: 'That would be fine.' He sat on the hard-knuckled chair while the pickpocket busied himself in the tiny kitchen. 'Is your father awake yet?'

'I warned you, he's not himself these days. He lives in the past.' Good, Michael thought. 'But it's muddled. He confuses the time when he was a boy wih the war.'

'How old is he?'

'Seventy-nine. But he's had a hard life.'

So he would have been thirty or thereabouts in 1941 when the Germans were outside Moscow. When Vasily disappeared.

The pickpocket emerged carrying two glasses of tea. He handed one to Michael and opened a door. The bedroom beyond wasn't much bigger than a closet, the bed as narrow as a coffin. The old man sitting upright against two pillows had been prepared for his visitor. Feathery grey hair combed, autumn face freshly washed, striped pyjamas pressed. But they couldn't do anything about the eyes which, milky with cataracts, stared gravely into the past.

Michael sat beside him and told him who he was.

'Vysotsky? He was a movie star. I did time with him in a camp.'

'Not that Vysotsky,' said the pickpocket. 'He's dead. A hero of the people,' he told Michael. 'Actor, poet . . . drank himself to death and on the day he died 30,000 people packed Taganka Square near the theatre where he performed. No, not that Vysotsky,' he said to his father.

Michael said: 'You used to meet my family in the banya. My mother and father and their son Vasily. I wasn't born. . . .'

The old man smiled gummily. 'Those were the days. Stalin was a great man. He saved Russia.'

'He sent you to the camp,' the pickpocket said.

'Whipped us into shape. Got rid of all the wasters in the army.'

44

Michael moved his chair closer to the bed. 'My brother disappeared. Do you know what happened to him?'

'I knew your father. A good soldier. In charge of the Tropinin Museum before that. Came from a good family.'

'A lot of *blat*,' Michael conceded. 'That's how he got to New York. . . . Did you know Vasily too?'

'Everyone talks about the Tretyakov Gallery. Me, I prefer the Tropinin. If you want to see old Moscow go to the Tropinin.'

'You've never been to Tretyakov,' the pickpocket said. 'Nor have I,' he said to Michael.

'Your father took me to the Tropinin once,' the old man said. 'Isn't there a bar called Vysotsky's?'

'Near the Taganka Theatre,' the pickpocket said. 'It's got an ornamental pool full of frogs. I've never been there either.'

Michael said: 'Vasily must have been very young. Seventeen or eighteen.'

'I don't remember him,' the old man said abruptly. Michael, judicial hearing tuned to evasion, gazed into the milky depths of his eyes. The old man looked back with directness that Michael had learned to associate with a too-firm handshake. Or was he being too acute? Why should the old man remember Vasily?

'He was about my height. Fair hair,' Michael said, remembering the photograph that had stared across the room in New York at Stalin. 'A mole on his cheek.' He must have hated that, Michael thought – like a beauty spot.

'In the camp we had to carry scoops of melted aluminium from the furnaces. Temperatures of 700 degrees. If we splashed any of it on our bodies the burns were treated as self-inflicted wounds.'

The pickpocket whispered: 'He wasn't in the camp with Vysotsky. Vysotsky was long after his time.'

'And for punishment we were thrown in a cell two metres long with a plank to sleep on. Protest and wham,' clapping fragile hands, 'they'd beat you with rubber truncheons.'

'You and Vasily must have visited the banya at about the same time,' Michael said.

'I didn't meet him.'

'How do you know?' asked Michael, interrogator.

'I don't remember anyone answering his description.'

45

'It was a long time ago,' the pickpocket said.

'But he remembers my father.'

'Their ages were closer. They had a lot in common.'

'I fought with the Communist Battalions in Moscow,' the old man said. 'Men, women and kids. How they fought. With old rifles, home-made bombs, sharpened spades. . . .'

'In case you're wondering why he wasn't in the army,' the pickpocket said to Michael, 'he was in charge of a whole floor in the Hammer and Sickle Factory. They made anti-tank hedgehogs which were placed round the outskirts of the city.'

Michael said quickly: 'Did Vasily fight with the Communist Battalions?'

'I told you, I didn't know him,' the old man said.

'I really don't think he can help you,' the pickpocket said. 'We mustn't excite him too much.'

Michael stood up. Looked for a last time into the opaque eyes, the jumbled past, more vivid than the present, sealed behind the cataracts.

'Vasily used to be a mimic,' Michael said. 'Charlie Chaplin, Churchill, Hitler. . . . He could do them all.'

'Perhaps that's why I don't remember him,' the old man said. 'Because he was never himself.'

It seemed to Michael to be a particularly lucid observation from someone adjudged to be senile.

In the living room the pickpocket produced a bottle of Hunter's vodka, mineral water, dark bread and gherkins.

'Stolen from a professor's briefcase?' Michael held up the bottle of vodka.

'I bought it,' the pickpocket said with dignity. 'With money from a professor's wallet.'

Michael tossed back a measure of vodka, extinguished its flames with mineral water. 'Don't you ever feel guilty?' he asked curiously.

The pickpocket clasped and unclasped his working fingers. 'The guilt,' he said, 'is the best part of it.'

There was a message waiting for Michael when he got back to the hotel to call 204–4008 and ask for a Magda Larionova.

Michael showed the message to the girl at reception. 'Mean anything to you?'

'The Intourist Hotel,' she said. 'Our skyscraper neighbour. But if you really want a call-girl try the Mezh.' She smiled at him brightly.

Michael called the number from his high-ceilinged room and was put straight through to Magda Larionova.

'Ah. Mr Cooper. Welcome to Moscow.' Like many Russian linguists she spoke English with a slight American accent. 'Are you free for dinner?'

'Do you mind telling me who you are?'

'I'm from Intourist. The State Committee for Tourism, not the hotel.'

'How did you know I was here?'

'Please, Mr Cooper, do not be suspicious – that is our prerogative,' a tentative chord of laughter in her voice.

'Okay, where are we going? The Aragvi?'

'You're out of date, Mr Cooper. It's gone downhill and you don't even have to bribe the doorman to get in any more.'

'*Glasnost?*'

'The Tsentralny on Gorky Street. 8.00.'

'I'll be there,' Michael said.

He hung up wondering why a girl working for Intourist should be so interested in an American travelling independently.

He lay on his bed and tried to picture her. Shrewd, indoctrinated, adaptable to the vagaries of visitors from the West, attractive in an unambitious sort of way.

He was wrong, except for the shrewdness that was. In the first place although she was a citizen of the Soviet Union she wasn't Russian: she was Ukrainian and uncommonly proud of it. She wasn't indoctrinated, except in Ukrainian chauvinism; she wasn't adaptable to visitors' vagaries – contemptuous rather of his incomplete knowledge of her land; and she wasn't attractive – she was beautiful.

But not stereotyped good looks: there was too much character there. Wisdom in the broad set of the blue eyes, concessions to experience in the line between nose and mouth. When she laughed her helmet of fair hair laughed with her.

They sat in one of the private booths on one side of the ornate restaurant. She ordered 200 grams of vodka, devilled eggs, poached sturgeon, jam pancakes and red Georgian wine, Hvanhkara.

'Stalin's favourite,' she said.

'That makes it good?'

'Strong,' she said.

'You admire him?'

'If it hadn't been for him there would be no need for *glasnost*.'

'I don't understand.'

'If Lenin had lived longer he would have got rid of Stalin. Without Stalin communism might have worked. He tried to starve Ukraine to death.'

Michael tossed back a measure of vodka. 'You're really allowed to talk like this?'

'Wonderful, isn't it?'

'What are you, Ukrainian or Russian?'

She regarded him steadily. 'Both.'

'That's why you're in Moscow?'

'A shrewd question,' she said. 'You probably don't know how shrewd.' She drank some vodka; like a professional, he thought. 'I was moved here because I was too outspoken.'

'Ukraine for the Ukrainians?'

'Why not? Within the Soviet Union, that is. After all we are a separate nation, fifty-three million of us. And Kiev was the first capital of the people who came to be known as the Russians.'

'You're admitting you're the same people?'

'Do not, Mr Cooper, try to put me on. We have our own language – similar to Russian, I agree – and our own culture. And our own borders.'

'And you've had many masters. Tartars, Cossacks, Poles. . . .'

'A little knowledge is a dangerous thing, Mr Cooper.'

'I was born on the Lower East Side of New York. There are a whole lot of Ukrainians there.'

'That makes you an authority on Ukraine?'

Michael held up his hands. 'Tell me about it.'

'The Tsars tried to make us Russians because they were scared of us. Then the western part of Ukraine, fifteen per cent of it, came under Austrian rule in the eighteenth century. when Austria–Hungary fell at the end of the First World War and in

48

the chaos after the Russian Revolution we became united and independent.'

'Then you got the Russians again?'

'Lenin promised to leave us alone; he broke his promise, of course. The Bolsheviks took most of the country; the Poles got the western reaches; the Czechs and Romanians a few crumbs.'

'Then World War II?'

She began to eat the poached sturgeon. 'Just before it. The Hitler–Stalin pact. The carve-up of Poland. Stalin got back the western part of Ukraine. You know the rest.'

'Hitler invaded, took back *all* of it. Then Russia took back *all* of it when Hitler lost the war.' He drank some of Stalin's wine. 'Do you ever have an identity problem, Miss Larionova?'

She regarded him steadily. 'Do you, Mr Cooper?'

Ukraine – 'Not *the* Ukraine, it's not a desert' – expanded across the dinner table with the consumption of wine.

Michael saw fields of grain rippling on the black-earthed steppe. Stood on the ramparts of Swallow's Nest castle and stared across the Black Sea. Ascended the 192 Potemkin steps at Odessa which he remembered in Eisenstein's *Battleship Potemkin*. Descended into the Monastery of the Caves in Kiev. Heard the hoofbeat of Cossack horses. Breathed the contamination from Chernobyl.

'We're represented at the United Nations,' Magda said. 'Why shouldn't we have our freedom?'

'It wasn't what Stalin had in mind, I guess. He wangled three seats, including Byelorussia, from Roosevelt and Churchill because he didn't want to be outvoted.'

'And where did he wangle – wangle, I like that – this concession?'

'In Ukraine. At Yalta. Where else?'

'He was a great wangler,' Magda said. 'A monster, too. What are you, Michael, American or Russian?'

'I'll tell you when I leave.'

He told her about his brother and fleetingly gained the impression that she wasn't as surprised as she might have been.

'Why is it so important to you?'

49

'Because I promised my father.'

'You're a man of integrity, I can feel that.'

But what was she? he asked himself as they collected their coats and walked into Gorky Street. It had stopped raining. Tyres hissed with purpose, stars shone in pools in the night sky and the air smelled clean. She took his arm, leaning against him a little tipsily.

'Let's walk,' she said, guiding him in the direction of Pushkin Square. 'Why don't you come on one of my guided tours? I'll slip you into my party. No problem.'

No time, he told her.

She walked in silence nursing the refusal. An airliner flew winking across one of the dark pools.

She pointed at some buildings fronted with arches leading into side-streets. 'Chekhov and Chaliapin both lived down there. And that's Gastronome No. 1 once known as the Elisseev Grocery Store. See what you're missing?'

'Maybe when I've found out what happened to Vasily.'

'And how are you going to do that?'

He told her about the bath-house.

They crossed the street and began to walk back to Marx Prospect. When they reached the Intourist she said: 'Maybe I can help you. . . .' She didn't elaborate. 'And then I can really show you the city.'

'Moscow?'

'Kiev,' she said.

This autumn the weather repented for a couple of days and fragile sunshine lit the city. On the second of these intermissions Michael played chess with Robert Hanson in Gorky Park.

He had already discovered the park; its beer and chess halls, its mossy lakes, pergolas, arbours and halls of culture; its flavour of the aristocratic and servile past that still pervaded the converted pastures of the Golitsin Hospital and the Alexander Palace and the Neskuchny Gardens. He enjoyed its weekday loneliness – the limping rotations of the ferris wheel, the companionship of men with their dogs.

Today there were disturbing nuances abroad, a lurking fur-

50

tiveness. Was he being followed? He made elaborate detours and felt stupid – he was only going to play chess with an English defector.

He found Hanson sitting at one of the outdoor tables in a row where black and white are engaged in interminable warfare until winter drives them indoors. Arrogant new recruits played scowling veterans; spectators wandered from battlefield to battlefield.

The first nine moves of a Ruy Lopez were played at a cracking pace then Michael, with black, played a variation. Hanson, chin cupped in his hands, paused and Michael studied him. There was about him an air of premeditated waste. Vestiges of nobility on his features, now pouchy, eyes that had lost a discerning focus. And yet how old was he, forty-seven or so?

Hanson moved, an unexpected reply, and Michael took his time responding. Long ago he had played café chess in New York, winning a few dollars more often than he lost. He moved a bishop.

He glanced along the row of tables. A black-haired man with folds in his face who looked as though he should have been wearing a fedora had taken his place at the end table where he was playing checkers. Have I seen him before? Michael frowned as though anticipating Hanson's next move.

Hanson brought up a knight, then lit a yellow cigarette with a cardboard tip. Michael moved with the sort of bluffing speed that, in times of uncertainty, had helped him to win a few bucks.

Not today it wouldn't have done.

'Check,' Hanson said.

The game took forty-five minutes longer and Michael lost. He got the impression that Hanson hadn't been playing an individual: he had been playing an uncharitable fate.

The second game was more convivial. The black-haired checkers player glanced in their direction, then set up the pieces again with his opponent, a delicately-boned man with pale hair, wearing a raincoat that was too large for him.

'Okay,' Michael said, 'I know you've been asked a hundred times before but, just the same, what made you do it?'

'Leave England? Because I didn't belong.'

'And you do here?'

'I pretended I did. People like me delude ourselves, you know. That's why I go to the bath-house. But the Russians see me as a member of the Twilight Brigade. That's what they call the circle of defectors. Strong on mushroom collecting, amateur theatricals and character assassination. Would you care for an introduction?'

'I'll pass,' Michael said. He moved his queen's pawn two squares. 'Did you know Burgess and Maclean and Philby?'

'Not Burgess, he was before my time. Maclean a little, Philby reasonably well. He had always had ideals, you know; I envied him for that. I had nothing, you see. I was a void waiting to be filled. Can you tell me, Mr Cooper, why in 1939 a young Englishman who had been taught patriotism should have been expected to hate a young German who had been taught patriotism? Why were they expected to kill each other?'

'You know as well as I do that wars are waged by a self-appointed few. The rest of us are lambs to the slaughter.'

'It is the educationalists who are to blame. I believe that sincerely. The glory of war. Criminal indoctrination.'

Ten moves later Michael said: 'The black-haired man at the end of the row playing checkers. Take a casual look at him and tell me if you know him.'

'He looks,' Hanson said, 'like every cartoonist's idea of a Soviet citizen. I do think cartoonists should pay a visit to Samarkand.'

'You don't know him?'

'If he's a patron of the bath-house I might recognise him if he was semi or totally naked. Shall I ask him to take his clothes off?'

Michael sacrificed a pawn. 'Was Philby really an idealist?'

'He believed he was. Isn't that the same?'

'Or did *he* delude himself? Can betraying secrets really be idealistic?'

'Betraying secrets? Have you forgotten that Russia was our ally in the last war?'

Michael moved a bishop. 'Check.' And then: 'Don't give me shit, Hanson. Russia wasn't anyone's ally after 1945.' He leaned back, hands behind his head. 'Were you a spy?'

'I admire your court-room advocacy.' Hanson smoothed the

creases of his forehead with the tips of his fingers. 'The only person I ever spied upon was myself and I failed.'

'Which is why you want out of the Soviet Union?'

'You should prosecute, Mr Cooper, not defend.'

'I pursue truth. An option open to prosecution and defence.'

'Odd,' Hanson said, 'how pompous people become when they talk about truth.'

'And ideals?'

'Chess,' Hanson said, 'is the nearest I've ever come to truth.'

'Which is why you just lost?'

'Check,' murmured Hanson sweeping a rock forward.

Michael studied the board. 'I quit.'

They shook hands.

'We must play again,' Hanson said.

Michael stood up and walked across the damp grass. When he was one hundred yards away he glanced back. Hanson was still sitting at the table but the black-haired checkers player had disappeared.

Outside the bath-house Michael was accosted by a vibrant girl with shining black hair. What did she want, he wondered. Dollars, jeans, cassettes. . . .

What she wanted, she told him, was a favour. Her name was Tanya Agursky and she had heard about his quest. Through her parents she might be able to help him. And in return? He was a lawyer, he could make representations to the International Olympic Committee on her behalf.

Michael stared at her in astonishment. When she explained he thought: why not? If *blat* was currency why not spend it?

5

The protest meeting was held in the men's steam-room. The fire-bricks were cold, the steam condensed to a few pendulous drops of water on the ceiling; with the tiers of marble benches rising on either side the chamber looked like a Roman forum. Patrons, men and women, occupied the benches; the preservation committee sat at a trestle table on the floor. Outside the hesitant rain had stopped and Muscovites who can smell snow on the march knew that winter would arrive that night. In case it made a premature appearance some of the patrons carried *shapkas*, fur hats, and a few women wore headscarves.

The laundress and the stallholder presided, the latter theatrically suffering the laundress's polemics, pinching the bridge of his robust nose, sighing heavily between draughts of beer.

The laundress, wearing her brown Fighting Comrades uniform, beehive of red hair freshly dyed, patrolled the floor, pausing occasionally in front of a section of the audience that might harbour opposition.

'First,' she said, 'a warning. Don't forget that there is at least one informer among us.' She stopped in front of the section where the sallow-faced hairdresser from the Ukraine Hotel was sitting. 'Even today there are some who are still prepared to lick the ass of officialdom.'

'How does she know that?' Michael Cooper asked Robert Hanson.

'A fair bet. It used to be estimated that one out of every twelve Soviet citizens had some sort of KGB connection.'

'But haven't the KGB's teeth been drawn?'

Hanson shrugged. 'Who knows. Outwardly, of course. But how can a secret service really be anything but secret? The

KGB probably poses the greatest threat to the Soviet leader. Particularly with the Old Guard as their front. He's purged the hard-liners from the Politburo but they still prowl the corridors of the Kremlin.'

The laundress pointed an imperious finger at them. 'Perhaps you two gentlemen would like to adjourn to the changing-room to continue your private debate.'

Michael raised a flat-palmed hand. 'Sorry,' he said.

'As it happens,' the laundress went on, encompassing everyone with a sweep of a dimpled hand, 'Comrade Cooper is here to help us.'

'My idea,' said the stallholder.

'Our idea.'

'Then you must both be crazy.' The voice of the miner who had been on strike in the Ukraine staying in Moscow without a *probiska* stamped in his internal passport. 'Why should an American help us?'

'Because,' the laundress said, arms folded across her bosom, 'he's Russian. Unlike you.'

'Shit, don't start that,' the miner said.

The stallholder wiped beer foam from his lips and sighed heavily.

The laundress swept on. 'I have news for you, comrades. They,' pointing vaguely towards the citadels of bureaucracy, 'are stooping to underhand tactics. I have been threatened.' She paused with the timing of a seasoned orator. 'I have been told that I may be banned from Gum for queue-jumping. Now that has never never happened before. Isn't the message clear? Abandon your fight for the banya and we will continue to let you operate in Gum.' She pleaded with her hands. 'What should I do, comrades?'

The seamstress, blue-rinse curls bobbing, rose to her feet. 'Let them do what they wish. Never admit defeat.'

'But you would have to go without. Gum is a good source of *defitsitny* goods.'

'We will manage without black market merchandise,' the seamstress shouted. 'Won't we?'

The Fighting Comrades rose to a woman.

The laundress's medals jingled. 'Comrade Cooper has drawn up a petition for us.'

Hanson whispered: 'Isn't that dangerous?'

'Over a bath-house? I doubt it. In any case they've promised to help me find my brother if I help them.'

The laundress said: 'It is to be handed to everyone concerned in mismanaging this city and the media – TV, radio, press – and foreign correspondents stationed here.'

She sat down abruptly and began to fan herself with a copy of the petition. The stallholder rose and his voice, deep and articulate, punctuated occasionally with oaths, rose from his beer belly.

'Comrades, I too have been threatened.' He had them. 'As you know I and other fellow workers have taken advantage of *perestroika* to open our own co-operatives, in my case a stall that sells pies and *shashlik*. Soon we will take on the State stalls and sell fruit drinks and ice-cream. A whole meal served in minutes.'

The Kremlin chauffeur said: 'This is not the place, comrade, to advertise your wares.'

The stallholder ignored him. 'This morning my stall was forcibly moved by the militia from the entrance to Sokolniki Park. Now what harm could I have been doing there?'

'Poisoning people?' inquired the bodybuilder.

'What about the threats?' asked the Kremlin chauffeur.

A drop of condensed steam fell from the ceiling and splashed on the trestle-table. 'While the militia were taking away my stall I was approached by a man in plain clothes. One of Vilkin's men; I'm sure of it. He suggested in a devious way that if I abandoned the campaign to save the bath-house I could operate my stall. Ah, that Vilkin, that shit.'

A murmur of contempt rose from the benches.

'Even if you did abandon the campaign,' the laundress said, 'we would fight on.'

The stallholder leaned on the table and regarded her speculatively. 'In Siberia they say geese are the doorknockers of the *izbas*. With a voice like yours they would require neither geese nor doorknockers.'

'What I do know,' the laundress said, 'is that when a man has lost an argument he resorts to abuse. Why not leave the whole campaign to us, the Fighting Comrades? We know how to deal with men, even Vilkin. Then you can get on with your drinking and brawling.'

'And fornicating,' the hairdresser said.

'Or perhaps,' the stallholder said, 'we should take over and leave you to gossip and knit shawls.'

The seamstress restored order. 'This isn't the Kremlin, no in-fighting.' She spoke with quick, needle-sharp words. 'If we are to beat Vilkin, we must have unity. And if we are to enjoy equal rights with men,' nodding at the laundress, 'we must behave with dignity.'

'What I don't understand,' Michael whispered to Hanson, 'is why this guy Vilkin is being so stubborn. Wouldn't it make sense to admit defeat? The will of the people. . . .'

'The trouble,' Hanson said, is that it's got out of hand. His honour is at stake. At the best of times he's a five-year-plan plodder. And a toad as well.'

'So are we agreed?' the stallholder demanded. 'First a concentrated campaign of publicity. Then demonstrations.'

'And then?' the Kremlin chauffeur asked.

The laundress stood up. 'We do battle.' Drops of water shivered on the ceiling and splashed around her.

From the banya Hanson drove to a defectors' party in a twenty-two storey Stalinist block of apartments near the Planetarium.

'Any news?' asked the hostess, a West German with capable shoulders and greying blonde hair skittishly styled.

'Nothing yet,' replied Hanson guessing that she had been primed by one of the resident foreign correspondents to find out if he had got his exit visa. He wasn't big game among defectors – scarcely a defector at all in his view – but the return to Britain of a prodigal after twenty years would make good copy.

He thought: if only they knew who had persuaded me to stay here.

'We're all praying for you,' the hostess said. 'Don't forget Sunday, a mushroom hunt.'

'I'll take a rain-check on it,' aware that his turn of phrase, like his clothes – today a frayed Prince of Wales check – was dated.

'Lunch at Tony and Sheila's place afterwards. Roast beef and Yorkshire,' the ultimate inducement to an Englishman.

Hanson who disliked Yorkshire pudding made his way across the cavernous living room, acknowledging other guests, but proceeding inexorably towards the bar, which was backed by a blown-up photograph of Chi Chi, one of two pandas who, more than twenty years earlier, had declined to mate in Moscow Zoo with a panda named An An.

He poured himself a vodka. He had once vowed to cut down his daily drinking but had finally abandoned the delusion. Alcohol subdued his doubts, stilled his trembling hands.

He was joined by a middle-aged Englishman, tentative and homosexual, who had survived some narrow squeaks in the vicinity of the Bolshoi. 'Glad you could make it,' he said. 'You're a bit of a recluse these days.'

'A lot on my mind.'

'So I hear. Anything positive?'

'This and that.' Hanson glanced over the Englishman's shoulder, looking for a pretext to escape, but the interrogators were closing in. An Australian journalist who wrote occasional pieces for the *Morning Star*. An American wounded more than fifty years ago fighting for the International Brigades in Spain. A Scottish seaman who had served with the Red Army in World War II and been dispatched to a penal camp for his pains. An eavesdropper from the British Embassy diffidently tuning his scrum-battered ears to any intelligence that might reach him on the outcasts' grapevine.

The ex-seaman, owner of hard, shiny-palmed hands and a bald scalp that wrinkled expressively, tried a clumsy ruse. 'Lucky bastard, wish to Christ I was going with you.'

Hanson ignored him.

'When, more like,' said the Australian. He was gingery and laid-back, so unlike the popular conception of an Australian that he could trap the unwary into indiscretions.

The British diplomat pulled at one ear that looked as though it had been gnawed by a rat.

The American who had once met Hemingway in Madrid said: 'Let's cut the crap, Bob. Have you got a visa or not?'

Hanson said: 'No comment. Speak to my secretary in the morning.' He smiled. 'Nothing definite.'

'On the level?' Sometimes the American's idiom was, like his own, an echo from the past.

'Undulating.'

They regarded him uncertainly. His responses sometimes unsettled his companions which was, perhaps, what he had intended long ago when his tongue had been timid.

The ex-seaman, believing steadfastly in his guile, said: 'The Press will be at Heathrow. The whole pack.'

'I'm famished,' Hanson said.

He broke through the cordon and took his place in a queue at a table covered with a cerise paper table-cloth. The food looked filling although not of the quality provided by some capitalist residents with hard currency to spend. Red caviar, black bread, a shark-faced fish that looked as though it had been lifted from a showcase, pale ham, potato salad, a trifle that wobbled to faint tremors said to originate in the metro.

He took his plate to a sofa where he could survey the company. Defectors, becalmed spies, unquestioning communists from the West who had settled at the fount of their beliefs, a few mid-Europeans uneasily following events in their countries, a couple of KGB visitors mingling politely. KGB apart, what bothered them was that if he went back to Britain he might talk – not about clandestine matters of which he knew nothing but about their lives in Moscow.

He was joined by Mayhew, a hearty Yorkshireman with a pendulous lower lip who reminded him of J. B. Priestley. Such was the calibre of his bonhomie that no one in the trade mission visiting the Soviet Union long ago had suspected any duplicity until he had eloped with a feline blonde interpreter from Riga. He was tolerated by the community but not well liked because he was considered vulgar. Hanson admired his perverse exuberance.

Mayhew washed down a mouthful of potato salad with vodka and tonic – a reprehensible mix in Russian eyes – and began to talk expansively about the twins *glasnost* and *perestroika*.

'Look at the poor buggers.' He waved a smeared glass at the other guests. 'Came here to escape democracy and capitalism, and what are they getting? What they fled from, aye that's what. Must make 'em wonder if it was all worthwhile. Was it,

59

Bob?' And before Hanson could reply: 'If it was why the bloody heck do you want to go back?'

'Out of curiosity.' Hanson, who believed that you could only be a traitor to yourself, always tried hard to be truthful, honesty being his only luxury these days. 'To see if I would do it again. To see if I was right.'

'Coming back here are you?'

'Of course.' He wasn't absolutely sure if this was the truth but the apartment was almost certainly bugged so, sadly, he couldn't say anything else. Mayhew often talked indiscreetly within the earshot of the microphones and occasionally directed jocular obscenities at the hidden listeners.

'And why not? To the new freedoms which were once the prerogative of the West. To riots, demonstrations and dissent. Ironic, isn't it, that our leader is trying to do the decent thing and getting kicked in the teeth for his pains. Makes you wonder which was right, the American Dream or the Russian Revolution. What do you think, Bob?'

'All that matters is that *we* did what we thought was right.'

'And did we? Did your left hand know what your right was doing?'

'You forget, I'm left-handed,' Hanson said.

'Don't play fucking word games with me, lad.' Mayhew prodded a finger of black bread into his mouth, bottom lip wet and porcine.

Hanson excused himself and picked his way through the throng to the bathroom. He washed his hands and, as he dried them, stole a glance in the mirror. He was the sole occupant but he could sense a presence. There was so much to tell the stranger but he was determined not to share the boldly surfacing past with him, not yet.

He remembered the date, the turning point. July 31st 1969. The day halfpennies were no longer accepted as legal tender in Britain.

And he was at Moscow University, studying for his Cambridge postgraduate degree.

The speaker in the lecture room below the extravagant Stalinist spires was a lawyer-politician from a city eight hundred miles east of Moscow who, at the age of forty, had just been elected to the Central Committee of the Communist Party.

He was chunkily built, richly voiced, mesmeric. And he spoke of communism in a simple and golden fashion that scythed through Party dogma. Listening to him, Robert Hanson was conscious of an all-pervading sense of peace as though he were deep in a forest, and his worries about identity and loyalty dissolved in this pure vision of equality.

After the lecture the politician, First Secretary of his territory, was introduced to the foreign students and Hanson, aware that he was in the presence of a luminary, asked for his autograph.

The First Secretary asked him his name and, when Hanson told him, he smiled and said: 'I might just remember that.'

By the time Hanson got back to Britain his fiancée had married a banker with prospects and his father had been framed by his partner on fraud charges.

One year later Hanson returned to the source of his vision and took out Soviet citizenship.

An impatient rapping on the bathroom door. 'Come on whoever you are, I'm bursting.' As he emerged a young woman wearing granny spectacles swept past him.

On his way out of the apartment he was intercepted by the hostess. 'Not going already, Bob?' She tossed her grey-blonde hair.

'A business appointment.'

'Ah.' She smiled conspiratorially. 'I understand. Good luck. But don't forget Sunday. Mushrooms.' She winked, admitting edible fungi into the conspiracy.

From the apartment block he drove to the offices of OVIR which was handling his application for an exit visa. He sat at a metal, jungle-green desk facing a woman wearing a work-shined navy suit and a white blouse with a lace collar. Pretty enough with bobbed hair and kind eyes, she was an old adversary and confidante. No, she said, there hadn't been any further news.

'Any idea how long it will be?'

'These matters take time.'

'Six months? Is there really any reason why I shouldn't be allowed to return to my own country?'

'But, Comrade Hanson, you made the Soviet Union your own country.'

'I only want to visit Britain.'

'Do you?' She regarded him wisely. 'And the reason for your visit . . . . '

'You know perfectly well. My mother is very old and ill.'

She picked up a pink dossier and opened it. 'After your father went to prison . . . . '

' . . . on a trumped-up charge.'

' . . . your mother obtained a divorce and remarried. She was reported at the time as saying she had *disowned you*.' She uttered the last two words in English.

'A quaint and old-fashioned phrase. Like me.' He smiled at her, the smile a relic of the days when he had discovered to his surprise that he was attractive to women. He clasped his hands and leaned across the table. 'Now tell me truthfully why you won't let me go. You can be quite open these days, you know.'

'It isn't me, Comrade Hanson.'

'I wasn't a spy. I'm not a colonel in the KGB, not even a private soldier. I am nothing. All I want to do is see my mother, drink a pint of English beer and watch a cricket match.'

'But it's almost winter. Isn't cricket a summer game?'

'*Touché*. A soccer match then.'

'And your wife, Comrade Hanson, what does she think about you going?'

Hanson, certain that she knew exactly what Lena thought, said: 'She has no objections.'

'I really don't understand you.' She leaned back in her chair appraising him. She was childless and recently divorced and she lived in a cramped apartment near the Olympic Village. 'You have a dacha outside Moscow and an apartment inside. Your life is very . . . snug,' she said wistfully.

'I merely want to see the country of my birth before I die.'

She consulted the dossier. 'But you're only forty-seven. And you have gone on record as saying that patriotism' – she returned to English again – 'is merely an excuse for hostile intent.'

'The last refuge of a scoundrel,' according to Johnson. 'But you haven't answered my question. Why can't I go?'

'Has it occurred to you, Comrade Hanson, that some of your fellow defectors may have something to do with it? That they may have approached someone in State Security?'

'Why would they do that?' If it were true it was because they didn't want him to broadcast to the West the poverty of their existence in Russia. But he wanted to hear her say it.

'Some of them are, perhaps, discontented – I can't see why they should be – and they don't want you to tell tales in England. *Sour grapes.* Isn't that the expression?'

Hanson embarked on mild and familiar flirtation. 'You're not deliberately withholding the visa are you?'

'Of course.'

'Then we will elope to the Black Sea. Are you packed?'

'But you are happily married, Comrade Hanson. Aren't you?'

Was he? Back at the dacha he picked up a photograph of Lena from the sideboard. She looked back at him steadily, plump-breasted but sharp-framed with a martyr's eyes. How would her life have developed if she hadn't been urged into a marriage of convenience to monitor the behaviour of a defector who was not, perhaps, as idealistic as he seemed? Married contentedly, producing two children, both Young Pioneers, later members of the Komsomol?

Instead she had been politely ostracised by her own kind and remained childless. But there had been compensations: she had enjoyed a higher standard of living than the average Soviet housewife and she had, presumably, fulfilled her duty to State and Party. To what extent he had never been sure. In the early days, reported his moods and confidences, eavesdropped on his dreams. . . . And now? Perhaps she had been told to find out if he intended to stay in Britain. To seek asylum in his own country!

Poor Lena. You will be rewarded in the Elysian fields of Marxist-Leninism.

He replaced the photograph, fetched the vodka from the kitchen and switched on the television to catch *Vremya*, the nine o'clock news. References to unrest in Ukraine and appeals to keep ethnic aspirations within the framework of the system.

Hanson knew that he was witnessing the end of communism and mourned the tarnishing of the bright visions struck here in the Soviet Union more than seventy years ago, the visions that the young politician had burnished fifty years later at Moscow University.

He switched off the TV, drank more vodka. He went into the bedroom, sat on the edge of the unmade bed, glanced into the mirror on the inside of the wardrobe door. *'So you're back.'*

'I'm never far away.'

'You remind me of a success story that no one bothered to write. A conquistador with a pot of fool's gold. A lord mayor without a banquet.'

'You know who I am.'

'What I might have been?'

'We all have a choice.'

'No one does. Not from the moment we're born.'

'What did you want to be?'

'A creator. Novelist, playwright . . . . '

'Then that's what I am.'

Hanson slammed the door of the wardrobe. Heard the mirror shatter inside.

Then he went to one of the bedside tables and from the drawer took out an autograph book with a punished leather cover. It contained just one signature. At least the stranger didn't possess the autograph of the leader of the Soviet Union.

6

And indeed the Muscovites were right: it snowed overnight with gentle persistence and at dawn the city emerged in soft and secret light. Snow-ploughs went ponderously about their business; pavements rang to the scrape of *babushkas'* shovels; citizens who all summer had confided their dread of winter rejoiced.

Tanya Agursky welcomed the snow from the window of her partitioned bedroom. She bathed and dressed quietly, took her fur hat and coat, hanging beside her old school uniform – brown dress and white pinafore – and, skates in hand, stole from the awakening apartment.

As usual Komsomol Square was busy with peasants who had converged on the three railway stations to buy, sell or barter. Today the women wore felt boots, the men hats with spaniel ears. The snow fell lightly and skittishly.

She caught the metro to Dynamo Stadium and took to the ice searching the other side of the barrier for the piratical figure of Lev Grechko who had once been one half of the world champion figure-skating pair. Without Lev she wouldn't have won a place at a special school where winter sports were encouraged – excel in sport in the Soviet Union and privileges unfurled before you. Without Lev there would be no hope of competing in the Olympics.

She accelerated round the almost deserted rink, loving the song of the skates, and executed a couple of upright spins. Then she saw him, swathed in grey scarf, a grin lodged between his wagging beard and his audacious nose.

He coached her for an hour, then beckoned her off the ice. She changed her skates and they went to the cafeteria where he drank tea, she Pepsi Cola.

'Well,' he said, unwinding a metre of scarf, 'winter's here. Our season. A lake isn't a lake until it's frozen.'

'Any news?'

'The Olympics? Nothing. And there won't be until that obstinate father of yours agrees to go quietly.'

'He says that's defeat. He says he can't cringe away after two years in a camp.'

'So he sticks a Star of David on the Kremlin wall. That wasn't smart, was it?'

'He's incorrigible.'

'So was Trotsky. He was Jewish and look what happened to him.' His laughter, which often issued at incongruous moments, boomed round the cafeteria. 'Can't you persuade him to accept compromise? Or is it the protest that matters? There are people like that, you know.'

'That's what my mother says. That doesn't help.'

'He's a selfish man.'

'A proud man.'

'Defensive? I like that.' Lev stilled his beard with one hand. 'But unless he changes his stance the news isn't good.' He drank some tea. 'The school isn't happy about the affair of the Star of David.'

'They've always known what he's like.'

'Indeed they have. I persuaded them that he would see reason. But here he is still creating trouble. It doesn't help the image of *glasnost*, does it?'

'They want to throw me out?'

'It's a possibility.'

Which would effectively end all her skating aspirations. She told him about her approach to the Olympic Committee through Michael Cooper, the American.

'Might help. Doubt it though. The committee here will just say you're not good enough.'

'You could write and tell them just how good I am.'

'If it would help. But I'm an old man, a has-been.'

'They still respect your opinion.'

'You might,' Lev said, 'have told me that I'm not a has-been.'

She choked over her Pepsi. 'Come to the banya more often and you'll look younger.'

'I hear we're organising a protest, too. It's infectious.' He picked a slice of lemon from his tea and ate it. 'Take my advice, have nothing to do with it. One protester in the family is enough.'

'Will you write to the Olympic Committee?'

He clasped her hand and she noticed how slender his fingers were. 'Of course I will,' he said.

The lake – little more than a pond, but love can make a carriage out of a cart – was cupped by gentle hills not far from the writers' colony at Peredelkino where Pasternak was buried. There was a dacha there too which the unromantic might have demoted to a log-cabin, where friends of Yury's parents spent the fleeting summer months. With the first snow-smelling breath of winter the friends had returned to their apartment in Moscow and Yury had the key.

He drove Tanya there in his tan Zhiguli – young Olympic hopefuls are entitled to modest automobiles – which he parked among the pine trees shouldering the dacha towards the lake. The fringes of the water were already laced with ice; soon it would be frozen solid and they would skate on it together.

They walked beside the lake. Moths of snow fluttered around them. He slipped his arm round her waist. She leaned against him and found that her thoughts were making their way to the bedroom of the dacha that smelled of resin and lavender. A ration of sunshine found its way through the bruised clouds; his green eyes shone with it. He opened the door of the dacha. In the 'fridge he found a bottle of sweet Sladkoye champagne. Found or expected to find? He lit a fire with yellowing copies of *Pravda* and *Trud*, pine cones and logs and poured the champagne. 'To us.' They sat opposite each other in front of the labouring fire. She saw them sitting thus in forty years' time. Content but unambitious. Youth had to be given its rein; as the flames caught she felt sexual excitement stir.

He poured her a second glass of champagne. You're trying to seduce me, she thought. Well, I'm nearly eighteen. She knew girls younger than that who had made love. Gone all the way, as they put it. But what if she became pregnant? That, surely, was an end to Olympic dreams. . . . But I can have an abortion.

Some women had eight or nine. Why think such things? Love is what I should be thinking about. The champagne laughed inside her.

A finger of ash fell from a log. Outside the afternoon began to summon night. Mauve shadows assembled in the fallen snow. She imagined the frieze of ice on the lake broadening as the cold knitted it. The time of the wolf. Champagne bubbles fizzed deliciously on her tongue. He kissed her and felt for her breasts under her sweater.

'Let's go upstairs,' she said.

She lay naked under a patched sheet. Gazed at a print of a poppy field on the wall, wandered through the fragile blossoms, feeling the petals brush her legs. Where was Yury? She heard water gush from a tap. Stretched out a hand, found her glass and drank a little more champagne. What was it like, this miracle of love and life without which none of us would be here? Painful the first time? Who cared?

She heard her mother. 'I have only ever loved one man.' Their apartment was a cabinet of marital rectitude. Would Yury leave the light on or switch it off? She smelled the lovely faded smell of lavender; through a slit in the curtains she could see a star pinned beneath a new moon; the snow must have stopped. The door opened. He was beside her, his body hard and warm. But she was drifting into sleep. In her dreams she heard the cry of a wolf.

Wolf-dogs, progeny of wolves and stray dogs, roam in packs outside Moscow. There are said to be between 1,000 and 2,000 of them, varying in ferocity according to the breed of the stray.

The bodybuilder bred his own wolf-dogs in a compound to the west of the city which was guarded by an old man who had known Michael's parents, possibly his brother too, during the war. The bodybuilder drove Michael there one October day when the snow lay flat and obdurate on the fields and at the side of the roads untouched by snow-ploughs.

The bodybuilder's aim, he told Michael, was to produce new breeds of dogs, crosses between wolves and strays. 'Wolf and South Caucasian sheepdog, that will be some dog,' the bodybuilder said, as his old grey Volga slithered round a bend. 'Wolf and Dobermann. How about that?'

'They'll all be fierce dogs?'

'I'll breed the finest guard dogs in the whole of the Soviet Union.'

'What about the strays? Surely the owner of a Dobermann would look for it.'

'Dog-catchers pick up 70,000 strays a year in Moscow alone.'

'And you buy them from the dog-catchers?'

'Something like that,' the bodybuilder said vaguely. He glanced at the black diver's watch on his wrist. 'We should be there in ten minutes.' He corrected a skid.

'And you're sure the old man who knew my parents will be there?'

'If the old bastard isn't he's out of a job. He may be drunk, of course.' Above the sound of the geriatric engine Michael heard barking. 'What about your other leads?'

'They all dried up.' Unsatisfactorily, Michael thought, as though they had suddenly lost direction.

'The Jew?'

'Wouldn't even see me.'

'You were lucky. Who wants to meet a trouble-making *zhid*.'

The Volga skidded to a halt outside a row of low concrete buildings on one side of a snow-covered enclosure caged by a wire fence. At one end of the row stood a wooden hut, its roof fanged with icicles. Wolf-dogs, whining and barking, clawed the fence as the bodybuilder stepped out of the Volga.

He pointed at the flattened and fouled snow. 'Where is that drunken bastard?' He put on a black, peaked cap and took a whippy leather cane from the trunk of the car. 'They don't look as though they've been fed for a week.'

The dogs howled.

The bodybuilder unlocked the gate. The wolf-dogs, each with lupine fur, physique determined by the stray in them, ran at him. He pointed the leather cane. They stopped; some grovelling, bellies pressed into the snow.

A wolf-dog with yellow eyes padded forward, teeth bared. The bodybuilder hit it across the muzzle with the cane. Blood ran. The wolf-dog slunk away.

'Did you have to hit it so hard?'

69

'They've got to respect me. They're beautiful animals but they've got to learn respect.' He snapped his fingers and the wolf-dog he had hit came to him, belly on the snow. He stroked it and the wolf-dog wagged its tail. 'I love these animals,' the bodybuilder said. 'In their way they love me.'

'They might love you more if you fed them.'

'They get meat,' the bodybuilder said. 'And they don't have to queue for it in the central market. Do you hunt, Mikhail?'

'I fish,' Michael said. In Canada once, he remembered, with Barbara. A lake rippled with shoals of sunshine, the trout biting, an insect murmur in the forest. . . . Barbara didn't enjoy it. She had wanted a vacation in California. Who could blame her?

'Would you like to see my guns?'

'I want to see the old man.'

'He can wait. He's drunk all right.'

The bodybuilder walked past the dogs to the last concrete building. He walked with a slight bounce, arms hanging away from his body as though he were holding invisible weights.

The building was so low that they had to crouch to get in. It was stuffed with straw. The bodybuilder plunged one arm into the straw and produced a long wooden box. From the box he produced a gun.

'A 7.62mm Dragunov sniper's rifle. Beautiful, isn't it?' He stroked the barrel. 'Gas operated, semi-automatic, effective range 1,300 metres.'

'You *acquired* it?'

'Afghanistan,' the bodybuilder said. 'Every motor rifle platoon had one. This one went missing.' He replaced the gun. 'Okay, beauties,' he said to the wolf-dogs pacing outside. 'Now you get to eat.'

He unlocked the door of another building. Meat hung from hooks, blood pinkly frozen. The air smelled raw. 'Moose,' the bodybuilder said. 'I got it with one shot from the Dragunov.'

'Aren't you going to heat it for them?'

'Over the old man's stove.'

He filled a sack with meat and headed for the wooden hut. The wolf-dogs jumped and sniffed. He hit one of them with the cane but the smell of meat was so strong in its nostrils that it jumped higher. He cracked it across the back and it subsided.

He hammered on the door of the hut. Icicles snapped and

70

fell around him. 'Shit,' said the bodybuilder. 'Here, hold this.'
He handed the sack of meat to Michael. He selected another
key from the heavy bunch and opened the door.

Heat leaped out.

The old man was lying on a bed covered with sacking. His
unshaven cheeks were sunken; metal teeth gleamed in his
half-open mouth. Two empty, unlabelled bottles stood on a
cigarette-scarred card table. In one corner the stove glowed.

'Out of his skull,' the bodybuilder said.

Michael put down the sack and went over to the old man.
He stared at him for a few moments. Then he said: 'This man
isn't drunk, he's dead.'

Back in the city Michael went straight to the bath-house to rid
himself of the smell of raw meat, dogs and death. He sat on
the top tier and let the rising heat open his pores. Who else
was there to help him? Even the initial enthusiasm of the
patrons had evaporated. Or was this his imagination? He
breathed deeply of the eucalyptus steam; it scorched his nostrils.
But I mustn't give up, he thought. Then the words of Magda
Larionova came to him. 'Maybe I can help you. . . .' Well, hell,
maybe she could.

He escaped to the changing-room where a skinny brewer was
dispensing blackcurrant *kvas*. He accepted a mug of it and sat
at a table opposite Hanson.

'Any luck?' he asked him.

'Lots of it if you consider staying in Russia lucky. Oh yes,'
Hanson said, staring into the mauve depths of his drink, 'I'm
inundated with luck.'

Had he always spoken like that? Or did affectations finally
become part of your character? Michael had once known a
generous man who had pretended to be mean and had become
a skinflint.

'But you only want to go for a visit. You are happy here,
aren't you?'

'I don't know. I never have known. That's why I want to go
back, to find out.'

'You're not the only one who wants to get out. I met a Jewish girl the other week whose father's been trying to emigrate since for ever.'

'Agursky? He'll never make it unless he stops shouting the odds. Perhaps he doesn't want to make it. Perhaps I don't. Would you like to come to my apartment for dinner one day? I'm moving into the city from the dacha.'

'I'd like that,' Michael said. 'A dacha *and* an apartment?'

'Like tourists, defectors have certain advantages over Russians.'

'You regard yourself as a defector?'

'For want of a better word. Pariah.'

'You can do better than that.'

'Dilettante,' Hanson said.

They were interrupted by the arrival of the pickpocket, hands fluttering. 'Have you heard the news?'

Conversation stopped because he sometimes stole thoughts as well as wallets.

'Guess where the stallholder is planning to set up shop?'

'In the Kremlin?' The Kremlin chauffeur winked at the other patrons.

'Close. In Red Square.'

7

A few hundred yards from the site where the stallholder planned to stage his act of defiance, Viktor Petrov, leader of the Soviet Union, sat in a modest office among the architectural glories of the Kremlin and agonised.

Autumnal shades prevailed. Russet cloth across the table-desk, scuffed leather chair, shelves of leather-bound books, a weary hand palm in a wooden tub.

It wasn't Petrov's study. It had once been occupied by Lenin and Petrov came here to meditate and question whether he was betraying the visions once seen by the Bolshevik leader.

Standing at the window overlooking the Kremlin grounds, Petrov shared the visions, returned with Lenin from exile in 1917 to Petrograd, now Leningrad, acknowledged the ecstatic greeting of the crowds at Finland Station.

Ah, such a night. Petrograd taken with scarcely a dozen lives lost. Then Moscow. The Bolsheviks in power. Peace, bread, land.

Then three years of remorseless civil war. Which we won. And then what happened? Joseph Stalin happened. Purges and policies of economic ruin.

Even now, thirty-five years later, Petrov felt his faith shudder with the 'secret' revelations of Stalin's crimes by Nikita Khrushchev at the twentieth Party Congress. It was as though a devout Christian in his mid-twenties had suddenly learned that Christ was a crook.

Which was when my crusade was born. And re-affirmed in 1961 at the twenty-second Party Congress when it was agreed that Stalin's body should be removed from the mausoleum in Red Square where it had rested beside Lenin's.

But should I reverse the principles of Marxist-Leninism just

73

because one man corrupted them? Petrov walked round the small room and, through an open door, contemplated the telephone switchboard that had been Lenin's link with the battlefields of the Civil War. What am I expecting? A call from Lenin?

But there was no dusty voice from the heroic past.

He closed his eyes and saw a dark-haired boy wearing a peaked cap that was too big for him kneeling outside a barn. He was compactly built but there was a frailty about his expression that was disturbing and Petrov fancied that his most precious possession, trust, was contained inside the cap.

But even then the trust was under insidious assault.

Peering through a slit in the wall of the barn, Viktor Petrov tugged at the peak of the cap; it gave him more years than the seven he owned and it gave him courage.

The five men sitting around a bale of mouldering hay were discussing a goat and a kid and the direction of their debate worried Viktor because both animals belonged to his father.

Well, not strictly speaking because, according to his father, they belonged to the State. 'That's collectivization. One day you will understand.'

'But Misha' – that was the kid – 'belongs to his mother.'

'And his mother belongs to the State therefore Misha belongs to the State.'

'I don't understand,' Viktor complained as they walked along a lane towards the village south of the Don near the city of Stalingrad named after the illustrious leader of the Soviet Union. The dried black mud was slippery from a summer shower and elderberries hung in clusters from the overhanging trees; ahead a derelict wooden church, its domes perched precariously, steamed in the sunshine.

'Well, you know about the hard times when we worked under the yoke of the landowners and the *kulaks*, the rich peasants. Well the Boss,' which was how he referred to Stalin, 'decided to change all that. He decided that all farmers should work for the State the same way factory workers do.'

'And was it a good idea?'

74

'It was a good idea,' his father replied unsatisfactorily.

'But it doesn't work?'

'You must never repeat any of this conversation. Do you understand?' Viktor thought that this was a strangely timorous remark to issue from the lips of a bearded giant who had fought for the Reds in the Civil War. 'Mistakes were made. . . .'

'Sergei says a lot of farmers only joined the Revolution so that they could own the land they worked on.'

'You must stop listening to your friend Sergei. He's too old for his years.'

'He's twelve,' Viktor said, switching at a clump of fireweed with a stick. 'He says that any farmers or peasants who refused to work for the State were either killed or sent to Siberia.'

His father rested one heavy hand on Viktor's shoulders. 'You must stop seeing your friend Sergei. Find someone your own age.' He stroked his grey-streaked beard. 'For your own good.'

Viktor said: 'If working for the State is such a good idea why are people starving?'

'Perhaps,' his father said carefully, 'because people lost initiative.'

'What's that, Papa?'

His father thought about it. 'Pride,' he finally said as though he were reassuring himself.

When they got back to the farmhouse Viktor's mother was sitting outside in the sunshine peeling potatoes. The potatoes, hoarded during the winter and spring, were wrinkled and sprouting. She dropped flesh into one saucepan, skin and sprouts into another for soup. She had taken off her headscarf and her grey hair stirred in the breeze; her cheeks, Viktor noted, were bunched like those of an older woman.

He crossed the yard to a corner where Misha lay asleep and stroked its mother's hard-knuckled head. The goat, skinny-ribbed from undernourishment and feeding the kid, stared at him ruminatively.

His father was talking to his mother and his voice reached him on the breeze. 'They're holding a meeting tonight . . . in Anatoly's barn . . . let's hope no one has said anything. . . .'

'About what?' Viktor asked, returning to his parents.

They looked at each other. His mother said: 'You haven't mentioned Misha to anyone, have you, Viktor?' She had told him that its birth was a secret but he hadn't understood why.

He shook his head because he didn't want to hear himself lie.

And now the men in the barn were discussing Misha and guilt stirred inside him. Anyone, he gathered, who had indulged in private enterprise, whatever that was, had to be reported to the local Party headquarters. And it was understood that in every village a minimum of two such delinquents had to be unmasked. The problem was that this village didn't harbour any such criminal elements. So how could the committee fulfil its quota?

Watching them debate by the light of a kerosene lamp, Viktor was struck by their unhappiness. Socialism, surely, was supposed to distribute happiness, albeit through toil and common endeavour. He had been taught this many times at school; once, memorably, when the class had been instructed to scratch out the eyes from a photograph of one of Stalin's enemies in a history book. Afterwards they had sung a hymn to Stalin.

The chairman of the committee, a cadaverous man with a head that was too heavy for his shoulders, said: 'The fact remains that Comrade Petrov has not declared the existence of the kid.' He drew on his pipe and blew smoke into the oily light.   .

'Perhaps he intends to.' The voice of the schoolmaster with the tobacco breath who every morning straightened the portrait of Stalin, smiling benevolently beneath his thick moustache, with his chalky fingers.

'That's not the point, comrade. The point is that we have to produce two enemies of the Cause. If we don't then we will suffer.'

Enemies? Viktor imagined his father with his eyes scratched out. All because of Misha? He remembered the kid's emergence into the world from its mother's stomach, slippery and defence-less. How could such a dainty-hooved animal pose a threat to his parents? He pulled at the peak of his cap.

The committee continued to agonise. Stars glittered thickly in the summer sky. One of the village drunks lurched past him on his way to the pump, the pivot of the clustered wooden cottages with their fretted eaves, where he snored and bubbled through the night. A rat paused in its foraging and stared at

Viktor hidden behind a water tank. If the rat could see him perhaps humans could too. He pressed himself close to the wet earth where the grass grew lushly after its winter hibernation.

'I ask you, comrades, who else is there?'

'Report me,' the schoolmaster said. 'I haven't declared the existence of my pupils' burgeoning knowledge.'

'Why report anyone?' The breathless voice of the cobbler, his crouching back turned away from Viktor.

'You know why,' the chairman said, words issuing in billows of pipe smoke.

'How can they argue? We are good citizens of the Soviet Union. So good that we are all blameless.'

'They will think it is a conspiracy.'

'So? They can't prove anything.'

'They can dispossess us all. Put us on a train to nowhere. It has happened. . . .'

Dispossessed? What did that mean? If socialism was sharing these men seemed to be sharing only misery.

The chairman said: 'When we planted the grain when the snow had melted there wasn't enough to go round. I wonder why, comrades. Had someone kept some back to be ground into flour?' He stared at the cobbler.

A pause. A star moved in the sky. The rat scuttered away. It was not a good time in history for hungry rats.

'I suppose you are right,' the cobbler said. 'As always. Comrade Petrov should have declared the kid.'

'Then we must report him?' The chairman looked from one member of the committee to the other, and when each nodded: 'Then it shall be done.'

'But that is only half our quota,' the schoolmaster said.

'It will do for the time being. What about the first five-year plan? That didn't work either, did it?'

'Shush,' the schoolmaster said.

When Viktor got home he told his parents what he had heard. His mother sat down in the creaking rocking-chair, hands tightly clenched. His father paced the room.

Finally he said: 'So you did tell someone.'

'I mentioned it at school.' Viktor wanted to cry but he was too appalled to do so. 'I didn't think it mattered. A baby goat. . . .'

77

'How many children know?'

'I told only one,' Viktor said. He took off his cap and felt the peak between thumb and forefinger. Without thinking he had told Pavel; Pavel was the *zvenovoi*, the group leader and informer. How could I have been so stupid? But who would have dreamt that a kid could be so important?

'But he would have told others. . . .'

Viktor's mother said quietly: 'Shall I pack?'

Pack? What was she talking about? Viktor began to tremble.

His father stroked his beard. 'Wait. Let me think.' The floorboards sighed beneath his tramping feet. 'This boy – '

'Pavel,' Viktor said.

' – might have told other children but he is the only real source the committee has. His word against yours,' looking intently at Viktor.

What was he expected to do? Deny the existence of Misha? A terrible certainty began to settle upon him.

His father told him to sit on the bench in front of the cold stove. His words were awesome, his tone gentle. Had he not always told Viktor to tell the truth? Viktor nodded. Well, sadly, there were times when other sins outweighed lies. If they wanted to stay in the cottage – Viktor gazed at the gingerbread eaves outlined through the window against the starlight sky – then he would have to tell an untruth.

'That Misha never existed?'

'That Misha's dead.'

'But Misha's alive,' as the certainty froze inside him.

'Misha died at birth.'

'No,' his mother cried out but his father, who usually listened to her, held up his hand, and said: 'This is the way it has to be.'

Viktor waited until he got to bed to weep.

When he went into the yard in the morning the goat was standing in its corner but of the kid there was no sign.

Viktor waited till lunch-break in the schoolyard to tackle Pavel who had that morning reported one boy for stealing purple ink powder and a girl for wetting herself.

Viktor, squaring his cap, said: 'We think our goat's going to have a kid.'

'But you've already got one.' Pavel, a crop-haired and freckled boy whose eyes shone with martyred zeal, frowned at Viktor.

'What makes you think that?'

'Because you told me, stupid.'

Memory returned miraculously to Viktor. 'Ah, that kid. Didn't I tell you? It was born dead.'

'But you described it to me.'

'Did I say it was alive?'

'You said it bleated.'

'As it died.'

'But I told – '

'Who, Pavel?'

'You lied to me,' Pavel said. 'Deliberately. I shall have to report you.'

'There is no kid. They will say it was you who lied. A *zvenovoi* who lies. Not much future there, Pavel.'

'You prick.' Pavel, freckles moving energetically, raised a fist and swung it.

Viktor ducked and hit him on the nose. Blood trickled from his nostrils. The freckles took up fresh positions as he began to cry. Lies, Viktor thought walking away, had their compensations.

Petrov left Lenin's study and made his way to his own office near the green-domed Council of Ministers building.

He had travelled to many august capitals and he wished that their citizens could see the Kremlin as it was. Its golden husks, its melody of towers, the Fabergé eggs in the Armoury, Tsar Bell and Tsar Cannon, the wandering flocks of tourists. Not the dark fortress of suspicious fancy.

He wished, too, that the guards in attendance weren't necessary but he had been warned that the more energetically he pursued his liberating policies the more endangered his life became.

He settled himself behind his desk on which his wife regarded him serenely, coyly almost, called for tea and, observed benignly by the omnipresent Lenin, considered the assembling crises.

The mounting agitation of countries in the Soviet bloc. First Poland making the break from doctrinaire rule, the rest in the queue. Hungary, East Germany, Bulgaria. . . . 'Let them go,'

79

he had said to the Old Guard who had urged him to send in the tanks. 'We want friends not colonies.' And when East Germany's time came he would try and persuade its dour leader to resign. If enlightened communism was to succeed it could do without such bleak stereotypes. A unified Germany? Well, it would divert a lot of the attention of the West from the Soviet Union. . . . He stared at a map of Europe on the wall. Who would linger longest under the old order? Czechoslavakia would take its time because dissent hadn't prospered since the Soviet crack-down in 1963 and Rumania, ruled by a madman protected by a 30,000-strong Praetorian Guard, might endure like a malignant cyst. But ultimately it would succumb because reform born in the Kremlin was compulsive.

When he paused to review what he had instigated he was awed. But the awe shrivelled when he considered the crises within his own boundaries. Soon he would have been in power five years and what had he achieved? Chronic shortages – coal supplies so short that heating in apartment blocks this winter was threatened – ethnic unrest, violent protest. He was under attack by diehards who believed his reforms were irresponsible, he was under attack by radicals who believed his reforms were inadequate. He didn't ask himself why he had failed because he didn't believe he had. Not yet. He had inherited a lumbering bureaucracy and he had known that it would take longer than five years to bring it to heel; meanwhile he would have to resort temporarily to production targets.

Petrov picked up a copy of *Pravda*. Now the people were protesting about co-operatives, the vanguards of free enterprise, claiming they were being exploited by them. Had they, he wondered, paused to reflect that at least they had the freedom to make their protest? He sipped his sharp and smoky tea. Why did you do it, Viktor Andreyevich Petrov? What possessed you to single-handedly challenge accepted values? Evening pressed down and snow collected in cushions in the corners of the windows.

He heard about the heroic battles of the Great Patriotic War on the radio.

80

The 900-day siege of Leningrad in which half the 3,000,000 population died, most of them in the first winter when temperatures dropped to thirty degrees below zero. The defence of Moscow. And, of course, the frenzied struggle for Stalingrad; sometimes the bark and roar of the battle reached him on a breeze fanning the steppe; sometimes he saw Stukas on their way to the devastated city, once he saw Ilyushin dive-bombers drop from low clouds to attack a German armoured column; he was a keen aircraft spotter and he recorded these sightings in a red exercise book.

He heard about German atrocities, felt the noose at his neck, the bayonet in his belly, as the stories were told. He waited fearfully – and with a measure of excitement – for the arrival of the strutting warriors who would exact a terrible vengeance on the villagers for the crime of being Russian. The arrival of a troop of weary young men led by an equally fatigued lieutenant who asked politely for food and then fell asleep was disconcerting. Disappointing too. How could you hate them as they dozed in the sun guarded by a yawning sentry? One even gave him a bar of bitter chocolate.

Nevertheless he was ordered to hate them and did his best to obey, sharing the chocolate with Sergei, now aged fourteen, flaxen-haired and speculative, before getting down to the tricky business of loathing.

The orders came from the heavy-headed chairman of the committee that had once made Misha the kid an instrument of capitalism. He hinted that he was a member of Laventry Beria's secret police, the NKVD – although what sinister purpose he could have served in a cluster of pink and blue cottages isolated in the steppe defied conjecture – and from his headquarters in the barn issued clandestine instructions to resist. These worried the villagers. To resist there surely had to be an oppressor in evidence, but there was nothing oppressive about the home-sick young men loitering in their midst. In fact they reminded some of the older inhabitants of their own sons fighting far away from home. When the chairman demanded fiercely: 'How much longer can we endure these privations?' the schoolmaster observed mildly: 'To be honest, comrade, the privations are no worse than they were before the war.'

Viktor's test came when he was summoned to the barn at the

81

behest of the chairman who had harboured resentment towards the Petrov family since the affair of the kid.

'The time is now,' said the chairman, raising his ponderous head. 'Are you prepared to fight for Mother Russia?'

'Of course.'

'To make sacrifices?'

'I will do anything for the Soviet Union,' knowing this to be the burning if confused truth.

'You must swear that what I am about to say will always be a secret.'

'I swear,' Viktor said.

The chairman lit a cigarette and coughed importantly. Then he said: 'We must kill the leader of the insurgents.'

'The lieutenant?' Viktor had surprised the German the other day writing a letter in a grove among the birch trees and when he had asked him about it the lieutenant, his thin face still shocked by battle, had replied in Russian: 'I'm writing to my sweetheart.'

'You will lure him to his place of execution,' the chairman said. 'It is the least you can do.'

'Does he have to die?'

'He is the enemy. Do you shirk the task?'

'I will do my duty,' Viktor said hopelessly.

'Don't tell your parents.'

'Why can't they know?' asked Viktor, sensing that the long-dead kid was somehow involved.

'It is your own crusade.'

The following morning Viktor approached the lieutenant who was sitting beside the village pump, tunic of his field-grey uniform open at the neck, writing yet another letter.

'To your sweetheart?'

The lieutenant smiled and the smile momentarily wiped the fatigue from his face. 'One day you will have a sweetheart and you will feel the wound of parting. Tears instead of blood.'

'Some letters have arrived in the village,' Viktor said, hoping his shame didn't show in his face.

'Letters? What letters?'

'For you, for the Fritzes.'

'How do you know this?'

'Everyone in the village knows it.'

'Then why haven't they been delivered to us?'

'They were intercepted,' Viktor said, swallowing his voice. 'By partisans. They dumped them here. They have no use for letters for Fritzes from Germany. Where are you from?' he asked slyly.

'From Berlin. Why do you ask?'

'There are letters from Berlin. Is that where your sweetheart lives?'

The lieutenant stood up, one hand on the pistol in the holster attached to his belt. 'Show me these letters,' he said. His fingers, Viktor thought, should have been resting on a quill, not a pistol.

'They're in the woods. A whole sack of them.'

'Take me to them.'

Viktor led the way past the school-house, past Sergei's cottage where in the garden cats had prowled before they had been eaten, past the barn – was the chairman of the committee peering at them through the crack in the wall? – to the glade in the birch trees where he had first disturbed the lieutenant, where two villagers armed with PPSh machine-pistols lay in wait.

The lieutenant walked behind Viktor. 'Have you ever wondered,' the lieutenant asked, 'why we should be fighting each other?'

Viktor, who wished that the lieutenant had committed at least one act of brutality, said yes it had occurred to him. But not, he admitted to himself, until these tired young men had entered the village.

'Do you hate me?'

'You are the invader.'

'That wasn't what I asked.'

'Millions of Russians have died because you invaded.'

'As a matter of fact I was quite happy in Berlin. I was going to be a librarian. What do you want to be when you're grown up, Viktor?'

'I don't know.' Why did adults always ask this?

'You would make a good diplomat.'

'That's for people who can't make up their minds one way or the other, isn't it?'

They were near the wood now. The two villagers would be holding their machine-pistols tightly.

'Better to negotiate than to fight, Viktor. Never forget that. Maybe one day you will become a great negotiator.'

Heat rose from the hard-rutted track. A green dragonfly hovered. Immediately ahead lay the birch trees with their parchment bark, leaves like coins.

The lieutenant said: 'Are the letters really there, Viktor?'

What was it that the chairman of the committee had said? 'If you don't go through with it I can't be responsible for your parents' safety.'

'That's where they were dumped.'

'Very well.'

A bird began to sing among the trees.

There were Stukas far away in the blue sky; he could identify their engines even from here.

'This way,' Viktor said.

The birch trees closed around them.

'Are we nearly there?'

'Nearly,' Viktor said.

The burst of gunfire startled him even though he expected it. Bullets ripped through the trees and their thin branches trembled.

Slowly he turned to look at the lieutenant. 'We may be tired,' the lieutenant said, 'but we're not completely stupid.' He pointed at the bodies of the two villagers, machine-pistols still in their hands, lying among the first fallen leaves of late summer.

He pointed the pistol at Viktor's head. 'I asked you before, do you hate me?'

Viktor didn't reply.

'Sad, isn't it, that we're taught to hate. Really they could do a better job at school. And now I should shoot you. Except that I can't. Because of that stupid cap. That wasn't fair, you know. Did you have to wear it on a hot day like this?'

The lieutenant thrust the pistol into the holster, turned on his heel and walked back towards the village. Viktor touched the peak of the cap; it felt like a blade.

*

Maybe one day you will become a great negotiator. . . .

Where are you now, lieutenant? An old man wearing a woolly cardigan watching your grandchildren build a snowman while your sweetheart cuts slices of creamy gâteau in the kitchen? Or did you die, frost-bitten and starving, in a slit trench as our tanks pushed you out of our land?

A great negotiator? Perhaps. But what matters is the fruits of the negotiations and so many of those are sour. Is my crusade truly the answer to the Soviet Union's torment? Or should I have remained a good communist and let the country stagger from one five-year plan to another?

Viktor Petrov, you were never a good communist: you are a good Russian.

He picked up *Pravda* again. An apology for carrying a report from an Italian newspaper that Nikolai Razin, the reformist who was snapping at his heels, had boozed his way through the United States on a recent tour. An apology! Unprecedented. So I am achieving something for my people.

My people? What was he, a Tsar? 'The history of the people belongs to their Tsar.' The words of Nicholas Karamzin that had contributed to the suppression of his history of Russia. Ivan the Great, Ivan the Terrible, Peter the Great, Catherine the Great. . . . Seated at his throne within the walls where these caesars had reigned, Petrov experienced a shrinking within his stocky body. Such achievements since the Tartars were sent packing and Muscovy became a kingdom. And yet I still have to order grain from the United States. God Almighty, can't the most powerful nation in the world grow enough corn to feed its own people?

Tsar Petrov smote the table with his fist. The photograph of his wife trembled. He steadied it. Where would I be without you? Then he remembered that it was his wedding anniversary. And he remembered the day he had met her.

March, 1953. Crowds gathering in the cold in Red Square to see the funeral procession for Joseph Stalin. Some had come to pay homage to the son of a Georgian cobbler who had brought order to his disparate people and shepherded them to victory in the Great Patriotic War; others had come to make sure he was good and dead. What everyone shared was shock that, after thirty years of dictatorship, the country was now in limbo.

Viktor, standing opposite the walls of the Kremlin, the spun-sugar baubles of St Basil's Cathedral to one side of him, was excited by the possibilities. He was twenty-two years old, a law student at Moscow University, and it seemed to him that if the right successor to Stalin was found, Lenin's visions might be realised.

He was conscious of pressure from the crowd behind but he was not alarmed: Red Square was big enough to accommodate legions of mourners. The girl beside him gave a little shrug of her shoulders as if to shake off the pressure. Viktor smiled at her. She acknowledged the smile, a small tilt of her face, nothing more. She had sensible features which could become beautiful when she wanted them to be; they were framed by a fur hat that imparted an air of innocence that he suspected was not wholly justified.

The pressure from behind increased. A cordon of militia in long grey coats and fur hats braced their shoulders but it didn't seem to Petrov that there were enough of them. From the front of the crowd a murmur as the cortège approached; from behind a surge. And a suffocating presentiment that any moment now he wouldn't be able to move freely.

'I think we'd better get out of here,' he said to the girl.

'You get out,' she said pleasantly. 'I'm staying.'

A woman slipped on the cobblestones in front of them and disappeared. The crowd filled the space. Viktor heard a muffled scream. The plugging of the gap created space beside the girl. That, too, had to be filled – Viktor felt inexorable pressure behind him.

A disturbance to the left. More heads vanished. Screams. A woman's voice: 'My little girl. . . .'

The collapse briefly created a corridor. Viktor turned the girl around and thrust her forwards. But the corridor was closing. Fists and elbows dug him. Bodies closed upon him. Faces were mauve, contorted with fear.

The girl looked round. He gripped her shoulders and pushed her brutally forward. A boy fell. He saw a pair of felt boots descend on him.

86

And then, like a bar of soap projected from a clenched fist, she was out of the crowd and he was with her. 'Are you all right?' Her face was scratched, eyes shocked. 'I'm all right,' she said.

'Stay here.' He only understood vaguely that he wanted her there when he came back. He fought his way back into the crowd looking for the boy. Seeing him lying still among the frantic legs, he managed to kneel to protect him. Feet came at him, knocking him to one side, but he managed to regain his postion. A boot struck his cheekbone. Cold filled his skull. But the boy was breathing.

The feet accelerated as though there had been another collapse in the crowd. But now they were thinning out, leaving bodies like litter on the cobblestones. The boy opened his eyes and stared at Viktor; his eyes were blue and calm. Then he was alone with the boy and the girl was walking towards him, limping a little.

Viktor told Natalia what the future held in store for them one Sunday afternoon in the following spring as they walked in Hermitage Park. The thaw was under way and the park was filled with the music of running water. Wafers of ice floated on the ponds, wigs of soiled snow slid from statues.

'It's not very exciting,' he said. 'We'll have to go back to my *krai* and I'll get a job with the Komsomol. I've got connections and I've been told I'll be First Secretary within a year.'

'You resorting to *blat*? You disappoint me,' but the disappointment in her voice was minimal. She wore a loose grey jacket and a cornflower-blue dress and the sunlight shone in her hair.

'It's the system. I have no choice. After that I'll become a Party Organiser. Then First Party Secretary in the area, then perhaps, a member of the Central Committee in Moscow. . . .'

'What do you really want to be, Viktor? President of the Soviet Union, General Secretary of the Party?'

'Why not? Someone has to be.'

She took his arm. 'I've never thought of you as a Party man. Are you a good communist, Viktor?'

'I believe in what it stood for once upon a time.'

'Do you know why I don't truly believe?'

Viktor, mildly shocked, said he had no idea.

'Because it teaches you not to think,' said Natalia who was studying philosophy at Moscow University.

'So you don't want to be the wife of a good Party member?'

'If you allow yourself to think.' They passed a couple of vodka drunks and a soldier in a crumpled uniform with his arm round the waist of an adoring girl with flushed cheeks. 'But haven't you left out something?'

'Have I?' sensing that he might occasionally feel inadequate in the presence of the forthright young woman at his side.

'You haven't asked me to marry you,' Natalia said.

He had forgotten to ask her to marry him and now he had forgotten their wedding anniversary. How many years was it? Thirty-five? He sent out for two bottles of sparkling Novi Svyet wine from the Crimea, champagne in all but name.

He told his driver to take him to the small apartment he sometimes used in Alexei Tolstoy Street near the headquarters of *Tass*. Seated in the back of the Zil, he watched the darkening street scenes flit past like strips of old black-and-white film.

It had stopped snowing and, even at this hour, he could hear the scrape of babushkas' shovels on the pavements. Pedestrians leaned into the cold, children slithered home, militia on point duty stamped their feet. And not a drunk to be seen. Well, not on the route taken by his Zil.

But were the people grateful to him for his campaign against alcoholism which had rid the metro, streets, parks, restaurants of many of the lurching boozers that had infested them? There had been reports of resentment, stories that alcoholics now drank industrial alcohol and after-shave!

And were they grateful for his drive, spear-headed in Moscow by Nikolai Razin, to stamp out the corruption that pervaded the Soviet Union from the borders with Eastern Europe to the North Pacific, from the Arctic Circle to the Chinese frontier?

Corruption, of course, bred on shortages and there were plenty of those. Who could blame the people for complaining about them?

Razin had tried to gauge public opinion – and pick up leads – by riding the buses and the metro, by striking up conversations in Gorky Park and drinking in the beer parlours that prospered behind Moscow's broad boulevards. But he had been forced to abandon these tactics because he was now easily recognisable. What chance would I stand?

Natalia was in the kitchen of the apartment, which they had occupied before he became General Secretary, when she had been a lecturer at Moscow University. She was wearing a black cocktail dress and pearls at her throat. She had remembered.

He poured sparkling wine and they toasted each other. Thirty-five years and she was still sensible at all times, beautiful tonight. He was as lucky that day in Red Square as others had been terminally unlucky. The little boy had lived: that had been their augury.

'I didn't think you had remembered,' she said, leading him into the richly-hued living room where comfort and refinement co-existed.

'I hadn't,' he said because lies hung and withered between them. 'What's for dinner?'

'You know what's for dinner. Borscht, Chicken Kiev and ice-cream. The same menu every anniversary.'

He patted his stomach. He had a little weight problem, nothing serious. He wished he had more hair but it had re-treated since he took over the leadership of the nation. Next year he would be sixty.

Over the dessert he confided his doubts about the mood of the people. Did they at least respect him for what he was trying to do? 'Because that's what really matters,' he told her.

She put down the spoon. 'There's only one place to find out,' she said, 'and that's in a banya.'

8

Vilkin came to the banya during an intermission in winter when the sky was light-blue and the sun was smoothing the surface of the snow into icing-sugar.

'Come into the steam-room,' the stallholder said. 'Leave your clothes there,' pointing at the abused hangers.

'I don't wish to go to the steam-room,' said Vilkin. 'I've come here to force some sense down your throats.'

He was in his mid-forties, the owner of a small and damp moustache and a truculent manner that did service for determination. The editor of *Pravda* had been fired the previous day and it was apparent to everyone in the changing-room that Vilkin was deeply affected by this: he didn't wish to follow the editor, dismissed because he favoured the Old Guard and because he was unable to shake off a lifetime diet of indigestible Party dogma, on the other hand he didn't want to follow any course that might offend Petrov's successor should Petrov's rule come to an untimely end.

'You have come at our invitation,' the stallholder said, 'to discuss the future of the banya. We are the hosts: we will decide where we talk. In any case women can't come into the mens' changing-room.'

'Women?' Vilkin stared at him aghast.

'Woman,' the stallholder corrected himself. 'They have equal rights in the banya just as they do all over Russia. Haven't you read the Marxist-Leninist view on womens' equality?'

'The laundress?'

'How did you guess?'

'Because she's a trouble-maker like you and both of you will be in the shit if you continue to oppose the development of the city for the benefit of the Soviet people.'

90

'The editor of *Pravda* was fired for using phrases like that.'

'Who's that?' demanded Vilkin, pointing at Michael Cooper who was making notes.

'Our lawyer.'

'I don't want any moronic lawyers around.'

'The Leader of the Soviet Union is a lawyer,' the stallholder said.

Vilkin pulled at his moustache as though trying to remove it. 'I'm not saying anything against lawyers as a whole.'

'Good because our lawyer is coming into the steam-room.'

'I'm not going into the steam-room.'

The stallholder beckoned Michael. 'Read him paragraph fourteen of the Press release.'

'Civilised attempts were made to discuss the proposed demolition of the banya with Comrade Vilkin from the House of the Moscow Soviet but he declined to take his place at the very heart of the controversy, the steam-room of the banya. Could it be that Comrade Vilkin who is on the portly side was afraid of melting?'

'You will make me a laughing stock.'

'So nothing will change,' the bodybuilder said.

'I suggest,' the stallholder said, 'that you get undressed.' He fingered the cloth of Vilkin's suit. 'From the German Democratic Republic, comrade?'

'Can't you turn off the steam?'

'Then we would have to tell the media that you couldn't take the heat.'

Vilkin began to undress.

The laundress was waiting for them on the top tier where the steam from the fire-bricks, heated to ambitious temperatures for this occasion, would be at its fiercest. She wore a pink bath towel and her shoulders bulged meatily above it. She patted the bench beside her. 'Sit here, comrade.'

The stallholder sat next to Vilkin, Michael gravitated to the bottom tier.

'So what is your proposition?' the laundress asked.

'That you drop this ridiculous campaign. We must progress, not stagnate,' his voice adopting the timbre of a platform speaker. 'What would have happened if people had opposed the construction of the Congress Building in the Kremlin, the Pioneers' Palace, the Exhibition Hall in Sokolniki Park?'

'We aren't here for a history lesson,' the stallholder interrupted, nodding to Michael who threw water and beer on the fire-bricks. 'Those buildings were constructed thirty years ago.' Steam rose in searing clouds.

'The people need a new store.' Moisture beaded Vilkin's moustache. 'But perhaps you don't,' to the laundress. 'More provisions might interfere with your business?'

'Another store lined with empty shelves? What difference would it make?' She touched the hive of her red hair which was beginning to wilt. 'I hear they've introduced tea rationing in Vladimir.'

'Stern measures have to be taken. One way or the other,' looking anxiously at Michael who was taking notes.

With a flourish of his sheet, the stallholder said: 'Demolish this banya and you demolish part of the heritage of Moscow.'

'There are other bath-houses.'

'This one belongs to the past.'

'The decadent past?'

Michael tossed more water on the bricks. Sweat trickled down Vilkin's forehead into his eyes.

The laundress said: 'You haven't stated your conditions.'

'Ah, conditions.' Glancing at Michael, Vilkin dropped his voice. 'I understand the management at GUM is prepared to be reasonable.'

'To let me queue legally? How considerate.'

'Louder,' the stallholder said. 'Our lawyer can't hear you.'

'Who needs lawyers in the Soviet Union?' Vilkin demanded.

'Did you get that?' the stallholder shouted to Michael.

'With so much justice they are not necessary,' Vilkin said hastily.

'Sweet Mother of God,' exclaimed the laundress who came from a generation when religious oaths had the added dimension of the forbidden.

More beer-smelling steam climbed the benches. Vilkin rubbed his eyes. 'Can't we go into the changing-room?'

'Have you no sense of decency?'

'You needn't come,' Vilkin told her. He appealed to the stallholder. 'Let's go, I'm being roasted alive.'

'Not if she won't come.'

'Then we stay,' the laundress said.

Vilkin said to the stallholder: 'We are prepared to be reasonable in your case, too.'

'Blackmail, Comrade Vilkin?'

'We're not saying you can park your stall in Red Square but there wouldn't be any objection to Kazan Station.'

'There *was* an objection.'

'Circumstances change.'

'If the co-operative can get meat for pies and *shashlik* why can't the State-owned shops?' the laundress demanded.

The stallholder held up one shiny-palmed hand. 'Not now, woman. The future of the banya is more important than your carping.'

'You look as though you get enough meat,' the laundress said.

'And you do not starve.'

More steam, scented with eucalyptus this time but even hotter, billowed. Vilkin coughed and loosened an invisible collar. His postage-stamp moustache dripped.

He said in a hoarse voice: 'It could be that you,' pointing at the laundress, 'will encounter difficulties at more stores, and you,' indicating the stallholder, 'might find more sites inaccessible . . . and that's off the record,' to Michael who was writing energetically.

'How can it be?' Michael asked. 'I've just recorded it.'

'Are you a Soviet citizen? I can't place your accent.'

'Scarcely surprising,' the stallholder said. 'We speak more than 100 tongues.'

'I'm American,' Michael said. 'And Russian,' he added.

'An American taking notes of what I say? This is an outrage.' Vilkin stood up, pulling the damp sheet around his body. 'I'm leaving.'

'I agree,' the laundress said, 'that it won't help your image in the media. Negotiating, threatening, in front of an American. Readers, listeners, viewers will think it very odd.'

'So will the Politburo,' said the stallholder. 'And by the way the door is locked. Mikhail, more water. Make the steam as hot as pepper vodka from Poland.'

Vilkin sat down. 'I have a bad heart,' he said. 'How about an extension? I can't authorise more.' He placed one hand on his chest.

'How long?' the laundress asked.

'One month. No petitions, no statements to the media during that time.'

'No other strings attached?'

'We will leave it open to negotiation.'

'Mikhail, write that down.'

'I feel as if I'm going to have a coronary,' Vilkin said.

'That would solve everything,' the stallholder said. 'Here, sign this,' handing Michael's hand-written agreement to Vilkin.

'I can't read it. The steam. . . .'

'Don't worry,' Michael said. 'No tricks.' He handed Vilkin a pen.

Vilkin made a wet, sprawling signature. 'Now unlock the door.'

'It's open,' the stallholder said.

'But you said – '

'Circumstances change,' the stallholder said.

Michael told Magda Larionova about the stay of execution in the open-air swimming pool opposite Kropotkinskaya metro station. The temperature was -10°C but the water was warm and snowflakes melted in the halo of steam high above it. Swimmers wearing bathing caps bobbed around like corks.

'Don't trust him,' Magda said in Russian. She was wearing a black, seal-sleek bathing costume; it flattened her breasts a little and Michael imagined them released. It was the fifth time they had met and he was conscious of a sense of sharing.

'Why not?'

'I know his kind. He's waiting to see which way the wind blows. So is the whole of the Soviet Union come to that.'

'Time is what I don't have.' His visa expired in five days and he had a seat on a Pan Am flight to New York. He asked her if he could get the visa extended.

'Anything is possible in this country.'

'Can you fix it?'

'You think I'm KGB?'

'You're Intourist,' he said.

'I'm Ukrainian.'

'So?'

'We Ukrainians get things done.'

'Just like that?'

'We'll have to work out a strategy.' She swam away from him, a leisurely and sinuous crawl; wisps of blonde hair protruded from the back of her bathing cap making her look vulnerable.

'So, do we have a strategy?' he asked when she returned.

'Perhaps,' and for reasons that he couldn't immediately identify the reply disappointed him. 'As you know the Kremlin is trying to present the KGB with a new image. To do that it's got to purge its Stalinist past. Raoul Wallenberg, the Swedish diplomat who saved thousands of Jews from the Nazis, is a case in point. He was arrested by the Red Army when they entered Budapest in 1945 on suspicion of being an American spy and thrown into gaol. His family think he's still alive. The authorities have apologised for the treatment he received and allowed the family into Russia to investigate. So maybe they'll let you stay longer. . . .'

She began to swim towards the tunnel leading to the changing-rooms where, in the men's section, Michael had been required to wash himself with a bar of carbolic soap monitored by a stolid female attendant.

'We will talk more outside,' Magda announced and swam into the tunnel.

They walked through sparsely falling snow along the narrow promenade of Gogol Boulevard. Two youths offered them badges – one of a sputnik, the other, furtively, of Stalin; Michael, wearing a sheepskin coat and *shapka*, gave them gum.

'So what we've got to do,' Magda said, tucking her hand beneath his arm, 'is publicise your mission. Get comments from someone with. . . .'

'Clout,' he said in English.

'And then go to the OVIR offices. I have a friend there. He might help but, as you know, nothing will be done without KGB permission. And they're not sure these days what's right or wrong. No one knows any more.'

'Where are we going?' he asked.

'Home to my apartment for lunch. Now hold out a packet of Winston or Marlboro and hail a taxi.'

As the taxi drew up, the driver's eyes hypnotised by the pack of cigarettes, Michael glanced behind him. A grey Volga was cruising. The driver looked like the man who had been playing draughts in Gorky Park. But many Muscovites looked alike to him.

Now Tanya Argusky skated freely. Along the hosed paths in Gorky Park where ice-dust sparkled in the air, on lakes and ponds that creaked as her skates cut them, in the courtyard behind the dismal apartment block where she lived. And at the Dynamo Stadium.

Her life was a figure-of-eight, the pattern from which jumps, spins and steps evolve. Her problem was partners. How could she practise pairs skating – a star lift or a double lutz twist – when she only skated with Yury once a week, if that, on the lake outside Moscow?

She consulted Lev Grechko one day when he was sitting behind the barrier at the Dynamo rink, beard at rest on the coils of his grey scarf. 'I've got just the right partner for you,' he said as she leaned on the barrier, jabbing the ice with her skates.

'There's only one right partner for me.' She smoothed her short white skirt which, like the skates, had become shabby; she couldn't afford new skates but in any case the best models were snapped up by the committee cossetting the teams for the European, World and Olympic championships.

'Yury? Be realistic, Tanya. When you're a pair you're one; it's the ultimate achievement in skating. Practising once a week with a partner isn't enough. How can you get your steps right, your counters, rockers, choctaws, let alone your jumps and spins?'

'Then what good will it do me skating with a stranger?'

'You've got to skate with someone.' His beard wagged.

'So you don't think I will skate with Yury in the Olympics?'

'Ask your obstinate father.'

'It must be just as difficult for Yury.'

96

Lev Grechko fingered his formidable nose. 'Not quite,' he said after a while.

'What do you mean?'

'You must realise that Yury doesn't skate alone.'

'Of course. He will have to find substitutes for me.'

'Just one,' Lev said.

She stared at him. A girl skated into her vision. Her hair was blonde and her eyes were green like Yury's. Yury's arm was round her waist as they circled a rink and the scar at the side of his mouth was smiling.

'Of course,' she said, 'one partner is better.'

'Her name is Nina and she has been chosen to skate in the Olympics in Albertville in France.'

'With Yury?'

Lev Grechko pulled at his beard. 'Who else?'

Cold from the ice crept up her body. 'Have you asked the Olympic Committee to re-open my case?'

'They say there's no case to re-open. You weren't selected; that's all there is to it.'

'Did they mention my father?'

'That's understood,' Lev Grechko said. 'But time's running out. I hear he's organising a protest march in Red Square. Protests about out-dated causes are what the militia can do without. Can't anyone beat some sense into the old fool's head?'

'Perhaps you can,' Tanya said and skated away, skates hissing on the opaque ice. It was lunch-time and the rink was crowded with skaters gliding and tottering in anti-clockwise circles. In the centre a handful of young men and women practised upright and sit spins. Some of the plodders protested as she swayed past them but she scarcely heard them; she was alone.

From Dynamo she caught the metro to Sportivnaya, emerging at Lenin Stadium nestling in the south-west loop of the Moskva River opposite the Lenin Hills and went into the Sports Palace beside the vast arena. The rink was occupied by the elite, skaters who had been plucked from childhood and launched into infinite figures of eight of application and endurance at one of the many academies for the professional amateurs of Soviet sport.

Tanya, attracting little notice in her shabby black coat, focused

97

her eyes on the centre of the rink. And there was Yury skating with leisurely grace. ALONE. Tanya smiled secretly. So much for Lev Grechko and his gossip. Yury completed a tight circle, fair hair, a little too long for Tanya's liking, fanning out behind him. And then with practised fluency, he was no longer alone. His arm was round the waist of a girl, a Siberian blonde, wearing a pink outfit and white boots, new skates – Canadian? – flashing daggers of light, finely muscled legs thrusting forward in unison with Yury's.

Tanya left the stadium and walked toward the domes and bell-towers of Novodevichy Monastery. Her mood was funereal so she walked among the graves of illustrious incumbents. Gogol, Chekhov, Eisenstein, Nikita Khrushchev at rest beneath a bronze headstone, a few flowers probably laid on October 14th, the anniversary of his death, frozen in an alabaster vase.

But this afternoon the graves were contrary: they invested Tanya with spirit. She turned on her heel beside the gravestone of the inventor of the Katyusha Rocket, lorry and rockets carved from marble, made her way along Novodevichy Proyezd and waited outside the stadium beneath the numbed sky. No scenes, no admission of grief, merely dignified reproof.

She saw the blonde first. Her fur hat was mink – Tanya's, bought at Tsum, was rabbit and had been infested with fleas – and her long coat was wolf. She walked with the careless swagger of a woman who has grown weary of admiration but she was surely a little too tall for Yury who was walking – no, hurrying – beside her.

When Yury saw her he slowed down, smiled, gave a little shrug. *So, you caught me, so what?* He pointed her out to the blonde. She, too, shrugged. *That little creature in the pauper's coat? Was she really your partner?*

Yury kissed her on the cheeks: at least he did that. 'Tanya, I want you to meet Nina Zelenaya.'

The blonde nodded at her, her eyes focussed on the balding lapels of the black coat. 'Same time tomorrow,' she said to Yury. 'We've got to work on that salchow.' She strode away, boots crunching on the snow.

'So your salchow hasn't improved?' Tanya moved away from him as he tried to take her arm.

'I know what you're thinking,' he said as they walked towards the metro station.

'Haven't I heard that line before? Along with "You're not going to like this," and "Tell me the truth, doctor." '

'Nothing has changed.'

'Some script-writer,' Tanya remarked.

'Look, I must have a partner to practise with. How else can I train for the Olympics? But that doesn't mean that we won't skate together on the lake.'

'What will Nina think?'

'Don't be bitchy,' he said, 'be reasonable. If your father was reasonable we would be skating together. Olympic champions, world champions. . . . I can see him now, the day we won the Olympics, staggering across the ice waving a banner GIVE ME A TICKET FOR JERUSALEM. Why doesn't he drop it, for God's sake? Other Jews are being allowed to go to the Promised Land. Why can't he go quietly?'

'Because he's suffered,' Tanya said. 'But you wouldn't understand that and don't say, "Try me." '

'So, he's suffered. All the more reason to put the suffering behind him and go where he believes he belongs.'

'You don't understand. They took away years of his life. He wants a public apology. He wants justice to be seen to be done. You see he doesn't believe *glasnost* has really arrived. What's changed? he asks. The military still put down uprisings, shortages are worse than they were before. . . . How many people are still imprisoned in camps? No one ever gives a figure.'

'Is that you speaking or your father?'

'A father's daughter.'

They stared into the mouth of Sportivnaya metro station. 'Let's walk,' Yury said. He reached for her arm but she kept her distance. They struck north towards the eight-lane Garden Ring Road.

Yury spoke logically and reasonably. There was no reason why he and Tanya shouldn't compete in the Olympics if her father abandoned his flamboyant protests. But she must surely realise that he couldn't practise with a phantom? Of course not, she agreed. It was merely that she had never envisaged Yury competing with anyone else. Stupid. Why should he abandon everything because she was the daughter of a bloody-minded Zionist?

'So you do understand?'

'Is she a good skater?'

'She's good.'

'Isn't she too tall for you?'

'Almost, not quite.'

'No difficulty with the lifts?'

'We manage,' he said.

They walked past the house where Tolstoy had lived. She had been there with her mother. The table was still set for dinner and the piano on which Rachmaninov and Rubinstein had played still waited silently. She had peered into the little room, next to his study, where Tolstoy had made shoes. She had been five years old and the ice hadn't yet called her and her father had been in a penal camp.

Were the two of them, Yury and Nina Zelenaya, ear-marked for the Olympics? Early days, Yury said. He took her hand. With his peaked cap at a jaunty angle, wings of fair hair sweeping over his ears, he cut quite a dash and she noticed girls looking at him.

He made the announcement when they reached the Garden Ring: he couldn't take her to the lake next Sunday.

'Why?'

'Judging at the Lenin Stadium. For the Olympics. Only preliminaries though. Nothing to worry about.'

'But you've got to be there?'

'Naturally.'

'With Nina Zelenaya?'

'She will be there, yes.'

'I wish you luck,' she said.

'Speak to your father.'

'You look very good together.'

'Not as good – ' but she was on her way, heading for a metro station, head averted so that he couldn't see her lips trembling. She turned at the entrance to the station but his jaunty cap had disappeared among the purposeful crowds.

*

Robert Hanson left his dacha late that year. On a mid-December day when the sun was bright on the soiled snow.

I wish, he thought, packing blue pyjamas with navy piping into an old BOAC flight-bag, that I had been born with one major talent instead of a clutch of mediocre aptitudes.

I wish I had been able to play the piano. At parties, glass of champagne on top of the Steinway, playing notes like melting ice cubes, Cole Porter perhaps, while adoring girls gaze at my nimble fingers and, from time to time, into my eyes.

I wish I had been good at cricket. A left-arm spin-bowler of impenetrable guile. Or an opening bat with a classic off-drive, the ball springing from the bat with a life of its own. But never an all-rounder. Too close to the truth.

Hanson slipped a pair of scuffed leather slippers into the bag. An old man's possessions. Only the chest-rub and frayed club tie were missing.

Christ how I worked at urbanity. A crash course in aphorisms. 'As Wilde put it etcetera, etcetera.' A few words of musical appreciation. . . . Amazing how you can impress with re-hearsed trivia. Stare into bovine eyes and see footlights.

Hanson went into the kitchen and poured himself vodka from the bottle in the 'fridge. He couldn't be bothered with bread or mineral water. The burn of the liquor lingered in his stomach.

The stranger appeared in the splashed mirror above the plate-rack. *'Sex appeal?'*

'I didn't realise I had it until my second year at Cambridge. . . .'

'Always an older woman?'

'Until I was older myself.'

'You should have been an actor.'

'I have been all my life.'

'You really do loathe yourself, don't you?'

'Shorthand, another of my minor accomplishments – Loathe is a very similar outline to love.'

'What is your greatest regret in life?'

'You.'

*

101

He drove the grey Zhuguli steadily along one of the main streets that converge like spokes from the perimeter, crossing the garden and boulevard rings, to the centre of the city.

On a fat curve of the river he saw men fishing in holes in the ice into the dark blood below. They sat motionless, swaddled in felt and fur, peering into the past and the precarious future. They were there at night, too, hunched beside charcoal braziers waiting for the fish to rise to the light from their kerosene flares.

As he approached the city centre he saw pedestrians carrying parcels as though they were souvenirs of war. Shopping for the New Year had started early in the bankrupt stores of Moscow. He noticed a bugle protruding from a knapsack, a badly-wrapped plastic rifle perched on a string-bag bulging with potatoes . . . .

He parked outside the apartment in a side street near the embassies, once the residences of aristocrats, in Vorovsky Street. The building was sturdy and square – it reminded him of a Victorian house in Dulwich – and was divided into six small apartments. Not the sort of home an illustrious defector might expect but better than most of the old apartment blocks. The garden, a starved expanse in summer planted with a few gasping roses, lay at peace under the snow.

As he walked down the path carrying a bruised suitcase and the flight-bag, lace curtains moved in the window of one of the ground-floor apartments. The old woman who lived there with four cats had been, it was rumoured, the mistress of the father of a government minister; she had never spoken to Hanson but had on occasions favoured him with a rheumy wink.

He climbed the stairs slowly, resting on the first-floor landing. He glanced at the grubby visiting card stuck on the door. No change there either. Nicolai Frolov was presumably still writing his definitive account of the Revolution and taking his time about it. Hanson knew from his own work translating Russian into English for the magazine *Sputnik*, published by Novosti Press Agency, that the earners these days were rewrites of Soviet history since the Revolution.

The door opened and Frolov peered out. He reminded Hanson of a tortoise. 'Welcome back, Comrade Hanson.' He was deeply suspicious of Hanson and elaborately polite with it.

'How was summer here?' Hanson asked.

'Close, very close. You're lucky to have a place in the country,' said Frolov who had never been able to reconcile the privileges accorded to foreigners with the ideals of the Revolution.

'How is the great work coming along?' Frolov had been working on the book for five years.

'Slowly,' Frolov told him. 'But with a certain majesty.'

'Many revisions?'

'Revisions?' Frolov frowned, stroking his stringy neck.

'*Glasnost*. Haven't you had to re-think the aims of the Bolsheviks? After all, they weren't fighting for democracy, were they?'

'I write the truth, Comrade Hanson.' The reptilian head withdrew, the door closed softly.

Hanson mounted the last flight of stairs and entered his apartment. Patina of dust apart, it was as neat as Lena had left it in the spring. Books, classics mostly, from the Soviet Union's 3,200 state publishing houses, and paperbacks brought by a dwindling succession of visitors, in disciplined rows; icons bought in commission shops making a chapel of the living room; shiny furniture in showroom formation.

Hanson dusted the furniture accepting that Lena, who was due back tomorrow, would dust it again. Then he sat down and sorted the mail that hadn't been re-directed to the dacha. *New Statesman, Spectator* and *Economist*; registration and automobile documents; a letter from his tutor at Cambridge who had gamely corresponded in Russian, sometimes in Ukrainian, occasionally in Georgian, down the years; mail-order catalogues. Hanson knew of one defector who applied for dozens of catalogues because without them he would have no mail at all; he knew of another who carried around with him a matchbox filled with American soil.

He went into the kitchen and made himself a pot of tea. Just as he had during one of the de-briefings before the KGB had finally become convinced he wasn't a spy.

'What do you think of the apartment?' The interrogator had been burly with thin, glossy hair that smelled of brilliantine.

'Is it bugged?'

'Of course.'

'Books,' Hanson had said. 'I need books. And carpets and warm furniture.'

'Many people live three to a room sharing a bathroom with other families.'

'And some, so I've been told, have penthouses on Kutuzovsky, palaces in Zhukovka.'

'Don't be deceived by loaded comparisons, my friend. I've lived in London and New York. I've seen race-riots. I've seen ghettos. I've seen poverty.'

'You forget, I'm on your side.'

'Are you quite sure?'

Hanson brought his mug of tea into the living room. The windows were still sealed with strips of newspaper. On the opposite side of the street oxyacetylene sparks dripped from the window of a small museum that was being restored.

He sat down, opened the suitcase and picked up the script of a video movie written by the Australian journalist who wrote for the *Morning Star*. It was to be produced by the West German hostess, directed by the American who had been wounded in the Spanish Civil War. It was a thriller about an assassination attempt on the president of the United States – the American was a fan of Alfred Hitchcock and had introduced a walk-on part for himself – and Hanson was to play the president.

God willing, Hanson thought, I won't be here to be assassinated. He glanced at his watch. 3.00 p.m. He had an appointment at OVIR in half an hour. The sparks spilling into the darkening air from the oxyacetylene torch as he left the block reminded him of fireworks in the back garden in Muswell Hill.

The woman with the bobbed hair shook her head slowly and sorrowfully.

'But this is a farce,' Hanson said. 'Whatever happened to *glasnost*?'

'Maybe you should ask your friends.'

'I have no friends.'

'Acquaintances then.'

'You really think one of the defectors is blocking my application?'

She spread her hands.

'What do you suggest I do?'

'Persevere. What else can you do?'

'Escape?'

'Don't be ridiculous.'

'There must be something I can do?'

'Why don't you . . . sound out . . . some of your colleagues. As is well known,' smiling as she quoted the familiar platitude of Party dogma, 'there is a skeleton in everyone's cupboard. Why don't you make them rattle a little?'

Hanson considered the homosexual's encounters in the environs of the Bolshoi. The Yorkshireman's anti-Soviet bravado. The hostess's sexual rapacity, particularly with young Russians. The Australian journalist who earned a little hard currency on the side telephoning tips to right-wing newspapers. The ex-seaman's black market deals. . . .

'You have a devious mind,' he said.

'As is well known the end justifies the means.'

'Where shall we go, Paris?'

'Paris would be nice,' she said sadly.

On the way back to the apartment Hanson stopped at one of the few liquor shops left in the wake of Petrov's crusade. He queued for half an hour and left with half a dozen bottles of Kolos beer.

He drank the first watching *Travellers' Club* on television, Geology in Siberia.

He remembered his first night in the apartment. He had opened the drawer of the bedside table. Inside a pack of black-and-white pornographic photographs of a young man with a large penis fucking a girl in textbook positions. The young man had been wearing his socks. Would the KGB burst into the apartment and catch him vicariously *flagrante delicto*?

He had taken the prints into the bathroom and tried to burn them, but they were resilient. Holding a charred penis and an accommodating vulva over the sink, he had reflected that if the police charged down the door now he would be accused of perversion that would confound even Kinsey.

He opened another bottle of beer, stood up and parted a chink in the curtain. A red star on the Kremlin glowed brightly, a winking airliner flew through the stars. To where? London?

Across the street the flow of liquid sparks faltered and stopped.

105

9

As soon as stories about his mission appeared in the media Michael Cooper was granted an extension of his visa by OVIR. Officials questioned him vigorously. Did he think of himself as Russian or American? *Russian*, they pleaded wordlessly but in truth he still didn't know, although echoes of his ancestry reached him on every street corner. What if he had grown up in the Arbat? Would he now be a Party stalwart grappling with the contradictions of *glasnost*?

He told Magda about the extension while she cooked dinner – fried sturgeon in breadcrumbs – in the kitchen of her modern apartment in a white and pink block with a view of the Ostankino television tower. The smell of cooking relaxed him. He sat on a red plastic chair opposite a shelf of family photographs, Magda's stocky parents on the banks of the Dnieper challenging the photographer to do his worst, Magda frozen in timorous childhood. A rubber plant grew shinily in one corner. A print of a painting by a Ukrainian artist, Malevich, hung on the wall; it was called *Girls in a Field*; the girls were brightly coloured, faceless automatons. 'He was banned by the Stalinists,' Magda said, following his gaze. 'What would Stalin have made of *Rukh*, the movement of change in Ukraine? Did you know that the Party stalwarts in Kiev allowed May Day rallies to go ahead within days of Chernobyl without telling the people just how bad it was?'

'Are we witnessing the break-up of the Soviet Union?' Michael asked in Russian.

'No, we're just becoming more like the United States.' The sturgeon sizzled in the pan. 'The country you in the West will have to watch, now that the Wall has finally been breached, is a re-unified Germany.'

'More than forty-five years after the war and you're all still paranoid about the Germans. . . . How long before a war becomes history?'

'When parents who lived in that war die.' She served the sturgeon with cabbage and sauté potatoes. It tasted like chicken.

She poured a Georgian white wine. 'So, how is the mission progressing?'

'Like an obstacle race. The old man guarding the dogs died of natural causes, by the way. If cirrhosis of the liver is natural. . . .'

'You're a very determined man.'

'I made a promise,' Michael said, sipping the dry wine. 'All right, I tried and I could have quit. But lawyers don't like doing that. And there is another factor – I want to see what I might have grown up like.'

'You think your brother's still alive?'

'A lot of people lay low while Stalin was still in power.'

'But what would your brother have feared?'

'He was the son of my father who was wanted by the NKVD for allegedly collaborating with the Germans.'

'But after Stalin died, why didn't he surface then?'

'Maybe he did. Maybe he lives in Samarkand. Or Moldavia or Irkutsk.'

'Or Mirny?' She stared into her wine and her fine, fair hair slipped forward framing her face.

Michael frowned. 'Where's that?'

'In Siberia. One of the coldest places on earth.'

'Why Mirny?' Michael shivered.

'I told you I might be able to help. Well, I made some inquiries. . . .' She raised her head and her hair fell back into place. 'Does the name Repin mean anything to you?'

'Vaguely. I think I heard my father speak about him.'

'He was a friend of the family. He's dead now but his son lives in Mirny. It's a diamond city. He went there in the sixties, one of the young pioneers opening up new frontiers. Siberia is the biggest treasure chest in the world and they get double, treble, the wages they get here. When they get there they become another breed. And why not? They've built cities in

107

permafrost, carved railways through the taiga. Siberia is the future,' Magda said.

'Not Ukraine?' Despite his excitement he couldn't resist it.

She ignored him. 'They have a saying there. "A hundred versts isn't far, a hundred grams of vodka isn't a drink and a hundred roubles isn't money." A far cry from salt mines and convicts. . . .'

'This Repin, would he see me?'

'Why not? Just remember you're dealing with a Texan of the Soviet Union even though he's an old man by now by the standards of the new Siberians, fifty-eight or so.'

'So he would have been about seven when my brother disappeared.'

'Old enough to help defend Moscow. Old enough to know your brother. It's a chance, nothing more.'

'How would I get there?'

'Trans-Siberian to Chita. Everyone should travel on it once. Then fly north. It's so cold,' Magda said, 'that tree trunks explode. Ice-cream?'

'Just coffee,' Michael said. 'Can you fix it?'

'Intourist can fix anything.'

She went into the kitchen to make coffee looking sensible and came out beautiful.

'You're lucky,' she said. 'Coffee is rationed. Soap and sugar too. A bit different to New York?'

'I don't think my wife would settle here,' Michael said. Why hadn't Magda asked more about Barbara? Because she didn't care? 'We're getting divorced,' he said, surprised to hear himself offering unsolicited information.

'Could you settle here?'

'I don't know yet. I'd like to show you America.'

'One day maybe. There isn't time now.'

'Why not, for God's sake?' He found it difficult to comprehend that anyone could be so indifferent to America. 'Surely you've got to see the other side of the coin?'

'For me,' she said, 'the two sides are the Soviet Union and Ukraine. Why should I be interested in the United States? For us it's another planet we see on the movies.'

Michael, appalled, said: 'How can you assess the world if you haven't seen America?'

'Have you been to China?'

'You should be a lawyer.' Lights glimmered beyond the TV tower. 'What happened in the kitchen?'

'How did you know?'

'You looked different when you came out.'

'God help a witness when you're questioning him. What is it, body language?'

'Something like that. As though you had reached a decision.'

'Do you want to make love to me?'

'From the moment I saw you,' he said.

The pea-green engine of the Trans-Siberian, resplendent with yellow flashes, a red star and a waterproof picture of Lenin, nosed out of Moscow's Yaroslav Station at 2.05 in the afternoon. Averaging thirty-seven m.p.h., it would travel the 5,778 miles to Vladivostock in seven days sixteen-and-a-half hours and across eight time zones.

Michael shared a four-berth, soft-class compartment with a burly Russian trapper, flamboyantly healthy, on his way to the village of Erbogachon in eastern Siberia to hunt fox, wolf and sable. In his punished suitcase he carried bottles of *spirt*, almost pure alcohol, which, he said, Siberians preferred to vodka which they considered effete.

Between swigs of *spirt*, the trapper talked about the superlatives of Siberia – Irkutsk, forty million roubles worth of furs in one warehouse, Baikal, the deepest lake in the world, a fifth of the world's fresh water. And hunting.

'For sable I take two dogs with me, both trained not to pierce the skin with their teeth. The best sable is Barguzin from the taiga near Baikal. They should be pure black but they're turning brown. They employ me to catch pure black Barguzin to be mated. I take the sables from the dogs and squeeze them until their hearts stop beating; that way you don't harm the fur.'

The hunting talk gave Michael a sense of persecution. Had he seen the draughts-player from Gorky Park on the train? He had noticed a man very much like him wearing a blue track-suit but every other Russian on the train was wearing one. He left the compartment and glanced up and down the corridor where passengers were gazing at the fleeing suburbs of Moscow.

He made his way through the coaches, each heated with a solid-fuel boiler, each with its own samovar for tea, wincing at the cold knifing through the connecting gangways. He navigated two second-class cars before reaching the hard class where the less privileged of this classless society slept and ate and drank in glorious communal confusion. He was stopped by an implacable woman attendant. 'Go back to where you belong,' she commanded him.

As he turned he saw a blue track-suit disappear into a compartment.

He asked the attendant in his own coach for a glass of tea and, holding it in its container printed with rockets and stars, went back into the compartment. The trapper looked startled, as though a sable had bitten him on the thumb. 'I think those are mine,' Michael said, pointing to the travel documents in his hand.

'They fell on the floor,' the trapper said.

Michael looked at his bunk – ground-level because he didn't want anyone beneath him. His briefcase, perched on his coat, was open and papers were protruding from it. Had he left it like that?

'Thank you,' he said, taking the documents.

'You should be more careful,' the trapper admonished him. 'In Siberia no one steals. But here. . . .' He shrugged his wrestler's shoulders. 'Do you know which fur gives you least protection against the cold?'

Michael didn't.

'Mink.' The trapper closed his eyes and began to snore.

At Danilov where the train stopped for twelve minutes Michael took a stroll on the platform. Men in blue track-suits jogged. Women bought boiled potatoes sprinkled with herbs, and pickled mushrooms from a co-operative stall; children bought gingerbread and sunflower seeds.

As the joggers passed and re-passed him, breath smoking on the freezing air, he searched for the draughts-player but the track-suits made them look-alikes.

As the train inched forward he made his way to the dining-car where he was handed a comprehensive menu. He ordered caviar and Chicken Kiev and was told that he could have

110

borscht, beefsteak or Stroganov. The car was dry but, fore-warned, he had brought Georgian wine; the waitress watched him grimly as he poured it and toasted her.

The trapper joined him and stuck out his glass. He wore jeans and an open-neck shirt and his chest was as hairy as the breast of a Barguzin sable. His black hair was dishevelled, his manner ponderous. As he waited for his soup he rolled bread into bullets and fired them into his mouth. He poured himself more of Michael's wine and said: 'When we get back to the compartment we will have a real drink.'

Phantom birch trees flitted past the window, their matchstick progress interrupted from time to time by the whoosh of a goods train, wagons loaded with coal.

The trapper fell into a reverie. The swaying of the coach made purple waves in Michael's borscht. A blue track-suit stumbled down the aisle.

An air of unreality settled on Michael. What was he doing burrowing through the taiga when he should have been in court in New York defending some victimised Armenian or Pole? Why was everyone so evasive?

The borscht was whisked away and replaced by a steak. He drank some wine. At the bottom of an embankment he saw an illuminated graveyard of old steam locomotives.

The trapper helped himself to wine and said lugubriously: 'Tomorrow we cross the Urals into Siberia, through the Monument of Tears. Know what that is?'

'Where the Siberians ran out of *spirit*?'

The trapper stared at him suspiciously. 'You trying to be funny, comrade?'

'The point where the prisoners used to say farewell to their families before marching into slavery?'

Mollified, the trapper said: 'Where the *plet*, a three-thonged whip, ruled. Where you worked in a mine sunk in permafrost, where home was a sod hut. Where the only reward for life was death.' His eyes watered.

Back in the compartment the trapper stripped off his trousers and shirt. Beneath them he was wearing long johns. He put on striped pyjamas and lay on the bottom bunk opposite Michael. Beside him lay an open canvas bag. Inside it a pistol.

The trapper handed him the bottle of *spirit*. 'Have a real

drink, comrade.' And when Michael refused. 'I said drink.'

'In the States,' Michael said, 'we use that as after-shave.'

The trapper reclaimed the bottle, tipped some down his throat and coughed. Then he said: 'I know who you are.'

'So you should – you read all my documents.'

'Knew before that.' He reached vaguely for the canvas bag. 'Comrade Michael Cooper in search of his long-lost brother. Well I'll tell you this, comrade, you'll never find him. No one who was wanted by Stalin's murder squads ever came back. Know where he is? Buried in the permafrost, that's where, alongside the convicts.'

'How did you know who I was?'

The trapper's hand settled on to the canvas bag and Michael tensed himself.

The trapper took out a cutting from the *Moscow News*. And there was Michael's photograph beside a two-column story about his mission. Odd – he didn't remember anyone taking a picture.

'Easy,' the trapper said, belching. 'Now get to bed, the cold can find its way through double windows. Know what the temperature is out there? Fifty degrees, maybe more.' He strangled a smile with a yawn. 'In Siberia we don't bother to say minus.'

Michael stripped down to his underwear and climbed into his bunk. When the trapper was asleep, breath plopping from between slack lips, he leaned across and removed the pistol from his bag.

Then he closed his eyes. Birch trees stutter across his closed vision. They transport him to a classroom on the Lower East Side. A teacher with hair sprouting from his nostrils: 'If you, Vysotsky, are so Russian why don't you go back to Russia?' A lecturer at Columbia Law School, stooping and brilliant-eyed: 'You've got a fine legal brain, don't waste it on those who can afford it.' He is admitted to the Racquet and Tennis Club but the lecturer's eyes glitter and he takes himself to Brooklyn, the Bronx, Queens. . . . A judge, bowed by the antagonism of ethnic minorities – by which he means people – addresses him outside the Bronx County Building: 'Don't bother to come slumming, boy, no one will thank you for it.' He is in bed reaching for the warm curve of Barbara's back; she turns and he smells Magda's perfume. . . .

'Don't ever do that again.' The trapper knelt beside his bunk pointing the pistol at his head. 'No one touches my guns, ever.'

'It looked dangerous; it was pointing at you,' ever the astute lawyer. But no judge or jury would buy that. He stared into the barrel's dark orifice.

'Okay.' The trapper straightened up. 'But next time. . . .' He pulled the trigger and the hammer clicked impotently.

Michael swung his legs off the bunk. Cold had filtered into the compartment and filled the space between the bunks. It was still dark outside but he sensed that dawn was about to yawn through the taiga. He put on a towelling robe and went to the cramped toilet and washroom at the end of the corridor.

After breakfast and during lunch he locked himself into a paperback edition of *Dr Zhivago*, emerging as the train pulled into Sverdlovsk at 3.51 in the afternoon, exactly on time. The trapper, queuing with him for beer on the platform, was expansive about Sverdlovsk. 'Know what happened here?'

'Of course. Tsar Nicholas II and his family were murdered here when it was called Ekaterinburg.'

'Something more important than that.'

Michael looked at him in astonishment. 'What can be more important than that?'

'Your spy, Gary Powers, was brought down here in his U2.'

For the rest of the journey Michael kept company with Zhivago as often as he could. On the fifth day he alighted at Chita, 6,200 kilometres from Moscow.

On the platform the trapper held his hand in a finger-breaking clasp. 'I have enjoyed your company,' he said. 'Here, take this,' handing him a bottle of *spirt*. 'It will keep you warm until you get back to your woman in Moscow.'

'What woman?'

The trapper winked theatrically and climbed back into the carriage.

From Chita, Michael flew north in a Yak-42 to Yakutsk. From Yakutsk to Mirny, normally out-of-bounds to tourists. The cold, minus fifty degrees fahrenheit and dropping, assaulted him, creeping inside his sheepskin coat and *valenki* boots, tweaking his ears beneath the flaps of his *shapka*. His breath froze and dropped softly to the ground.

He found a taxi and told the driver to take him to the address Magda had given him. Trucks loaded with kimberlite from the diamond mines to the north trundled past; body mist hung in the air; he saw a stall piled with blocks of frozen milk, sticks doing duty as handles protruding from each.

Repin lived in a small apartment block built on stilts so that it didn't melt the permafrost beneath. He opened the double-doors and pulled Michael inside. The windows were triple-glazed and the living room glowed.

He was a tall man, quick with youth that he was loathe to relinquish, and with his crinkled grey hair he reminded Michael of a retired cowboy. His speech was quick and nervous, a contradiction of his craggy image.

'Come in,' he said when Michael was already inside. 'Let me take your coat. A young woman from Intourist in Moscow telephoned to tell me you were coming. What can I do for you?' as though he wanted to get it over quickly. 'A drink?'

Michael handed him the bottle of *spirt*. Repin took the bottle, massaging it with his fingers. 'We use it as anti-freeze but when it gets really cold – minus sixty or seventy – we have to keep the engines of the automobiles running all night. Please sit down.' He patted the back of an uncomfortable-looking chair with wooden arm-rests.

Michael sat down. 'Didn't the girl tell you?'

'What? Ah, the purpose of your visit. Something to do with your parents, wasn't it? I can hardly remember them. . . .' He disappeared into the kitchen with the bottle of *spirt*, returning with two glasses of beer. 'From our own brewery here in Mirny. Did you know Mirny means peaceful?'

'I speak Russian,' Michael said. 'Hadn't you noticed?'

'Hasn't been built long. Thirty-five years or so. I worked at the Lucky Diamond Mine 400 kilometres north of here.' He pointed at photographs of the mine on the walls above the sturdy furniture. 'A wonderful life, nearly 600 roubles a month. . . . The cold is good for you, comrade, look at me.' He expanded his chest and Michael half expected him to beat it. 'I'm retired now, of course; I'm chairman of the Mirny Garden Club.'

Michael sipped his tepid beer.

'We sow and gather crops within three months.'

114

'What sort of vegetables did you grow in Moscow in the war?'
Michael asked abruptly.

'Moscow?' Repin drank some beer, wiping the froth from his
upper lip with the tip of his tongue. 'I can't remember; I was
only a child.'

'Seven I believe. In 1941, that is. Did you ever go to the
banya?'

'My parents did.'

'Which is where they met my mother and father.'

'What's this all about?' Repin demanded.

'You really don't know?' cross-examining but careful not to
offend.

'Something to do with your brother Vasily. . . .'

'I want to trace him. I promised my father in New York.'

'He seemed like a man to me but of course he was very
young.'

'Seventeen.' Michael said.

'Something of a hero to a seven-year-old.'

'Why?'

'Why? Because he joined the Communist Battalions of course.
Volunteered to fight the Germans even though he was medically
unfit.'

'What was wrong with him?'

'Tuberculosis, I think. That was the great killer in those
days.'

Michael who hadn't known that Vasily had been unfit said:
'Stalin was exempt from military service in 1916. An infirmity
in the left arm. Supposing he had been fit? He might have been
killed by the Germans and then what would have happened to
history?'

A mistake. The same feeling when you realise that you have
pursued a cross-examination too assiduously and a witness is
about to give the response the other side has been praying for.

Repin said: 'Stalin was good for the Soviet Union.'

Drop it. Regain the witness's confidence. 'So, despite his
illness, Vasily was prepared to fight for his country?'

'I helped him dig trenches,' Repin said.

'And your parents?'

'My mother worked in the Trekhgorka Cotton Mill. When it
was closed down she unravelled coils of barbed wire. Her hands

115

were caked with dried blood. That's how I met my wife. She helped my mother.'

'And your father?'

'He was in the Army. He fought at Viazma. We held up the Germans there for a week. Saved Moscow perhaps.'

'So he didn't go to the banya in 1941?'

'Earlier,' Repin said. 'Before the Germans attacked. Before he was conscripted.'

'Did they give Vasily a weapon?'

'I remember him showing me a really old gun. A Dragoon rifle. I doubt if he had any ammunition for it.'

'And then the Germans attacked Moscow?'

'They underestimated the will of the people. They fought like tigers.' His knuckles shone bone-bright. 'My mother took soup to the trenches. I remember the German planes dodging the barrage balloons. . . .' Repin breathed quickly.

'And Vasily?'

Michael sensed that he was on the verge of a reluctant disclosure.

The twist of a key in a lock. A bar of icy air as the front door opened. 'Dima,' said a small, swaddled figure, obviously Repin's wife, 'who is this?' She stared at Michael.

'The phone call, I told you. . . .'

'Ah, the American. . . .' She took off her fur hat and, beneath it, a grey-wool Balaclava. Button-black eyes regarded him angrily. 'What can we do for you?'

'Didn't your husband mention Vasily?'

'It was all very vague. What have you been telling him, Dima?'

'Nothing.' Repin's cowboy face relaxed. 'We were talking about the Great Patriotic War.'

'What do you know about that? You were only seven – '

'In 1941,' Michael said.

'A child.' She regarded him warily. 'A wasted visit, I'm afraid . . . such a long way to come,' she said with relish.

'Not necessarily – a child's memory can be more vivid than an adult's.'

'But Dima doesn't remember your brother.'

'The Dragoon rifle?'

She turned on Repin. 'What nonsense is this?'

116

'He had an antique rifle,' Repin said. 'Maybe it blew up in his face.'

'I wish we could offer you something,' Repin's wife said to Michael, 'but we have an appointment at the Mirny Garden Club. . . . Dima hopes to grow 1,000 tons of potatoes next year. Don't you, Dima?' She stared stonily at her husband.

'That's the Club's target,' Repin said.

'Dima tells me you unwound barbed wire during the defence of Moscow,' Michael said.

The spider-web lines at the corners of her eyes relaxed. 'They were hard times, brave times, especially when the snow came. Food was delivered on horse-drawn sleighs and there were no trains. Do you know what Lenin said about trains, Comrade Cooper?' She settled herself in another uncomfortable chair opposite him. ' "When the trains stop that will be the end." Well he was wrong that time. And who saved us?'

'Stalin?'

'He rallied us. Such a speech in Red Square on the anniversary of the Revolution. Fighter planes scurrying across the sky, the Germans at the gates of the city. And he talked about the heroes who had saved us in the past. Nevsky, Suvorov, Kutuzov. . . . He reached the soul of us Russians.'

'As opposed to citizens of the Soviet Union?'

'Ukraine had fallen, the Baltic States. . . . It was Old Muscovy that was threatened.'

Her husband raised his grizzled head. 'I remember Siberian troops arriving in the city. They attacked the Germans with bottles of petrol. Such bravery. That's when I first thought about living here.'

'I've regretted it ever since,' his wife said looking at him fondly. His only act of defiance and she respected him for it?

'The money was good,' he said.

'Money isn't everything,' not totally convinced.

'So you remember my brother in the Communist Battalions?' Michael said to Repin.

'We counter-attacked on December sixth,' he said. 'The campaign lasted till the end of spring.'

'Was my brother killed in the counter-attack?'

Repin's wife consulted her wrist-watch. 'Dima, the Garden Club.'

117

Repin stood up. 'I'm sorry, Comrade Cooper, we have to go.'

His wife opened the double-doors. The cold leaped in. 'Now you can go back to Moscow,' she said. 'I envy you.'

Michael put on his sheepskin coat and *shapka* and walked into the street. The brief daylight squeezed between dawn and dusk was fading. A light came on in the apartment. He saw Repin staring into the twilight. The appointment at Mirny Garden Club no longer seemed quite so urgent.

He boarded the west-bound Trans-Siberian at Chita. A flirtatious attendant told him he was lucky: a sailor had mysteriously jumped train at Belogorsk and he had a compartment to himself. She almost winked.

He turned down the taped music, a woman's choir singing soulfully about a willow tree, and lay down on his bunk. A knock at the door. The attendant entered carrying a glass of tea in a container. To keep him warm, she said smiling.

The rhythm of the wheels on the track was slow waves licking a beach . . . the lonely cries of seagulls . . . shingle moving underfoot. . . .

Another knock. Blouse unbuttoned? Lips parted, puppy tongue licking them? A few dollars would be greatly appreciated. . . .

He switched on the light and opened the door.

The man's bulk filled the frame. Below his *shapka* he wore a woollen anti-frost mask. He switched off the light and said: 'I have a message for you, comrade.' His voice was muffled but vaguely familiar. 'Drop this stupid mission; your brother is dead.'

'Who is the message from?' asked Michael, vulnerable in singlet and jockey shorts.

'No business of yours. Just do as you're told.'

The train passed a village. Lights glittered in the intruder's eyes. He smelled of moss. His jacket was padded; you could lose your fist in it. Kick? Bare foot against *valenki* . . . had to be the face . . . surprise. . . .

'You understand?' the man asked.

'I understand.'

118

Michael jabbed with two fingers at the glittering eyes but his arms were lovingly enfolded. Then he was turned around, gently. The padded arms encircled his chest and began to squeeze.

. . . *until their hearts stop beating.*

He heard a rib crack.

Part II

10

GUM, pronounced GOOM, is a nineteenth-century shopping mall, long, ornate and glass-roofed with two elevated arcades joined above the main concourse by bridges. It stands on Red Square and is famed for its fountain, its ice-cream and its dearth of anything worth buying. When anything worthwhile does appear in one of its shops queues form as quickly as rent-a-crowds.

The Fighting Comrades, frustrated by a second postponement of a decision on the fate of the bath-house, struck three days before Christmas which has been replaced in the Soviet Union by the New Year. Led by the laundress, a platoon of Comrades in brown uniforms, medals on their breasts, patrolled the arcades waiting for windfalls. Other shoppers, some bearing New Year pine trees, followed them believing that they knew a thing or two.

The laundress, acting on a tip-off, stopped suddenly outside a shop on the arcade above the ground floor. The marauders piled up behind the Comrades. A pale-faced shop assistant with finger-combed ringlets and smudged make-up gazed at them apprehensively from behind an empty counter.

A few minutes later two men in brown overalls deposited three cardboard packing cases on the floor. They were upside down and the writing was in English. 'Natural fabrics perhaps,' the seamstress said wistfully. 'Linen?' 'Or condoms?' said the hairdresser. 'Not far wrong,' the laundress said. 'Passion-killers,' as the men tipped a container onto a display counter in the window and packs of tights slid out like fish from a net.

Women in the queue outside sighed. The shop assistant stared at them defiantly. They began to hammer on the window.

She walked furiously to the door and opened it. The Comrades swept in, laundress at their head.

The girl folded her arms. 'I'm sorry,' she said to the laundress, 'I've been ordered not to serve you.'

'Whose orders?'

'The manager's.'

'Fetch the manager.'

'I can't.' She pointed at the slithery pile of packaged tights. 'I can't leave them, can I?'

'That's up to you,' the laundress said, loosening her headscarf. 'I can stay here all day.'

'We can't,' said a voice in the queue.

The Comrades turned and the voice faltered.

The assistant was saved by the arrival of the manager, a middle-aged and bespectacled bureaucrat who carried himself importantly and wore a Red Star pin in the lapel of his charcoal-grey suit.

'What's going on here?' he demanded.

'Are you blind,' the laundress said. 'Or are you wearing your wife's glasses?'

The manager stabbed a plump finger at her. 'You're banned.'

'On whose orders?'

'You know whose orders.'

'Vilkin's?'

The manager shrugged.

'You can't ban me: it's unconstitutional.'

'We reserve the right of admission.'

'Bullshit,' the laundress said. 'A murderer could walk into GUM and you'd sell him an ice-cream.' She placed six roubles on the counter. 'I want three pairs of tights,' she said to the assistant.

'You'll have to leave,' the manager said. He placed one hand on her arm.

'Physical assault. Did you see that Comrades?'

'Do you want me to call the militia?'

'Call the President – he's just across the square.'

The manager turned to the crowd. 'This woman,' he said, pointing at the laundress, 'has been abusing her privileges in this store for years. Paying for information, installing accomplices in the queues while she joins others. . . .' He took off his glasses. 'She has also been robbing you of what is rightly

124

yours and selling it to her cronies in the banya. I ask you, is that just?'

The seamstress spoke up. 'If you and your sort did your jobs properly she wouldn't have to do it. How many containers of food and clothes are stuck in ports and railway stations at this minute? It's because of people like you that people like us have to scavenge.'

The laundress fingered the lapel of his suit. 'A fine cloth, comrade. Where did you get it? On a State-sponsored trip to London or New York, all expenses paid? Don't talk to us about privileges, stick them where the monkey puts his nuts. Now give me my tights before my colleagues,' nodding at the Comrades, 'get really angry.'

'Give her the tights,' shouted a woman in the queue. 'We can't stay here till the New Year.'

'I can't,' the manager said.

The crowd became vociferous. 'Give her the tights . . . couldn't organise a piss-up in a brewery . . . throw him off the balcony. . . .'

The hairdresser poked him in the chest. 'You're useless, do you know that? Like all men.'

The manager said to the assistant: 'Telephone the militia.' And when she hesitated: 'Do what I tell you. Do you want to lose your job?'

A woman shouted: 'Why should she lose her job? What about yours? What about all the empty counters? What about the cubes of concrete sugar from Cuba, the gold-fish disguised as peaches, anti-freeze that freezes. . . .'

The seamstress said: 'Don't involve her,' nodding at the flustered girl. 'If you want the militia you call them.'

The manager hesitated: 'Can't we settle this reasonably?'

'Of course we can,' the laundress told him. 'Give me the tights.'

The manager took a step backwards. The jingling bosoms of the Comrades bore down upon him. He stared wildly into the arcade towards one of the footbridges spanning the concourse.

He picked up the phone, dialled a number. 'He must be there. . . . Tell him it's urgent. . . . His authority is being defied.'

A pause. The crowd grew silent.

125

'Yes, comrade, she's here. Yes, I have relayed your orders. No, she won't move . . . insists we sell her. . . .' He whispered into the receiver. 'Yes, comrade, you heard correctly, tights.' He glared at the Fighting Comrades. 'It is not my intention to make a fool of anyone. . . .' He straightened up and pressed the receiver against his ear. 'I can't help it if they were the commodity that became available. . . . Very well, I will do what you suggest.'

He replaced the receiver. Closed his eyes for a moment as if he were enduring a stab of cranial pain. Opened them and smiled wisely at the laundress. 'The, ah, official dealing more directly with your problem has decided to compromise. And don't forget that compromise should not be confused with weakness.' He compressed his lips. 'In fact it is a device employed by the greatest statesmen in the world.'

The laundress said: 'Do I get my tights?'

'One pair.'

The assistant handed her a pack containing a pair of black tights, large size.

'Three pairs,' the laundress said.

'Two.'

'Three.'

'Very well.' The manager picked up two more packs and threw them at her. She fielded them neatly in her string-bag. 'But don't think this is defeat. It's a compromise and you're still banned. Understand?'

He turned and pushed his way through the queue to the crowd outside. On the arcade a woman stuck out her foot. The manager lurched and fell, jack-knifed across the balustrade three metres or so above the ground floor.

The crowd on the arcade pressed forward. The manager swung his legs over the balustrade, hung for a moment by his hands, dropped, bounced on his feet and sloped away among the predatory shoppers below.

The stallholder was proud of the laundress. He told her so outside the banya. 'Wonderful, wonderful. That will show them they can't patronise us.'

126

'Us?'

'Everyone at the banya.'

'Patronise? You use some weird words. . . .'

'What I'm trying to say is you did well. I couldn't have done better myself.'

'I'm flattered,' the laundress said warily.

'Did you make any sort of statement afterwards?'

'I read what the American had prepared. Well some of it. . . . I said I refused to be persecuted. That we in the banya refused to be persecuted.'

'Was there anyone there to take it down?'

'I don't think so,' the laundress said.

The stallholder squeezed her arm and went into the mens' changing-room. 'The red-haired bitch forgot to inform the Press,' he announced. 'Now it's up to us.'

'So what do you propose?' the Kremlin chauffeur asked.

'Red Square?' The pickpocket knitted and unknitted his fingers.

'Where else? Does any other city have such a fulcrum? The heart of Mother Russia.'

'You can't expect me to go,' the Kremlin chauffeur said.

'You are exempt. What about the rest of you?'

'Why not?' The Ukrainian miner who was on strike again pulled a coarse grey shirt over his muscular shoulders. 'Red Square. Where else?'

'Where else?' said a lusty Georgian who had begun to frequent the banya. 'I will protest there too. Freedom for Georgia.'

'Forgive me,' said a lanky Estonian, 'but wasn't Stalin a Georgian? Isn't he still a hero in your part of the world?'

The Georgian ignored him. 'We had three years of independence under the Mensheviks, the minority. Then the Bolsheviks, the majority, sent in the Red Army in 1921 to re-occupy our land. Seventy years of tyranny. . . .'

'Not to mention crime and corruption,' the Latvian said. 'Why are you here? To sell carnations for the New Year at a 200 per cent mark-up?'

The stallholder held up his arms. 'Just this once,' deep voice filling the room, 'let's be united.' Silence. Then: 'Follow me.'

He led the way down the street, fur hat at a jaunty angle, to a parked van bonneted with dirty snow, unloaded the dismantled

127

sections of a trestle table, a charcoal burner, and two trays of *shashlik* and meat pies covered with silver foil and handed them out.

The daylight was beginning to lose its icy radiance when they reached Red Square. Clusters of tourists roamed the cobblestones, peering at the baubles of St Basil's, the red-granite mausoleum where the body of Lenin lay, the walls of the Kremlin and the area where, in May 1987, the young German pilot, Mathias Rust, landed a Cessna.

The militia were there too.

'Shit,' said the bodybuilder. 'Who told them?'

The policemen walked towards the stallholder and his supporters, boots beneath their long coats ringing crisply on the cobblestones.

'Put up the table,' the stallholder ordered. 'Quickly.' He placed the burner and the trays of *shashlik* and pies on the scarred surface.

An officer stood in front of him, arms folded. 'So what the hell do you think you're doing?'

'Selling pies,' the stallholder told him. 'And *shashlik*.'

'Well, you can't sell them here. Are you crazy?'

'I understood it was a free country.'

'Could you sell meat pies in the forecourt of Buckingham Palace?'

'Who knows. Perhaps the Queen likes meat pies.'

'Shit,' the officer said, 'a comedian. There's only one human being I detest more than a drug-pusher or a child-abuser and that's a comedian.' His face beneath his fur hat was young and keen but he didn't look as tough as his talk.

'Would you like to try a pie? Beef, potatoes, lots of spice, just the thing for a cold afternoon on duty.'

The officer unfolded his arms, placed one hand on the holster of his pistol, and sighed. 'Right, I don't want to hand you over to Petrovka. I believe in *glasnost* just as much as you. But I don't think it should be abused. The authorities,' nodding towards the Kremlin where the red stars on the towers had just come alight, 'are doing their best to cope. Comedians are what they can do without. So why don't you pack up your pies and piss off before I get really angry?'

The Georgian, standing to the front of the stallholder's henchmen, said: 'Doing their best to cope? Killing demonstrators in Tbilisi with sharpened spades?'

'Do you see any sharpened spades here?'

'No, but – '

'Then shut your mouth.'

The stallholder said: 'I'm not doing any harm. . . .'

'Listen, I know what you're doing. You're protesting about the decision to demolish your banya. . . .'

'So someone did rat on us,' the bodybuilder said.

A lone star pricked the greening sky. The last group of tourists trooped obediently away behind their courier. An iced breeze explored the square which wasn't square at all.

'Well, it sounds a fair enough cause to me,' the policeman went on. 'I like to feel steam heat cleansing me as much as anyone. But this isn't the place to protest. You must see that,' he appealed to the stallholder.

The stallholder turned and said: 'Is the reporter here?'

No one replied.

'I telephoned the *Moscow News*.'

'They probably thought you were crazy,' the officer said. 'You are, aren't you?'

'Shit,' said the stallholder.

'So take your stall somewhere else. The Arbat?'

'I'm staying,' the stallholder said. He took a box of matches from the pocket of his padded jacket.

'Oh no you don't,' the officer said. 'Are you really going to be so stupid?'

'We might as well go home,' the Ukrainian miner said. 'No point, is there, if the Press aren't here?'

The stallholder struck a match and stepped towards the charcoal burner.

'That's it,' the officer said. He waved his hand and a police car materialised out of the dusk. 'Petrovka,' he told the driver. Two militiamen bundled the stallholder into the back; the match went out.

The bodybuilder picked up the tray of meat. 'For the dogs,' he said.

*

Tanya Argusky made *her* protest while cross-country ski-ing with her parents. Her skis were old-fashioned and cumbersome but the exercise was good for her leg muscles. The snow on the fields was bright with the blue of the sky; bare trees bloomed with frost; a church with gold and azure domes like lacquered mushrooms sprouted from a village.

She stopped to wait for her parents. Her father wore a red and white woollen hat which contradicted the suffering on his bearded face, her mother a fur *shapka* that, hiding her tired grey hair, gave her back ten years of her life.

As she waited Tanya summoned courage. In truth it was perfectly simple. 'If you don't abandon your campaign, Papa, I shall leave home.' Until, that was, she was in the presence of her father.

That morning she had skated with the young man chosen by Lev Grechko as his answer to Nina Zelenaya. He skated well enough but he lacked Yury's instinctive graces.

Afterwards he had said: 'We go well together, you and I?' He was as dark as Yury was fair with handsome, set-piece features.

'You skate well,' she said. *But not well enough.* But she had to have a partner to practise with. 'Tomorrow?'

'I'll be here,' he said. 'Maybe one day we'll win some championships.'

Her mother said: 'Is anything the matter, dear?'

Nothing more than usual, Tanya thought. Snow fell from the branch of a tree; the sun found jewels in the snow. How could her father want to leave Russia?

'How did it go this morning?'

'I've got a new partner.'

Her father leaned against a tree. 'That's sensible. What's he like?'

'Adequate.' They both suspected that she saw Yury when she said she was visiting Lev Grechko's niece, Zina. Her mother even asked camouflaged questions about pregnancy in the guise of instruction. And here she was, still a virgin. 'His technique is good.'

'Does this mean,' her mother said carefully, 'that he is going to be your full-time partner?' *That you won't see Yury again.*

'We'll see,' Tanya said.

They moved off again, pushing their skis through the snow at a leisurely pace. A dog, or it may have been a wolf, howled in the distance.

After a while her father said: 'I'm glad you're being sensible, Tanya.'

So the time had come. She thrust herself forward and spoke over her shoulder. 'Abandoning any hope of skating in the Olympics? That's sensible?'

'And have you abandoned hope?' Her father caught up with her.

'If you had your way I would have done.'

'So nothing has changed.'

'Not unless you've changed.'

'You know that's impossible.'

'But why, Papa?'

'You know why,' he said. 'Twenty years ago in a courtroom in Leningrad. . . .'

Tanya stared at the snow in front of her. She had heard the story repeated since childhood. Two Jews sentenced to death, nine to imprisonment, for trying to hijack a twelve-seater AN-2 from Priozersk to Israel via Sweden. A weeping woman at the back of the court crying: 'Children, we shall be waiting for you in Israel. All the Jews are with you. The world is with you. Together we shall build our Jewish home. Tanya could recite the story.

Tanya said: 'But they did commit a crime. And the death sentences *were* commuted.'

'To long terms in strict regime camps. And who helped to get those sentences commuted.'

'You, Papa,' Tanya said bleakly.

'And went to a camp for my pains.'

Tanya listened to the swish of the antique skis on the snow. Then she said: 'But that was a long time ago. Before I was born. . . .'

'So it was all in vain?'

'You've got what you wanted.'

'No. Emigrants must be seen to be leaving beneath the Star of David. We must be seen to be victors not unwelcome visitors slipping out of the side door.'

They ski-ed slowly into the village. Young men were playing ice-hockey on a frozen pond, their shouts sharp on the bright air. They stopped at a café where a stove surrounded by wooden tables and benches glowed. An old woman with snapping gums served them mugs of hot chocolate. Tanya thought: I am Jewish but I love this country. Why can't I be Jewish *and* Russian?

'. . . always persecuted,' her father was saying. He had removed his woollen hat and his bald patch was white above his polished cheeks. 'Your ancestors in the Pale of Settlement, confined there by the Tsars. . . . sent to Siberia after the murder of Alexander II. . . . Jews in Russia blamed for the defeat by the Germans in the First World War. . . .'

Tanya interrupted. 'Who said, "Shame on accursed Tsarism which tortured and persecuted the Jews?" '

'Lenin?' Her mother took off her fur hat and looked ten years older.

'We all know who said it,' Tanya's father snapped. 'And then what happened? Stalin! He was frightened of us, our brains, our initiative, and off we went to the camps once more . . . until the Great Patriotic War. Then we were useful again fighting the Germans. They even allowed us to form the Jewish Anti-Fascist Committee of the Soviet Union. And then what happened?'

'We know what happened,' Tanya said.

'Once again we were a threat. Solomon Mikhoels, director of the Moscow Yiddish State Theatre who had spread the good word to the world in 1943, was murdered in Minsk. The Committee was broken up, the persecution began again. . . .'

'That,' Tanya said, 'was nearly fifty years ago. Khrushchev did his best for us, didn't he?'

'They never forgave the Israelis for smashing the armies of Egypt, Syria and Jordan in 1967 in the Six Day War. Those armies were equipped by the Soviet Union. . . .'

'Ah yes, 1967. . . . I still hadn't been born.'

Her mother said wearily: 'Do I have to listen to all this once again? Can't we enjoy the day? It's short enough.'

Tanya said: 'You should have put a stop to it years ago.'

Her father's beard came up. 'Don't speak to your mother like that.'

'I'm sorry, Mama.' Tanya touched her mother's hand. 'But it's true. You should have spoken out.'

'Against what? I agreed with your father.'

'But not any longer, surely?'

'You don't understand. The indignities he has suffered, they are indelible.'

Tanya turned to her father who was rubbing his bald skull-cap with the palm of his hand. 'Then you won't give up your . . . your crusade?'

'You know I won't.'

'Then that is very sad.' She finished her chocolate. 'I'm leaving home,' she said.

Her mother put on her hat. This time the years stayed with her.

11

In his weekend retreat Tsar Petrov considered his responsibilities and was intimidated by them. No emperor of Holy Russia had ever presided at the liberation of an empire; no Romanov had ever loosened the bounds of repression so energetically within the homeland.

I must practise humility, Petrov counselled himself as he prowled the ground floor of the sleeping dacha at Zhukovka, thirty kilometres outside Moscow. And honour my late mentors – Nicolai Zorin, First Secretary of the *krai* near Stalingrad, now Volgograd, and Yury Ivan Abramov, head of the KGB before his brief reign as leader of the Soviet Union.

But it wasn't easy to be humble when you controlled so many destinies. Only when he was here, where he could hear the countryside breathing, could he elude the responsibilities he had manufactured. But even here the tranquillity was fractured by pending decisions.

He paused in front of the log fire. It was 7.30 in the morning but the embers were still glowing. He poked them and butterflies of flame came to life casting reflections on icons and Palekh boxes in the darkened room. He tightened the belt of his dressing-gown and sat in front of the struggling flames.

Sometimes he felt young and quick with life, sometimes middle-aged; this morning, after dreaming that ballistic missiles dangling from a net of radiation emanating from Chernobyl, were about to drop on Moscow, he felt elderly. His eyes were still tired, his head ached.

Did anyone watching him on television shaking hands and kissing heads of state comprehend the turmoil within him? Why did you do it, Viktor Petrov? A flame clung to an ember for a moment, then died.

He padded into the kitchen, past the cold samovar, and made himself a pot of tea. He raised a slat on a shutter and stared into the lingering night towards the dachas of Zhukovka where the privileged slept. Lying out there, stirring in their uneasy dreams, they comforted Petrov; they were the living proof of the betrayal of socialism. They were his rationale.

Snowflakes hovered at the window. Through them he saw the blurred silhouette of one of his guards investigating the beam of light.

Glass of tea in his hand, he made his way to his pine-walled study. Faintly he heard snoring. His wife or his daughter, taking a break from medical research, or her husband, a surgeon. What must it be like to be the daughter or son-in-law of the author of *glasnost* and *perestroika*? Sometimes, because he valued family life above everything, Petrov wished there had been more children.

On his desk were the weeklies and monthlies. *Ogonyok, Moscow News, Literaturnaya Gazeta, Novy Mir, Oktyabr, Kommunist, Pamyat, Molodaya Gvardia*. . . . He threw the prepared digests which he didn't trust into the wastepaper basket and began to read.

One journal analysed his foreign policy. The withdrawal from Afghanistan. His disarmament initiative. But it was the disintegration of unity in the Soviet bloc, the breaching of the Berlin Wall, that really made the writer's adrenalin bubble. Whether he was for or against it was difficult to determine. Understandably – all Russians under fifty had grown up to accept that half a dozen or more disparate countries co-existed. The writer was bewildered. He hoped that socialism would continue to prosper – *which it manifestly hadn't* – in the countries seeking their identity.

Petrov sipped his tea. He heard footsteps upstairs. The dacha continued to breathe in the darkness. When light came the garden reaching down to the river would be gentle with the new snow.

Petrov prayed that the writer's hopes would be realised because they were the foundations of his policies. That men and women would embrace a qualified socialism in which initiative was rewarded.

Another magazine examined the domestic policies. The

attempt to lift the heavy hand of the State from the economy. The birth of the co-operatives. Electoral reforms. Human rights recognised. The drawing of the KGB's teeth. *Had the roots been extracted?* The granting of autonomy to the Baltic States. Did this, the author demanded, presage the beginning of the end of the Soviet Union?

Petrov lowered his head. It was weighted with contradictions – and the knowledge that so far his reforms had failed: that the economy of the Soviet Union was floundering.

He picked up the translation of an article from an American news magazine. Meat ration a mere two and one fifth pounds in some parts of the Soviet Union . . . soap four ounces . . . 40,000,000 farm workers controlled by 3,000,000 bureaucrats . . . public bored to distraction by his long-winded speeches. . . . *Well, they had a point there* . . . in a poll fifty-seven per cent of the people pessimistic about the future.

Petrov rubbed his tired eyes. Surely Russians, although extrovert, were intrinsically pessimistic; it was their historic legacy. So what did the pollsters expect? I don't need moribund statistics: what I want are the opinions of actual people. I want to know if they believe that, errors apart, I am doing my best for their country. That they are grateful that I have given them back their birthright, freedom. What I need, decided Tsar Petrov – Petrov the Benevolent – is a cross-section of opinion. His wife's words came back to him. 'There's only one way to find out and that's in a banya.' Advice he hadn't yet taken because he had been in Washington, London, Warsaw. . . . He picked up the telephone and called the head of the KGB, Vladimir Kirov, at his nearby dacha.

Kirov's voice yawned with sleep. 'Wake up, Dima,' Petrov said. 'I've got a job for you.'

'On Sunday?' To Kirov who worked fifteen hours a day at his desk in Dzerzhinsky Square, Sunday was a sacred oasis. Everyone knew that – he had said so in a televised interview with Novosti. The head of the KGB confessing that he had a wife and children, admitting that he enjoyed the theatre, divulging that he read Bertolt Brecht. . . . The people were stunned.

'Nothing to extend you,' Petrov said. 'Just get someone to check out the regulars at a banya. Isn't there one just north of

136

the Kremlin? Then drop round for a drink before lunch.'

'A banya?' The man who controlled a secret service 500,000 strong sounded bemused.

'Just do it,' Petrov said. 'The vodka's in the freezer.' He hung up as Natalia came into the study. 'I couldn't sleep,' he told her.

'Who was that?'

'Kirov.'

'On Sunday?'

'The banya. Remember?'

'Couldn't it have waited until tomorrow?' On Sundays Natalia tried to re-direct stress.

'Perhaps. But it's a relaxing worry,' he said craftily. 'A banya. The heat. . . .' He flexed his shoulders. 'And Kirov is just down the road. . . . He's coming round for a drink.'

'You look tired,' she said. She stroked his cheek. 'Breakfast?'

He pressed her hand against his cheek. '*Kasha*,' he said. 'With butter.'

'Your diet?'

'No stress on Sundays.'

In the kitchen she raised the shutters. The clean light came in cautiously. There were ferns of frost on the double-glazed windows; beyond them the garden was at peace. Errant wisps of snow hung in the air; dawn lingered on the horizon in grey and winter-pink slates.

Natalia busied herself with the porridge. Petrov enjoyed the kitchen; it wasn't too modern – bunches of dried herbs hung from the ceiling – and Cossack ancestors would have approved. He smoothed the grey hair above his ears, regressed from old to middle age. In two days he would be meeting the Pope in the Vatican, three days later the President of the United States: at times like this such encounters were difficult to comprehend.

He said: 'On Tuesday we'll be in Rome.' *We*, thank God. There were times – 3.00 a.m. for instance, with doubt levering him from his dreams – when he didn't think he could contemplate any diplomacy without her.

'Remember the first time?' she said.

'Paris? Of course. Our first excursion outside the Soviet Union. Nearly twenty years ago, when I was still Second Secretary of the *krai*.'

137

'The stores. . . . I couldn't believe that there could be so much for sale. The shoes. . . . Why do I remember shoes?'

'Because they weren't made of cardboard,' Petrov said, dipping a spoon into his porridge. 'People still say I was converted on that vacation. Well, they're right but not in the way they think. The excesses sickened me.'

'Those shoes. . . . And there I was writing a thesis about peasant customs. . . . '

'What impressed me were the books. The newspapers actually criticising the government. Five years in a camp in the Soviet Union for that. Article 70. . . .' Butter melted on his tongue. 'The freedom. . .' his voice slippery with the butter. 'And now the ultimate irony, I'm more popular abroad than I am in my own country.'

'Inevitable. People haven't had to make decisions for seventy years. Now, suddenly, you've handed them responsibility. It scares them.'

'Such initiative,' Petrov said. 'Do you know what I heard in Tyumen? The incentive to drill for more oil, more gas, was a free ticket to the cinema! I wonder what the film was. *War and Peace?*' He pushed the empty bowl aside.

'It will take time,' Natalia said. She sat opposite him sipping a mug of tea.

'Why don't they trust me? Aren't I a man of the people?'

'Meeting the President of the United States, the Pope. . . . They don't understand, not yet.'

'But how much time have I got?'

'Not long enough,' she said. 'If you don't relax on Sundays.'

Their daughter and her husband came yawning into the kitchen. He regarded them with pride. Handsome young people aloof from politics. Sitting beneath the bundled herbs of long-ago summers, Tsar Petrov tried hard to be a family man.

Kirov arrived at 11.30 at the wheel of a humble Volga. His secret features beneath his fur hat had been aged by frank disclosures and his heavy spectacles rested loosely above his cheekbones. But Petrov respected him; his willingness, occasionally sabotaged by his years, to be a celebrant of *glasnost*. In fact Petrov did not subscribe to the revulsion generated by successive heads of the KGB; that was Beria's legacy, their misfortune; Yury Abramov, who had become his mentor after visiting the *krai*, had done his best to exorcise some of its more grotesque follies.

'First,' Petrov said, 'a stroll. Then a nip of firewater.'

'A stroll?' Kirov shivered.

'Cold stimulates the brain,' said Petrov who liked to isolate the dacha from intrigue.

'I have those names for you,' Kirov said, as they skirted a clump of pines. He handed Petrov an envelope.

'Such service!' Petrov slipped the envelope into the pocket of his heavy coat. 'I want you to put an observer in there, Dima.'

'An observer? But we already have someone there. In every bar and every banya.' Kirov grimaced apologetically.

They reached the river. The snow on the far bank was rutted by the remains of trenches dug in 1941.

But I don't want a spy, Petrov thought. I want an impartial referee. He touched the envelope. 'Do you know the occupations of these people?'

'Most of them,' Kirov said. 'It's all in the envelope. Is it really so important? You're about to meet the Pope, the American president. . . . I worry about you, Viktor.'

'What the people of the Soviet Union think about me is important, yes?'

'I worry about your safety. The company you're keeping. . . . The Pope was shot, so was the President's predecessor. . . .'

They made their way through a copse of birch trees, parchment barks peeling, where in the summer Natalia fed the squirrels.

Kirov pointed with a black-gloved hand towards tall trees screening grand dachas. 'You have enemies there, too. Men who can feel you pulling privileges from under their feet. Men who think your reforms are too hasty, men who think they're too slow. As you know, we've already uncovered two plots to depose you.'

'Every leader lives with threats.'

'I have names,' Kirov murmured.

'I could recite them,' Petrov said.

'You must be more careful.' Kirov adjusted his ponderous spectacles. 'Some are old but they employ young men.'

139

'Assassins?'

Kirov rubbed his gloved hands together and examined them as if he expected sparks to fly. 'Time for that firewater, Comrade President?'

They walked back to the dacha followed by two guards. Petrov felt sorry for them. Lose the Soviet leader and your own Commander-in-Chief and what did the future hold for you?

They adjourned to Petrov's study where the periodicals were still sprawled on the desk. Petrov fetched vodka from the freezer in the kitchen, Narzan water, gherkins and bread.

They each had a shot. Sluiced down the mineral water, snapped at the food.

Natalia materialised in the doorway. Kirov glanced at his watch. 'I didn't realise it was so late,' he said. He gave a small, Prussian-style bow and made for the front door.

Petrov opened the envelope in his study in the soporific aftermath of lunch. Twenty or so names typed with a machine badly in need of a new ribbon, occupations bracketed beside a dozen of them. Bricklayer, architect, stallholder, Red Army colonel, laundress, a miner who believed that his illegal presence in Moscow had gone undetected, Kremlin driver, seamstress. . . . Beside one name was a cross made with a red ball-point, presumably the KGB operative. The last name: Hanson, Robert. And in brackets *defector*. Hanson? Knowledge, as yet unfathomed, stirred in the recesses of Petrov's memory. Frowning, he leaned back in his chair and closed his eyes.

12

Nowhere was Christmas celebrated more resolutely than in the homes of the Twilight Brigade. Pine trees harvested from State plantations were potted and bedizened prematurely; cards mail-ordered from abandoned homelands were posted with premeditated despatch; plum puddings were made with improvised recipes and doused with Georgian brandy; carols were sung tearfully.

This year one of the most prestigious Christmas lunches was served at the cavernous apartment where the West German widow lived. On his way Hanson stopped at the bath-house to see if Michael Cooper wanted to join him for a festive drink in a hotel bar. But Cooper, even more of a celebrity since he had been squeezed almost to death on the Trans-Siberian, had other plans. This didn't surprise Hanson: visitors or diplomats in Western embassies rarely had time to mix with defectors. Nor, for that matter, did Russians. He wished Cooper a merry Christmas and drove to the apartment.

He gave the widow an imitation amber brooch, fulvous plastic containing some sort of foreign body. 'Bob,' she said, 'you shouldn't have,' and in a stage whisper: 'Any luck?'

'Keeping my fingers crossed.' Hanson kissed her deftly on the cheek, and made his way to the Chi-Chi bar where sparkling Crimean wine was being served.

Glass in hand, he surveyed the yuletide gathering animated this year by the possibilities of the video movie. The gingery Australian who had written the script had expanded with creativity and was showing his screenplay to a knot of hopefuls – to be left out of the production altogether was the ultimate rejection.

Joe Palmer, the American veteran from the Spanish Civil War

who was directing, was explaining a suspense sequence. 'Just like Hitch did it in *Vertigo*. Remember that movie? Jimmy Stewart and Grace Kelly. I always figured Hitch had a thing about Grace.'

'Wasn't it Kim Novak?' asked an earnest Belgian dispatching any chance he might have had of taking part.

'Kim, Grace. . . . It matters?'

The widow, who was the producer, circulated speculatively, a galleon in full sail. Behind her floated her latest house-guest, a morose Rumanian.

The Yorkshireman, Mayhew, eating a cracker smeared with lumpfish caviar – in Russia! – joined Hanson. 'Ah,' he said, 'the American President, the victim. Where are you going to be shot? Between the eyes? I'm told that's the most effective for special effects.'

'You should know,' Hanson said. 'You're the assistant script-writer.'

'Or would you like it in the back? Stumbling forward, pitching head first into snow.' Mayhew licked buck-shot vestiges of caviar from his fingers. 'I can fix it you know. A word in the ear of our director. . . .'

The Scottish ex-seaman approached them hugging his guile. 'Maybe that won't be necessary, eh, Robbie?' He rubbed his shiny hands together. 'Maybe they will just have to find another victim.'

Mayhew gulped sparkling wine. 'You?'

'Hadn't you heard? I might be the assassin.'

'Eight years in a fucking labour camp. Don't you feel like knocking off a Russian instead of an American?'

The seaman glanced uneasily behind him. 'Watch it, some of our friends are here.'

'Spooks?'

'They'll do for you one of these days,' the ex-seaman said and thrust his way through the guests towards Joe Palmer.

The widow pointed at the black-and-white photograph of the panda covering the wall behind the bar. 'Don't you just want to cuddle him?' She tossed her grey-blonde hair.

'It would tear you to shreds,' Mayhew told her.

'Ooh.' She shivered, licked her lips with the tip of her tongue. Behind her the Rumanian took cat-sips of wine and nibbled fussily at a cracker. 'Pretor! Music.' The Rumanian made his way to an ancient record-player and Bing Crosby began to dream of a white Christmas.

'Jesus!' exclaimed Mayhew.

'It is Jesus's birthday,' Hanson said.

'Droll, that's what you are,' the widow said in her comprehensive English.

An apt description? Wit imagined by the listener? The humourless laugh in case a subtle quip had been missed. . . . How he had worked at it, second-hand aphorisms, implied jests. . . .

Why had he bothered? Why manufacture your character? I was different enough as it was. He massaged the palm of his left hand. Or was that the crux of it? So different that I couldn't integrate with any society? So I became . . . urbane. . . .

He made his way to the bathroom. Stared in the mirror, but of the stranger there was no sign; washed his hands methodically and passed some of the blame onto Weinreb.

Weinreb whose brother had in all innocence fought for the Germans, papers falsified in anticipation of the Holocaust.

Weinreb, pint of bitter in hand behind the red curtains of the Polar Bear in Soho says: 'There isn't anything you want to tell me, is there, Robert?' He sips mightily and grimaces: Weinreb is not a beer drinker but a tankard in his paw is part of his new image, jovial entrepreneur who likes to drink with the boys from the band of the Talk of the Town.

'Nothing, *de rien. Nada*,' says Hanson who is tremulously contemplating perfecting his Russian in the Soviet Union and staying there.

'Come off it – we've always known what the other was thinking.' Weinreb, exuberantly handsome but already losing his waistline, hails a gasping saxophonist and orders him a pint. 'You're worried, Roberto. In a funk. What is it, got that girl from Bottisham in the family way?'

'There's nothing the matter, honestly.'

'Remember when you had a crush on Miss Holtby? Didn't tell you at the time but I fancied her myself.'

'So did the games master,' Hanson says.

A little drunk, he regards Weinreb over the rim of his tankard. He still loves him but inevitably they have come to a cross-roads.

It was written; it is immeasurably sad; he raises his tankard and Weinreb's face dissolves in its depths.

'Come on,' Weinreb urges, 'out with it.'

'I feel a bit unsure of myself.'

'Should have done your national service.' Hand to his mouth. 'Sorry, your lungs. . . . .'

'Bellows. They sound like a church organ sometimes.'

'You'll get over it,' Weinreb says dismissively.

'Don't you ever wonder . . . you know . . . about who you are. . . .'

'Used to,' says Weinreb. 'But I grew out of it.'

'I may be going away,' Hanson says tentatively.

'Teaching job?' Weinreb always associates a degree in languages with tuition. 'During vacation?'

'For a long time.'

'Private tutor? Lucky sod.'

And Hanson realises that there is no one outside the Soviet Union with whom he can share his pure visions.

From behind the bar a weary voice: 'Time gentlemen, please.'

Hanson slides his half-full tankard behind a collection of empties, hopes Weinreb doesn't notice, observes Weinreb doing the same.

Weinreb clumps various musicians on the shoulder, winks at a couple of them for no apparent reason. 'Come on, Roberto, time for you to hit the sack.'

'Up the wooden stairs to Bedfordshire. My mother used to say that.' Hanson closes his eyes and sees the capillaries of blood from her apron in the sink. 'I feel sick.'

Weinreb leads him to the lavatory – the bog, as he calls it – where Hanson throws up and vows never to drink again.

Weinreb sticks two one pound notes in the breast pocket of his jacket, hails a cab and tells the driver to take him to the address in South Kensington where he is staying with friends.

That evening Weinreb takes an out-of-work drummer to an Italian restaurant in Soho, eats a surfeit of pasta, suffers a precocious heart attack and dies in Charing Cross Hospital.

Hanson finished drying his hands in the widow's bathroom, and opened the door. 'I know,' he said to the girl outside. 'You're bursting.'

144

At lunch – turkey brought from Helsinki by a Finnish journalist, and plum pudding – Hanson sat between the English homosexual and Mayhew. Opposite him Joe Palmer and the Australian.

A Frenchman who reminded Hanson of the late Maurice Chevalier carved the turkey. The wine was Moldavian red. A Santa Claus with a yellowing beard beamed from the wall; lights on the pine tree stuttered. The ex-seaman lit the candles on the trestle tables placed end to end and covered with maroon paper.

The widow rapped the table with a spoon. 'Under starter's orders,' murmured the homosexual. 'After the meal,' the widow said, 'there will be the usual games – and a surprise.'

Smiling secretly, she sat at the head of the table, the Rumanian on one side of her, on the other a theatrically vivacious Mexican whose husband had in his time made a pass at half a dozen of the women in the room.

'A surprise?' Penrose, the homosexual, spooned cranberry sauce onto his plate. 'Now what can that be, an exhibition? The Rumanian position over the turkey carcass?' He was middle-aged with a well-preserved physique and a pugilist's features who had been compromised years ago by a male interpreter and had, to the consternation of the KGB, elected to stay in Moscow.

'Back home,' the Australian said, 'we used to eat Christmas dinner outside in ninety degrees of heat.'

Palmer raised his eyebrows and rubbed the grey stubble that grew patchily on his liver-spotted scalp. 'Isn't this home?'

'You know what I mean. Figuratively speaking.' The Australian searched meticulously for his words since he had become a screen-writer.

'Moscow's more home to me than Los Angeles ever was. What about you, Bob?'

'It's the only home I've got,' Hanson said.

'Then why the hell are you trying to get back to Britain?' Palmer stared at him accusingly.

'Any reason why I shouldn't?'

'Not if you intend to come back, I guess. Do you?'

'I don't think the Brits would let me stay.'

'And if they did?'

145

'I'd still come back,' Hanson said, hoping that no one detected the uncertainty in his voice.

'But what would you tell the Brits?' Penrose asked. 'About us, I mean.'

Mayhew, picking a fragment of turkey from between his teeth with a fingernail, said: 'He'd tell them about the fabulous times we have, wouldn't you, Bob. Amateur dramatics, mushroom hunts. . . .'

'I'd tell them about the banya,' Hanson said. 'Pity none of you go to it. Or is it too Russian for you?'

Palmer said: 'You're the one who wants to go home. Wants to go back to England,' he corrected himself.

'And when I'm there I'll think about the banya. No class warfare in the banya, comrades. More levelling than any British pub. Do they still have saloon bars and public bars?' he asked Penrose.

'I don't know,' Penrose said. 'I wasn't a pub man.' He drank some wine. 'Has it occurred to you that it might not be the Russians who are delaying you?'

'The British Embassy you mean? Why would they do that? I wasn't a Blake or a Philby.'

'An undesirable alien? After all, you abandoned ship. Why should they have you back?'

'Compassionate grounds?' suggested the Australian. 'The Brits *are* compassionate, aren't they?'

'In any case,' Hanson said, 'it's all academic. I'll get my visa.'

'In that case,' Palmer said, 'we'd better shoot your video takes as soon as possible. It's no big deal: you're the justification for the movie but you're not the star. No way,' he said with satisfaction.

'Can't you find someone else to play the part? An American, for instance?'

'No one in the right age group. In any case you can act, i.e. *Uncle Vanya*. . . . You were really something in that.'

With a few vodkas inside me, Hanson remembered. Leadenly sober, not so inspiring. The committee of the Muscovy Players had chosen Chekhov to ingratiate themselves with the Russians but not one had turned up for the first night.

'What's more,' Palmer said, 'you look presidential . . . in silhouette anyway.'

146

'Which president? Lincoln?'

'In fact,' the Australian said, 'we only need you for three takes.'

'Possibly, but let me be the judge of that.' Palmer raised his eyebrows again. Writers, his eyebrows said, could be a pain in the ass. 'Three, maybe four. You know the storyline?'

'I know I get shot,' Hanson said.

'Not necessarily.'

The Australian put down his knife and fork. 'What do you mean not necessarily? Of course he gets shot; that's the climax of the movie.' His laid-back voice had acquired an edge.

'I've played around with it a little, Tom.'

'You had no right.'

'I've improved it, okay?' Palmer held up one hand. 'Do we want a run-of-the-mill whodunnit? Do we really want that, Tom? Now just supposing two guys want to kill two separate individuals. Just suppose those two individuals meet towards the end of the movie. I don't know, maybe the American President and a Russian. They meet someplace and leave in different automobiles, right? Now we are with one of the assassins. Which one we don't know. Jesus, the camera angles, the little touches. . . . It begins to snow . . . the blurred silhouette of the intended victim . . . the wheels of the limousine failing to grip, spewing up snow . . . departure delayed . . . the killer waiting in the cold – shit, you can *feel* that cold – begins to shiver. Shivering is all a marksman needs, right?'

'I didn't write anything like this,' the Australian said.

'It's yours in essence, Tom. A director and his writers have got to work together. Right, Mayhew?'

'What's he got to do with it?' the Australian demanded. 'He's my assistant.'

'Your *eminence grise*,' Mayhew said picking up a drumstick bone and gnawing it.

'Finally,' Palmer said, 'the limo takes off. A snowflake falls on the telescopic sights of the rifle. The killer has to wipe it clean. It's almost too late . . . the blurred silhouette of the victim . . . the gunshot . . . its echoes burying themselves in the falling snow. . . .'

'So who gets killed?' Penrose asked.

147

'Tom here, and Mayhew and I are going to talk about that. How would Hitch have ended it?'

'Why don't I get a first name?' Mayhew asked. 'I've got one, you know.'

'There are a couple of possibilities,' Palmer said. 'One, we never get to know who was killed, the President or the Russian. Everyone guessing as the lights come on. Or two, a lingering close-up of the body as the credits roll.'

'But whose body?' Penrose asked.

Palmer said: 'Whoever you least expected.' He frowned, bringing the liver spots on his scalp into play. 'Or maybe it's some other guy. You know, the President or the Russian – hey, the Russian President, how about that? – got wind of the plot and sent out someone else in the limo. One of the heavies, someone the viewers recognise. . . .'

'Why did you ask me to write a script?' the Australian asked.

'You've got to improvise as you go along, Tom. Perfection is what we're aiming for. Did you ever see *Psycho*?'

'The heroine got killed half-way through the movie,' the Australian said. 'What kind of a screenplay was that?'

'Not stereotyped,' Palmer said. 'Never let yourself get stereotyped, Tom. Airplanes landing, airplanes taking off, guys getting in and out of automobiles, into elevators, pouring drinks in apartments. . . .'

'How about breathing?' the Australian asked. 'Are they allowed to do that?'

'I thought,' Hanson said, 'that I was going to stop breathing. Now it doesn't seem quite so certain.'

Palmer looked at him thoughtfully. 'We need an understudy,' he said. 'In case you go *home*.' He turned his head to Penrose. 'Maybe. . . .'

'Why not?' Penrose pushed aside his plate. 'Use real bullets if you must.'

Two volunteers cleared away the plates. The Rumanian appeared from the kitchen holding aloft the plum pudding. The widow poured brandy over it and struck a match. A wing of flame crawled up the side of the pudding and, having reached the heights, died. More brandy. Blue flames flapped bravely. The widow cut slivers of pudding. Raising her glass, she said: 'To the spirit of Christmas everywhere in the world.'

148

'Even in China?' asked the ex-seaman.

'There is only one God,' the widow said, smiling at him fondly. 'He comes in many guises.' With a swish of her hair she sat down.

Hanson stared into the gathering dusk in the direction of the Kremlin where, unseen from the apartment, the red stars of another faith, not wavering like the flames of the candles on the tables, would now be glowing.

The widow played a worn cassette, *Christmas with Mantovani. Mary's Boy Child. . . . O Come All Ye Faithful.* Home-made crackers that didn't crack were pulled, contents – button badges mostly – pocketed, paper hats donned, mottoes and proverbs read. . . . 'Mostly Russian,' said the Australian who had compiled them. 'One or two of my own.'

'The Russians have a proverb for everything,' Palmer said. 'We'll use one in the script.'

'I have,' the Australian said.

'The trouble with proverbs,' Hanson said, 'is that they contradict each other. Many hands make light work, too many cooks spoil the broth. . . . He lit one of the cheap cigars, leaf adhering to the cellophane, with which the Cubans seemed to repay Soviet aid.

'How about this,' the Australian said. 'People who seek advice only want to hear what they were going to do anyway. One of mine,' he added.

'It's okay,' Palmer said. He mouthed the words. 'With a little tightening up, that is.'

It was dark outside now. The widow drew the curtains and turned the tape. *Jingle Bells. . . . Silent Night.*

The vivacious Mexican began to sob.

'We mustn't forget the Queen's speech,' the ex-seaman said.

'And now some games,' announced the widow. '*Give Us a Clue.* It's a television game. I saw it on a video. Brought here in the bag.' She winked.

Penrose said: 'Is she trying to tell us she's got contacts at her embassy?'

'On the end of a porno video, most like,' Mayhew said. 'You can make a bloody fortune with them.'

'Book, film, song. . . . ' The widow made expansive gestures. 'You do a little bit of acting – rather like charades – for each

149

word or syllable. Right, who's first?' She clapped her hands.

Mayhew stood up. 'Best get it over,' he said. A book, spreading two hands, indicating two words with two fingers. First word. . . . He manipulated an invisible stethoscope.

'Doctor!' from all quarters of the table.

Second word, first syllable. . . . He trembled vigorously, jowels wobbling.

'Shiver,' from the earnest Belgian.

'*Dr Zhivago*,' said the Mexican in between sobs.

The Bible, A Christmas Carol, The Cherry Orchard, Mrs Beeton's Cookery Book and *The Brothers Karamazov* (unguessed) followed.

Then the widow stood up. 'And now,' she announced, 'it is my turn.' Film, one word. She smiled and pointed at Palmer.

Palmer spread his hands modestly. '*Thriller?*'

'In one,' the widow said.

'Our movie?' The Australian frowned. 'That wasn't what I called it.'

'Terse and apt,' Palmer said.

'Which brings me to the surprise,' the widow said. 'We're going to film a take. Now.'

The cassette whirred and stopped.

Palmer talked using his hands as camera and clapperboard, panning, zooming, cutting.

'As you know, takes aren't necessarily filmed in sequence. We might film one near the end of the screenplay on the third or fourth day's shooting. Of course everything's got to gel. No virgin snow one second, footprints of the abominable snowman the next. That's where you come in,' to the Mexican. 'Continuity.' She put away her handkerchief. 'So what we're going to put on video now is a sequence near the end of the movie. Robert here,' panning to Hanson, 'getting ready to go out. He's in a dacha someplace outside Moscow. He's alone in a bedroom and he's nervous. Why? Well, you'll have to see the movie. . . .'

The Australian said: 'I thought the assassination was in the daylight.'

'Did you, Tom?' He appealed to Mayhew. 'Have I said this

is a sequence immediately before the assassination?' He turned to Hanson. 'When you're in that bedroom putting on your topcoat I want you to feel you're in danger. You know, it's evening and it's cold outside and you're in an alien land. You look through a chink in the curtains. You see nothing suspicious but maybe *we* do. Maybe we see the killer.'

The widow said: 'You're certainly giving me the creeps.'

'Then I'm doing my job,' Palmer said. 'Okay, so the only member of the cast we want is you, Bob, Mr President.'

'Soon to be the late Mr President,' Hanson said.

Palmer put one finger to his lips. 'Who knows?'

The widow led the way along a corridor to a bedroom. Floodlights stood on one side; beside them two video cameras on tripods.

'All the property of our producer,' Palmer said. 'Without her there wouldn't be a movie.'

Penrose touched Hanson's arm, pointed to a pair of blue pyjamas protruding from a pillow. 'Rumanian?'

The guests clustered in the background while Palmer propelled Hanson across the room to the curtained windows. Shaggy rugs lay in soiled islands on the floor; on the walls were a couple of pastoral scenes from Bavaria and a lithograph of two bears which looked as though they might be mating.

'It's not my room,' the widow said.

'So what I want you to do,' Palmer said to Hanson, 'is walk across to the window, glance at your wrist-watch, hesitate as though you know what you're about to do is stupid but you're going to do it anyway, then part the drapes a little and peer through the chink. When you turn round you're a little reassured but apprehensive just the same. Think you can manage that? Between you and me,' Palmer whispered, 'it doesn't matter a goddam. We'll shoot it all again but she,' inclining his head towards the widow, 'wanted her surprise.'

'What about make-up?' Hanson asked, playing along with him.

'To tell you the truth we won't be using much of you in close-up. You know, you look presidential from a distance. . . .' He clumped Hanson on the shoulder. 'Okay, lights.' The Rumanian flipped a switch and the floodlights glared at Hanson. He shaded his eyes and peered across the room at the Twilight Brigade. Was the woman at OVIR right? Was one of them trying to stop him from returning to Britain?

'Quiet,' Palmer shouted. 'Action.' He peered into a view-finder, director *and* cameraman.

Hanson looked at his watch. It was 5.10. He frowned, placed the tips of three fingers on his forehead, thumb lightly on his cheek, took the hand away, made a chink in the drapes and peered through it, half expecting to see the stranger peering back at him. Below he saw the frozen and floodlit courtyard behind the block, half a dozen children skating on it. They had lit a bonfire and thick sparks floated like incandescent insects. He looked across the yard. Windows lit in another block, figures moving in some of them. *Rear Window.* James Stewart. He smiled despite everything and straightened up.

'Okay, cut.' Palmer strode across the room. 'Okay, that was great, Bob. Just one or two points. That hand to the forehead and cheek. A little theatrical? Too Muscovy Players. . . . And don't stare through the window too long. What are you looking at, some broad stripping off in the opposite block? So, let's try again. As if it matters,' softly to Hanson.

'Okay, action.'

The fire in the courtyard was blazing more hungrily, flames reaching for the sparks.

'Okay, cut.' Palmer turned to his fans. 'Don't forget that we, the viewers, are seeing what Bob sees.'

'What's that?' someone asked.

Palmer wagged a finger. *Wait and see.* 'Okay, that wraps it up for now. We'll be doing a lot of stuff on location during the next few weeks. You're welcome to come along but let's stagger it, a few at a time. I want the snow to stay pristine. . . .'

The widow led the way back to the dining-room.

Hanson lingered in the bedroom. *White Christmas* reached him from the dining-room. Why had Weinreb died so young? Why did I listen so avidly to the burnished words of the lecturer whose destiny it was to change the course of history? For reasons he couldn't determine he leaned forward and peered into the lens of the camera.

*

152

'So, how did it go?' Lena, sitting on the stiff-backed sofa, knitting a shawl, switched down the volume of the television – *Health*, a programme that warned young people about AIDS, drugs and alcoholism.

'The usual scene,' Hanson said in Russian. He poured himself a vodka, sat down and regarded her affectionately as one might a long-serving secretary. She didn't mix with the expatriates and he didn't blame her. She had been born in Leningrad, a daughter of the siege in the Great Patriotic War, emerging into the world between the sharp haunches of a starving copy editor at the Soviet Pisatel Publishing House and she was singularly patriotic, marrying him from duty rather than choice. But he liked to think that she now regarded him fondly.

At this time of the year Lena became introspective; her body, or so it seemed to Hanson, thinner, her complexion more sallow. On December 25, 1941, the 116th day of the siege, Party workers at their headquarters at Smolny Institute had been told to spread the word throughout the frozen city that the bread ration was to be increased. 'A few crumbs,' Lena had told him. 'But children and grown men and women wept. They had been living on a slice of bread a day made from sawdust and flour brought across the frozen surface of Lake Ladoga, hot water and salt, linseed oil cake and, if they were lucky, a little stew made from pet dogs which had been put down. . . .'

The increase in the ration had been interpreted as a prophesy that Leningrad would soon be liberated. That its citizens would stop smoking Golden Autumn cigarettes made from fallen leaves, burning furniture to keep warm, dropping dead on the frozen Neva. That the crows that had deserted the city for the pickings in the German lines would return; that the currency in the Haymarket would cease to be the ration cards of the dead.

The interpretation was wrong, the siege lasted 900 days. But on that December day Lena's mother went forth to collect her extra ration of bread. Taking a short cut across a patch of wasteland, she slipped on a frozen puddle, broke one wasted leg and fell into a snow-drift. From a distance she was taken to be a corpse and soon she was one.

'And that day we didn't get any bread at all,' Lena had told him.

Hanson poured himself another tot of vodka. She didn't seem to mind. Perhaps she didn't care. . . . No, she cared. He had given her security, and here he was home from an excursion into the hostile world outside, carrying its cold polish on his cheeks.

'I suppose they all asked whether you were going to England,' she said.

'I'm their principal topic of conversation.'

'You must enjoy that. . . .'

'It makes me feel important. I haven't felt important since I first came here.'

'And you'll feel important in England?'

He glanced at her speculatively. Did she know something? After all, she must have had KGB contacts, maybe still did. 'Possibly.'

'Why do you want to go back?' she asked.

'To find out if what I did was right.' A sort of truth. 'To re-examine the accident of birth.' He was a little drunk.

'You make Russia' – not the Soviet Union – 'sound like another planet.'

'To most people in the West it is. Or was. *Glasnost* is changing all that. Soon you'll be living in a capitalist democracy. Just like the one I escaped from. . . .' Petrov, he thought as the vodka burned, you betrayed me.

'So there will be nothing to choose between the Soviet Union and Britain?' She placed her knitting on her lap and considered her own question. She had a graceful neck and sometimes in bed Hanson considered kissing it and slipping his hands beneath her sensible nightdress and cupping her breasts, but he never did. 'Maybe you want to return. . . .'

Even now was he being screened? Hanson said quickly: 'This is my home.'

'England was your brithplace.'

'So? Wherever you go in the world you'll find an Englishman being buried.'

'Would the British give you asylum?'

Asylum in my own country! 'I don't know. But I keep telling you, this is my home.'

The evasion hung between them.

On the screen a young man with a shaven scalp wearing a

154

studded leather jacket picked up a used syringe and injected himself with heroin.

Lena regarded Hanson wisely. 'You can't possibly know, can you.'

'The dacha, the apartment. . . . Why shouldn't I come back?'

'I notice you didn't include me.'

'And you.'

'You know I do understand,' she said, picking up the half-finished shawl and beginning to knit more busily than before. 'Really I do.'

'We've shared a lot. . . .' He stood up because he was committing their relationship to the past and went to the bathroom. His face in the mirror was slipshod; pink blotches glowed on his cheeks. The face that materialised beside him was, as usual, benign with conviction.

New Yorker or Muscovite? Christmas Day sharpened Michael Cooper's doubts as he made his way briskly through the frost-crackling streets to the banya. He imagined the lavish decorations at the Rockefeller Center, the icily elegant display in Tiffanys, carols drifting above the counters of the big stores. Striking deeper into his youth, he sauntered through Stuyvesant Square where festive snowflakes, soft and wet, were bandaging Peter Stuyvesant's peg-leg; walked with his father along the bleak reaches of the Bowery which, so he had learned at school, the one-legged Governor of the then New Amsterdam had built to reach his homestead. 'Bouwerie, Papa, Dutch for farm.' He dodged into Delancey Street, bouncing off an ancient, orthodox Jew, bearded and black-garbed, and sniffed the multi-national breath of Essex Street Market. He stared through the window of a tenement and saw the Ghost of Christmas Present detached from *A Christmas Carol* which he had been reading at school; but his father stared at him uncomprehendingly when he told him about the ghosts, about Scrooge, Bob Cratchit and Tiny Tim. Christmas for his parents was pre-revolutionary, its message lost in the years of Bolshevism. But the feel and smell of the cramped apartment had been Russian enough and that compounded Michael's dilemma: for even when he parted the

155

years to spy on his childhood Russia was lodged there in New York.

He skirted an autumn-leaf old woman scraping at the side-walk with a shovel, even though it hadn't snowed during the night, as though she had been wound up with a key. Plunged down a side street into a beer hall with a yeast breath and a sharp tongue. Empty, it would have been soulless; full, as it was now, it transported Michael back to the raucous, hope-filled days of the Revolution. Men in rough clothes argued with virile abandon; a young man with wet eyes was singing about lost love; the floor was littered with discarded shrimp shells.

I am Russian, he assured himself. Then he remembered the two phone calls he had received that morning from New York. God knows what time it had been there, still Christmas Eve probably. First Barbara from the house on Long Island.

'Hi, Michael . . . just called to wish you a merry Christmas. . . . Can it be merry in Russia?' That irritated him. 'No, I didn't mean that. . . . How's it going, the search for your long-lost brother. . . .'

He could hear her being the dutiful wife which, he had to admit, she always had been. Which was crazy: they were getting a divorce.

'I'm working on it,' he said.

'But you've been away – '

'A long time. I know. But the bureaucracy here. . . .' He felt treacherous. 'Not much different, I guess, to New York. . . .'

'Michael, when will you be back?'

Did it matter? 'I don't know . . . a few more weeks.' She wasn't, surely, going to say: 'I miss you.'

'Has Dick called yet?'

'No, why should he?'

'Two cases he wants to talk to you about. One a wealthy client – real estate, I think – accused of evading tax.'

'It can wait,' Michael said. He had a banya to save first.

'Secondly a family of seven being evicted from their home.'

'Nationality?'

'Russian,' she said. 'Second generation. Like you.'

'Kids?'

'Your age.' She had smiled then, he could feel it, sunlight on her careful features. 'And grandchildren.'

156

Shit. 'Is it snowing?'

'Not yet but it's cold. The wind coming in from the sea. . . .'

Colder on the Lower East Side, he thought. If you had been thrown out of your home and were standing on the sidewalk. He saw them – grandparents, parents, three kids, in a line, shivering. Tiny Tim at the end.

'Dick can handle it,' he said.

'He says it's your kind of case. You know, the kind that never makes any money.'

'The kind you never wanted me to take.'

'I know I'm perverse but I do want you to now.'

'You're perverse all right,' he said.

'Michael. . . .' A long pause. 'Merry Christmas, Michael.' Then the sound of silence across Europe and the Atlantic. But not a complete severance. He could feel the wind fanning across Long Island from the ocean.

He replaced the receiver. A chambermaid unlocked the door and backed out in confusion when she saw him. He told her she could stay and get on with her job and she retreated even more precipitously.

So Dick Kavanagh wanted him back. Two baits. One materialistic, the other compassionate; jurisprudence was flourishing in the offices of Kavanagh, Cooper and Fraser. And I am wanted urgently to take over non-profit-making compassion. If I don't go back will Dick quietly drop all cases involving Russians, Armenians, Ukrainians, Poles, Latvians . . . ? Dick with his fine blonde fuzz on the barren pastures above his monk's fringe, brown eyes full of pain, teeth small and sharp, pointing out that they weren't a charity organisation, God knows, there were enough of those. And as for ethnic minorities, hell, weren't we all ethnic, Irish, Italian, English. . . ?

The phone rang. Michael picked up the receiver. 'Hi, Dick.'

'How did you know?'

'I know your ring.'

'Yeah, well. . . . I called to wish you everything you wish yourself.'

'Not to mention the intricacies of tax avoidance in real estate and the plight of a Russian family about to be cast onto the streets. . . .'

'Barbara called you.'

157

'On the button, Dick. As always.'

'Why so hostile? It's Christmas. Just because they don't celebrate it over there. . . .'

'Merry Christmas, Dick.'

'Haven't you forgotten the prosperous New Year bit?'

'What about the Russian family. Are they going to have a prosperous New Year?'

'Come back, Mike. Make sure they do.'

'Come on, Dick, someone else can handle that.'

'You're the one who speaks Russian.'

'Second generation Russians don't speak English?'

'The old people – and I mean old – still struggle.'

'Then you or Max or Phillip can deal with the second generation.'

'You're the one, you know that.' *Without you we wouldn't have to bother.*

'Why don't you play the violin? Hearts and flowers. . . .'

'So what's keeping you in Russia?'

'I haven't traced my brother yet.'

'It's occurred to you he's probably dead?'

'There is an element of doubt, Your Honour.'

'So when are you going to call it a day?'

'I'm going to give it a little longer, Dick.'

'We need you here. And Barbara. . . . She misses you too.'

'Knock it off. We're getting divorced, remember?'

'Supposing she's gone cold on the idea?'

'Has she said that?'

'Not in as many words but. . . .'

'You're not a divorce lawyer, Dick. Forget it.'

'She was a good wife. . . .'

'I would be the first to admit it. Now off you go for Christmas drinks with Mr Real Estate.'

'In the middle of the night?'

'I'd forgotten,' Michael said. 'Merry Christmas, Dick,' and this time it was he who cut the connection. But Kavanagh had aroused professional instincts. The courts, the sighting of a half-truth, the bladed exchanges, the unravelling of a truth in which you had uncertainly believed; the incisive formality clouded occasionally by the suspicion that you were representing the wrong party. . . .

An inquisitive breeze blew along the street, brightening the lights in stores and offices that stayed burning during the rationed daylight. Where was he? To his left stood a cavernous building with a glass facade. The scent of flowers reached him. The central market. Behind the flowers, vegetables and meat, cheese and butter, were sold privately and exorbitantly. In this age of *perestroika* it was easier to buy flowers than food.

He paused and looked around. Since the incident on the Trans-Siberian he no longer cared whether he was being followed; would have welcomed the opportunity to tackle a substantial shadow. But there was no furtive movement. Classic tourist, he consulted a street map. He was approached immediately by a willowy young man offering roubles for dollars at a festive exchange rate. Do I look that American?

Michael retraced his steps in the direction of Trubnaya Ploshchad where brothels had once flourished. Boots crunched on the snow, the sour smell of 76 octane gasolene hung on the air. By the time he reached the banya the breeze had matured into a wind which was blowing away the heavy clouds.

He was greeted warmly. The bodybuilder examined the adhesive bandage round his chest. 'We'll get you exercising when that comes off,' he said. 'I've got some good equipment. You can use it.'

Hanson came in and offered to buy him a drink. At this time in the morning? He declined politely.

The Kremlin chauffeur interrogated him once more about his assailant, the pickpocket tentatively fingered the bandage and the newcomer, the Georgian who carried with him vestments of intrigue, the national garb of his land, fingered his abundant moustache.

'I understand,' the Georgian said, 'that you are a lawyer like our illustrious leader. My profession is far more elementary – I grow carnations.'

'I know an old joke about Georgians,' the Kremlin chauffeur said to Michael.

'If it's a Moscow joke it's bound to be old,' the Georgian said.

'There was a plane bound for Moscow,' the chauffeur persisted. 'On board a hijacker who told the pilot to fly to Paris.'

'London the way I heard it,' the bodybuilder said.

'Then a Georgian grabbed the gun and said, "Fly to Moscow."

159

"Why Moscow for God's sake?" the first hijacker demanded. And the Georgian replied "What would I do with two thousand carnations in Paris?"'

'You are right, comrade,' the Georgian said, 'it is an old joke.' He turned to Michael. 'Would you like to buy a carnation?'

'How much?'

'For you two roubles.'

'For one carnation?'

'It will soon be the New Year.'

'By which time your carnation will be dead,' the chauffeur said.

'But Comrade Cooper celebrates Christmas. And I'm sure he knows a lady who would appreciate a red carnation, its stem wrapped in silver foil, accompanied by a sprig of maidenhair fern. One rouble fifty kopeks,' the Georgian said.

Michael gave him the money and went into the steam-room. The heat was fierce, the steam sharp with eucalyptus. The bodybuilder, steroid muscles leaping with a life of their own, beat the chauffeur soundly with a birch switch. The chauffeur's angelic shoulder-blades moved piteously.

The pickpocket said to Michael: 'We're worried about the stallholder. He's being held hostage in Petrovka.'

'Hostage? All he did was trade illegally.'

'In Red Square?' The pickpocket massaged his fingers. 'That was blasphemy. They – Vilkin, that is – want a written undertaking that we won't oppose the demolition of the banya before they release him.'

'So,' the bodybuilder said, putting down his switch, 'he will have to stay in a cell in Petrovka. Did anyone ask the old fool to park his barrow in Red Square?'

They were joined by the miner, his white skin ingrained in places by coal dust trapped in healed wounds. 'He did it for us,' he said, wiping sweat from his brow.

'Us?' The chauffeur sat down, pushing his shoulders back so that the reddened wings folded. 'You are a stranger.'

'A stranger? How long does it take to become accepted in this doomed place? Aren't we all members of the Union of Soviet Socialist Republics? Aren't we all comrades?'

'Take no notice of him,' the bodybuilder said. 'He once drove Brezhnev and he thinks he's taken his place.' He addressed

160

Michael. 'But the miner is right and I was wrong. We must free the stallholder.'

Michael summoned legal acumen; it certainly wasn't the first time he had been asked to spring a client from police custody. 'Was anyone present when Vilkin threatened to hold the stallholder until we agreed to let him pull down the banya?'

'I was,' the chauffeur told him.

'Anyone else?'

They shook their heads.

'Then we shall have to force his hand.'

'And how will we do that?' the chauffeur asked.

'We'll have to wire someone up,' Michael told him.

The Georgian stopped Michael on his way from the changing-room to the street. 'Are you still determined to find your brother?' Beneath his moustache his teeth were dental white.

'More than ever.' Michael pointed at his ribs, one fractured, two cracked.

'Then I may be able to help you.'

'But you've only just got here.'

'Why do you think I came straight here?'

Michael had no idea.

'Part of my family used to live in Moscow.'

'Carnations?'

'We grew them in Georgia and my aunt and uncle sold them in the Central Market. But finally they gave up that outlet – the bribes for a stall were too steep. . . . Anyway, I used to stay with them and they used to use this banya.'

'How old are they now?' Michael asked.

'Who knows? There are many people in Georgia over the age of 100. I met an old woman who reckons she was born the year Russia sold Alaska to America for $7 million and that would make her 123.'

'I'm interested in 1941,' Michael told him.

'They would have been striplings in their seventies.'

'Do you really believe that?'

The Georgian shrugged eloquently. 'Who knows? They are very old, I do know that. Twenty years ago a doctor from your

161

Harvard University studied an old woman living in a village named Kutol and decided she was between 131 and 141. It's difficult to say. . . . A lot of births weren't registered.'

'But your aunt and uncle remember the war?'

'Oh they remember all right. Old people don't remember what happened yesterday but they remember what happened when they were kids.'

'Can you take me to see them?'

'Of course. When do you want to go?'

Magda picked him up from the banya in her ancient but lovingly tended Moskvich. Although it was a dumpy saloon it was blood-red and looked dangerous against the snow.

Magda had the necessary travel permits for him and they left Moscow by Entusiastov Prospect and headed east on the Vladimir Road, the M8, towards Suzdal, which, Magda said, was a congregation of churches, where religion, Russian Orthodoxy, was rising once more from its knees after the persecution by Stalin and Khrushchev. This meant, she added, that onion domes were now being refurbished for God as well as tourists. Did he know why the Bolsheviks had been so rabidly anti-Church? Because it threatened their authority? he suggested. Perhaps, she conceded, but there were more pertinent motives: religion was considered to be an instrument of tsarist rule. Had the Church ever done anything for the peasants before the Revolution? Magda demanded.

Probably not, said Michael, who did not want any more argument this Christmas Day. He glanced at Magda in profile and realised that, apart from her Ukrainian nationalism, he knew little about her. Nor, he suspected, did she know too much about herself. Like so many Soviet citizens at this time of change she was bewildered by the emotions she was allowed to display. How many of them were genuine? How many were as unstable as a drunken man's tears? She was, after all, in her late twenties and what she had absorbed in adolescence was indelible because we are all what we were when we were young. Did a part of her even now want to revert to the predictable days of the past?

162

At Petushki, 120 kilometres from Moscow, she pointed to a red-brick church to the left of the road. 'There's an inscription outside,' she said. *Faith without work is dead.* Bad luck if you're a cripple. . . .'

They reached Suzdal, thirty-five kilometres north of Vladimir, its historic rival, at 2.00 pm. It was once the capital of old Russia and possessed fifty churches. Magda took him to one of them in the market-place, snug inside its white walls. A handful of old women in black knelt in the devout gloom.

'Not much of a turn-out for Christmas,' Michael whispered.

She led him outside into the blue, gold and white day. 'It isn't Christmas Day, you see.'

'They've been kidding me all these years?'

'The Soviet Union changed the calendar after the Revolution. The Church didn't. For them Christmas Day is our January 6 i.e. December 25 in the old calendar.'

'No wonder you Russians get confused.'

'Soviet citizens,' she said.

They walked the length of Lenina Street, the little town's main artery, and she showed him fourteen churches including the Uspenskaya Refectory where, she told him, Field Marshal Friedrich von Paulus, vanquished at Stalingrad, had been imprisoned.

'You're a credit to Intourist,' he told her.

'And now we eat,' she said.

She drove to a small restaurant in Frunze Street in Vladimir. It was spartan to an obsessional degree. White walls hung with a single print of skeletal birch trees in the snow, tables and chairs arranged in cafeteria formation; only the table-cloths, freshly laundered and pressed, showed any signs of concern.

The two waiters competed with each other in the art of treating customers with indifference. One was sturdy with soulful brown eyes that gazed beyond the walls; the other was quick and bitter and bowed. They both wore black trousers, white shirts and aprons.

'So what would you like?' Michael asked as the sturdy waiter, frowning at whatever he perceived through the wall, threw cutlery in front of them.

'You eat what they give you,' Magda told him.

The other waiter, put on his mettle by the careless disposal

163

of the knives and forks, trundled two bread rolls across the table.

'To drink?'

'What they think fit.'

'Merry Christmas,' Michael said.

The first waiter thumped a jug and two glasses in front of them. Michael poured amber liquid. He drank some; it tasted of honey.

'Mead,' she said. 'Part of Christmas long ago. You're honoured – it isn't their Christmas.'

Two bowls of borsch with islands of cream floating on its surface materialised. It had a deep purple colour and it was the best soup he had ever tasted.

He looked at her through the steam and thought: I want to go on sharing surprises with you – rude waiters and the sudden melting of spring and laughter in adversity. And he steeled himself to ask the question that had been on his tongue all morning.

The second waiter snatched the empty soup bowls away; the first stared towards Siberia.

'So,' she said, 'what do you think?'

'I like it here in our own capsule.'

'We're lucky to be together. Not so long ago they would have made it impossible for us. Perhaps they will again. Who knows? The Soviet Union is unstable these days, dangerous even. No one knows what's going to happen. Can freedom really compensate for hardship? If not it's back to the old days of repression. Perhaps even more ruthlessly imposed than before. Because the old hard-liners will be the victors and hell hath no fury like a victorious Russian. Ask the Germans. You would probably be accused of being a spy, using the search for your long-lost brother as a front, and I would be accused of collaborating. Did you take any photographs on the Trans-Siberian?' she asked him brightly.

'A Russian bear took them away from me.' He breathed in deeply and winced. 'Why would anyone go to such pains to stop me looking for Vasily?'

The first waiter, intent on retrieving the initiative, dumped two earthenware pots in front of them as though he were ridding himself of garbage. They contained mushrooms and

164

onions in sour cream that had been sprinkled with cheese and toasted.

'You really are honoured,' Magda said.

'This is the main course?'

'Intermission.' She sipped mead. 'How's the *belonging* coming along?'

'Right now in top gear.' He told her about the two calls from New York. 'Whatever happens I'll have to go back. Temporarily anyway.'

She regarded him wisely. 'Once you got back you'd stay. Your birthplace. . . .'

The cue to ask the question. . . . The second waiter whipped away his earthenware pot, not quite empty, as he placed his spoon in it. The first waiter, intimidated, flung two plates at them; the second replied with a fiercely projected dish containing roast duck and apple sauce.

The moment was lost.

She served the duck. 'We don't bring tourists here,' she said. Trying to help him to belong?

The other tables were filling up with Russians, their cheeks polished with cold. The second waiter regarded them contemptuously, the first not at all. Body heat from the new arrivals permeated the room. He washed down tender meat with mead and felt his cheeks flush.

'Blinys afterwards,' she said.

He held up his hand. 'No more.'

Outraged, the second waiter snatched away his plate, the second susbstituted a glass of tea, spilling some on Michael's jacket. Then they stepped back waiting for an unseen judge to award points. Michael left a 10 per cent tip, 5 per cent more than was expected.

Sleigh-bells jingled in the fading daylight as Magda unlocked her audaciously red car. She drove back from Vladimir with a verve she hadn't displayed on the way; once, slithering round a bend, she was stopped by the GAI, the traffic police, but she charmed them apologetically but not too breathily because driving with any liquor inside you was an offence.

As they approached the lights of Moscow he at last made his approach. 'I wondered,' he said, as she drove round a drunk, 'if you could come back to New York with me.'

'Defect?'

'Just see the city that made me what I am.'

He waited.

The car burrowed into the city, bore right towards Magda's apartment.

Finally she said: 'You should see my city, too. Kiev.'

'A deal?'

'Perhaps. It depends what happens to this country of mine. The Soviet Union, that is.'

They made love that night in the narrow bed in her apartment and they slept soundly and it wasn't until the following morning that they heard that, on Christmas Day, the president of Rumania and his wife had been executed by a firing squad. What, Michael wondered, would happen to this country of hers.

13

Christmas was over, snuffed out like a candle, only a few traces of greasy smoke awaiting the arrival of the Magi. So why in the Kremlin, in the Palace of Congress where the Bolshoi Ballet was performing, did a towering pine tree glow with coloured lights and why in windows all over the city did its progeny beckon cosily? And, in the name of St Nicholas, who was the white-bearded old trouper in red who, summoned by telephone, delivered sacks of presents for a small fee to city dwellers' homes? Grandfather Frost paying his New Year visit? Or could it be Santa Claus unavoidably detained? After all St Nicholas is protector of children *and* patron saint of Russia.

A small tree adorned with scratched lights even glowed this first day of January, 1990, in the car lot on the banks of the River Moskva where Hanson had arranged to meet the Twilight Brigade's film crew. Having parked his Zhiguli a safe distance from avaricious eyes – windscreen wipers were still at a pre-mium – he made a tour of the automobiles which were all for sale, privately and illegally, above the price fixed by the State. Some were spanking new, purchasers willing to pay over the odds to by-pass waiting lists; some were aged but pert enough; others should have been driven to the knacker's yard. But a car was still a status symbol and, who knows, if you had accumulated enough money in your own scam, you could depart in an expelled diplomat's hastily sold Volvo.

On the extremities of the lot other branches of commerce had gained footholds. Dogs waiting to be sold, anything from Afghans to mongrels, barking frostily; stalls selling button badges which were collected as avidly as coins or stamps, Palekh boxes and beaming Matrioshka dolls, brass candlesticks, a 'Tsar's chess-set', a chipped bust of Stalin, a pile of newspapers

as dusty as gunpowder published during the Revolution. . . .
In a corner behind a rusting Mercedes a vendor with a brigand's
face sold *shashlik* spitting over a charcoal brazier.

Hanson glanced at his wrist-watch. Directors were punctual
individuals who berated stars for being late; Joe Palmer was
three minutes overdue. He kicked the tyres of the Mercedes
and a wing-mirror fell off. He stopped beside a canary, its cage
covered with a brown blanket, singing gamely through its cold
beak. The notes sprang from the garden in Surrey after a
shower. Snapshots of England surfaced readily these days. The
used smell of much-read books in the public library in Muswell
Hill . . . loneliness in a playground . . . a girl at Cambridge
whose lips tasted of strawberries . . . the sour and nutty taste
of his first beer drunk with Weinreb, the connoisseur . . . the
first sigh of the sea on shingle on a fortnight's holiday and
saucy postcards furtively observed. . . .

'Sorry we're late,' Palmer said. 'A hiccup with the script.
Nothing that Tom here,' slapping the Australian on the back,
'can't put right. Or Mayhew for that matter.'

'Still no first name,' Mayhew said to Hanson. 'What do I have
to do?'

Palmer herded his team to the entrance of the site, a plot of
waste ground on which the oil-stained snow was as hard as
ice. He wore a scuffed bomber jacket and a baseball cap.

'Okay,' he said, 'so the assassin sells used automobiles so
he's a crook, i.e. he asks more than the controlled price. Who
doesn't? So that's his front, a small-time racket diverting attention from his greater designs. This man is a professional killer.'

'Who employs him?' Hanson asked. 'I'd like to know who
wants to kill me.'

'Ask Tom.'

'Why bother?' the Australian said.

'The CIA,' Palmer said. '*And* the KGB? Who knows. Who
knows who gets killed, the American or the Russian President.
Supposing the KGB want to kill their own man because they
believe *glasnost* is laying waste their country and see the American President's visit to Moscow as a golden opportunity to
blame the CIA. Mayhew here came up with that angle.'
Mayhew, sunk in a frayed Crombie and looking not unlike
Brezhnev beneath his black fur hat, suffered a clump on the

back. 'And just supposing the CIA want to kill their own man and blame the KGB?

'Why would they want to do that?' Penrose asked. The cold had aged his warily pugnacious features.

'Because they believe *their* President is selling America down the river. Rapprochement with the Russians? They don't buy that.'

'Sure you're not personally involved?' Mayhew asked, popping a peppermint into his mouth.

'What the hell is that supposed to mean?'

'If the West gets too friendly with the Kremlin then you and I are going to look pretty bloody silly sitting on our arses here. Why did we bother to come? So why not bump off the President of the United States and get Moscow and Washington at each other's throats once again?'

'You know, Ted, sometimes you talk a lot of crap,' Palmer said.

'Recognition at last,' Mayhew said to Hanson. 'By the way, where's our producer?'

'She'll be here any minute,' Palmer said without enthusiasm. 'Without Pretor, of course – he's back in Bucharest helping to put his country back on its feet. Which means, thank God, he can't play the lead. Any ideas, Bob?'

'I don't know enough about the plot,' Hanson said.

'You don't have to. What we're looking for is someone with sex appeal who is tough enough to stand up to our Mexican who has been promoted to leading lady.'

A young man with furtive eyes and a junkie's pallor approached offering to sell them a Volga limousine. Giveaway price if they paid in dollars. His lips trembled and his nose ran. When Palmer threatened to call the militia he spat at them. 'Fucking mongrels,' he said and walked jerkily away.

Palmer who had never conquered Russian looked at Hanson. 'What did he say?'

'He implied we were neither Westerners nor Russians.'

'True, I guess. An enlightened breed. . . .'

'I don't think that's what he had in mind,' Hanson said.

The Australian said: 'Here comes our producer. Maybe she's got another star in tow.'

An old BMW drew up and the West German widow stepped

out. Dealers and customers stared at the automobile hungrily. She squeezed Hanson's arm. 'So, let the cameras roll. They're in the trunk,' she said to Palmer.

'Okay,' Palmer said, 'this is what I want. The assassin is approaching the lot so we see it through his eyes. Then a few atmospheric shots. A tyre spitting snow, wipers clearing a windshield and some close-ups. That guy, for instance,' pointing at the *shashlik* vendor. 'Jesus, what a face. . . . Remember Akim Tamiroff?

'So who's the brutal assassin?' the widow asked.

'We haven't cast him yet. Maybe our sea-faring friend. Maybe Penrose here if he's not standing in for Bob, i.e. if Bob hasn't defected to England. Any news, Bob?'

'*Nyet*,' Hanson said.

'And we haven't got a leading man,' Palmer said to the widow. 'Any ideas?'

'An East German has joined our circle,' the widow said. 'Or maybe these days I should just say German. Confusing, isn't it. And everything used to be so simple, so clear-cut. Anyway,' she said brightly, 'he's very dishy.' She hugged her moulting mink to her body and stamped her bushy boots.

The *shashlik* vendor approached and, pointing at the BMW, said: 'I'll give you twice what it's worth.'

The widow favoured him with a winsome smile. 'It's not for sale.'

'Three times.'

'Bob, tell him to piss off,' and when he had gone: 'What a villain, what a face. . . . He reminds me of someone.'

'Akim Tamiroff,' Palmer said.

'Before my time,' the widow said.

Palmer fetched a video camera from the BMW. 'So what I'm going to do,' he said, 'is back off, then walk towards the lot shooting. There'll be a bit of camera movement but that's okay because we don't want it too smooth. You know, as though it were being shot from an automobile. Okay Tom?'

'You're the director.'

'And maybe I'll stop at the *shashlik* stall and let him buy himself a kebab. Did you ever see that Hitchcock movie when everything is shot through the protagonist's eyes?'

No one had.

'Why don't you play the killer?' Hanson asked.

'No way – Hitch only appeared as an extra. I guess I was the only one in the movie theatre to spot him in *Foreign Correspondent* with William Holden.'

'Joel McCrea,' Penrose said, thus diminishing his chances of playing the assassin.

Palmer, camera tucked into his shoulder, retreated. His team dispersed to give him a clear approach.

Dealers, sellers and purchasers melted away into a cafeteria with steamed-up windows.

'Shit,' said Palmer as, filming, he passed Hanson.

'I should have warned you,' the Australian said. 'Never point a camera at a Russian.'

Palmer continued his approach, finishing at the unattended *shashlik* stall.

When he returned he said: 'Jesus, what atmosphere! The killer approaches, right, expecting to find everyone wheeling and dealing as usual. And what does he find? Not a goddam soul in sight, a ghost lot. It scares the pants off him, right? Where the hell have they all gone? Do they know something he doesn't? Has his cover been blown? Is there going to be a shoot-out?'

'Is there?' Mayhew asked.

'That's for you and Tom to work on. But that's what this game is all about. Luck, right? But everyone has luck. The trick is knowing what to do with it.' He replaced the camera in the BMW. 'Now let's get into the countryside while the weather holds. The build-up to Hanson's death. Or whoever gets killed. . . .'

They met up in a restaurant near the Arkhangelskoye estate twenty or so kilometres west of Moscow on the Volokolamsk highway. On her way the widow had acquired the newcomer, the East German. He was sturdy and blond and sleepy and Hanson wondered why, at this critical time in his country's destiny, he had chosen to come to Moscow.

He sat opposite Hanson in the restaurant, the Russkaya Izba, a log cabin with a metal roof that could make a cloud-burst out of a shower, and assured him, unsolicited, that there was nothing sinister about his arrival. He had a disconcerting habit of laughing lazily at humour that wasn't shared, not even

171

sighted, and Penrose, sitting admiringly beside him, had a hard job anticipating when he was expected to laugh.

'You see,' the East German said, spooning soup into his mouth, 'my father was part of the old discredited regime. Discredited, is that right?' He spoke English slowly and carefully. 'As there was no future for me in Dresden I decided to come to Moscow to perfect my Russian. They could hardly refuse me. . . .' He laughed at some oblique irony. 'I'm not qualified to go to university so I have a private tutor.'

'And private means?' Hanson asked.

'My father was not without means. But, you will understand, I do not have much in common with the staff of my embassy in Moscow these days and the Russians as you know,' smiling sideways at Penrose who grinned gamely, 'don't always take to foreigners. So, I was very lucky to meet our mutual friend,' smiling this time at the widow who was sitting next to Hanson.

'And now you're going to become a film star,' the widow said.

'Fantastic.' Hanson half expected a burst of laughter but he was disappointed.

A troupe of Russians, cross-country skis discarded, tramped into the restaurant accompanied by gusts of cold air. They occupied three tables, ordered *zakuski* and vodka and toasted the New Year. One of them began to play a guitar and folk songs rose from deep in their souls.

'I am going to enjoy Russia, too,' the East German said, laughing. 'Who is my co-star?'

'A vivacious Mexican,' the widow told him. 'You'll like her.' She frowned.

'Fantastic.' He tossed vodka down his throat. 'Just like schnapps. Have you been to the German Democratic Republic, Herr Hanson?'

'East Germany? I get confused with the Federal Republic.'

A familiar sense of intimidation settled on Hanson. He wasn't always sure of its source but he usually tried to disguise it with irreverent humour.

'Yes, East Germany, Herr Hanson.'

'Never.'

'It's a terrible thing to lose faith in your country. You see everyone sympathises with the revolutionaries and no one gives a shit about the good men who have been overthrown.'

'I suspect you're a dedicated communist, Herr – '

'The communists were once the revolutionaries. I hear you want to return to England, Herr Hanson.'

Hanson glanced at the widow but she was conferring with Palmer who was making alterations to a page of the screenplay. 'Just for a visit,' he said.

'That's what citizens of the German Democratic Republic used to say if they managed to visit the Federal Republic. They didn't always return.'

'Does it concern you whether or not I return?'

The East German uttered a measured laugh. 'What concerns me is the movie. Whether or not you get killed. What part I play in the killing.'

The guitarist had changed tempo and a young man with a pointed beard was squatting in the throes of a Cossack dance.

'Are you going to stay here?' Hanson asked.

'It depends on what happens in Russia. If there is a counter-revolution. Anything could happen in this moment of time. Is that good English?'

'No,' Hanson said.

Palmer stood up and rapped on the table with a spoon. 'After lunch,' he said above the guitarist's frenetic music, 'we're going to the palace of Arkhangelskoye for location shots.' He consulted a bunch of notes. 'The palace was built at the end of the eighteenth century for Prince Golitsyn. It was bought in 1810 by Prince Yusupov, a millionaire landlord of his time. We've got some of those in New York right now,' he said to polite laughter. 'It was burned down twice, once by the French and once by a bunch of serfs. It's stuffed full of treasures.' He peered at his notes. 'Paintings by Van Dyck and Roslin, precious china and glass. More importantly it's ideal for our purpose – the location where the Presidents of the United States and the Soviet Union rendezvous.'

'They'd meet at the Kremlin,' the Australian objected.

'For informal talks?'

'Nothing informal about Arkhangelskoye.'

'Let me be the judge of that, Tom. Okay?'

'Do we have permission?'

'No permission needed – it's open to the public. In any case all we need are outside shots. Homing down on the window of the room where they're supposed to be meeting and the room where the American President is spending the night. Remember the shot of Bob in the apartment on Christmas Day?'

'A dacha would have been better,' the Australian said.

'The Russians won't give us permission to film any.'

'Some of us have got dachas. What about Bob's?'

'Not quite grand enough, Bob. Sorry. Really, Arkhangelskoye has got everything. Views of the river from a terrace. A pavilion dedicated to Catherine the Great, a serf theatre, avenues of monuments, a statue of Pushkin. . . . It's normally closed Monday and Tuesday but it's open today because it's New Year.'

Snow was peeling from the sky when they presented themselves outside the palace and Palmer welcomed it. If the palace had been razed, Hanson decided, he would have been gratified.

The Mexican whose husband wasn't appearing in the movie – he was said to be involved with an interpreter – was waiting for them, abundant black hair tucked into a sable hat, betrayed features resolutely animated.

'So this is my leading man,' she said in Spanish-accented English. She surveyed the East German as a farmer surveys a bull. 'I think we will work very well together.'

The East German bowed. 'My pleasure.'

Mayhew sighed theatrically and selected another peppermint. A promenading family of five who reminded Hanson of Edwardians perambulating in a London park took their time passing the palace. Palmer waited indulgently beside a camera.

The ex-seaman who had arrived by metro and No. 541 bus snapped a clapperboard and Palmer began to film, panning from one end of the palace to the other.

The Mexican tried to tuck her hand under the East German's arm but the widow took him away to meet the rest of the crew.

'And now,' Palmer said, 'a few shots of Bob in the grounds, i.e. the grounds of the dacha where he's staying with the Soviet President. We've got to shoot as much as we can of Bob before . . . well, you know.'

They made their way down an avenue of statues and took up positions on a terrace overlooking the River Moskva between two buildings that had once been sanatoriums.

'Okay,' Palmer said, 'let's move it before the light goes. You, Bob, are walking in the grounds brooding. Your gooks have heard whispers of a plot and they aren't happy with security. It's all a little scary but you aren't the sort of guy to lock yourself away. Nor was Jack Kennedy. . . .'

'Is this where I get killed? Or someone gets killed?'

'It's where you think you might get killed despite the guards in the grounds. You stop on the terrace and stare across the river. A perfect target.'

'I didn't write this,' the Australian said.

'As a matter of fact,' Mayhew said, 'I did.'

Hanson paced the terrace and brooded over the river. 'Just once more,' Palmer said. 'Don't look so goddam indifferent to your fate.' He snapped his fingers. 'Try thinking about your exit visa. The possibility that you won't get it. . . .' He peered into the view-finder. 'That's it. Terrific.'

Penrose said: 'What happens if Bob does get his visa half-way through the shooting?'

'Then you'll take over and we'll have to do these takes again. No sweat – and you dress more like a president than Bob. That black coat of his is pretty tacky. Although maybe your neckwear is a little too fancy.' Palmer fingered Penrose's paisley scarf.

As they trooped back to the palace Hanson wandered through the gardens. Ornamental trees wadded with snow closed around him as the afternoon assembled. Statues peered at him. He thought of cottage windows snugly lit beneath thatched roofs. The muffled silence blocked his hearing. He imagined an assassin peering through the sights of a rifle fitted with a silencer. . . . Do I really care if I die here, now?

'*Oh you care all right,*' the stranger whispered. '*You want to know if there was ever any point to any of it.*'

A bird took to the sky scattering snow which dropped softly, reinforcing the silence. The flakes fell more loosely and, in their midst, Hanson thought he distinguished a human shape.

The East German lowered his rifle. 'I was sent to find you,' he said. He tapped the barrel of the rifle. 'Don't worry, it's a replica.'

*

175

Tanya Agursky spent New Year's Eve in Lev Grechko's apartment near the block at 12, Sadovaya-Samotyochnaya which housed many of the representatives of the Western media. It was a widower's home, cluttered with memories of a dashing career and a happy marriage. Trophies shouldered each other along dusty shelves and photographs of Lev and his wife skating together, imprisoned in time and motion, were pinned haphazardly on the walls. 'It isn't just youth that the camera freezes,' Lev said, pulling at his beard. 'It's the present. We're there now, she and I, on the ice. Don't have any dealings with time, Tanya, it's an illusion.' He smiled at his wife who had died ten years earlier from tuberculosis. 'She was the best,' he said. 'We were one, you know; that's why we were champions.'

'Yury and I are one,' she said, listening to the tumult of a party in the apartment next door.

'Then you will skate together again,' he said.

She spent New Year's Day on the rink at the Dynamo Stadium with her new partner, Lazar. And made him toil. A coalescence of figure eights, spins, jumps and lifts.

'For God's sake, Tanya,' Lazar said after they had been skating for two hours, 'let's take a break.'

'Too much for you?'

'You're punishing me for not being Yury. I can take it all right but it's not good for either of us. We'll get cramps. Didn't Yury ever get cramps?'

'Not that I remember,' Tanya said, gliding beside him.

'Look,' he said, 'I know Yury is better than me. I'm competent, nothing more. But I'm trying. For your sake. Maybe we'll win some cups. But not the Olympics, I'm not good enough for that.'

His humility irritated her. Like his dark and handsome features it came from a predictable mould. 'Let's try some more lifts,' she said.

'We've done enough.'

'Then I'll practise by myself.'

'All right,' he said, 'a few more lifts. But I've warned you. . . .'

The rink was filling with circling skaters who cramped their movements. Were Yury and Nina even now skimming round some uncluttered expanse of ice? The lake? She stumbled, almost fell. Lazar glanced at her and frowned. 'Are you sure. . . .?'

'A twist lift,' she said.

They narrowed their orbit, heading for the centre of the rink where a couple of hopefuls were practising. The pain knifed the calf of her right leg as Lazar prepared to lift her. She fell sideways. Her leg burned but the humiliation was worse. Like a child who falls and runs away to escape ridicule she stood up and began to stumble towards the exit. But her leg had no substance. She fell again, fingers, spider-like, feeling the ice. Faces peering at her. Her calf felt as though someone was searing it with a blow-torch.

Lazar knelt beside her. 'Stand up slowly,' he said, 'and hold onto me. Balance on one skate – you've done it before – and I'll take you off the rink.'

'I can manage by myself,' she said.

'Do what I say.'

'I don't need your help.'

He lifted her and guided her towards the barrier.

He sat her on a spectator's seat and took off her boots. He bent her foot up at the ankle and straightened the leg. The pain eased.

They went on the metro to Lev Grechko's apartment.

'You'll have to rest,' Lazar told her, looming over her seat on the train so that she could see the tiny mends in his jacket, as neat as embroidery.

'It will be all right tomorrow.'

'Then you can skate by yourself.'

'Very well.'

'You really shouldn't,' he said earnestly.

'It's *my* leg.'

'You're *my* partner.'

Lev Grechko gave them tea and made her sit on a sofa with her legs on the cushions. He had been polishing his trophies and they stood on the table beside a bowl containing a small pumpkin and some shrivelled apples.

Carefully rubbing polish from a cup bearing his name beside his wife's, he said: 'I warned you not to over-train.'

No sympathy, merely criticism. The unfairness of life over-whelmed her. Her eyes smarted with self-pity.

Lazar said: 'I've told her to rest.'

'Of course she must rest. Supposing she got cramp in a competition.'

Now they were talking about her as though she wasn't there, the way people sometimes talked about the aged.

'Does it matter?' she demanded. 'I can't enter competitions.'

'Not the Olympics,' Lev Grechko said, gently dusting his wife's name on the cup. 'Not yet. But I've entered you for the national championships. They can't stop you entering for those. And when you've won how can they ban you from the Olympics?'

How could she have been so churlish? Why did her emotions change so dramatically these days? She said tremulously: 'That's wonderful. Will Yury be able to skate with me?'

Lev, staring at his piratical features contracted in the depths of the rose-bowl, shook his head slowly.

'I'll do my best,' Lazar said.

'I know you will.' She smiled at him graciously.

'Don't underrate him,' Lev said. 'He's championship material. He might not have Yury's natural abilities but he's got style and he's dedicated. He could become just as good as Yury, better. . . .'

Never.

'Do what he tells you,' Lev said. 'Rest that leg.'

The door-bell rang, an ancient and dislocated sound. Lev opened it and Tanya's mother said: 'I thought I'd find you here.'

Twelve days into the New Year. In the north-west of the Soviet Union the Republic of Lithuania was poised to secede; in the south-west Azerbaijan and Armenia were at each other's throats; elsewhere across the eleven time zones in the largest country in the world disparate races zestfully and sometimes murderously pursued their identities. And even if motives were occasionally questionable – egotism struts close to terrorism – the possibilities of their combined zeals, the dissolution of the Soviet Union, were only too real.

In the mens' changing-room of the banya these possibilities were discussed as vigorously as the wiring-up of the Kremlin chauffeur who, it had been agreed by everyone except the chauffeur, was the most plausible agent of entrapment.

Even as the small microphone was taped to his chest, the chauffeur, standing beside the moulting New Year pine, pilfered from the forest by the bodybuilder, protested. 'Why me? Surely I am the most obvious *agent provocateur*,' a reference to the conspiratorial airs he brought with him from the drivers' pool at the Kremlin.

Standing back to observe his handiwork, Michael Cooper said: 'You are the only one Vilkin respects. You have the presence of a diplomat, a true negotiator.'

'Even if that were true,' and the chauffeur showed no signs of disputing it, 'my future will be in jeopardy. When we play the tape to Vilkin he will know who betrayed him – an employee at the Kremlin: for me kaput.' He drew one finger across his protuberant Adam's apple.

'Or,' Michael said, brushing against the tree and scattering pine needles on the floor, 'you could become a figurehead in the new order.'

'New order? What new order?' The chauffeur pulled on his shirt over the microphone.

'Communism is dead,' Michael said. Quiet breathed around him. 'And with it bureaucracy as you know it. The Vilkins of the Soviet Union are finished. And people like you will be recognised as the revolutionaries who made this possible.'

The chauffeur tucked in his small shoulder-blades. 'But when will all this happen? I could lose my job. . . .'

'Or your head,' the bodybuilder said.

'The change is happening now,' Michael said. 'You're its vanguard.'

The chauffeur, not convinced that he wanted to be, said: 'We could have wired you up.'

'An American leading the delegation? It's tricky enough being your lawyer.'

'Or you,' the chauffeur said, pointing at the miner.

'Without my *propiska*? Are you crazy?' Draping a sheet round his coal-scarred body, the miner turned to Michael. 'And who says communism is dead? In Rumania, maybe. And other old puppet states. The Kremlin is glad to get them off its back – let them fight among themselves, like they did before the Great

179

Patriotic War, become a pain in the ass for the West instead of the Soviet Union. . . . But communism dead here? Don't kid yourself, comrade. Not even our illustrious leader wants to see an end to communism. What he wants is a return of those early ideals. Nothing much wrong with them, was there? And if he fails – which he looks like doing – then the old hard-liners will come back and we'll step back ten years into communism old-style.'

A newcomer, an intense Lithuanian who frowned as though he were tasting his words, said: 'He's right – there was nothing wrong with communism before Stalin put it through the mangle. Maybe we'll even keep it in our country. Our country. . . .' sampling the two words incredulously. 'We were told for decades that Party came before country but we never bought that. Why should we? We had known freedom for twenty years after the First World War when Britain made sure that the Russians didn't take over the Baltic States instead of the Germans. Then Stalin made his deal with Hitler and the Russians moved into Lithuania again. But we always reminded ourselves of those years of freedom.'

'The way I heard it,' the miner said, 'you had a bunch of fascists in charge during those years of freedom and were only too happy for the Soviets to take over.'

Here we go again, Michael thought. He had once spent a vacation in a village in Quebec where the French-speaking Canadians could hardly bring themselves to talk to the English speakers, where the demarcation line was a garden fence. Here there was now a Russia-for-the-Russians movement.

The Lithuanian said: 'A few fascists, maybe. But that wasn't the point – '

'So what was?'

'That we had a choice. Then after the Great Patriotic War, in which a lot of you Ukrainians fought for the Germans, Stalin crushed the breath out of us.'

The bodybuilder, lifting weights in his undisputed corner of the room, said: 'Shit, why don't we debate Kirgizia, Uzbekistan, Turkmenistan. . . . I read that they'll soon outnumber the Russians and then Islam will take over from Lenin.'

The chauffeur said: 'Why don't you wear the microphone?' He put on his jacket and poured himself some beer.

'His muscles would get in the way,' the miner said.

'I've heard rumours,' the chauffeur said, tone pitched somewhere between clandestine knowledge and apprehension, 'that Vilkin reports directly back to the KGB.'

'Well he won't this time,' Michael said. 'We'll have his threats on tape. And we'll tell him, "Go ratting to anyone and the whole of the Soviet Union will hear about your . . . indiscretions." And you,' to the chauffeur, 'will make your mark in history beside the President and General Secretary, whichever you prefer to call him.'

'Now that,' the miner said, 'is a man I really feel sorry for. Poor bastard. He gives the people freedom and they reward him with shit.'

'Now this is how we do it,' Michael said. He led the delegation out to the bodybuilder's Volga where the recording equipment bought in a store on Kalinina Prospect had been installed.

Vilkin's office was his desk, a great slab of polished oak, supported by sturdy legs carved with vines heavy with grapes, on which lay architects' plans tightly rolled or waywardly uncurling to give a comprehensive impression of his powers to develop or destroy. To these powers he brought dental application, treating old buildings as rotten teeth to be extracted and filling the cavities with uncomplicated, decay-proof molars. He greatly admired his predecessor who had drawn the teeth of the historic Arbat and capped their roots with skyscrapers and was himself responsible for much of the city's uncompromising bridgework. When the deputation from the banya arrived he was reading a report on the condition of their unforgivably old institution which was, according to the surveyor who was anxious to install his son in the city planning department, on the point of collapse. Caries, Vilkin thought. A couple of nudges with a ball and chain and this affront to his authority would be demolished and in its place would rise a pearly white monument to his enlightenment. Dabbing with one finger at his diminutive moustache, he pressed a button on the intercom and told his secretary to usher the five defenders of the bath-house into the office.

They sat on stiff-backed chairs, their seats considerably lower than his own, and regarded him speculatively across the acres of the desk.

'All right,' Vilkin said, glancing at the surveyor's reassuring conclusion that the bath-house was a threat to public safety, 'let's get on with it; I haven't got much time.'

The Kremlin chauffeur stood up.

'You may sit down,' Vilkin said irritably.

'I prefer to stand.' The chauffeur cleared a nervous quaver from his voice and began to read from a prepared statement. 'We have noted the views of Comrade Leonid Vilkin concerning the future of the banya . . . has been our avowed intention to preserve this historic relic of Moscow's architectural glory . . . note certain conditions that have arisen during negotiations. . . .'

'Conditions? What conditions?' Vilkin noticed that the chauffeur's hand kept straying to his chest; perhaps, hopefully, he had a heart condition that would terminate his address. And what the hell is the American doing in my office taking notes? I should throw him out on his ear. AMERICAN PATRON BARRED FROM BANYA TALKS. The *Moscow News* would gobble that up.

'You must remember the conditions, Comrade Vilkin. A member of our committee is in gaol. . . .'

'Quite rightly by all accounts.'

'But you said – '

'New evidence has come to light.' Vilkin held up the surveyor's report. 'I have here conclusive proof that the banya must be demolished.'

'What's that, a surveyor's report?' The speaker was a muscular young man with oiled hair and Adonis looks that Vilkin considered vulgar. He consulted his notes on the delegates: the young man had once been a member of the Lyubertsi gang of bodybuilders who had terrorised hippies and the like on the streets of Moscow. Vilkin underlined his name with a red ball-point.

'Exactly so,' Vilkin said, smiling at the delegates benignly.

The deputation went into a huddle. At least they hadn't insulted his intelligence by bringing along the pickpocket. But why no women? Didn't the red-haired bitch know about the meeting? He made a note: *Divide and conquer*.

The chauffeur, still standing, said: 'May we have the name of the surveyor?'

'You may,' said Vilkin who had decided to recommend the chauffeur's removal from the Kremlin drivers' pool to a snow-clearing depot. 'Vladimir Panov.'

They went into a huddle again while Vilkin fumed because that morning he was trading a building permit for a hotel reservation overlooking the Black Sea at Sochi in the summer.

While the American made notes on his pad the chauffeur said: 'We know of him, Comrade Vilkin.'

'I'm sure he will be honoured. Do you want to hear his report?'

'We presume it says the banya must be knocked down for safety reasons.'

'How perceptive. A hazard to the public. Now is there anything else?'

'We also understand,' said the chauffeur, hand to his chest, 'that his son has been promised a job in your department.'

And you, you bastard, will be on a snow-plough without protective clothing by tomorrow. Vilkin threw down his ball-point. 'Who says so?'

'I say so,' the bodybuilder said. 'We go to the same gymnasium.'

'And what if he has proved himself to be competent to join my staff?'

'He told me he had failed his examinations.'

'Then he lied.'

'I don't think so – he showed me his papers. He seemed rather proud that he had failed. Said he'd get a job anyway. . . .'

Vilkin said: 'I don't listen to hearsay evidence.'

'Don't let it worry you,' the miner said, 'I expect we can get copies of the examination papers. I expect *Ogonyok* would publish them.'

'Threats, comrade?'

'Exactly so.'

Vilkin plucked at a damp corner of his moustache. 'Why should I bother with a bunch of shit-heads like you?'

'*Blat?*'

'*Blat?* What do you mean, *blat?*'

'You raised it last time we met,' the chauffeur said clearing his throat. 'You said that if we abandoned our fight for the banya you would get the stallholder released.'

Vilkin stared at a photograph of the Soviet President hanging on the wall beside a photograph of a cavity in the ground where a glass-blowing factory had once stood. The President returned his stare equably.

'Very well,' Vilkin said, 'that still stands. But you must promise to keep your end of the bargain.'

The chauffeur, voice gaining power, said: 'First release the stallholder.'

Vilkin swept aside the plans arranged with such precision on the desk. 'Get out of here all of you.'

Hand to his breast, the chauffeur bowed. 'You have been most considerate, Comrade Vilkin.'

Vilkin, holding onto the edge of the desk as though it were slipping away from him, took control of his voice and said evenly: 'I'm looking forward to seeing the foundations of the new store laid. Have you ever had your feet trapped in wet concrete, comrade?'

The stallholder was released from Petrovka police headquarters the following day on a technicality concerning the wording of the charge against him. That night a small package was delivered to the spacious apartment on Kutuzovsky where Vilkin lived with his extravagant wife and two exuberant sons. He played it in his study with a lurching sense of doom. First the chauffeur's voice, now bounding with confidence: 'Don't forget, Comrade Vilkin, that we promised nothing.'

A pause. Then the resonance changed. His office, his voice. 'All right, let's get on with it; I haven't got much time.' Vilkin poured himself a vodka and tossed it down his throat. He pressed the FORWARD button. The miner: 'I expect I can get copies of the examination papers. . . .' FORWARD. The chauffeur: '. . . get the stallholder released.' FORWARD. Vilkin: 'Have you ever had your feet trapped in wet concrete, comrade?'

184

14

The Aeroflot jet taking Michael Cooper and the carnation-seller to Tbilisi was packed with swarthy Georgians and a sprinkling of pale Russians. The carnation-seller, nodding at a clutch of grey-suited Russians, told Michael that it was their kind, jealous of the expansive Georgians' life-style, who had tried to put an end to southern enterprise and that, although they were proud that their former Party Chief had become Foreign Minister of the Soviet Union, they still spoke more reverently of Otari Lazishvili.

Plucking at Michael's sleeve, occasionally whispering warmly into his ear, the carnation-seller recounted the exploits of Comrade Lazishvili, a lapsed student of economics and owner of a modest synthetics laboratory, who had been able in his heyday to demand the head of any Party *apparatchik* rash enough to inquire into his business interests. Lazishvili and his henchmen, said the carnation-seller, voice phlegmy with admiration, had appropriated 2,000,000 roubles' worth of State property. How? He massaged his hands so that his rings clicked softly together. By taking advantage of Moscow's inept central planning, that was how – the same behemoth that was today sabotaging *glasnost*. With surplus materials that weren't accountable he had manufactured clothes that were in short supply and sold them at ambitious profits and bought property, feasts and favour. 'He even had a factory hidden in the Caucasus,' the carnation-seller said.

'So what went wrong?'

The carnation-seller's voice took on the tone of one who has lost a near relative. Five-year plans went wrong, he said, invoking them as instruments of persecution. Because of Lazishvili's enterprises Georgia couldn't fulfil the plans and

185

the Kremlin had appointed a new and incorruptible Party Chief who these days kept company with presidents and premiers in Washington, Paris and London. Lazishvili had been arrested and jailed for fifteen years. 'If he hadn't been the man he was he would have been shot,' the carnation-seller said proudly.

A stewardess served roll-mop fish, dark bread, fizzy water and fruit. The carnation-seller pushed his plate aside and from his flight-bag produced a cheese-filled *khachapuri* roll. 'You will like Georgia,' he said, chewing, 'the people are as warm as the climate.'

Michael consulted a guide that informed him that, at the end of the nineteenth century the capital, Tbilisi, had accommodated more than 100 shoemakers and 125 tailors.

'Of course we want our independence,' the carnation-seller said.

'Who doesn't?' Michael read about Tbilisi rescued by the Russians from the Persians at the end of the eighteenth century, then fell into a reverie as the jet flew parallel with the Don. What was he doing heading for the peaks of the Caucasus? He finished eating a banana, presumably from Georgia, and folded the bruised skin. Keeping a futile promise made to a dying old man in Bellevue Hospital, New York. . . . Any rational investigator would have given up by now. . . . Michael closed his eyes. But he had been misled, threatened, hurt. . . .

He was in the back of a cab taking him from his office to a tenement on the Lower East Side from which an old and bewildered Russian who had never quite got his tongue round the English language was about to be evicted. 'Why should you worry about me?' demanded the old man and threw a jar of Beluga caviar at Michael's head.

He booked into the Hotel Adzharia on Constitution Square and went for a stroll beneath the balconies of Tbilisi's poetic and teeming streets. It was evening and he smelled kebab and brilliantine. He visited a bakery on the banks of the River Kura where flat bread was baked on the sides of an underground oven, promenaded Rustaveli Prospect and took a cable-car up

186

Mount David. He knew he was vulnerable to attack but he had become cavalier about his safety; nevertheless he carried himself vigilantly in the capital of the republic that had spawned Stalin, Beria and more than its fair share of gangsters.

He slept easily and met the carnation-seller in the foyer of the hotel the following morning. He was wearing long black boots and, striding out of the hotel, he greeted the day as though it had just returned from a long absence. Long fingers rippling, he said: 'Georgia is sunshine, wine and music. Did you know we even wrestle to music?'

They took a train to Sukhumi on the Black Sea and wandered round its balmy streets where jasmine still bloomed sparsely, blossoms lying on the sidewalks like stars that had fallen out of the night, and a breeze coming in from the sea rustled the palms and ragged fronds of banana trees. They visited one of its spas, drank Borzhomi water and dined in a restaurant on a hill overlooking the sea.

The following day the carnation-seller borrowed a friend's black Volga and drove them into the hills where apple trees grew alongside parade grounds of tea bushes.

'What are you looking for?' the carnation-seller asked as Michael scanned the hillsides.

'Just looking,' Michael told him.

'Sometimes you act like a fugitive. Are you scared that brother of yours doesn't want you to find him? Wants to kill you?'

'Why would he want to do that?'

The carnation-seller flung the Volga round a serpentine bend in the dusty road. 'Why should brothers and sisters love each other? Look at them at each other's funerals. "Thank you, dear God, for letting him go first," is what they're thinking. In Georgia we don't have time for hypocrisy, only intrigue.'

'It must be wonderful,' Michael said, 'to be so sure of yourself.'

'If you're Georgian it's not difficult.'

Or Ukrainian, Michael thought. Second generation American–Russian was more tricky.

'Stalin was a Georgian. What a man. The whole world feared him.'

A gun-shot. Echoes bouncing around the valleys. Pellets pattering on the roof of the Volga.

The carnation-seller patted Michael's arm. 'Just a hunter shooting small birds for his supper.' A man wearing a camouflage jacket and lace-up boots appeared on the road in front of them and saluted, rifle raised high.

Ahead a cluster of buildings lodged on a hillside. 'That's where my aunt lives,' the carnation-seller said. 'Her husband is bed-ridden. I suggest you pretend you've come to interview her for a Western magazine. She's very proud of her age, whatever that is. But no one likes questions about the war.'

'Not even Georgians?'

'Her name is Ekaterina, the same as Stalin's mother.'

The Volga skidded to a dusty halt outside a white-washed cottage with leaning walls and high, rheumy windows. Stepping out, Michael reflected that, in his time, he had interrogated many aged witnesses but never one who was, at a conservative estimate, 120 years old.

Inside the cottage that smelled of old fires and distemper a feast had been laid out on a long table. Flat cheeses, olives, unleavened bread, beans in walnut sauce, bowls of apples and black grapes. Ekaterina sat at the head of the table flanked by guardian relatives of indecipherable ages. She wore a blue scarf round her hair and her brown eyes, set in the features of a canny old saint, regarded him warily.

Michael turned to the carnation-seller. 'You didn't tell me there was a reception committee.'

'Greet her in Georgian, the way I taught you, and everything will be fine.'

Michael bowed to the matriarch. *'Rogor brdzandebit.'*

'And now you must drink a toast,' the carnation-seller said. 'And it won't be the last.'

A man with pepper-and-salt stubble on his cheeks and the face of a village wastrel filled everyone's glasses with vodka.

'You don't mean *she's* going to drink that stuff?'

'What else?'

'Welcome to Georgia,' Ekaterina said in Russian and tossed the vodka past teeth the colour of old piano keys.

Everyone ate an olive and a morsel of bread.

'Now sit opposite her,' the carnation-seller instructed Michael.

Michael laid a pad and a ball-point on the table-cloth. What should he ask her? To what do you attribute your longevity? His glass was refilled by the wastrel.

'To American–Georgian friendship,' said a man of about fifty – or he may have been seventy – with carefully combed grey hair sitting next to Ekaterina.

Michael drank the vodka, chased it with mineral water. 'I can't go on like this,' he whispered to the carnation-seller.

'They will be very upset if you refuse. I did warn you. . . .'

'About thirty seconds ago. And you didn't warn me about all the guests. . . . I'm surprised the local Party boss isn't here.'

'Over there,' said the carnation-seller pointing at the grey-haired man who would always make others look untidy.

'Surely she can't take much more vodka.'

'Of course not,' the carnation-seller said. 'She'll start on red wine in a minute.'

The wastrel served Michael beans in walnut sauce.

'I think,' the carnation-seller said, pulling at Michael's sleeve, 'that you should propose a toast.'

A girl in a green dress with flirtatious eyes smiled at him across the table. Finding his glass full again, he stood up. 'To the people of Abkhazia,' the autonomous republic in which the village was situated in Georgia. 'The land of the Golden Fleece,' because, according to his guidebook, this was where Jason had come in search of it.

Vodka hit the backs of their collective throats. There was a moment's silence. Then a burst of clapping. Ekaterina stared at him ruminatively. The girl in green seemed to wink although he could not be sure.

'And now let's drink wine,' Michael said.

Sweet red wine was poured from earthenware jugs, skewers of kebab brought from the kitchen. Chickens strutted into the room. An old and arthritic dog rose painfully to its feet, smelled the spicy steam and dragged itself to the table.

Michael drank wine, leaned across the table and said to his ancient interviewee: 'To what to you attribute your longevity?' She stared at him down through the years, mottled flesh bunched on her cheekbones.

'Speak simple Russian, for God's sake,' the carnation-seller said.

189

'I'm sorry,' words loud inside his mouth. 'How is it that you have lived so long?'

She spoke rapidly in Georgian.

'What did she say?' Michael asked.

'She said she has lived a long time because she does not waste precious breath answering stupid questions.'

'You ask her.'

Michael waited, pen poised over the pad.

The carnation-seller said: 'She says one of the secrets is never to lose your temper but she thinks she might at any moment now.'

The girl in green burst into laughter. Ekaterina bared her eroded teeth; her fragile shoulders shook beneath her shawl. How had she looked when she was a mere ninety? How old would she look in ten years' time?

'Laugh with her,' the carnation-seller urged.

Michael chuckled elaborately and raised his glass of wine.

'You've got her now,' the carnation-seller whispered. 'But lead her gently. She's not stupid. It takes brains to conquer so many years.'

'How old are *you*?' the old woman asked.

'A third of your age,' Michael said.

'It isn't the years that matter,' she said. 'What are they but the passing of the seasons? Years are what Man invented and they have no meaning. Never listen to the ticking of a clock, young man – the seconds are the burden that squeezes life from us.'

A young man with a bandit's face and a bandolier of bullets across his chest rose to his feet. 'To old age,' he shouted.

Michael, raising his glass, was conscious that everyone was staring at him.

'You've got to drain your glass,' the carnation-seller whispered.

'I can't.'

'Then you can forget your questions.'

Michael gulped the honeyed wine and made swift and wayward notes on his pad. 'Tell her in Georgian,' he said, 'that I appreciate her philosophy but my magazine must have practical advice about living longer.'

Ekaterina regarded him scornfully and spoke rapidly in

Georgian. Too much sleep, Michael gathered from the translation, was one of the greatest threats to a long life. That and failing to give the stomach a rest. 'Fasting,' the carnation-seller explained. 'One day a week. And don't eat before going to bed.'

'Anything else?'

Work hard, he was told, at a labour you don't consider to be a burden. Eat vegetables and fruit, and dairy products such as the soft cheeses on the table. Breathe fresh air and drink clean water; sing and dance and love.

'What about booze?' Michael asked as the red wine rose to his brain.

'On occasions that merit it,' the carnation-seller translated. 'Like today.'

'To fraternal comrades in the United States of America,' the immaculate Party Chief said, raising his glass.

The wine tasted more stable this time and Michael thought he could handle it. 'We have a Georgia in the States,' he said and they nodded wisely.

He eased goat's meat, green pepper and onion from the skewer and chewed it vigorously. Still chewing, he said to his hostess: 'I understand that when you were in your seventies you lived in Moscow,' congratulating himself on his subtlety.

'I knew your parents if that's what you mean.'

Michael, jolted, said: 'How did you know?'

'That they were your parents? Because they ran away to America and you are American and I can see them in the set of your eyes. It's the eyes that tell everything, not the nose or the mouth. Look into a man's eyes and you see his soul.'

'And what do you see in mine?'

'Doubt,' she said.

'Here's to the Georgian soul,' said a man with dark, dusty hair and a couple of metal, Moscow teeth shining in his mouth. The girl in green ran the tip of her tongue round her lips and smiled secretly.

Ekaterina, sipping spring water, said to Michael: 'So what do you want to know? What happened to your brother?'

'You're very shrewd.'

'Why else would you come to see me? You're not a writer.

191

Those notes. . . . They look as though a fly has had a fit.' She smiled a yellow smile. 'And isn't it natural that brother should follow the fate of brother?'

'To brotherly love,' roared the wastrel.

'So what happened to him?' Michael asked.

'He fought against the Germans in Moscow.'

'And died?'

'Disappeared. Does that disappoint you?'

'I don't know,' Michael said hearing the words as though they belonged to someone else. 'Do you think he's dead?' He stared into her brown eyes to see if there was any duplicity in *her* soul.

'I cannot help you,' she said. 'I'm sorry – you have come a long way.'

'But you would have known whether he was killed: you were there in Moscow when the Germans were at the gates.' His cheeks burned.

'That was 200 seasons ago. Now I remember what happened when I was a little girl more clearly than what happened then. I remember when electric light was invented. We never had it, of course, but I remember its dawning. It lights the past, you see.'

'Didn't they talk about Vasily's disappearance in the banya?'

'They handed out ammunition in the banya,' the old, old woman said.

A deliberate evasion, Michael Cooper, advocate, told himself. He tried to put this to her but his tongue couldn't keep pace with his instincts.

The wastrel put his hand on Michael's shoulder. 'She can't remember. . . . Don't upset her.'

The Party Chief said: 'We understand as much as anyone about fraternal love. But she cannot help you anymore.'

So drop it, the hand on Michael's shoulder said.

Ekaterina's smile moved the lines of the season on her forehead. 'Don't ever forget, Comrade Cooper, that it's the clocks that kill.'

'But – '

The hand on his shoulder was a vice.

'To the brotherhood of socialists all over the world,' said the Party Chief.

Michael drained his glass. The girl popped a grape into her mouth and sucked the tip of her finger.

'It's over,' the carnation-seller said. 'We must go.'

Chairs scraped. The dog limped back to its corner. The chickens retreated into the sunlight where they pecked diligently in the dust.

Michael shook many hands. On the way back to the Volga he leaned against a fig tree and consulted his wrist-watch. Its ticking seemed unduly loud.

While Michael Cooper was listening to the measurement of time Robert Hanson was reviewing its headlong passage. Months, weeks and days melting as though he were being bundled towards a predetermined fate. During pauses in this unseemly despatch he worried; about gentle and occasional pains in his chest, about cruelties and injustices that he read about when old British newspapers came his way. When nothing precise presented itself for concern he worried about insubstantial premonitions.

He worked steadily enough translating Russian into English for *Sputnik* at Novosti's offices on Bolshaya Pochtovaya; he went filming with Palmer and his crew and drinking with Mayhew; he remained a dutiful husband discovering a steadfast affection born, perhaps, of habit; he went fishing at night in black holes in the ice on the Moskva.

Sitting swaddled beside his brazier one night when the sky was scattered with watching stars, he gazed into his cavity in the ice and saw instead of the face of the stranger the face of Weinreb.

Weird, Weinreb's brother fighting for the Germans. Weinreb never really explained. But if you were rich enough you could buy false papers. Presumably he hadn't been circumcised. . . . Did I at the time realise how profoundly Weinreb's revelation affected me? Moonlight shivered on the water and the stranger replaced Weinreb.

'Are you trying to say that if it hadn't been for that you wouldn't be here today?'

193

'Just one of the ifs, one of the marker buoys. . . . If I had children I would teach them, "Beware of unswerving loyalty." '

'Swerving loyalty doesn't seem to have been an unqualified success otherwise you wouldn't be going back to England to see if you did the right thing. . . .'

'It doesn't look as though I will be going back,' Hanson pulled in his line. One of the hooks had gone. He began to thread another with nylon.

'Has it occurred to you that Perfidious Albion might be conspiring against you? Why don't you pay a visit to the British Embassy where "there's some corner of a foreign field that is for ever England"?'

The stranger disappeared but the moon remained captured in the black orb. Hanson fed his line back into the water. It tugged immediately. He hauled it in and a fish leaped and slithered in the glow of the brazier. He gazed at it for a moment, tomorrow's lunch. Then he removed the hook from its mouth and dropped it into the water.

Lena said: 'Where are you going?'

She stood at the front door of the apartment like a wife seeing her husband off to work, familiar dressing-gown over her sensible night-dress.

'You don't usually ask.'

'You're leaving earlier than usual.'

'I'm going to the British Embassy. Catch them before they've put their protocol on.'

'About your visit to England?'

'Someone's trying to stop me. Why not the British?'

'Why would they do that?'

'Because anyone who severs their allegiance to the Queen is a traitor whether they've escaped with State secrets or a packet of Kleenex. Because although I'm a Soviet citizen I'm a mongrel, Slavic–British, and can't be classified. Because I could cause a modicum of trouble by not turning up for my return flight to Moscow. But most importantly because I just don't matter.'

'You matter,' Lena said.

'Ah, but to whom?'

'To yourself. In the end that's all that counts.'

He kissed her and let himself out of the apartment. On the floor below the tortoise-head of Frolov, the historian, emerged. 'So early, Comrade Hanson?'

'A business appointment.'

'Lucky to have business these hard days. What is there left to buy and sell?' Frolov, having finally acquitted Hanson of espionage, assumed he was a black marketeer.

'How's the Revolution going?'

'I write the truth. . . . But these days it is difficult to reach conclusions – they change every day.'

Frolov's head withdrew into his apartment. Hanson ran down the last flight of stairs, navigated two cats, opened the double-doors and, observed by a single eye peering from between heavy curtains, made his way to his car.

The British Embassy stood on a coveted site across the river from the Kremlin. It had been built by a sugar baron in the nineteenth century for his mistress and was baronial in a cosy sort of way. Here successions of diplomats had pussy-footed with the Kremlin leaders across the water, stoically endured predictable snubs, and eaten strawberries on the Queen's birthday with hostile emissaries including almost everyone except the Russians who, isolated from the forums of international debate, were most friendly.

A militiaman at the gate demanded identification papers and regarded him speculatively as he perused them.

'They're expecting me,' Hanson told him. 'I telephoned yesterday – I need permission to do some filming here.'

The militiaman made a call and, with a jerk of his head, let him go.

A receptionist, retired army NCO by the look of him, said a Mr Jarvis was expecting him and, tightening his lips, withdrew from his contaminating presence.

Jarvis, young with clipped woolly hair and big, eavesdropping ears, led Hanson to a small office proportionate to his lowly rank. He sat behind a modest desk and said: 'So we're making a movie, are we.'

'Why don't you relax,' Hanson said, settling himself on the other side of the desk. 'I haven't come here to subvert you.'

'You'd have a hard job.' He pulled uneasily at his lower lip that had been cracked by the cold.

'I'm sure I would.'

'So let's get to the point, shall we,' his voice searching for an authoritative pitch. 'What do you want to film and why?'

'The white ballroom?'

'Impossible,' Jarvis said with satisfaction.

'The landing where a young officer once blew out his brains because his girlfriend had found another lover?'

'Out of the question.' Jarvis glanced at a photograph of a girl who looked like an aristocratic milkmaid as though he half expected a nod and a wink.

'Exterior shots?'

'A possibility. But, really, you must let me know what this film is all about. HE is adamant that the Embassy mustn't be compromised.'

'I should have thought HE had more important things on his mind – there is a civil war raging in Azerbaijan.'

'I don't think the ambassador's priorities need concern us,' Jarvis said. He picked up a small puzzle and began to coax silver balls into cups hollowed in black plastic. 'What sort of a thriller? A whodunnit?'

'Sort of. We are only interested in the embassy because of its juxtaposition with the Kremlin. An ironic commentary on international hostilities.'

'Who's we?'

'Members of the foreign community in Moscow.'

'Which members would those be?'

'You know perfectly well which members.'

'Ah, those members. . . .' Jarvis, gaining assurance, tut-tutted at an errant silver ball.

'So will that be all right, exterior shots I mean?'

'We'll consider your application.' He smiled, drawing the girl in the photograph into the decision-making, and his ears moved infinitesimally. 'Now if you'll excuse me. . . .'

'There is one more thing.'

'Really?' Jarvis consulted a schedule on his desk. 'I don't think – '

'I want to see Gordon. And don't say Gordon who. I want to see Alistair Gordon, Flash as I believe he's known.'

'*Mister* Gordon is in Chancery.'

'I don't care whether he's in the potting shed,' Hanson said, 'I want to see him.'

'I'm afraid that's impossible.'

'Why don't you pick up the phone and ask Flash?'

'As you rightly pointed out there are more important things to hand.' He stood up. 'I'll see you out.'

'I'm staying put.'

Jarvis pulled at his lip, blood oozed from the crack. He licked it. 'I can have you thrown out.'

'A scene? I don't think HE would like that. Violence and originality are a diplomat's cardinal crimes.'

Jarvis sat down. 'Why do you want to see Fl – Mr Gordon?'

'Why don't you just pick up that phone?'

Jarvis glanced at the girl in the photograph. She must have nodded because he picked up the phone. 'Alistair? Brian Jarvis here. There's a chap called Hanson in my office who wants to see you. No, HANSON . . . yes, that Hanson . . . no, I don't know what he wants . . . you will?' He replaced the receiver. 'Mr Gordon is coming to see you,' he said incredulously.

He can't afford not to, Hanson thought. Gordon was a Second Secretary whose brief included surveillance of defectors in case any intelligence came their way. It almost never did but Gordon couldn't take any risks. Supposing I had wind of another Philby?

The door opened and Gordon came in. He reminded Hanson of a Swedish tennis-player whose Wimbledon hopes had been impaired by a predilection for intrigue. He was blond and boyish and his pin-striped suit was decently crumpled.

He said to Jarvis:'Could you leave us together for a few minutes, Brian. See you at the Down-Under tonight?' reminding Hanson that the beery club under the Australian Embassy was one of the many outposts of the West where he and his ilk were not welcome.

'Right you are, Alistair.' Jarvis took a last glance at the photograph of the girl and exited gratefully.

'Hallo, Bob,' Gordon said with a familiarity scarcely merited by their one previous meeting. 'What can I do for you?' He sat in Jarvis's chair.

'I want to know why you've put the block on my return to England.'

197

'Do you now. To tell you the truth, Bob, I had no idea you wanted to go back. I thought you were more than happy in the country of your adoption.'

'Spare me the bullshit, *Alistair*. You knew as soon as my application came before the consul.'

'Did I? Perhaps. It probably didn't seem all that important at the time.'

'The KGB have put a block on it, too.'

'Then why bother to come to me, old son?'

'If I'm right one of my people – '

'Your people?'

'Those you choose to call the Twilight Brigade?'

'Really? I hadn't heard that. But where the cap fits, eh?'

'One of my people who was, possibly still is, an officer in the KGB has been in touch with his superiors and they have instructed OVIR not to give me an exit visa.'

'You chose to be a Russian, old son.'

'Now why would he do that?'

'Search me.' Gordon put his feet on the desk and leaned back audaciously in the chair. 'Nothing sinister, I shouldn't think. You only came across with ideals.'

'Sorry about those,' Hanson said.

'So what do you want me to do? We haven't put a block on you, as you put it. No need. Our friends are doing that for us.'

'But if they did give me an exit visa you would – '

'Put a block on it? That eventuality hasn't arisen. Probably never will. You see in cases like this we work together, a sort of old boys' network, if you follow me.' He toyed with the tip of his tie, silver crown on navy blue, Vincent's, Oxford.

'So if one gives permission the other follows suit?'

'Something like that.' Gordon transferred his attentions from his tie to his carefully dishevelled hair.

'So if you gave me the okay they might do the same?'

'They might,' Gordon conceded. 'But why should we give you the okay? I can see no good reason, can you?'

'Humanitarian grounds?'

'Spare me your aged mother. She disowned you a quarter of a bloody century ago.'

'How about a poor old sod who just wants to see England once more before he falls off the perch?'

'You're not that old,' said Gordon. 'Anyway, what have you got to offer?'

'Offer? How can I have anything to offer? I came here with nothing and I've got even less now.'

'You say you may have a KGB officer in your midst. His name would be marginally interesting.'

'Then why don't you ask your friends.'

'They are,' Gordon said, 'remarkably reticent about certain matters.'

'I thought the espionage game was over.'

'That's what our friends would like you to think. What would happen to the unemployment figures if they disbanded the KGB?'

'How can the identity of some has-been KGB officer among the defectors possibly interest you?'

'Always a few ends to be tied up,' Gordon said. 'It's not that important, of course, but we do like to know who stole the family silver.'

'Someone who was more important than he appeared to be?'

'Put out a few feelers, old son. And don't forget the female of the species. Cambridge, weren't you?'

'I don't betray people,' Hanson said.

'No question of betrayal.' Gordon crossed his legs which were in disrespectful proximity to the milkmaid. 'What's past is past. And I don't mean only Brits – Americans, Europeans . . . any nationality. Why, incidentally, do you think any of them would want to stop you going back?'

'Because they think I'm betraying them?'

'You seem to be obsessed with betrayal.'

'Telling the truth about their lives here. . . .'

'But isn't this the fount of your beliefs? Isn't this your rationale, your *raison d'être*? I thought you all fairly wallowed in equality.'

'You wouldn't understand,' Hanson said.

'Oh I understand all right. Lack of initiative, lack of identity. . . . Join the Party and we'll bury your character defects in dogma. Why not be a star? A defector? A spy even. Fulfilment, meaning . . . until your mentors cross the street when you try and shake them by the hand.'

'I hope for your sake,' Hanson said, 'that this room isn't bugged.'

'Don't you worry about me, Bob. I look after number One.' Gordon swung his legs off the desk. 'Are you game?'

'I suppose so, provided you keep your end of the bargain.'

'Well said, old man.'

Old man . . . promoted from son. Old boy, chap, fellow . . . . There was no knowing where it might end.

Random anarchy ruled in the banya. Hanson gathered from Michael Cooper, just back from Georgia, that it had begun with the return from prison of the stallholder. Celebrations given an edge by the new freedom of expression had spawned emotional debate and a fight had broken out in the steam-room.

The origins of the fight, Michael said, had been complex. An Armenian who now attended the bath-house regularly had taken advantage of the jubilant mood to launch a diatribe against his neighbours in Transcaucasia, the Azerbaijanis.

What had been lacking was an Azerbaijani to take up the ancient feud. No problem. A member of a delegation visiting Moscow from Alma-Ata, capital of Kazakhstan, had stepped into the breach. A Muslim? Hanson inquired, recalling the Kremlin fear that within the next thirty years Muslims in the Soviet Union – if it still existed – might outnumber ethnic Russians. Negative. The patron from Kazakhstan was Russian Orthodox. And that had somehow brought the Russian Republic with its population of 145,000,000 into the hostilities.

In what context? The Baltic Republics seeking independence, the Ukraine with its separatists, Moldavia intoxicated by the collapse of communism in neighbouring Rumania, Transcaucasia already embroiled in civil war, the Muslims of the deep south who religiously had never been part of the Soviet ethos? Michael shook his head. Russia for the Russians, would you believe.

Who had fought whom? Bodybuilder versus Lithuanian? Half right. A pardonable misjudgement. Who in the circumstances would have picked Russian v. Russian? Bodybuilder v. stallholder. . . .

'Why, for God's sake?' Hanson asked. 'Weren't they both celebrating victory over Vilkin?'

'Great issues have a way of becoming personal, I guess.' Michael, sitting opposite Hanson across the scattered pieces on the chess-board, drank some beer; around them hostilities raged unabated. 'Toasts in vodka didn't help.'

'So who was the aggressor?'

'Verbally the bodybuilder. He accused the stallholder of taking advantage of *perestroika* and hiking the prices on his free-enterprise stall. The stallholder said he didn't take that sort of shit from a Lyuberite thug who had roamed the streets of Moscow beating up innocent citizens. A thug, what's more, who deprived starving families of meat by feeding it to his mongrel dogs. *Mongrel*, that's what did it. . . .'

'So who hit who?'

'They went into the steam-room. Jesus, it looked like some haunted arena. The steam . . . the tiers of seats . . . these two guys wearing only their underpants squaring up to each other. The stallholder got in first, bear-hug. But the *Lyuberite thug* has got muscles where God never put them. He broke free, caught the stallholder with a forearm smash. And then what happens? Enter the cops. . . .'

'Because of the fight?'

'Hell no. A professor had given a description of a pickpocket who had lifted a bottle of vodka from his bag on Biblioteka metro station. So the cops came straight here. But one bottle of vodka looks very much like another so they helped to drink the evidence and left.'

In one corner of the room the Lithuanian was brandishing his fist in the face of the Kremlin chauffeur; by the clothes hangers where the ancient attendant hovered uncertainly, the Ukrainian miner was shouting at Lev Grechko, the skating instructor.

'I hear,' Michael said, 'that there have been sporadic outbursts of hostilities across the border.' He aimed his thumb towards the womens' quarters.

The various altercations were interrupted by a pummelling on the door leading to the street. The stallholder, man of the moment, shouted: 'If you're the police you can piss off – there's no vodka left.'

201

The unmistakable voice of the laundress came back at him. 'Let us in you double-crossing sons-of-bitches.'

'Have you no shame, woman?'

'Cover up your miserable bodies and let us in.'

'And if we don't?' He wrapped a sheet round his considerable girth.

'We'll batter the door down.'

'She could do it single-handed,' the chauffeur observed.

The stallholder unlocked the door and the laundress, followed by the seamstress and the hairdresser pushed their way in. They wore their uniforms and their medals jingled indignantly. Behind them came Tanya Agursky.

The laundress surveyed the men who had abandoned their vendettas. 'What a pathetic bunch,' she said. 'I don't think any of these would do us much good, girls.' She turned to the bodybuilder. 'How did you get those?' pointing at his biceps. 'Blow them up with a bicycle pump?'

'If you've come here to swop insults you might as well leave,' said the chauffeur. Since his wired-up interview with Vilkin his prestige had grown and he exercised it thoroughly.

'We've come here to discuss justice,' said the seamstress.

'I've had a bellyful of justice,' the stallholder said.

'A lot of justice in that case,' the hairdresser said. She was not renowned for witticisms and, as she sat down at a table, a smile briefly lit her sallow features.

In the background Tanya Agursky scanned the faces of the men; then, quietly, opened the door and went out.

'So what's your problem?' the stallholder asked with elaborate weariness.

'You,' said the seamstress sitting beside the hairdresser, blue-rinsed curls moving springily.

'How could anyone be such a big fool?' The laundress stood in front of him, arms folded across her bosom. 'Setting up a stall in Red Square. . . .'

'Someone had to make a stand. Hooligan behaviour in GUM didn't help the Cause much, did it? Not without publicity, anyway.'

'You had publicity?'

'I made a call. . . .'

'No publicity,' the seamstress said, words needle-sharp. And to the laundress: 'Get on with it, we haven't come here to listen to you two scoring points.'

An air of resolute calm settled on the laundress. 'You,' to the stallholder, 'were packed off to prison quite rightly in my opinion.'

'Did anyone seek your opinion?'

'But it's not the fact that you went to gaol that concerns us: it's the fact that you got out. You men acted without consulting us, fellow members of the committee.'

'It was my ass that was in gaol,' the stallholder said.

'And there it would have stayed if someone hadn't interfered.' Her eyes found Michael Cooper.

'You would have preferred me to stay in prison?'

'You wouldn't have been able to act the big fool there. How did you get out?'

'We can be very persuasive,' the chauffeur said.

'Get to the point,' the seamstress said.

'In future all decisions must be agreed by the committee. Do you agree, you big fool?' the laundress said to the stallholder.

'We agree,' the chauffeur said. 'It just happened that this was a matter for men.' He tapped his chest where the cassette had rested.

'You were very clever doing a deal with Vilkin.' She smiled at the chauffeur, making him the personal recipient of her admiration. 'How did you do it?'

The chauffeur appealed to his fellows. 'Shall I tell her?'

Michael Cooper stood up. 'What is more important is how she knows that we approached Vilkin. Did he tell you?'

'I don't discuss my business with foreigners.'

'You see,' Michael said, addressing the men, 'Vilkin wants to divide us, weaken us. Set men and women at each other's throats. That's why he told them that we went to see him.'

Men and women stared at each other. Ah, that Vilkin, their looks said.

15

Tsar Petrov consulted Lenin first.

Leaving his own office, he made his way along red-carpeted corridors to the apartment where Lenin had lived for five years with his wife and his sister Maria.

He glanced at the piano at which Lenin had sung accompanied by the two women. Lingered in front of his books. Peered into the kitchen with its cracked plates and serviceable table.

Then he went to the study and sat at the table-desk and stared at the hand-palm in its wooden tub.

Vladimir Ilyich, would you send in the tanks?

The silence, disturbed by his intrusion, hovered resonantly.

You see it contradicts everything I've preached. A return to the blood-letting of my predecessors. Do I have to resort to the law of the gun, I who gave the people liberty instead of repression?

You forget – I fought a Civil War.

Petrov, skull aching with inchoate decisions, made his way back to his own office in the Council of Ministers building on which a red flag fluttered on a green dome. The yellow, snow-capped building was separated from the mausoleum where Lenin, head resting on a white pillow, red beard simultaneously avuncular and aggressive, lay at peace in a glass case, by the walls of the Kremlin. His brain was elsewhere – in the Institute of Neurosurgery.

Petrov sat at his desk and considered the unfinished business in its trays. Top priority: should he order KGB, Interior Ministry and Reservist troops to attack in Azerbaijan? He placed the document requiring his signature beside the photograph of his wife and consulted the next folio.

ENVIRONMENT. More desolate revelations that had surfaced from bureaucratic dross. Not merely Chernobyl. The Aral Sea leaking to death – fishing villages becalmed in desert. Air pollution in Archangel sometimes fifty times over the limit. A paper-pulping mill pumping 100,000,000 metric tons of inadequately, treated cellulose into Lake Baikal which held twenty per cent of the world's fresh water. Pesticides, pollution, erosion. . . . In Magnitogorsk life expectancy fifty-three years.

And all exposed by *glasnost*. Me.

Petrov returned to a report from the Kremlin Commandant. The crows that perched irreverently on the citadel's spires and domes were cawing louder than ever this year and the goshawks trained to send them packing weren't doing their job. Petrov scrawled on the bottom of the report *Send in the tanks* and smiled for the first time that day.

After he had signed all the documents on his desk – all that was, except the authority to send the army into Azerbaijan – he summoned one of his guards and told him he was going to walk among the visitors in the public areas of the Kremlin.

He put on his grey topcoat, scarf and FBI hat and emerged on one of the main thoroughfares near the thirty-five-inch bore Tsar Cannon which stood on a corner outside Cathedral Square's melody of golden domes and crosses.

At first no one believed what they saw; or if they did they hid recognition as a cold sufferer stifles a sneeze. They had come to see the cannon and the great broken Tsar Bell and the Amoury where the Fabergé eggs were displayed, not the leader of their land. They still hadn't adapted to a man of the people, if that's what he was, and his presence embarrassed and alarmed them. He approached the Church of the Twelve Apostles, turned into the square where he could scarcely be ignored and walked towards two of the towers that spiked the Kremlin walls – the Secret and the First Nameless. Half-way across a boy with a brace on his teeth pointed at him. His parents, both wearing cheap fur hats – the mother's like a grey chrysanthemum – whispered to him urgently. What were they saying? 'Don't point, it's rude?'

Petrov folded a smile and said: 'What's your name?'

'Viktor,' the boy told him, feeling for the brace with the tip of his tongue.

His mother hissed: 'Comrade President.' She and her husband stared intently at their felt boots.

Petrov wanted to say: 'Do you believe in me, Viktor? Have you heard good things about me? That I am an honourable man who means well?' Instead he said: 'That's my name, too. A good name, a man's name.'

'It's my father's name, too.'

'Where do you go to school, Viktor?'

'Work-Polytechnical Middle School Number Eight.'

'Comrade President,' muttered his mother.

'In Irkutsk, Comrade President,' said her husband, squaring his shoulders.

'And you, comrade, do you work on the hydro-electric scheme?' Petrov prided himself on his intuition.

'I do – '

'In this weather?'

The boy said: 'This isn't cold. In Siberia we say – '

'It doesn't matter what we say, Viktor,' his father interrupted.

'Come on,' Petrov said, 'what do you say?'

'That Moscow people are as soft as goat's cheese.'

Petrov, sighting an opening, said: 'And what do they say about Kremlin people?'

'I'm sure Viktor doesn't know, Comrade President,' his mother said, kicking a ridge of ice with the toe of her boot. 'He's making it all up.'

'But they must say something about the Kremlin,' Petrov said. *About me. . . .*

'I don't remember anything in particular.' The boy covered the brace with his tongue.

'Nothing? Come now, they must say something.'

He remained obdurately dumb, words trapped behind his inside-out tongue. Petrov remembered such moments in his youth: the desperate search to find just one articulate phrase.

He patted the boy's shoulder. 'Tell them at Work-Polytechnical Number Eight that you met me. And write to me. That's an order.' He smiled to show that it wasn't. 'Tell me what *you* think of the Kremlin people.' *Of me if I'm still there.*

A crowd, emboldened by the boy and his parents, had gathered. The plain-clothes guards, worried, stamped their feet.

Petrov shook the parents' hands. 'I'm glad it was only goat's cheese,' he said to the father and continued on his way through the hastily parting throng.

He stopped and talked to a group of Japanese, a couple of Australians and a party of shivering Uzbeks from Samarkand. Then, having learned nothing, he pulled the snap-brim of his hat low on his forehead and strode back to his office. There he ordered his limousine for five o'clock and waited impatiently to consult wih the one person whose opinion he valued as much as his own.

Natalia said: 'You look tired,' and instantly he did. He sat in an easy chair in the unpretentious apartment and listened to her preparing the evening meal in the kitchen. Homely sounds – the ring of crockery, a clatter of saucepans, the flare of a match. His eyes felt hot and he closed them. What he envied most in other men's lives was the uncomplicated evenings that followed a day's labour; the anticipation of such calm pleasure as you hurried homeward; the promise of sleep that wasn't knotted with doubt. Until recently he had been imperturbable in crisis; now, since he had carried his briefcase into his dreams, he was at war with himself.

Peaked cap firmly in place, he peered through the chink in the wall of the barn. The conspirators, debating the future of Misha the kid, stared back and aimed pistols at him. His limbs jerked as they fired and Natalia, hand to his forehead, said: 'I think you've got a fever. Do you want to go to bed?'

'Let's eat first,' he said because the meal was the foundation of secure evenings. Why had he chosen to be different on such an Olympian scale?

Soup stiff with nourishment, steak, red wine. He ate without appetite. His body felt dry and it shrank to the touch of his clothes. Natalia, wearing an old grey shirt and heather-coloured jersey, ate hungrily.

He put down his knife and fork. 'That day in Red Square. If you hadn't been so obstinate you might not be here now – I wouldn't have led you forcibly out of the crowd and laid claim to you.'

'I'm glad I was obstinate,' she said.

207

'Thank God you still are. And unpredictable and familiar.'

'I don't know that I want to be familiar.'

'A great compliment. The familiarity of sharing. Hearing what the other is thinking.' He sipped some wine but it was tasteless on his tongue. 'I couldn't do any of it without you.'

'Which makes me jointly responsible for the uproar you've caused.'

'Or the instigator?'

'Accomplice,' she said.

'Why do you look so young?'

'How can I be old married to a man who re-shuffles continents?'

'Don't you ever yearn for something more – ordinary. . . ?'

'A cat curled on the hearth-rug? I prefer a parrot squawking with invective. Although there are times. . . .' She shook her head and began to clear the dishes.

'I don't squawk,' Petrov said.

'You have been known to pound rostrums.'

'I feel like pounding one now. I give people freedom and they demand liberty.'

'There's a difference?'

'Of interpretation.'

'You sound like a reproving father.'

'One who's lost touch with the young?'

'With human frailty perhaps.'

'So what should I do about this frailty? Let the people founder on it?'

'Or send in the tanks. That's what you've been leading up to, isn't it.'

'You know me too well,' he said. His eyes ached and his head was heavy on his shoulders.

'How can I advise you?'

'You're my conscience.'

'More lives lost, Viktor, if you don't mobilise the troops. You don't have any choice, do you.'

His dreams were populated by soft-mouthed goats and conspirators bathed in kerosene-smelling light and weary German soldiers firing ancient muskets that exploded in their faces.

Twice he awoke, bathed in sweat. Reached for Natalia who

208

was falling beneath inexorable ranks of boots in Red Square. Plucked her from them. Felt her dry hand gripping his.

By morning, he had shed the fever. He dressed hurriedly, kissed his sleeping wife, drank two glasses of tea and summoned his driver.

At his office he authorised troops to go into Azerbaijan. Any rational tsar would surely have done the same.

The KGB Chief's dacha was a splendid indulgence – wooden turrets, parquet floors, pool room – and it was an embarrassment to him. But how could he vacate it? He had occupied it without noticeable guilt in the pre-*glasnost* days and departure to more lowly quarters would be interpreted as shameless boot-licking.

He talked round this predicament as he led Petrov across the forecourt, past the frozen fountain and the frost-bitten nymphs. 'Not my style really. A legacy of my position. . . .' His eyes watered behind his heavy spectacles.

'You could always move into the caretaker's cottage,' Petrov said. 'I might join you one day,' he added, as they took off their coats in the hall observed moodily by the glass-eyed heads of animals on the walls.

'A bad week, eh?' Kirov led Petrov into a baronial living-room. Logs burned and spat in a capacious fireplace and three leather armchairs had been arranged in a conspiracy in front of them.

'In the past three days I've been accused of being a mass-murderer, the re-incarnation of Hitler and Stalin – take your choice – and,' quoting, 'a hypocritical shepherd who has shamelessly betrayed his flock.'

'Vodka?' Kirov, confused features beginning to thaw, held up a bottle of Stolinchnaya.

'I'd prefer tea,' Petrov said. Half expecting Kirov to pull a bell-rope, he sat in one of the chairs which sighed under his weight.

Kirov went to the door and called to his wife.Then he sat opposite Petrov, looking pensively at the bottle.

'Don't let me stop you having a nip,' Petrov said.

'If the President drinks tea then I drink tea.' Kirov poked the fire; sparks chased each other up the chimney. 'I hear you took an unscheduled tour of the Kremlin the other day. That wasn't very wise. . . .'

'If I can't meet the people in my own fortress then I might as well give up.'

'Reassurance. . . . Is that what you were after?'

'I want to know the will of the people, Dima. You see it's not the Politburo who will get rid of me – they were wisely chosen.' He stared at Kirov's face that had so recently grown old, at the soft hair that had so precipitously turned from grey to white. How could a man who had been weaned in the dark places of intrigue be expected to flourish in the daylight? 'It's the people who will judge me through the duly elected parliament. Ironic, isn't it: I've given them the means to depose me.'

'It may never get that far,' Kirov said, 'if you insist on flouting security arrangements.' He picked up a briefcase from the floor. 'There was another plot to assassinate you last week.'

'I should be very upset if someone didn't want to kill me. What sort of leader is it whom no one hates? Always be suspicious of the man who's universally popular.'

'A well-conceived plot,' Kirov said, taking papers from the briefcase. 'A single shot while you were in Vilnius. Blame laid squarely on a crazy Russian who didn't want to see his language replaced with Baltic tongues.'

'I would prefer to die for a greater cause than that,' Petrov said as Kirov's wife, smile not quite concealing her taciturnity, came in with a silver tray bearing two glasses of tea and a plate of ginger-nuts.

When she had gone Kirov read aloud from one of the sheets of paper. Documents had been prepared incriminating the Russian; a sniper's rifle with one bullet fired hidden in his apartment. The Russian, of limited intelligence, was to have been a dispensable martyr.

'And who were the real assassins?'

Kirov read on. Actual killer disarmed and shot dead in struggle. Accomplice disturbed hiding behind the decorative shutters of a house in Stikliu Street. Turned his pistol on himself before he could be overcome.

'And the brains behind the attempt?'

'We don't know,' Kirov said. 'Except that he's a Muscovite

210

living in Moscow. He wouldn't care whether they spoke in Baltic, Russian or Chinese in Lithuania.'

'So what did he care about?'

Kirov took off his spectacles and pinched the bridge of his nose. 'Who knows. . . . Someone who thinks you're doing too much or someone who thinks you're doing too little. . . .'

'How did you find out about it?'

'An informer. Where would we be without them? Even though they might dirty our new image. How can you have a secret service if it isn't secret?'

Petrov picked up a ginger-nut. Worry had given him an unhealthy appetite and he would have to diet. He bit into the ginger-nut and chewed noisily.

He said: 'This organising genius . . . this mastermind. . . . Could he be in the Kremlin?'

'Could be in the Hammer and Sickle factory for all we know. But we'll keep after him.'

'Why this sudden and *important* invitation to your dacha, Dima?'

'I thought I should warn you – no more unscheduled stops, no more spontaneous walk-arounds in Cathedral Square. And talking about public places, what about the banya?'

Petrov, who had been thinking about Razin, his mercurial opponent who was enviably popular with the public, said: 'Too much on my mind lately. . . .'

'You said you didn't want a KGB informant. As distasteful, you implied, as the informer in Vilnius who saved your life.'

'Don't harrass me, Dima. I've got enough problems.'

'Remember I mentioned a defector named Hanson?'

'And I have remembered why I knew the name. He attended a lecture I gave at Moscow University. He was an idealist; I felt it. I remember thinking that if there were more Robert Hansons in the West and fewer Stalinists in the Soviet Union then there was hope.'

Kirov, too old to comprehend such heresy, stared into the caverns of the fire.

'He asked me for my autograph and I gave it to him.'

'You said you wanted someone to tell you what the people are really thinking. Why not this idealist, this Robert Hanson?'

'I wonder what I told him all those years ago.'

'Enough to make him defect apparently.'

'Was he a spy?'

'He was nothing,' Kirov said. 'And now he wants to go back to England.'

'For a visit?'

'Who knows.' Kirov's voice acquired clandestine authority. 'But he needs an exit visa. . . .'

A finger of ash fell thickly into the grate.

Petrov said: 'Once a secret policeman always a conspirator?'

Kirov nodded slowly. Odd, Petrov thought, how vulnerable he looked without his spectacles.

16

The best drinking chocolate in town was dispensed in a café opposite the French Embassy on Dmitrova Street. There once a week Tanya Agursky met her mother and, while she waited for her to arrive by bus or metro, reviewed the challenges facing her.

She and Lazar were skating competently enough. Or were they better than she believed? Perhaps they could win the National Championships. Would the Olympic Selection Committee then be forced to include her in the Squad?

If they did then the complications proliferated. She would, of course, want to skate with Yury. But would she and Lazar be regarded as an inseparable unit? And would they be pitted against Yury and Nina for a place in the Olympic Team?

She had skated with Yury only once since the New Year. On *their* lake one sparkling Sunday. Speed, spins, lifts – they shared an exhilaration that she had never experienced with Lazar.

As they skated, hands linked, he said: 'I hear you've entered for the National Championships. As you know the Olympic Squad is exempted. Do you think you'll win?'

'Of course.'

'Then they won't be able to overlook you for the Olympics.'

Unspoken questions hovered between them.

'This Lazar,' he said, 'he's good.'

'Oh yes,' she said, Lazar's very good.'

'So if you win the National Championships. . . .'

She waited.

'. . . perhaps he could skate with Nina?' The scar at the corner of his mouth smiled.

A surge of happiness.

'But it would be better,' he said, 'if it happened naturally.'

'If my father admitted defeat?'

'If he went quietly. God knows, Jews bound for Israel are swarming out of the Soviet Union now. This year they reckon 150,000 will go. You can't even get a flight to cities in transit to Israel. Leningrad–Budapest booked up until the summer of 1991. . . .'

'You know that isn't the point,' she said, happiness on the wane.

In the cottage, the dacha, as they took off their skates in front of the log fire Yury said: 'Know something? I think your father's a little crazy.'

'The authorities aren't letting everyone go.'

'Maybe not but they'd be delighted to let your father go.'

And so dogged was he that the clear light of perception suddenly illumined her thoughts. He was scared that she and Lazar might ease him out of the Olympics.

This fallibility touched her strangely. She reached out and touched his cheek.

He said: 'Remember that day when we came here when the lake was just beginning to freeze?'

'I remember.'

'You drank too much champagne.'

'And you just happen to have another bottle in the 'fridge?'

'I haven't checked. I hoped – '

'That it wouldn't be necessary?' She remembered the lavender smell of the bedclothes. You're trying to make me your property, she thought. 'Check the 'fridge and see if there's any champagne there and if there is we'll drink it and then when we're skating together in the Olympics. . . .'

And he had fetched the champagne, she remembered as she watched her mother crossing the street, and there had been no more hints about making love and she remembered how much she had wanted to and how prim and old-fashioned she had felt.

'I'm sorry I'm late,' her mother said. 'Your father isn't well.' She sipped her bitter-sweet chocolate and Tanya watched the steam wreathe her face that lately had acquired an autumnal frailty.

'What's the matter with him?' She suspected him of ploys to entice her back without losing face.

214

'It's something inside him. Defeat, I suppose. I'm worried about his state of mind.' Her usually severe grey hair was looser than usual and from time to time she fidgeted with it. Since her mother had found her in Lev Grechko's apartment Tanya had expected her to plead with her to go home but she never had.

'It's pathetic, isn't it,' Tanya said. 'He feels defeated and yet the Jews have won.'

'They haven't won,' her mother said. 'There isn't any battle any longer.'

'Do you want to go to Israel, Mama?'

'I go where he goes.'

'Does he ask after me?'

'In his way. Indirectly. *Tell her I'm sorry it had to be this way* but not in so many words.'

'It doesn't have to be.'

'He's been crucified and now they've taken away the cross.'

'If only he cared about me.'

'He cares,' her mother said, pushing an amber comb closer to the shiny fist of hair at the nape of her neck.

'Is he in bed?'

'He's on the prowl,' her mother said. 'Glancing at books, making notes, staring out of the window, talking to himself. There's a sickness inside him; I know the symptoms. I'm afraid he's planning something stupid. A last act of defiance, perhaps. He's an obstinate man, your father. Like his daughter.'

'How could I have stayed at home? I want to skate in the Olympics for Russia. He wants to destroy my hopes for the sake of Israel. Or his own ego. . . . I understand him but he makes no effort to understand me. I understand that because he is old – '

'Not so old.'

' – he wants to settle in the Promised Land. I would if I were him. Don't you understand that?' She found she was raising her voice and two French diplomats wearing fastidious suits and beautiful ties were staring at her. 'I'm Jewish. Not ultra-Orthodox, perhaps, despite the way you and Papa have brought me up. But I respect my faith and I will always defend it. But I am also Russian. That is the difference between Papa and me.'

One of the Frenchmen smiled at her.

215

'So I'll tell your father you're happy?'

'As I can be in the circumstances.'

'And that you've entered for the National Championships? That will please him. If you win you will be able to enter for the Olympics?'

'There isn't much time,' Tanya said. 'But, yes, tell him that. And tell him not to do anything . . . dramatic.'

'Have you ever known him take any notice of what I say?'

'Tell him just the same.'

'I must go now; I worry about him. And you.'

Tanya watched her cross the street, a breeze tugging at the hem of her brown coat, fur collar long since removed and laid to rest; it was the only coat that Tanya could remember her wearing. She walked cautiously, head lowered as though searching for lurking perils.

As Tanya walked out the Frenchman said: 'I come here every day at this time. Tomorrow, perhaps?' His teeth were a startling white, arranged for disarming smiles.

Tanya who had recently acquired the arrogance that is a necessary accomplice of beauty swept past him. She took the metro to the banya, arriving as a group of men emerged onto the street. She scanned them for Yury but he wasn't among them; nor had he been in their changing-room when she had accompanied the three members of the Fighting Comrades there. Olympic hopefuls, she supposed, had access to more ambitious therapy than a bath-house. Or was it that he didn't want her to accost him outside?

The American and the young man with the sculptured features and astonishing muscles were among the group. The American, spotting her, raised his shoulders and spread his hands. No success with the counsellors of the Olympics, the gesture said. She nodded at him and made her way to the womens' changing-room.

The organiser of the group was the bodybuilder. But it hadn't been easy to assemble them. No one had been noticeably enthusiastic about seeing a display of obedience by his wolf-dogs and the promise of a guest appearance by a Carpathian wolfhound hadn't weakened their resistance. A guarantee, however, that vodka, beer and *zakuski* would be available had aroused unsuspected canine appreciation.

'Just keep your hands to yourself,' the stallholder told the pickpocket, whose vows did not extend beyond the banya, as they climbed into his van.

Michael travelled with the bodybuilder in his Volga. First to his home in a ten-storey apartment block to the west of the city. The block, one of a complex, was hung with yellow balconies; shops, separated from a broad street by snow-patched grass, comprised the ground floor.

The door was opened by a young woman with plaits and assessing eyes. The bodybuilder introduced her as his sister, Lara. 'I share the apartment with her and her husband and their two children.' His sister nodded without enthusiasm. Photographs of a devoted, crew-cut husband with their two daughters, wearing frilly white aprons and bows in their hair, abounded in the unambitious but well-groomed room; but there were none of the bodybuilder. Muscles, Michael gathered, didn't count for much in this home. So why had he brought him here?

'Michael's an American,' the bodybuilder said as though he had arrived from outer space. And then Michael understood: a relationship with a foreigner, an American at that, which had hitherto aroused implacable suspicion was now prestigious; and prestige was what the bodybuilder needed in a lodging where he was a paying guest.

'Really?' She regarded him with minimal interest. 'What brings you here – ?'

'Mikhail.'

'A Russian name?'

'I'm known as Michael in America.'

'Ah.' She greeted this intelligence stoically.

'I'm taking Michael to see the dogs,' the bodybuilder said.

'They should be put down, eating all that meat when the butchers' counters are bare.'

'Michael might like some tea.'

'You know where the kitchen is. Now if you'll excuse me. . . .' She went into a room where bright-cheeked dolls lay on two bunk-beds.

The bodybuilder led Michael to his room. It was as trim as the quarters of a sailor home from the sea. Pictures of Lyuberites exhibiting their bodies adorned the walls; expanders and weights lay in one corner. The air was redolent of liniament.

'Lara has a lot of worries,' said the bodybuilder putting on a black leather jacket. 'Like all housewives. If anyone brings down this regime it will be the women.' Like many clients Michael had met the bodybuilder's image changed inside his home. 'Do you really want a cup of tea?'

Michael shook his head.

The bodybuilder toughened up again in the car. Driving it with the panache of one of the privileged – only forty-five in every 1,000 owned cars – protected by St Christopher hanging from the dashboard.

'How can you afford a car?' Michael asked as they drove into flat white countryside.

'Buying and selling,' the bodybuilder said vaguely.

Drugs? Michael wondered. He had known a pusher in New York who was so contemptuous of the way his clients insulted their bodies that he became a health fanatic.

'Army surplus mostly,' the bodybuilder said. 'There was a lot left over after Afghanistan. But soon I'm going to sell guard dogs. You wait until you see Sasha, the Carpathian wolfhound. I went all the way to the Hutsul highlands in the Ukraine to collect him.'

'Ukraine,' Michael said. 'Not *the* Ukraine.'

'Free people up there. Don't give a shit for communism. They paint eggs and weave carpets and make axes. I brought some axes back to Moscow and traded them.'

St Christopher swayed frantically as they slithered round a bend.

'And what will you do with Sasha?'

'Mate him first with a stray South Caucasian sheepdog. Ferocious bastards those,' he said fondly. 'The puppies will be piranhas.'

Michael glanced at the sky. It was grey and darkly smudged. Snow had been forecast but the Kremlin chauffeur who knew more about most subjects than recognised specialists was confident that it wouldn't arrive until nightfall.

'So what's the point of this show?' Michael asked.

218

'Spread the word. The patrons of a banya. . . . What better couriers? Who knows, I might sell my piranhas to the Kremlin.'

The other members of the group were waiting in the van as though they feared that the snarling wolf-dogs might jump the chain-link fence. Where, they demanded, was the promised sustenance?

'All in good time,' the bodybuilder assured them. 'First the show, then the reward.'

He let himself into the pound raising his leather cane as the dogs came at him, cracking one over the muzzle when it disobeyed him. As they lay down the wind rippled their fur, brown, fawn and white, exposing their skin.

He turned to the disgruntled spectators standing on the other side of the fence. 'These animals are all products of crossing wolf-dogs with pure-bred strays. They're the best guard dogs in the Soviet Union.'

Tongues hanging out, the wolf-dogs slavered.

He made them sit, chase, retrieve, drop.

'Shouldn't you reward them?' the stallholder asked.

'They know what their reward is. Meat. And they know their punishment if they don't obey. They go hungry.'

Snow began to fall lightly.

'I thought you said nightfall,' the miner said to the chauffeur.

'I keep them separate from the studs and the stray bitches,' the bodybuilder said. Cane raised, he shouted at the wolf-dogs and they ran to a concrete bunker. 'I also keep a few star turns by themselves. Sasha, for instance. He's too young to be used for stud, too old to be treated as a puppy.'

He opened a gate and a strapping, wolf-like dog hurtled out of another bunker. 'Stay.' The dog slowed down but the impetus of his release kept him going forward. The cane landed on his beautifully-marked flanks. 'Stay.' The dog whimpered and lay down. 'He's just a beginner,' the bodybuilder explained.

'Does he beg?' the miner asked.

'My dogs don't beg.'

He took a length of wood carved like a bone from his pocket. The dog ran round and round him barking excitedly. The bodybuilder raised the cane. The dog subsided. The bodybuilder threw the piece of wood. 'Stay.' The dog whined, half rose to its feet. 'Stay.' The dog sat. 'Fetch.' It bounded away.

'Drop it,' as it circled him, ears flattened. The bodybuilder eased the wooden bone from its jaws. 'That's how it's done,' he said, turning to the shivering group. 'He's learning.'

'Good dog,' the stallholder said.

'He will be one day.'

'Tell him that now.'

'I'll tell him when I think he's ready to be told.' The body-builder led the dog to its bunker.

The sky sank lower showering snow and the chauffeur kept his counsel.

The bodybuilder lifted two cartons from the trunk of the Volga and the group adjourned to the wooden hut where the caretaker had died.

The bodybuilder ripped open the cartons and pulled out unlabelled bottles of vodka. Not, Michael hoped, the moon-shine that had killed the old man. Soused herrings and dill pickle and glutinous brown bread followed; finally, fluted bottles of beer.

The bodybuilder handed out glasses. The first shots of vodka went down. Heat flowed from the glowing stove; snow began to gather in the corners of the neglected window where, on the inside, the husks of spiders and flies hung together on cobwebs.

More vodka dropped down their throats. 'To Sasha. . . . To *glasnost*. . . . To food in our bellies and peace in our hearts . . . . To Mother Russia . . . . To us. . . .'

Soon the window was masked with snow. The stallholder shoved a log in the mouth of the upturned stove. Sawdust glowed and died on its flanks.

Michael sat on the bed and felt a hard-edged object beneath him. A chest. 'What's in this?' he asked the bodybuilder.

'The old man's disgusting belongings. Take a look at them, Mr Investigator.'

Michael pulled the metal chest from under the bed. It was padlocked and there was no key. He found a chisel, thrust it under the lid and pressed the handle downwards; the lid gave way with small explosions of rust. Old and unsettling smells rose from its depths.

'You'd better put gloves on,' the bodybuilder said.

Michael put on a pair and pressed the surface of the dead man's possessions like a doctor examining an abdomen. On top a length of red satin curtaining; beneath it small objects like children's knuckles. He removed the curtaining. The knuckles were chess pieces, ivory and ebony, unblemished and worth a lot of money in a New York antique store. Why hadn't the old man sold them? Why had he preferred to poison himself with illicit hooch in a filthy shack surrounded by savage dogs? He took out the chess pieces and stood them in battle order.

A copy of *Nijinsky* by his wife, Romola, published in 1933 . . . lacquered music box, melody locked inside it . . . lace handkerchief . . . pair of chopsticks . . . necklaces with foggy glass beads . . . copy of a fifteenth-century Ukrainian ikon, *Mother of God* . . . identification papers of a German soldier from the 29th Motorised Division, *Stalingrad, Oct. 25, 1942* scrawled on top with mauve, indelible pencil . . . dinner jacket, mould feeding on the silk lapels. . . .

Michael remembered as a boy staring at the bundles of humanity on Skid Row and wondering if they had ever been young. What sort of man was it who had packed his life in this chest, padlocked it and abandoned it? A musician, he decided. A purveyor of martial airs, a bugler or a trumpeter. Conscripted in Moscow when the Germans attacked. Discharging brave notes of music across the humped remains of Stalingrad. Finding the papers of a young and dead German soldier slumped over the wheel of his truck. Returning to Moscow, to the ballet, perhaps, finding that his girl had been exiled to a penal camp in Siberia. . . .

The Ukrainian miner went outside to urinate. He had to push the door hard and snow whipped into the hut in his wake, sizzling on the stove. When he came back he was caked white.

'So what have you found?' the bodybuilder asked Michael.

'I wish I knew. Fragments of a life.'

If only he had looked more closely at the old man's ruined features. In the faces of some old people you discerned how they were when they were quick with youth. And sometimes they smiled at you knowingly. *Look what I might have been, look how I finished.* Michael drank a nip of vodka and the young bugler squared up the ragged infantry.

He dipped into the chest again. A ticket to the Hermitage . . . rapier with a bright and unsullied blade . . . glove with one finger missing . . . clockwork engine . . . flaking newspapers, one of them a copy of *Pravda* carrying the announcement of Churchill's death in 1965. . . .

But no letters which was what Michael had been hoping for. Had he destroyed them? Michael believed that he had withdrawn from life in middle-age, possibly earlier.

Outside the wolf-dogs howled.

'Are they warm enough?' the chauffeur inquired.

'Would I allow them to suffer?' the bodybuilder demanded. And when no one answered: 'I love those animals.'

At the bottom of the chest lay an album, brown leather binding spotted with mildew. Michael opened it. Sepia photographs of hirsute patriarchs and severe matriarchs stared at him outraged. He turned a page. A boy wearing a bulging cap and trousers down to his knees and a soldier smiling with nervous belligerence. Were they, man and boy, the antecedents of the corpse he had found on the bed? There was a young woman wearing a print frock, a breeze shaping it to the mould of her body, kerchief over her hair, smiling at the photographer with cheerful familiarity.

He turned another page. A teenager regarded him quizzically from a doorway. He wore a white, open-neck shirt and black trousers tightly belted across the waist. He was holding what looked like the fin of a bomb. His cropped hair was as shiny as needles and his expression was carefully composed of triumph and modesty. He was more easy to identify because Michael had seen the same face, albeit with a full head of hair, in a photograph in the apartment on the Lower East Side of New York.

The wind carrying the blizzard from Siberia whistled and moaned through the eaves of the hut.

The blizzard found Robert Hanson as he was driving his Zhiguli away from the Lenin Hills where he had been filming on location. He hadn't been required to appear in front of the cameras and his only function, as far as he could determine, was to give Palmer the pleasure of emphasising that he was not indispensable.

The first warning was a fusillade of hard snow against the windscreen as he left the East German and his Mexican co-star walking hand in hand through a copse of birch trees. As he drove down Vernadsky Prospect towards the river he noticed that there were fewer cars abroad than usual. This and the blurring of the city's silhouette should have alerted him but he was concentrating on a summons to OVIR. Had the bureaucrats finally conceded? Or was he on his way to be handed a conclusive *nyet*.

He was watching the grains of snow dancing on the bonnet when suddenly the windscreen became opaque. He switched on the wipers. Laboriously they pushed aside wads of snow swept there by a wind that had found the fat loop of the river in front of Lenin Stadium. Ghost cars, headlights peering short-sightedly, passed him. By the time he reached the bridge spanning the river the wipers were faltering. They stopped past the stadium. He pulled into the side of the road as the snow embraced the Zhiguli and began to engulf it.

He adjusted the rear-view mirror. The stranger smiled at him. *The decision is yours.* To sit here in an igloo or walk through the blizzard to the nearest metro station, Sportivnaya.

He looked at his watch; he was due at OVIR in fifteen minutes. Supposing his failure to keep the appointment was used against him?

Hanson half opened the door. Snow rushed into the car. He closed it again, resting his hands on the wheel. Fourteen minutes. At that moment the engine stopped. He turned the ignition key. Nothing. Cold began to find its way inside.

He put on his sheepskin mittens, raised the collar of his overcoat, wound the scarf round his neck, untied the flaps of his fur hat, tied the lace beneath his chin. He dropped the ignition keys into one pocket, took a last look in the rear-view mirror and, finding it unoccupied, opened the door again.

The snow pushed at his body, sealed his eyes, lodged in his nostrils. Where was the metro? Was he going in the wrong direction? He turned and let the wind thrust him forward, boots already ankle-deep in snow.

As he rounded a corner one foot slipped on a ridge of ice lurking like an iceberg. He fell, hitting his head against the stone buttress of a building. The blow administered a boozy sense of well-being. He got up and held out his arms. Victory

223

over the elements or defeat – he wasn't sure which. Snow plastered him, finding its way into his mouth as he opened his lips to utter some exultant cry of defiance. He turned again, snow heavy on his shoulders. It seemed to be pulling him forward so that he was bent double as though searching for tracks. When he fell the snow was warm and flakes pirouetted among his thoughts.

Michael levered the photograph from the album. His brother wasn't named but on the back of the picture was an oval, passport-type stamp bearing the name of a photographic studio on Solyanka Street.

Outside the blizzard howled. The stove still glowed but the vodka was low in the last bottle.

'Relax, Mikhail,' the bodybuilder said. 'We can keep each other warm and one day the snow will stop.' He drank some beer.

'Who's going to feed the dogs?' the chauffeur asked.

'Don't worry about the dogs. They're tough. Carpathian wolf-hound and South Russian sheepdog. . . . One day I'll breed the toughest dogs in Russia.'

'If Sasha lives.'

'You think it's a picnic up in the Carpathians?'

'Ah, the cold,' the stallholder murmured drowsily. 'That's what makes us Russians so tough.'

'Not as tough as Ukrainians,' the miner said.

'I could have sworn,' the chauffeur said, 'that there was another bottle of beer.'

They stared at the pickpocket. He handed them the bottle. 'Sometimes,' he said, 'my fingers have a life of their own.'

They nipped the last vodka bottle dry and handed round the bottle of beer. Then one by one they fell into stertorous sleep. Michael stared at the photograph of Vasily for a moment, then slipped it into his wallet.

Hanson partially regained consciousness in the casualty department of the Sklifosovsky Institute. He heard voices like the

224

chatter of birds in an aviary, saw tendrils of blood in a bowl of water, felt the blows of the metal-edged ruler on his left hand . . . . Hypothermia, he heard dreamily, and facial frostbite. He looked undernourished, he learned without indignation, and there was a possibility that he would not survive. 'Unless,' said a woman's voice, 'he has some incentive.' Well, he had that all right – to go home. He remembered a men's outfitters in which unfashionable clothes were obstinately arrayed in a village in Surrey and he smelled the organic scents of a small gardening shop where plants overflowed their pots in fertilised profusion. Were they still there? He would have to find out. 'What's the time?' he asked.

'Six o'clock,' the woman said. 'In the evening.'

Too late. For what? He returned to the village but the shops were no longer there. In their place a squat office block, windows bearing the names of solicitors and surveyors in gold and black italics. On one such window in ornate script OVIR.

He opened his eyes and saw the patient features of his wife. He turned and felt the pull of a tube plugged into his wrist.

'Why did you do it?' she asked. She laid her hand on his and regarded him patiently. She would die patiently, he thought.

'Do what?'

'This . . . this stupid thing,' and he realised that she thought he had tried to commit suicide.

'I had to get to OVIR.'

'Was it so important that you had to walk through a blizzard?'

'The engine in the car broke down. I would have been frozen to death. I was trying to reach the metro.'

'You were going in the wrong direction.'

'I was disorientated,' he said.

'I suppose that if you were trying to reach OVIR. . . .'

'. . . .I wasn't trying to kill myself?'

'. . . .That in a way you were trying to escape.' Her hand moved drily on his.

'But not from you.'

She clasped her hands and rocked gently.

'You'll have to stay here for a while,' Lena said. 'Then we'll go home and I'll nurse you. The apartment and the dacha. . . . They are still your homes even though there isn't a pub on the corner,' and he realised how much he must have bored her.

225

'I'll be in good hands,' he said. What if his exit visa came through? Could the British really deny him admittance to the country of his birth?

She stood up. 'You must get some rest now.'

She picked up her coat and hat and stood hesitating and for one extraordinary moment he imagined her taking off her clothes and slipping into the bed beside him.

When he next awoke the young woman from OVIR was sitting beside his bed. 'Your wife telephoned me,' she said. 'She didn't seem to know we're planning to elope.'

He heaved himself upright on the pillows. 'You sent for me,' he said.

'Is that why you braved the blizzard?'

'Why did you want to see me?'

She poked at tendrils of hair that had escaped from her cheap fur hat; the fur was still wet with melted snow. 'It was only a formality,' she said. 'They want some more details. . . .'

He gave it a few moments. Then he said: 'The longer the better. Where shall we go, Frunze? I've always wanted to go to the races there.'

By dusk the fuel had run out and the blizzard was burying the hut, making wind instruments of the eaves. Everyone except Michael and the pickpocket was still asleep whimpering from time to time as though their predicament had penetrated their dreams.

'Don't worry,' said the pickpocket who feared the hazards of his occupation but not spectacular perils, 'it will stop.'

'And then how do we get out?'

'I'll think of a way,' the pickpocket said. 'Are you going to stay in Moscow?'

'If we get out of here? It depends. . . .'

'On whether you find your brother? I saw you take the picture from the album.' His little fingers curled. 'Was that him?'

'Here, take a look.' Michael handed him the photograph.

The pickpocket turned over the photograph and read the stamp. 'That's near the synagogue.'

'The studio may have some records,' Michael said doubtfully.

226

'I hope so,' the pickpocket said. 'Because if you find your brother you'll stay. And live with the girl from Intourist,' he added slyly. 'And continue visiting the banya. Do you have bath-houses in America?'

'We have saunas. They're not quite the same thing,' he said with great certainty.

'I'd like to visit New York some day.'

'Good pickings on the subway.'

'Then you'll have to go there on vacation and defend me if I get caught.' Resting his back against the wooden wall near the fading glow of the stove, he gazed fondly at Michael, his personal property.

A few minutes later the wind sighed and passed on its way leaving behind a silence that disturbed the men's sleep. They awoke coughing and wincing in the dying light.

The pickpocket, taking advantage of their confusion, lectured them. 'If we don't do something we'll freeze to death. But the door is jammed by a wall of snow that probably stretches as far as the forest. . . .'

The stallholder, one of those who revel in their hangovers, groaned. The bodybuilder, one of those who claim to be impervious to them, said: 'So what do you suggest?'

'Have you got a storm lantern?'

'Over there.' The bodybuilder pointed at a pile of sacking.

The pickpocket, picking up the lantern, said: 'A blizzard is a good time for my profession. People only think of escape: they don't notice if they lose anything. . . .' He paused with the timing of a seasoned orator. 'If the blizzard is behind them the front of their clothes where we usually ply our trade is dry – '

'Get on with it,' the bodybuilder said.

'If the front of the hut is piled high with snow then the back will have been sheltered.'

'And there's wood behind the hut,' said the bodybuilder, stealing the pickpocket's inspiration. He picked up a mallet and began hitting the louvred slats of wood nailed outside to the uprights. With a creak three slats swung outwards and cold rushed in. 'Out you go,' the bodybuilder said to the pickpocket.

The pickpocket handed in logs of pine and birch. When one corner was piled high with them the bodybuilder said: 'Now meat.' He handed the shivering pickpocket a key. 'Last bunker.

Bring six cuts.' The pickpocket, hands grazed, passed the hunks of frozen moose through the gap, then climbed back. The bodybuilder levered the slats from the points where they were still hinged to the uprights, pulled them into the hut and nailed them in place from the inside.

The miner split a log with an axe and dropped kindling wood into the embers at the bottom of the stove. Small flames fluttered into life, then roared. The miner tossed in logs and damped down the stove. The bodybuilder found the pan on which he thawed meat for the dogs, placed it on top of the stove and lay three cuts of meat on it. The deep-frozen ice hissed and bled. Then the meat began to fry and the hut was filled with greasy smoke. The men, huddled together in the camaraderie of deprivation, drooled.

When they had eaten, washing down the meat with melted snow, they gathered around the stove and talked about the great conquests of their lives; and such were their shared triumphs over adversity that they didn't argue and *glasnost* might never have been conceived. Then, one by one, they fell asleep and went their separate ways.

Dawn, viewed through the gap where the bodybuilder had again removed the slats, was mauve fading to lemon-yellow. A few stars still lingered; the dogs were quiet and silence lay thickly over the countryside. The van and the car, the pickpocket reported, were buried; the track leading to the pound and the road beyond it were waist-deep in snow. 'We're marooned,' the miner said with deep satisfaction.

But not for long, the bodybuilder assured them. He fired a Very light into the sky and they watched it hover burning bright red. While the sun rose and polished the sky they waited. A helicopter arrived within an hour, blades clattering briskly. As it settled it made its own small blizzards. The bodybuilder ran out to it and returned to the hut with the news. They could return to Moscow on the helicopter or wait till a snow-plough arrived. Still sharing, they elected to stay.

The snow-plough made its ponderous appearance at midday, swinging away from the road it had cleared and pushing its way down the track. The bodybuilder directed the driver across the pound to the bunkers where the wolf-dogs slavered. Then he heated more meat and threw it to them.

228

When the snow had been cleared from the Volga and the van they drove back to Moscow where ploughs, dumper trucks and chippers were clearing the last of the snow.

They went straight to the banya and into the steam-room. When he had thawed, Michael, two packs of Marlboro in his hand, hailed a taxi and told the driver to take him to the address on Solyanka Street.

Once in the changing-room the returning patrons entered into the discord unlocked by *glasnost* with renewed vigour, finding to their satisfaction that a new element had entered hostilities – the Volga German Republic.

When the Lithuanian stated unwisely that he had never heard of it a newcomer from the sprawling republic of Kazakhstan waved a copy of *Frankfurter Allgemeine* on which he had underlined a headline RUSSIA'S GERMANS WILL NO LONGER BE IGNORED.

The Germans, he said, had been invited to farm the steppe by Catherine the Great. Then Stalin, systematically ruining the economy with collectivisation, had also ruined their self-sufficiency.

Freed by the invading Germans in 1941, they had been punished by Stalin for their disloyalty and exiled to central Asia where the way of life was totally alien.

'Two million ethnic Germans,' the newcomer said. 'What's to become of us?'

'What, for that matter,' the stallholder said, 'is to become of 145,000,000 Russians?'

'What's to become of the Soviet Union?' the chauffeur demanded.

'What's to become of the banya?' the pickpocket murmured.

Part III

17

The womens' changing and steam rooms were less commodious than the mens' because married women, occupied with both job and home, had fewer opportunities to relax. But both were more decorous.

The steam-room was supported by Corinthian columns and the marble tiers were laid with linen which made voluptuaries of even the most amply designed women. The changing-room contained a samovar, two gold-framed mirrors and a pygmy fountain splashed in an alabaster bowl.

On the wall of the changing-room hung an extract from *The Travels of Olearius*, published in the seventeenth century, in which the delights of a contemporary bath-house were described. The steam-room was 'strewn with flowers and various aromatic grasses', And a woman or girl was assigned to attend bathers. 'When an acquaintance or a cherished guest bathes with them, he is looked after attentively, waited on, and cared for. The mistress of the house or her daughter usually brings or sends into the bath some pieces of radish sprinkled with salt. . . .'

Why this extract was displayed was as hotly debated as any topic touching on the role of women. The laundress maintained that it was evidence of long-ago equality among the sexes – mistress and daughter at the helm. The hairdresser asserted that it clearly demonstrated that, then as now, women were the victims of men's lust.

Privately the laundress saw no merit in displaying the extract because some of the observations of Adam Olearius, who had been in the service of Duke Frederick of Holstein, were too close for comfort. 'The Russians are in general a very quarrelsome people who assail each other like dogs, with fierce, harsh words.

Again and again on the streets one sees such quarrels, the old women shot with such fury that he who is unaccustomed to it expects them at any moment to seize each other's hair. They very rarely come to blows, however; but when they do, they strike with their fists beating one another with all their might on the sides and genitals.'

The Fighting Comrades and numerous other women patrons assembled in the changing-room to discuss the future of the banya on January 31st, the day when the first McDonald's hamburger restaurant in the Soviet Union opened in Moscow. Tea was available from the samovar, beer from a dispenser in a dark cavern down the street, blinys smeared with sour cream and mustard-smeared sausages from a steamy café for which the laundress was victualler.

'McDonald's seats 700,' said a slender interpreter with lustrous dark eyes whose ancestors, White Russians, had emigrated to Montreal. 'And a big hamburger costs half a day's pay.'

'So?' The seamstress sunk her sharp teeth into a bliny. 'Everyone's got plenty of money – there's nothing else to spend it on. And they're paying their staff 300 roubles a month. Incentive, that's what it's all about.'

'May I remind you,' said the laundress, taking her place at the head of a long table covered with a starched white cloth, 'that we're here to discuss the banya. If they pull it down you won't be able to steam yourself in McDonald's.'

'And let's make some positive decisions. It's about time the Fighting Comrades lived up to their name,' said the interpreter whose sexist outrage fluctuated.

'Vilkin thinks we've lived up to it,' the laundress said. 'That son of a whore.'

'Because a sycophant fell off a balcony and you got yourself three pairs of tights? What good did that do us?' The interpreter fixed her lustrous eyes on the laundress. 'It seems to me it's the men who have been getting results. . . .'

The laundress folded her arms tightly as though to control a snapping animal. 'One big fool sets up shop in Red Square and gets himself arrested. . . . What good has that done us?'

'The men got him released,' the hairdresser said.

'And the banya is still standing,' the seamstress said.

234

'As much our doing as theirs,' the laundress said.

Tanya Agursky, sipping tea and nibbling a small and obdurate sausage, said: 'What's the point of recriminations? We want action.'

'Well said.' The laundress smiled at her; the young still possess many attributes, the smile said. 'Any suggestions?'

'Don't you have any?' the seamstress inquired.

'I want to hear the others first,' the laundress said. 'What about you?' to the interpreter.

'What about publicity?' the interpreter suggested vaguely.

'We're going ahead with that. We've been waiting in case Vilkin changed his mind. Now the men have charged in – '

'Where angels fear to tread?'

'We don't fear anything. Do we?' the laundress said to the seamstress, evoking glorious deeds in which they had participated when they were girls. Their medals picked up the fractured light reflected from the chandelier.

'We must take the initiative,' the hairdresser said. 'The men will ruin everything.'

They all looked at the laundress. 'We mustn't be too hasty,' she said, fortifying suspicions that she was holding an impoverished hand. She was saved by the interpreter who worked for UPDK, the State agency that, among other services, provided translators for foreigners. 'Do we really want to keep the banya?' she asked.

The little fountain splashed prettily and the silence quivered around it.

The hairdresser was the first to speak. 'What has Vilkin done for you?' she asked.

'That little lavatory rat? I want more than a moustache the size of a postage-stamp to tickle my fancy.' She appeared unconcerned by the heresy she had just uttered. 'This place is old, run down, falling apart. Why should we stay here? Supposing they do build a new store. Supposing they install a sauna underneath it with cubicles and a splash pool and a stylish salon. . . .'

'She *has* been talking to Vilkin,' the hairdresser said and the seamstress said: 'The banya is history,' and Tanya Agursky said: 'It's home,' and the laundress smiled upon her once more.

'What makes you think they'll provide a sauna?' the hair-dresser demanded. 'Has Vilkin said so?'

'Just a thought,' the interpreter said, licking sour cream from her fingers. 'If we agreed to let the banya be knocked down provided a sauna is installed. . . .'

They drank tea and beer, coughed, rustled papers and conferred privately. Petitions, rallies, demonstrations? But whenever you watched television you saw riots – water-cannon, tear-gas, rubber bullets. . . . Only slaughter seemed to be effective in these days of far-flung and unrelated anarchy and a banya scarcely merited that.

Inevitably the debate embraced the men. What were they plotting to exploit in a chauvinistic society where, although women laboured unremittingly men got all the pickings? Whatever it might be it would be unilateral and sly.

When the blinys and sausages had all been despatched and the jugs were dry the seamstress went down the street for more beer. In the silence that lingered after her the laundress maintained a magisterial calm that aroused hopes that she might still have a card or two left to play.

'I suppose,' said the seamstress, entering with two brimming jugs, 'that we could petition the President.'

'You don't think he has enough on his mind?' the interpreter inquired but the laundress, visibly relaxing, nodded approvingly. 'At last you're being constructive,' she said.

'You think it's a good idea?' Frowning, the seamstress poured herself beer.

'A step in the right direction.'

'You can't step much higher,' the hairdresser said, reaching for a jug.

'Can't you?'

'God?' The interpreter narrowed her shining eyes. 'He has a few things on his mind, too.'

'Think,' commanded the laundress, dispelling suspicions that whatever she was contemplating had been suggested by the seamstress. 'Think as women. . . .'

Tanya Agursky got it first. 'The President's wife?'

'Who else?'

The laundress unfolded her arms and stood up. 'And now,' she said, 'I have to attend to two more casualties of *perestroika*

236

– sugar and flour.' Magnanimously she nodded towards those who might have doubted her. 'Don't worry, none of you will go short.'

The photographic studio was on the ground floor of an old building where salt had once been stored. Like many shops in Moscow it didn't advertise its presence – the window was grimy and the only visible wares were two antique, fold-up cameras. Michael pushed open the door; a bell jangled above him, its cracked notes losing themselves in the dusky interior. He waited. A cat materialised from the depths and pushed itself against his legs. Somewhere a clock ticked loudly. He opened and shut the door again; the bells clattered more loudly as though the previous outing had shaken the dust from them. A light appeared in the wings of the gloom. Footsteps measured and fatigued. 'Who is it?' A woman's voice faintly outraged at an unwarranted intrusion.

'A customer.'

The voice grumbled. Another light came on lighting up a history of photography. A camera on a tripod with a black hood attached, a movie camera labelled Mosfilms and trailing coils of film, boxes of photographic plates, a blistered panorama of Moscow taken from the Lenin Hills, a box of light-meters and lenses and, at the back of it all, studio props – half a row-boat, a wooden clown with a hole instead of a face for the subject's head, a stiff-backed chair beside a table on which stood a portrait of Stalin.

The woman emerged as though, Michael thought, she had been sitting among the props waiting for someone to call. She was in her sixties, dressed in black, with abundant grey hair and an indoor complexion; her features had an unrequited set to them, her head a tilt that might once have been flirtatious.

She inspected and, he felt, dismissed him. 'What can I do for you?' she asked, gazing over his shoulder.

'Have you worked here a long time?'

'All my life.' She toyed with a silver locket hanging from her neck. 'But I have a poor memory.'

'I'm sorry?'

'Gorky's slums are down the street, the silversmiths' church, Trinity, is round the corner.'

'I think we're at cross-purposes. . . .'

'You're not a tourist?'

'I *am* looking for information. I'm a lawyer. Do your records go back a long way?'

She brought him back into focus. 'For ever,' she said.

'The Great Patriotic War?'

'Even as far as that.'

'But you would only have been a baby.' He had long ago ceased to be ashamed of transparent flattery.

'I was sixteen when the Germans attacked Moscow. I'm sure you're aware that I wasn't in my cot. Now what do you want?'

Michael took his wallet from his hip pocket. 'I found a photograph; it had the name of your studio stamped on the back.'

'Let me see it please.'

He handed her the photograph.

She held it away from her in the manner of people who don't acknowledge failing eyesight. Her hand shook a little and when she spoke her voice had acquired immediacy. 'Where did you get this?'

He told her about the old man's chest. 'His name was Vlasov. Did you know him?'

'Was?'

'He's dead,' Michael told her. 'Poisoned himself with moonshine.'

'I have never heard of him,' she said and Michael knew with the weary instincts of the interrogator that she was lying. With professional diffidence he began to cross-examine.

'He was an old man. You can't really be sure, can you.'

'I don't remember ever knowing anyone of that name.'

'But you must have had thousands of customers in this studio. Can you remember all their names?'

'Why do you want to know?'

'I didn't catch your name,' he said.

'I didn't give it to you.'

'Yelena Orlova?' glancing at a scattering of unopened correspondence on the dusty counter.

'Look,' she said, 'I didn't know this old man – '

238

'But you did know him?' picking up the photograph hoping to catch her by surprise.

'This is ridiculous,' she said. 'That picture was taken fifty years ago. It isn't even in the studio.'

'What's he holding?'

'I don't know what he's holding,' she said.

'You said you were sixteen.'

'Just.'

'Just? You mean you remember the month the photograph was taken?'

'I'm sorry, I can't help you, Comrade – '

'Cooper – I'm American. Look, I'm sorry I'm so persistent. But it could be very important to me.'

'The old man must have had records. Try the State Statistical Service.'

'I have,' Michael lied. 'As far as they're concerned he didn't exist.'

'He existed all right.'

'But you've never heard of him. . . .'

'There *was* a body, wasn't there?'

'Was the young man in the photograph Vlasov's son?'

'No,' she said.

They stared at each other and the ticking of the clock seemed to grow louder.

'You tricked me,' she said.

'Why are you lying? Please tell me. Then I won't ask any more questions. I promise.'

'Why is it so important to you, Comrade Cooper?'

Michael turned and faced the jury. 'Because the young man in the photograph is my brother.'

The room upstairs was stuffed with the years. Chaise longue covered in green satin, upright piano with keys the colour of old tusks, stuffed Siberian tiger snarling at its long-ago fate, polished turtle shell, puppet with leering eyes, bird-cage, leaning piles of sheet music, half a dozen copies of a *Guide to the Great Siberian Railway* published in 1900 by the Ministry of Ways and Communications and printed in St Petersburg.

The old man sitting in an upright chair, arthritic hands clasped on the handle of an ebony cane, seemed to have been deposited there in the same haphazard way as the other antiques. His eyes were cloudy with cataracts, the flesh hung loosely on his face.

'My father,' said Yelena Orlova including him with the Siberian tiger. 'He will help you. He lives in the past – he's more comfortable there and he can remember what happened in 1941 better than what happened last night.'

'Of course he can. Why should he want to remember what happened last night?' Michael looked at the studio portraits on the walls; they possessed a glossy and private youth of their own. 'I thought *you* would be able to help me. You recognised my brother – I saw it in your eyes.'

'What did they do, leap out on organ stops?'

'You knew him, didn't you?'

'My father must have photographed him.'

Her father, scalp liver-spotted beneath his white, rationed hair, looked at the photograph and said: 'Outside the old orphanage. It became a barracks. Lots of the youngsters joining the Red Army or the Communist Battalions wanted to be photographed there.'

'You knew this young man?'

The old man looked vague. 'He was one of many. They all wanted their pictures taken in case they died. Then they gave one to their mother and one to their girl.'

'Do you have records?'

'There were too many of them. They picked up their pictures and ran. To make love to their girls before fighting the Germans.'

'He looks,' said Michael, examining the photograph, 'as though he knew who was taking the picture.'

'I was one of the last people they saw before dying.'

'He's holding the fin of a bomb.'

'They all held a fin of a bomb: it was one of my props. I see them still,' he said, 'through a view-finder. And Yelena as a girl. . . .'

'You didn't take many pictures of me,' she said. 'I wasn't important: I wasn't the flower of Soviet manhood.'

'You speak,' Michael said to the old man, 'as though they all died.'

'Not all of them. But they took their photographs with them and I didn't see them again.'

'Would this young man,' holding up the photograph, 'have fought in the Communist Battalions?'

The old man peered at it. 'Probably – he looks too young for the army.'

'Did many of them survive?' Michael asked Yelena Orlova.

'Of course. Moscow survived. But don't you see, we can't help you.'

You can, Michael thought. The emphasis was too heavy.

She said to her father: 'Comrade Cooper thinks this young man is his brother.' She spoke loudly although his hearing didn't seem to be impaired.

'Does he?' The intelligence left him unmoved; his chin sank towards his hands clasped on the handle of the cane. 'You're American?'

'I don't know what I am,' Michael told him. 'I was born in America.'

'The land of the free. . . . Soon we, too, will be free. But will we know what to do with freedom? It's a luxury and we mustn't over-indulge in it.'

'He'll be having his supper soon,' Yelena Orlova said as though it might tranquillise him. 'Boiled chicken,' she said to her father.

'I had that last night.'

'You're lucky to have anything – the market was bare. That's free enterprise for you,' she said to Michael. 'Give me back the bad old days.'

She sat upright on the chaise longue, stiff with challenge.

Michael said: 'But there is only the present. The past is a scrap-book.'

'The past is the present,' she retorted.

'And that's where you live?'

'I have had to look after my father. . . .' She spoke about him as many people speak about the aged – as though they aren't there.

Michael, continuing his cross-examination, said: 'Don't you prefer to live in the past?' and when she replied vehemently that she didn't he felt that he was approaching a dusty truth.

'Does the name Vysotsky mean anything to you?'

241

'Should it?'

Too brisk. Anticipated.

'Vasily Vysotsky.' Her father uttered the name with vague incredulity.

Michael turned to him excitedly. 'You remember him?'

'Just the name. An echo.' His knuckles shone bone-white on the cane.

'Why should it echo?'

'Because the name was uttered here,' the old man said.

'His mind wanders,' Yelena Orlova said but there was resignation in her tone.

'In what context?'

'Bombs,' the old man said. 'Gunfire. . . . I lost my wife, Yelena's mother. . . .'

'The name,' Michael said. *Brutal*, the jury would decide. 'Why do you remember the name?'

'It was part of that time. Before Yelena's mother was killed in an air-raid.'

'A friend of Yelena?'

Yelena Orlova stood up and, navigating the inanimate past, crossed the room to the piano. From the top, amid a clutter of portraits, she selected a picture of Emil Gilels, its silver frame more conscientiously tended than any of the others. Could Gilels have played on this relic? She undid the clasps at the back of the frame, removed a square of thin plywood and withdrew another photograph.

Michael was in the Federal District Court and the case was his: the photograph was identical to the photograph in his hand.

And now Yelena Orlova talked filling Michael's mind with images of Moscow in the spring of 1941.

Winter had melted and fled precipitiously and the boulevards were burgeoning. Wooden houses steamed in the sun after fleeting showers; sweating *kvas* vendors dispensed their cordial; children blossomed into the white shirts, pinafores and red sashes of the Young Pioneers and paraded exuberantly; the crab apples blossomed in the gardens opposite the Bolshoi and

242

in Gorky Park, on the banks of the slumbrous River Moskva, fortune-tellers sold prophecies to blissful lovers.

Yelena met Vasily outside the banya, while she was waiting for her father who had been photographing a group of patrons conscripted into the Red Army. Vasily, whose father was one of the conscripts, was idling in the sunshine beside a *kvas* van. He had one kopek in his pocket and he bought a mug of cordial; to her surprise he handed the mug, chained to the van, to her. They shared the drink and that evening hired bicycles and rode round Sokolniki Park where aristocrats had once paraded in their carriages. He showed her how accurately he could shoot at the gallery there – rifles, like the mug, on chains – and escorted her home by tram-car.

The next date was less ambitious because, being only an apprentice tool-maker, he was broke. They walked beside the mossy lakes in Gorky Park, fed the black swans and watched a puppet show. At dusk he kissed her under a rowan tree. It was the first time she had been kissed by a boy.

Silence expanded in the over-stuffed room. The old man grumbled for his supper and Yelena Orlova fetched a plate of boiled chicken, potatoes and woody carrot from the kitchen. The old man ate noisily, depositing chewed fibres of carrot on the side of the plate.

'What was my brother really like?' Michael asked.

'He was romantic,' Yelena Orlova said. 'But without realising it. That mole on his cheek. . . . With him everything was spontaneous. That kiss. . . . He would buy me a bunch of violets with his last kopek. And he was a wonderful mimic. But there was a darker side to him; sometimes he became very quiet and I used to be frightened that he was going to say he didn't want to see me anymore. But then I realised that it was just frustration. Not sexual, you understand – fulfilment. You see Vasily wanted to be a warrior not a tool-maker and he wanted a cause just as the Bolsheviks once had a cause. But there wasn't one, was there? Instead there was repression and mediocrity. I sometimes think that if it hadn't been for the Great Patriotic War *glasnost* would have happened much earlier. It was the war, you see, that made people worship Stalin again. . . . Whenever Vasily had a little money he took me to the shooting range in Sokolniki Park and when he shot well, which was almost always, he would be full of high spirits again, skipping along the paths with his arm round my waist. . . .'

The old man handed her the tray. 'Don't forget my tea,' he said. She took the tray into the kitchen and when she returned with the tea she struck a few cracked notes of Alexandrov's *Sacred War* on the piano.

Michael said: 'If he wanted to be a warrior he could have joined the Red Army, couldn't he? As a cadet?'

'He was nearly seventeen,' Yelena Orlova said. 'But that wasn't the point. The factory where he was learning his trade was being converted to munitions. You see, even though the German invasion was a shock, they knew in the Kremlin that, sooner or later, the Soviet Union and Germany would go to war – that was why men like your father were conscripted. But the men and women making the weapons for that war had to be exempt from military service. A young warrior who wanted to use weapons reduced to making them. . . . Ironic wasn't it. That's why he pretended he had tuberculosis and was unfit to join the army. His job was too humiliating.'

'Odd to think that my brother wanted to be a fighter,' Michael said.

'But you're a fighter: you're a lawyer. You found your fulfilment. Given the same circumstances you would have reacted the same way Vasily did.' She touched her hair fussily the way a girl does before going on a date.

'How did he react when Germany and Russia finally went to war in June?'

'He was shocked, of course. We all were – we had been cosseted by the non-aggression pact between Hitler and Stalin. We heard about it on the radio from Molotov. I can remember one sentence in particular "This unheard-of attack on our country is an unparalleled act of perfidy in the history of civilised nations" because I asked my parents what "perfidy" meant.

'I don't think anyone in Moscow, apart from the Kremlin leaders, understood how serious the invasion was. We certainly didn't know that within a week the Germans had advanced

244

nearly 300 miles. And in any case hadn't Molotov assured us that the enemy would be smashed? "Victory will be ours," he had said. And Stalin hadn't made any statement. Could it really be that serious? Do you know how long it took Stalin to tell us the truth? Twelve days. . . . And even then we forgave him because he spoke to us with affection. "Comrades, citizens, brothers and sisters. . . . I am speaking to you, my friends." Friends!' And even now there was wonderment in her voice. 'Yes, we worshipped him that day, the tyrant that Khrushchev raised from his grave.'

Michael, unsure whether even now she regarded Stalin as hero or despot, but anxious to know about his brother, urged her on. 'Were you with Vasily when you heard Stalin broadcast?'

'Here in this room. We had illegally kept a wireless – all sets should have been handed over to the militia in case we listened to German propaganda. My father was at the barracks down the street photographing recruits in their new uniforms.' She picked up her photograph of Vasily and studied it. 'I'm sorry to be taking so long; you see it's the first time I've spoken like this about those days. The first time for fifty years. . . .'

'I understand,' Michael said.

Vasily, she said, had been morbidly excited by the speech. He had found a map of the Soviet Union in an old copy of *Pravda* and had with an indelible pencil – she could still see the stains on the tip of his tongue – filled in the territories which Stalin said had been captured by Germans. Swathes of western Ukraine and Byelorussia, the whole of Lithuania, parts of Latvia. . . . On the names of cities that had been bombed – Kiev, Murmansk, Odessa and Sebastopol among them – he had slashed purple crosses. And all I'm doing is making rifle bolts, he had said, staring at the map.

Sitting beside each other on the chaise longue – 'Pink in those days and holed with cigarette burns' – they had continued to listen to Stalin telling the Soviet people in his thick Georgian accent what they had to do.

Scorched-earth policy – not leaving behind a shred of anything that could be used by the enemy, 'not a single pound of grain, a single gallon of fuel'.

Partisan warfare – And it was here, Yelena Orlova said, fingers

245

searching for cigarette burns that had been mended long ago, that Vasily had become agitated, clenching and unclenching his hands. In occupied areas, said Stalin with measured deliberation, roads, bridges, telephone and telegraph wires had to be blown up, enemy stores and convoys destroyed. 'Intolerable conditions' had to be created.

Scared, she had distanced herself from the frustrated young warrior beside her.

Then Stalin, with a reference to 'the insolent enemy', had talked about the formation of a home guard in cities such as Moscow and Leningrad, anywhere threatened by the Germans. A force recruited from the workers. . . . Then Vasily had smiled fiercely and, cautiously, she had edged closer to him. 'All the strength of the people must be used to smash the enemy. Onward to victory!'

'I honestly thought,' Yelena Orlova said, 'that Vasily was going to stand up and salute. I had never seen him so moved, so proud. . . .'

Her father said: 'Switch the television on, Yelena. It's football. Dynamo Moscow v. Dynamo Kiev.'

She switched on the black-and-white set, keeping the volume low.

'So what happened then?' asked Michael.

'Nothing much,' her tone so anti-climactic that he knew that, although she wasn't lying, she wasn't stitching in the embroidery of total truth. He also knew from court-room experience that it would be injudicious to pursue this line of questioning. 'Did you go out that day?' he asked. 'What day was it?'

'July the third. When my father came back Vasily and I went for a walk. Crossed the river on Ustinsky Bridge and strolled towards the centre of the city. You could hear everyone talking about Stalin's speech and you could feel their emotion. He was going to be their saviour and they loved him despite everything that had gone before. Hadn't all that been for the best, the purges, the collectivisation?'

Her father said: 'Kiev have scored; put the sound up a bit, there's a dear.'

When she didn't respond Michael switched up the volume and learned that it was Moscow who had scored.

Moscow, she said, was still an agreeable city in which to live

246

at the beginning of July, 1941. Word had it that the Germans had taken a beating at Smolensk, food and drink was still readily available – chocolates, even, in confectionery shops in Gorky Street – and the workers in essential industries were flocking to join the *opolchenye*, the home guard. But Vasily couldn't be spared from the factory.

On July 21st the Germans launched their first air-raid on the city. Search-lights switched across the sky; shrapnel from anti-aircraft guns clattered onto roof-tops. Ten days later there was another raid; it wasn't effective but one hundred people died when a bomb scored a direct hit on a shelter in Arbat Square. 'That day my father took Vasily's photograph in the doorway of the barracks even though he wasn't joining the Red Army. This man Vlasov was a friend of your parents; they gave him a copy.'

On September 30th, with Leningrad in a state of siege and the Soviet armies reeling, the Germans launched their first offensive against Moscow. By October 16th they were at the gates. The situation, Yelena Orlova said, was worse than they had ever dreamed it could be.

'And Vasily?' Michael urged as Dynamo Kiev equalised.

'He was a young man possessed,' she said. 'Most of the factories had been shifted from Moscow to the Urals, or even further east to Siberia, to be re-constructed in the snow and ice. What those construction workers did,' she said, 'was just as heroic as anything the Red Army did.'

'And Vasily?' He felt that he was losing vicarious contact with his brother and he wondered why.

'He showed great initiative. He was seventeen by then and he presented himself to one of the officers organising the defence of the city under General Zhukov and demonstrated to him what a good shot he was. That way he got a rifle instead of a lathe and taught the volunteer Communist Battalions – many of them old men and boys – how to shoot straight. If they were lucky enough to have rifles that was.'

Her father said: 'It was the mud that beat the Germans. Mud, *katyusha* rockets, T-34 tanks and Josef Stalin. Idiot,' he said as a Dynamo Moscow forward shot wide of goal.

'He's right in a way,' Yelena Orlova said. 'The mud was like glue and the Germans go stuck in it before the winter froze

247

them. He fought, too,' she said, nodding at the old man. 'In the Communist Battalions when he wasn't taking photographs.'

'And did Vasily fight as well as train volunteers?'

'He fought all right, sniping from the outer defence line while the women dug tank-traps and trenches. The Fritzes got to within ten miles of the boundary of the city, you know. At Lobnya railway station. Some people said a couple of German tanks actually got into the city – at Khimki in the north-west – but I never believed that.'

'Did you dig trenches?' asked Michael who believed in the value of diversions.

'I used to take food to the women. I remember barrage balloons like sausages and the smell of winter on its way. "The Fritzes are going to love this," we said when the first snow fell. You see they weren't prepared for it – some of them still wore summer uniforms when, with wind chill, temperatures dropped to minus forty. The grease froze in their guns and surgeons had to amputate their frost-bitten limbs. They were very brave, those Fritzes,' she said.

Michael, suspecting that she was on the brink of a revelation and not wanting to frighten her, said: 'Your father mentioned Stalin. . . .'

'November 7th, the twenty-fourth anniversary of the Revolution. His speech in Red Square. Guns booming in the distance, Soviet fighter planes in the skies. Addressing the troops, many of them on their way to be killed. He told them we were fighting a war of liberation, a just war. And he said they should be inspired by the heroic figures "of our great ancestors". Nevsky, Donskoi, Pozharsky, Suvorov and, of course, Kutuzov who sent Napoleon packing. "Under the banner of Lenin – onward to victory!" He inspired us the way Churchill inspired the British. We counter-attacked a month later and Moscow was saved.'

'Did you hear *that* speech with Vasily?'

She shook her head, a neat and certain movement, as she shed a memory. 'Vasily was dead,' she said.

With the tip of his cane her father switched off the television. Whether out of respect, or disgust at the match, Michael couldn't determine. Outside a girl's laugh, slithering footsteps and a man's whoop as he caught the girl.

Michael let the moments rest. Then he said: 'How did you know?'

'I knew. Don't you think I *knew*?' She struck a single bass note on the piano. Then began to slide the photograph of Vasily behind that of Emil Gilels.

'But there was never any proof?' Now the jury would be turning against him.

'Thousands died and their bodies were never found.'

'You checked the records? You must have known his birth date,' said Michael who had never known it exactly.

'October 10th, 1924,' she said promptly.

'And his address?'

'A wooden house on Russkovskaya Street.' Michael wrote down the number. 'It was pulled down years ago. But what does it matter? Your brother is dead. Although a little bit of him lingered on. . . .'

Her father stood up, and, leaning heavily on his cane, made his way to a room in which Michael glimpsed striped pyjamas folded on a neatly-made bed.

'. . . .I was pregnant, you see.' *That day, in this room.* 'And no, Comrade Cooper, I didn't have the baby. I wasn't sixteen, you see, I was only fifteen, so I took advantage of that great service available to Soviet womanhood – I had an abortion. Pathetic, isn't it.'

'I'm very sorry,' he said, appalled at the inadequacy of regret.

'After that I stayed and helped my father.' *There was no other man*, she was saying. *Ever.*

'May I ask you one more question?'

She slipped the clasps on the picture-frame back into place and restored Gilels to pride of place on top of the piano. 'It was a long time ago. Now everything is changing in Russia. It makes you wonder if anything is worthwhile, doesn't it, Comrade Cooper.'

Michael, renowned for his persistence in the pursuit of justice, said: 'Did you ever receive official notification of Vasily's death?'

'He was reported missing, that was all.'

And once again Michael became conscious that, although she wasn't lying, she was omitting the requisites of absolute truth.

In the clock-ticking gloom of the shop downstairs she paused,

249

fingers resting on the handle of the door. 'That rowan tree,' she said. 'It's still in Gorky Park, you know.'

The bells clattered and their discordant notes followed Michael down the street.

Lying in bed spooning potato broth, Robert Hanson worried about the two developments in his campaign. The extended details required by OVIR and the deal languidly proposed by Gordon at the British Embassy. OVIR he could handle – a few more statistics to be added to his *cv*. Gordon's proposal was more perplexing. Who do I know with KGB connections who might be able to find out the identity of a has-been spy in the Twilight Brigade? Finally, swallowing the last spoonful of broth, he called out: 'Lena, could you come here a minute.'

18

February 4th, 1990. A Sunday, grey and unsmiling, the first day of a week which, Great Patriotic War aside, promised to be the most heroic in the Soviet Union since the Revolution.

An end to absolute communist rule after seventy-two years. . . . Even Viktor Petrov, although it was his proposal which would be put before the 250-strong Central Committee meeting the following day, found it difficult to absorb such a heretical possibility.

He began the day in unheroic fashion. Ahead lay meetings with friends and enemies – it wasn't always easy to distinguish the two – and he liked to compose himself with domesticity. He swung himself out of bed, put on a tartan dressing-gown and made his way to the bath-room.

The man staring back at him from the mirror didn't look like a crusader, an iconoclast. His sparse grey hair was ruffled, his sleep-pouched face vulnerable, his stomach, which had not responded to a capricious diet, comfortably expanded. A hungry stomach, he thought, giving it a friendly pat.

Did the deviousness of political manoeuvring show in his face? Long ago he had worried about the intrigue that accompanied the pursuit of ideals. No longer; if he hadn't plotted he would be a lawyer working for a prosecutor in some indifferent little town dispatching drunken wife-beaters to gaol.

And he had plotted consummately, he conceded, as he stepped beneath the shower, sighing as the hot water hit the muscles below his neck. The Politburo was his; in two days' time the Central Committee would be his if it voted to abolish Article Six of the Constitution guaranteeing the Communist Party the monopoly of power. What alternative did they have? A return to the stagnant past in which the blow-flies of deprivation had bred? No, the restless subjects of his empire wouldn't wear that and the old guard knew it. Whatever happens I have consigned the past to its coffin.

He stepped out of the shower, dried himself and put on a blue towelling robe. Then he lathered his face with an old-fashioned stick of soap and a badger-fur brush and began to shave – carefully because his tired skin bled easily these days.

Was there any chance that his proposal would be thrown out? He cut a swathe through the foam on his cheek. He doubted it. The run-up to the session had been carefully orchestrated. Attacks on the hard-liners by Tass and *Pravda* whose new editor was an ally; an article in *New Times* advocating Petrov's role as President outside the Party, a survey in *Arguments and Facts* revealing that the Central Committee was still dominated by ageing hacks.

And later today a mass demonstration calling for democracy, time and venue disseminated by the media and word-of-mouth. Petrov's slightly blood-shot eyes stared craftily from the mirror above a half-mask of foam.

In any case, who was there to take over from him? Who would want to be saddled with the chaotic responsibilities he had created? No one. Not yet. Not until he had laid the foundations of prosperity. Then, by God, they would be after him.

He shaved industriously, rinsed his face, combed his wet hair, admired the restoration work, winked at himself and descended the stairs with a bouncy swagger that wasn't quite genuine.

Natalia was waiting in the kitchen.

'I don't approve,' she said, 'but I realise today is an exception.' She handed him a glass of tea.

'To what?' The aroma of the herbs suspended from the ceiling reached him faintly.

'To a normal Sunday. Who are you meeting?'

'Linitsky, of course.'

'He won't budge. How can an old Stalinist like him agree that the teeth of the Party should be pulled? He's the leader of the die-hards and he's got his pride; he'll never relinquish that.'

'He could moderate his pride,' Petrov said. 'Succumb to the inevitable.'

She looked at him doubtfully. 'I hope you're not becoming too arrogant, Viktor.'

'Maybe I am.' He raised the shutters on the window. Hesitant light crept into the kitchen. A guard retreated respectfully across the lawn. 'I've got enough people attacking me; don't you start.' He was surprised how brittle his voice sounded.

'And you're seeing Razin, I suppose?'

'Of course. Razin the maverick. Razin the radical. Razin scourge of authority.'

'Do you hate him?'

'I admire the bastard,' Petrov said. 'Razin man of the people. Has anyone ever called me that?'

Without replying she busied herself preparing the breakfast.

Hunched over his *kasha*, Petrov considered Razin, enemy of corruption, rabble-rousing revolutionary who accused Petrov of mis-managing his reforms, of not giving the people what they wanted most – the necessities of life. '*Perestroika* is for the economists and not the people,' he had thundered, his pugnacious, calculating face mauve-blotched by the wind nipping through an open-air rally. Well, it was easy to bellow when you were in opposition. Man of the people; that was what hurt.

Petrov laid down his spoon and said to Natalia: 'Do you hate Razin?'

'Because he said you were trying to make me into a first lady? That I was the power behind the throne. . . .'

'Well, aren't you?' Surely they weren't going to fight on the eve of such a critical occasion.

'You would have done it all without me.' She sat in front of him and peeled an apple. 'Nothing would have stopped you. It was written long before I met you. What else could I do except go along with you?'

He looked at her in astonishment. 'You've been happy with me, haven't you?'

'Married to the saviour of Mother Russia? To the man at the conference table, the man in the Zil, the man in the Kremlin? It would have been nice if you had occasionally worked in the garden. Painted the window-frames. Played dominoes. . . .'

'Put the cat out at night?'

'Enjoyed your home,' she said as the peel fell from the apple in the shape of a letter S.

'Sundays. . . .'

'Last week it was Kirov. This week Linitsky and Razin. You

253

see, Viktor, you've never enjoyed the cosiness of a peasant returning home from the fields and sometimes I wonder which is more important, your life or his.'

'One life is as important as another,' Petrov said.

'A private soldier's as important as a general's? I believe that because there is only one life and it might as well be the one the private perceives. But I don't think you really agree, Viktor. People are quantities to you. Republics, nationalities, ethnic groups, friends and foes. . . .'

Petrov felt confidence ebbing from him. 'I've dedicated my life to the people of the Soviet Union.'

'And your ego?'

'You sound like Razin.' Had she been simulating contentment all their married life? He pushed away his plate. 'What's got into you? I've been a good husband, haven't I? A good father. . . .'

'You've been dutiful and loving.'

'That isn't enough? You knew,' Petrov said measuring his words, 'what you were undertaking when you agreed to marry me. That day in Hermitage Park. . . .'

'I remember.'

'You asked me if I wanted to become President, General Secretary of the Party. . . .'

'And you said "Why not? Someone has to be." '

'So you accepted the consequences. . . .'

'I also said I didn't truly believe in communism. I remember that conversation well; I often run it through in my mind. I told you that communism teaches you not to think and you said something like, "So you don't want to marry a good Party man" and I said, "*If* you permit yourself to think," something like that.'

'I don't think?'

'About the end of communism as such. You're almost as obsessive about that as an ideologist is about the Party.'

'Perhaps I should do some gardening today. Paint a window-frame or two.'

'You really don't understand, do you.'

'I understand that I'm trying to save the Soviet Union from bankruptcy and you want me to plant potatoes.'

'Always *I*,' she said.

'*We* is all right?'

'Better,' she said. 'Marriage should make us an entity. Or is that too much for your macho Russian image?'

'This is crazy,' he said. 'You go with me everywhere, we're photographed everywhere together. . . .'

'I think I always came second to the Cause,' she said. 'A close second, perhaps. . . .'

'I suppose I've been like most husbands, most fathers. The job must come first otherwise there isn't any home.'

He was ashamed of the evasion.

'I often wonder,' she said, 'what it would have been like to be married to an ordinary man.' She took a bite out of the apple.

'Ordinary,' Petrov said. 'Why haven't you come out with any of this before? Why today of all days?'

'Because it's important today.'

'I don't understand.'

I've been worrying whether the people believe in me and now I find out that not even my wife does.

'I didn't think you would.'

'I'm so insensitive?'

'Pre-occupied.' She chewed crisply.

'Is that so surprising?' He astonished himself by hammering the table with his fist. 'Can you think of any man in the world at this moment with more on his mind?'

'No one. But that isn't the point. I don't want you to lose touch with yourself.'

'Power corrupting?'

'I don't think you're corrupted.'

'You're very kind!'

'I just think you lost Viktor Petrov somewhere on the way.'

'I'll go back and drag him from the gutter.'

'Don't be stupid and dramatic.' She took another bite from the apple.

'I don't understand,' he said again. 'I really don't.' Or did he? 'Why today? That's what I really don't understand.'

'I want you to go in there tomorrow prepared.'

'I am prepared.'

'To be truly prepared you must find yourself again. Be a man of the people.'

'Like Razin?'

'No,' she said, 'not like Razin. Like Viktor Petrov. Can you spare a couple of hours before you meet Linitsky, Razin, Kirov. . . ?'

'Anything,' he said warily, 'was possible.'

'I thought we might take a walk in Hermitage Park.'

'That would be nice,' he said.

She took a last snapping bite from the carcase of the apple. 'This is the best thing that's happened to us for years,' she said. 'We had a fight.'

To the south of the city that Sunday morning, in the working-class suburb of Taganka, another man sat at breakfast listening to a litany of complaints from his wife.

He, too, was stockily built and short on hair but he was thirty years younger than Petrov, eyes grey and hooded, and whereas Petrov listened with incredulity Leonid Lysenko heard out his spouse with despair.

Of course she was right. Why should they live in a two-roomed apartment in a seedy block within sight of modern high-rise when he was one of the State employees responsible for the safety of Party VIPs? Why should he and his wife sleep on a makeshift bed in the living-room because their two children occupied the only bedroom?

'Security guard . . . marksman . . . member of the elite, so you tell me, and we live in a hovel. . . .' Soft brown hair falling across her brow, eyes smudged with unremoved make-up, she regarded him with weary contempt.

'Don't worry,' he said, 'things are going to get better very soon,' and once again his thoughts reverted to the approach that had been made to him three weeks earlier in the pedestrian underpass between Gorky Street and Marx Prospect.

The man, wearing a fur-trimmed coat and a sealskin hat, had fallen in step with him as he passed a beggar with a bowl and Lysenko had assumed he was a black-marketeer.

'Something to your advantage, not mine,' the stranger had said when Lysenko had told him to piss off. '5,000 roubles to your advantage. . . .'

They had adjourned to a basement bar behind the Bolshoi where the stranger, middle-aged with a creased but undefeated face, had put his proposition.

He knew that Lysenko was a marksman. He knew his duties included manning vantage points when VIPs 'including our beloved leader' were in transit from one location to another. What he wanted Lysenko to do was commit a murder.

They walked together in the empty park, once the favourite promenade of the French, not hand-in-hand, but close to each other, and Petrov knew that once again he would be causing panic in Dzerzhinsky Square and that Kirov would have been roused, blinking and vulnerable, from his bed in his dacha. At the entrance to the park guards who had followed him stamped their feet and bear-hugged their bodies with mittened hands. He wouldn't be popular with them either, Petrov reflected as they passed the statues that had been witnesses to their courtship.

He said: 'You're right: when I see myself on television I see a stranger. Razin's lucky: he sees himself.'

She said: 'When you address the Central Committee see yourself as you are now. As you were that day when the snow was slipping from the statues.' They passed a wooden theatre where in the summer small companies played to audiences red-faced and happy with the day's heat.

Then, observed warily by their guards, they turned and headed for the exit. Natalia slipped her hand under his arm. Tsar Petrov pressed it against his body with his elbow.

Glass of tea in his hand, Leonid Lysenko sat in the chair beside the telephone where he could read the newspaper before the children awoke and filled the apartment with their quarrels. In the claustrophobic kitchen his wife clattered rebelliously. From time to time Lysenko touched the telephone; it was old-fashioned, the shiny black surface long since dulled by use, but it was the only status symbol he possessed. It was also the only phone in the block and neighbours regarded it with reverence, speculating what variety of *blat* might have been invoked to obtain it. He had never satisfied their curiosity, much more

257

gratifying to shroud himself in mystery rather than confess it was an ability to shoot straight.

He turned a page of *Sovyetsky Sport*. 'Who do I have to kill?' he had asked the stranger in the tone of a nurse humouring a demented patient and the stranger had replied in a voice of unassailable normality: 'All in good time, my friend. All I want to know now is whether you're interested.'

Interested! As though they were discussing the sale of a second-hand car. To maintain the level of the preposterous dialogue Lysenko had replied: 'The money. . . . How will it be paid?'

'A thousand roubles now. . . .' *Now!* '1,500 when you accept the contract. The balance on completion.'

Completion!

'What,' asked Lysenko, still playing the game, 'if I decide I don't want to accept the contract. What happens to that first thousand.'

'Non-returnable,' the stranger said, sipping his beer without apparent enjoyment. 'It's yours – buy yourself half a room.'

'Half a what?'

'I understand you want a new apartment. Or, rather, your wife does. . . . The going rate to get yourself to the head of the housing list is 2,000 roubles a room. Right?'

'Two thousand five hundred,' Lysenko was surprised to hear himself answer. 'Inflation.' He smiled, all part of the charade.

'So how many rooms in one of those nice new high-rise apartments you can see from the shitty coop you inhabit?'

'It's not that bad,' Lysenko said. 'Three,' he said, 'excluding the bath-room which in any case doesn't count in these estimates.'

Estimates!

The stranger massaged his hands as though he were drying them in a hot-air dispenser in a hotel lavatory. Lysenko would not have been surprised to see him produce a calculator.

'Okay,' the stranger said, '7,500 roubles.'

'In hard currency,' Lysenko said.

'That would be more difficult.'

'Dollars preferably,' Lysenko said – everyone who manipulated currency thought in dollars.

'That will take a little time.' Where was he going, the *Gosbank*, the State Bank? 'And the reward will be less – 6,000 roubles.'

A six-thousand-rouble bribe in dollars? That was worth an apartment on Kutuzovsky! The game had become absurd. . . .

The stranger slid a fawn envelope across the table. 'Count it. Non-returnable. Convertible into dollars if we do a deal.'

The envelope found its way into the inside pocket of Lysenko's jacket. 'Who?' he asked again.

'I'll be in touch,' the stranger said.

But he hadn't been and the 1,000 roubles was still in Lysenko's wallet behind his ID.

The children awoke and began to argue. His wife broke a plate. The walls of the apartment began to squeeze him.

The revered telephone rang. 'He's done it again,' a resigned male voice said. 'Departed from his schedule. Gone for a walk in Hermitage Park. You'd better get over here.'

'Sorry,' Lysenko said to his wife who was on her knees picking up shards of broken plate, 'I've got to go.'

He didn't hear what she replied but he could guess.

In his official Moscow residence, a spacious and fussily-appointed house near the Lenin Hills one and a half miles from his unofficial bolt-hole, Petrov waited for the first of his visitors.

Andrei Lenitsky. Seventy-five years old. Number Two in the Party hierarchy, Number One on the list of Petrov's enemies. Responsibility: ideology. But an ideology that was withering in the winds of *glasnost*. The set of his face was unrepentent but martyrdom had replaced fervour in his gaze.

Martyrs, however, can be vengeful. And tomorrow, when Petrov sought to emasculate communism, Lenitsky would seek revenge on those who sought to take his beliefs away from him. Unless, with Mother Russia as my accomplice, I can make him see reason, Petrov thought as the old man walked disdainfully across the echoing living-room.

'I'm glad you could make it,' he said as Lenitsky, wearing a funereal suit and silver tie, sat opposite him.

'You said a meeting would be in the best interests of the Soviet Union. I have those interests at heart.'

'I know you do,' said Petrov who had never doubted Lenitsky's sincerity.

259

'And do you have those interests at heart?'

Petrov waited while a maid served tea and biscuits. Then, leaning across the marble-topped coffee table, he said: 'We both do, Andrei, in our different ways. You believed in the Revolution and you have served it well. But time overtakes everything, even ideals. It's time for another revolution and I want you to be part of it.'

Lenitsky tested a chocolate biscuit with fragile teeth. 'Can you imagine what it's like to give your life to a Cause? To witness its destruction when you're too old to save it?'

'What I'm proposing is a continuation of that Cause. Communism served its purpose in a one-party system. The Soviet Union needed unequivocal rule. But not anymore. We have evolved: the people must choose who they want to rule. Good communists have the people's interests at heart, don't they, Andrei?'

'But do you? What have you given them? The freedom to riot until you decide to send in the tanks? A capricious authority they no longer respect? Economic chaos? Shortages on a scale unknown since the last war?'

'So what do you advocate, iron discipline, the mailed fist?'

'You have gone too fast and too far, my friend. I fear for our country.'

'Mistakes have been made.' He remembered Natalia's accusations. '*I* have made mistakes. *Perestroika* should have been aimed more at the immediate needs of the people instead of the economy. But don't forget, I was fishing in stagnant waters.' He was safe enough there: Lenitsky had viewed Brezhnev's predilection for awarding himself medals with contempt.

'So what do you want of me?' Lenitsky chewed the biscuit tentatively.

'Your support tomorrow,' knowing this was more than he could expect but hoping to abate Lenitsky's stony fury in the debate.

'You ask a lot.'

'There is a lot at stake.'

'I have to say what I believe to be true. You must allow me that – I have nothing else.'

'Then just tell the committee that you believe I am sincere. Misguided perhaps – in your view, that is – but honourable.'

'And you'll do the same for me?' His smile was wintry. 'A deal? *Blat?*'

'Of course – you are honourable.'

Alone in the house, Petrov waited for his second visitor.

Nikolai Razin. Aged fifty-eight. Member of the Central Committee. Candidate member of the Politburo until his dismissal, Moscow Party Chief until his removal. Man of the people. . . .

'I can't stay long,' Razin said as he stomped across the room, wearing an anorak and fashionably baggy trousers, wave of grey hair looping back from his forehead, face saved from all-out aggression by a connoisseur's appreciation of his own jokes.

'Another meeting?'

'I've got to prepare a speech in front of my favourite audience – the mirror.'

'Where are you speaking?'

'At the *spontaneous* rally later today. Where else?' He flung himself into a chair, waving aside tea and biscuits as though, like Rasputin's dainties, they had been dosed with cyanide.

Petrov said: 'Good of you to come, Nikolai.'

'I was curious to hear what sort of deal you are proposing.'

'No deal.' Petrov sat opposite Razin, intimidated by his flamboyant presence. 'Co-operation.'

'Between you and me? Have you been drinking, Viktor?'

'We both want to get rid of Article Six, don't we? The end of the communist monopoly. . . .'

'I want more: I want to rid the Party of the old hacks.'

'With a multi-party system they'll be thrown out at the next elections.'

'But not you. You've manipulated everyone beautifully. How can a rag-bag of opposition parties get rid of you? Well, you've reckoned without one factor. . . .'

'You?'

'If you don't stop compromising. If you don't stamp on the bureaucratic toads, eradicate privilege, then I'll fight you.'

'I'm fully aware,' Petrov said, 'that your wife shops with the ordinary housewives of Moscow.'

'Which is why I'm losing weight. Are you worried about your kilos, Viktor? Try sending Natalia to the market – she'll come back empty-handed.' Razin crossed his plump legs.

'Co-operation. . . . You mean you want me to keep my mouth shut tomorrow?'

'Muted – in our joint interests.'

'Bullshit. What a beautiful American invention. Can there be a more expressive word in any language?'

'You mean you won't co-operate?'

'Why should I? You need me: I don't need you. And, believe me, if I form a breakaway party I'll pull the votes. The common touch. . . .'

'I don't think so,' Petrov said. 'You see you're just a sniper. You might shout like a cannon but a sniper doesn't lead armies.'

'And you, Viktor, are a preacher. Know why the people have never taken to you? Because even when you step down from your pulpit you walk among your flock.'

This comprehensive truth saddened Petrov.

He said: 'Save your speech for tomorrow – and the mirror.'

From a small room high in the Kremlin Petrov observed the demonstrators in Manezh Square – 300,000 of them, according to an assistant who prided himself on crowd assessment – through a pair of binoculars. Nothing like it had been seen on the streets of the city since the Revolution. Adjusting the focus of the binoculars, faulty because Russians made better rockets than optics, he studied some of the banners. IN SEVENTY-TWO YEARS WE HAVE ACHIEVED NOTHING. Wrong – they had achieved the right to hold this demonstration. WE WANT DEMOCRACY. Well they were going to get it but not at a perilous speed. Whatever happened in the next two days, whatever happened at the Party congress in a few months' time, the communists were still in the majority in the new parliament.

Petrov refocussed the binoculars and saw Razin in full flood. What was he expounding to his rapt audience? The evils of Party privilege? Grand dachas, *special* rations – the special grocery store on Granovsky Street had been closed but the rations continued – exclusive clinics, private aircraft, holiday homes on the Black Sea or the Valdai Hills. . . . That will all go, Nikolai, I promise you.

262

Or, more probably, was he attacking the faltering authority of Tsar Petrov?

Your problem, Nikolai, is that you can't distinguish compromise from political wisdom. You are a naive rabble-rouser although one day you will be President of the Russian Republic to satisfy your ego. Careful, Viktor – see yourself as you were that long-ago day in Hermitage Park.

Petrov made his way through the Kremlin thoroughfares to Lenin's study. He sat for a few minutes behind the table-desk, laid his hands flat on the russet cloth and stared at the scuffed books. 'Another revolution was due,' he said softly.

Then he went into the corridor, closed the door firmly behind him and gave the key to an attendant.

From the third-floor window of a granite block constructed as solemnly as a sermon Leonid Lysenko surveyed the street below. According to the voice on the handset the Soviet leader's Zil was due to pass beneath the window in three minutes time if, that was, he hadn't stopped for a picnic on the way from the Kremlin! The voice on the handset had been edgy; in fact everyone involved in protecting Petrov was nervous this traumatic day. No leader had been harmed since Lenin had been wounded in 1918 – Brezhnev had emerged unscathed when, in 1969, an assassin had fired at the wrong target – but today was as good a day as any for that unblemished record to be terminated.

Rifle butt tucked into his shoulder, Lysenko studied the windows across the street looking for an assassin's giveaways. A half-open window, curtain drawn aside, glint of light on a telescopic sight. Nothing.

He relaxed a little. Why hadn't the stranger in the fur-trimmed coat made contact with him? An elaborate hoax, a KGB test of reliability? He shook his head. No one spent 1,000 roubles on a joke and if it had been the KGB he would have been busted by now for taking the money.

Who does he want me to kill? Lysenko wondered as, two blocks away, the Zil turned into the street and approached majestically. Once again he dismissed an awesome possibility. Not for a mere 6,000 roubles. Not even in dollars.

19

News of Petrov's comprehensive victory was brought to the banya by a Siberian oilman who had been invited to the meeting of the Central Committee as an observer.

The old hacks, said the Siberian who regarded anyone living west of the Urals with expansive pity, had spent three days snarling at Petrov before lying down like whipped curs.

The Siberian, blond with diamond eyes and long-sheathed muscles, favoured the occupants of the mens' changing-room with a look of deep compassion. Only one member had abstained; only one had voted against the proposals. Nikolai Razin, who else? Former First Secretary in Sverdlovsk in Siberia, where else?

The Siberian handed round bottles of *spirt*, advised Muscovites and other less hardy breeds to dilute it with equal quantities of water, and enlightened them about the bountiful qualities of his vast homeland.

The patrons, listening readily while there was still raw spirit in the bottles, learned about the perils of exploration for oil in the north where, in winter, the permafrost was three metres deep, where trees exploded with the cold, where spit froze before it hit the ground. 'Smart-asses are soon put in their place on construction sites,' said the Siberian, striding naked around the room, bottle in one hand. "Hold these", we say, handing him a couple of nails. And like any construction worker with a tool in his hand he holds them between his lips. So when he takes them out what happens? He takes part of his lips with them.'

Before the patrons had managed to absorb the perils of deep-freeze exploration the Siberian had informed them that it was nothing compared with drilling in the bogs of western Siberia. 'We use amphibious ferries, GSPs – they can carry fifty tons – and army carriers, APCs, and hovercraft. In the summer, mosquitoes as big as Ilyushins. . . . But we get paid for it, four times what you earn in Moscow.'

The Ukrainian miner, discovering that the bottle in his hand was also empty, said: 'You mentioned Sverdlovsk just now. . . .' His squat, half-clothed body invested the Siberian's with lithe grace. 'Scarcely Siberia, is it?'

'Where are you from, comrade?' The Siberian sat down and regarded the Ukrainian solicitously.

'Kiev.'

'Scarcely the Soviet Union, is it?'

'Certainly not the Russian Republic. Not like Siberia.'

'For your information,' said the Siberian, 'there is a monument near Pervoralsk. On one side it says Europe, on the other Asia. Now Sverdlovsk, as I'm sure you know, is forty kilometres *east* of that monument. Do I make myself plain?' The other patrons, interest in the wonders of Siberia diminished by the lack of *spirit*, nodded lethargically.

'Ah, Asia. What has that to do with the boundaries of Siberia? I have heard Sverdlovsk described as the Pittsburgh of the Urals,' the Ukrainian said.

'It is certainly in the Urals. On the eastern side. . . .'

'Of a range of miserable slopes as gentle as the Lenin Hills? What about the Column of Tears?'

'What about it?'

'Two hundred and forty miles *east* of Sverdlovsk. Isn't that where the exiles said goodbye – for ever usually – to their families? Before they disappeared *into* Siberia?'

'I don't give a shit about the Column of Tears,' said the Siberian indulgently. 'I'm not talking about history: I'm talking about now. And now Siberia begins near Pervoralsk.'

'I feel sorry for the Siberians,' the Ukrainian said.

'You do?'

'Because of their history. They can't escape it. The convicts, the rule of the *plet*. The Decembrists banished to Irkutsk. Dostoyevsky flogged almost to death because he complained about his soup. . . .'

'I feel sorry for Ukrainians,' the Siberian said. 'Fighting for the Germans in the Great Patriotic War until the Russians won it.'

'Such a vast land, Siberia, to be part of the Russian Republic.

To be ruled from Moscow where salaries are so pathetic. . . .'

'Everyone is ruled from Moscow,' said the Siberian. 'That's what's wrong with the economy.'

'It's your capital: it isn't mine.'

'Nor mine,' said the Lithuanian.

'Nor mine,' said the Armenian.

'Certainly not mine,' said the newcomer with German origins from Kazakhstan. 'Berlin is my capital. What a man,' he said, neat features flushed with *spirt* and hope.

'Who, Hitler?' the bodybuilder asked.

'Viktor Petrov, Man of the Century.'

'What a people we are,' the stallholder said. 'We're taught to worship Lenin, then Stalin. And we do so as if they were the children of the God our ancestors worshipped. Then, suddenly, Stalin becomes the devil. Now Lenin? You wouldn't think, would you, that we could believe in anyone anymore. But we will, of course. As long as he's ruthless.'

'Petrov?' The ethnic German looked doubtful.

'Not ruthless enough yet. He's a manipulator: we Russians need a tyrant.'

'Give him time,' the bodybuilder said.

'Time is what he hasn't got,' said the chauffeur who these days offered opinions as facts.

'What you need,' the Siberian said to no one's surprise, 'is a Siberian. Nicolai Razin. . . .'

'Ah, the man from the Urals,' the Ukrainian said.

'Who do you suggest, a Nazi collaborator from Kiev?'

'If it were colder I'd give you some nails to hold.' The Ukrainian, black scars dancing, hooked one foot under the Siberian's chair and pulled it.

The Siberian fell easily to the floor, almost gratefully, then stood and smiled, a re-incarnation of one of the Cossacks who 400 years earlier had struck east and discovered Siberia and followed its boundless horizons across the Pacific to Alaska.

The Ukrainian threw the empty bottle of *spirt* on the floor. As he and the Siberian advanced on each other their feet bled.

Hanson said to Michael Cooper: 'The end of seventy years of totalitarian rule. You are witnessing the advent of democracy.'

*

266

Excitement at the impending abolition of one-party rule was muted in the womens' changing-room by the arrival in the Dobryninskaya Square branch of Gum of bales of material lavishly printed with flowers. Encouraged by the seamstress who envisaged a whole rack of frocks, half a dozen Fighting Comrades descended on the store from which the laundress had not as yet been banned, returning with a herbacious border of fabrics.

'At least we have plenty of money to pay you,' said the lustrous-eyed interpreter as the seamstress began the comprehensive task of measuring up the laundress for a dress.

'Money? Who wants money? I've got buckets of it. What else have you got to offer?'

'An American journalist I was working for gave me a Michael Jackson cassette. A Swedish diplomat gave me some blank cassettes in return for some favours. . . .'

'Ah, favours,' the hairdresser murmured.

'. . . I took some *samizdat* home and translated it for him and then copied Michael Jackson onto the blank tapes.'

'All right,' said the seamstress, straining to stretch a tape-measure round the laundress. 'I've heard my daughter talk about him.'

The seamstress turned to Tanya Agursky. 'Do you want a dress?'

'I'd like one for my mother,' said Tanya who did not want to walk down Gorky Street dressed like a flower-garden. She handed the seamstress her mother's measurements.

'And what will you pay with?' And when Tanya flushed: 'Don't worry – just let me touch your gold medal when you win it.'

'An historic day,' remarked the interpreter as the seamstress began to measure her.

'Much the same as any other,' said the laundress pouring herself tea and sitting beside the fountain. 'Who cares about votes in the Kremlin? What we want is food in the stores.'

'In a land of plenty,' the seamstress said, 'you would be out of a job.'

'And gladly,' the laundress said. 'They say Petrov is giving himself even more power than he had before. For me Razin is the man.'

'I find that difficult to believe,' said the seamstress. 'He's against corruption.'

'He's one of us; he knows what we want. Bellies full of potatoes, not heads full of ideas.'

Tanya Agursky said carefully: 'You wouldn't even be able to hear what Comrade Razin had to say if it wasn't for Petrov.'

'Well put,' said the seamstress, writing down the interpreter's slender measurements. 'He's given us back the right to be people again.'

'What's he done for Tanya Agursky?' the laundress demanded. 'Is she free to skate for her country? Perhaps she should take her case to Comrade Petrov.'

'I thought,' said the interpreter, 'that we were going to petition Petrov's wife to save the banya.'

'So this is the time, is it?' The laundress folded her arms. 'When she's worried out of her wits about her husband's future. When he's just put a revolution through the Central Committee. This is the moment, is it, to go up to her and say, "Can you please save our banya"?'

'Next week?' the interpreter suggested mildly.

'Don't worry,' the laundress said, placing her hands on her thighs. 'I shall decide when the time is right.'

'Well it had better be soon,' the interpreter said. 'There's a bulldozer parked round the corner.'

The seamstress began to cut the cloth with her scissors and from time to time bright petals of it fell at her feet.

A false spring visited Moscow for a few days and its drip and splash made soft music in the streets. Armadas of cloud sailed in from the steppe, ice floes on the river ran for the sea and it was rumoured that a policeman on point duty had been seen to smile.

On one of these days, when her school was closed because of leaking pipes, Tanya Agursky spent the morning and afternoon practising with Lazar on the Dynamo rink.

As they walked into the melting street Lazar said: 'I think we've earned a meal. How about the Hard Rock Café?'

She shook her head. 'Lev's prepared soup.'

'Oh no he hasn't – I told him I was taking you out.'

'You had no right – '

'I want to talk to you.'

'Talk away.'

'Look, Tanya, just this once climb off your iceberg.'

'How can you afford the Hard Rock?' Lazar worked on a building site but he had been suspended because he spent more time on the ice.

'My brother's got a car, an old Volga. We're running it as a taxi.'

'Pirate taxi?'

Lazar shrugged. 'Free enterprise.'

'I didn't know you could drive.'

Lazar grinned. 'I'm learning.'

'At night?'

'When else?'

'You must be exhausted.' She noticed the smudges beneath his eyes.

'Nothing that a good meal won't put right. Are you coming or do I have to take that blonde who kept falling in front of us on the ice?'

'A pirate taxi and already you can afford the Hard Rock?' It was in the basement of an open-air theatre in Gorky Park where, in the summer, heavy metal called the young and dispatched the middle-aged and elderly, and she had always wanted to go there, even in the winter.

'I had a good night. Australians – they wanted to do the town.'

'So where did you take them?'

'A couple of beer bars, jazz session at the Bluebird, night-cap at the Mezh to give the call-girls a chance. . . .'

'And you get paid for that?'

'Australians are very generous,' Lazar said. 'Are you coming or does it have to be the blonde?'

'We'll go to the Stolishniki,' said Tanya who was starving. 'As much as you can eat for five roubles.'

They took their place in the inevitable queue outside the restaurant beneath the gatehouse of an old mansion and Tanya noticed girls glancing at Lazar's routine good looks and she wondered whether features necessarily reflected character. She knew several young men with growling faces who, when

269

coaxed from their gruffness, displayed unsuspected sensibilities. Perhaps the stereotyped perfection that characterised the male models in *Burda* was equally misleading. It took strength of character to drive a taxi for most of the night and skate for most of the day.

She said: 'What do you want to talk about?'

'Later, on a full stomach.' He took her arm as they inched forward in the line. Dusk was thickening and the wet ice beneath their feet was crisping. 'How's that father of yours?' he asked.

'Angry. He reckons anti-Semitism is breaking out again. A by-product of *perestroika*. Blame the Jews for all its short-comings. That's what he says anyway.'

'Do you believe it?'

'He says he's got proof.'

'You can always find the proof you want to find. Have you experienced anti-Semitism?'

'Only because of my father.'

'And that's only because he creates trouble for the State.'

'I've never understood anti-Semitism,' she said. 'Have you?'

'Easy,' Lazar said. 'Failures have to have scapegoats.'

'Sometimes, Lazar, you amaze me.'

'Because, just occasionally, I think?'

'You should have been born ugly, then people would listen to you.'

'So people with blue eyes are cold, people with brown eyes warm?'

'That's what we're led to believe.'

'The people who lead us have a lot to answer for.'

'But they were led, too.'

'Aren't you excited to be alive today?'

'Of course.'

'Because, you see, we aren't being led anymore. And we're young enough to shake off what we were led to believe. People with blue eyes can be soft.'

Yury had blue eyes, she remembered. God she was hungry. And then they were inside. She sat opposite Lazar who was wearing a suit, dark blue with thin lapels, white shirt with a frayed collar and a grey, knitted tie. And she was wearing a track-suit!

'Finnish,' he said, fondling a lapel of the suit. 'Helsinki.'

270

'Taxi money?'

'My money. Not the State's, not the Party's. Mine.'

'Have you got a licence to drive?'

'A licence to exist,' which she thought was evasive and not very smart but by that time she was tucking into the *zakuski*, herring, pickled mushrooms and red caviar.

When the meat, vegetable and plum stew arrived he said: 'So where are we going, Tanya?'

'To the National Championships?'

'And if we win them?'

'The Olympics?'

'To the Squad, you mean. *We* will have got there together. Does that mean we'll compete for the Olympic Team together? Or will you skate with Yury?'

'Whatever the Committee thinks best.'

'Don't give me that, Tanya. I think occasionally. Remember?'

'Yury and I have been skating together for a long time.'

'You're not eighteen yet.'

'And we have an understanding. . . .'

'We don't? The double lutz? Look, I know Yury is a better skater than me. But I'm working at it. I can be as good as him. With application. And, by God, I'm giving it that. So why shouldn't I skate with you in the Olympics?'

'Maybe neither of us will skate in the Olympics.'

'They can't ignore us if we win the National Championships.'

'But Yury and Nina have been training with the Olympic Squad.'

'So?'

'Yury will have been taught what to expect in the Olympics.'

'But you won't.' He sipped a spoonful of gravy. 'Nina will, though.'

'I can soon adapt.'

'Are you sure that's what Yury will want?'

'Of course,' Tanya said without conviction.

'So you expect me to go on training with you day after day, week after week, to win the National Championships only to be discarded like an old skate?'

'You would be a National Champion.'

Lazar pushed his empty plate away. 'Not good enough, Tanya.'

'Then find another partner.'

'The blonde?'

'She kept falling over.'

'I could pick her up. Then who would you have?'

'I would find someone.'

'Tanya Agursky looking for yet another partner?'

'You're right,' Tanya said, 'you do think occasionally.'

'All I ask is this. You're the best. No doubt about it. Streets ahead of Nina. But when it comes to making a choice promise me you'll compare me with Yury. His natural talents – wasted a little with Nina? – compared with my application. And if I compare favourably you'll choose me to skate for a place in the Olympics?'

'I promise,' she said. Not that there would be any comparison.

Later he took her to the Bluebird to listen to jazz. When they emerged his brother was waiting with the Volga. Lazar drove her home in it and kissed her before departing for the Mezhdunarodnaya, the Mezh, to make another killing.

When she walked into the apartment it was in a state of melancholy chaos. There was a doctor in attendance, a policeman – even though he was in plain clothes, heavy topcoat and tartan scarf, she knew what he was – an ambulance driver and a young man with a zealot's face wearing a seaman's cap – a witness? Her mother was wearing suffering like a shawl.

'What happened?' she demanded.

'Your mother will tell you.' The policeman, pugnaciously built but with features that were not unkind, stood beside her chair like a waiter poised to take an order.

Her father, it transpired, had decided to make another protest. Had been planning it for days, her mother said stoically. Not in Red Square, not outside OVIR. What he had done was tell the media and set out for Viktor Petrov's residence near the Lenin Hills. But someone had been tipped off.

The policeman said: 'Ever heard of *Pamyat*?'

'An anti-Semitic organisation?'

'They wouldn't call it that. They would say it was Russian nationalist. But, yes, it's anti-Semitic all right. They see the Jews as the cuckoos in the nest.' He looked as though he might apologise for their views. 'There have been a couple of killings in Leningrad. . . .'

272

So her father had set off, banner under his arm, for Kazan station where he had arranged to meet other protesters. There they had been waylaid by a gang of thugs shouting anti-Semitic taunts. 'Get out of Russia you *zhids*,' the very worst abuse to hurl at a man who, for two decades, had been trying to do just that. So immediately the area outside the station, crowded with soldiers and peasants loaded with merchandise, had become a platform for Tanya's father.

'According to a witness,' said her mother, nodding towards the young man in the seaman's cap, 'he loved it. Really entered into the spirit of it. I can believe that, can't you?'

Tanya said she could readily believe it. 'But he wasn't hurt, was he?'

'Roughed up,' the policeman said. 'Grotesque but nothing serious.'

'What do you mean grotesque?'

'Your father got really excited,' the young man in the cap said. 'You know how he is. . . .'

'I know, but how do you?'

'I'm a member of his committee.'

'Maybe,' said the policeman, 'if you made less noise you might all be allowed to go to Israel. The biggest exodus, I read, since the Jews left Spain in the Middle Ages. Or maybe the Israelis don't want you? Too many mouths to feed?'

'Anyway,' said the young man, 'your father started to sing *Hava Nagila*. That did it. You know, as though he was mocking them. Or maybe they intended to do it all the time; I don't know.'

'Intended to do what?'

'You'd better see for yourself,' the policeman said.

Her father was sitting up in bed wearing striped pyjamas, beard jutting aggressively. One eye was blue-black and slitted and there was a plaster on his cheek; otherwise he didn't appear to be in bad shape.

'They did a good job,' he said.

'Good job? What kind of talk is that?'

He lowered his head. On his bald patch, his personal skull-cap, someone had cut a Star of David, its geometric triangles already coagulating healthily.

20

Robert Hanson dreamed that he was making love to a girl named Ruth. She was green-eyed and her body was neatly sensuous and she laughed at secret jokes. In the dream she discarded him for another man leaving him bleakly alone; in truth he had met her after the break-up of his engagement and abandoned her when he went to Moscow. She stayed with him in the transition of waking and he tried to re-trace his way through the dream; he found himself walking with her on a beach on a desolately beautiful day in winter. . . . Or had they in fact strolled together on just such a beach beside the hissing waves?

He stretched out one hand and touched Lena still asleep beside him. Where was she in her dreams?

He swung his legs out of bed and opened the curtains. It was dawn, a half moon and a single star discarded in the sky. A cat from the ground-floor apartment walked prissily across the garden; in the flat below Frolov frantically gunned his type-writer. What iconoclastic revisions would he have to make now if Lenin's role in the Revolution was to be played down?

Putting on his dressing-gown, Hanson went into the kitchen and made tea in the samovar, a majestic relic in which charcoal was fired in the centre to keep the water on the boil, teapot bearing heraldic eagles perched on top. He dropped slices of lemon into two glasses, placed cakes and apricot jam on a fragile plate and carried the tray into the bedroom.

She was sitting up in bed, snug and angular and familiar. He sat beside the bed sipping his tea. Had she returned from some long-ago assignation with a dashing lover? When it comes to dreams, he thought, we are dishonest by omission.

She said: 'I'll speak to Andrei today.'

'Andrei?'

'A friend. He may know whether you've ever had a super spy in your midst. But even if he knows I doubt whether he'll tell me. In any case it must have been a long time ago. I can't imagine why the British are still interested.'

'They're like the Russians: they love to discredit establishment figures from the past. Anthony Blunt, Surveyor of the Queen's Pictures, for instance. He was in his dotage before they knocked him off his perch. They're particularly fond of discrediting generals, too.'

'Ironic, isn't it, that I may be helping you to escape.' She smeared jam on a small cake shaped like a cottage loaf and took a bite out of it.

'I won't be escaping.'

'I don't think you'll come back.'

'I'll be back,' not sure whether this was true, wishing that he could be honest, unable to take the risk that his reply might be relayed to Andrei, whoever he was.

She licked jam from her fingers. 'I hope so,' she said. 'We're growing old together.'

'Poor Lena,' he said. He smiled at her, a small grimace stiffened by the frost-bite sustained when he had collapsed in the snow.

'I haven't been unhappy.'

'I wasn't much of a catch.'

'You've been a good husband.'

'In a desultory sort of way.'

'At least you questioned your values; that was something to be proud of. Now everyone in the Soviet Union is doing it.'

Her words pleased him immoderately. 'I could never understand why Doubting Thomas has always been vilified.'

He went into the bathroom to shower and shave. Of the stranger there was no sign. He put on an old jacket with leather stitched on the elbows, polo-neck sweater and flannel trousers.

Over breakfast she was solicitous and it seemed to him that her concern was more deeply felt than the mere fear of being alone that often keeps couples together.

She said: 'I worry about you.'

'No need to,' buttering a rough-hewn slice of toast.

275

'If someone is so anxious to stop you going back isn't it possible that they may do you some harm?'

'Kill me? I don't think so. I haven't any secrets to take back with me.'

'Be careful, Robert.'

He swaddled himself against the cold which, according to the radio, was regrouping over the steppe, kissed her and let himself out of the apartment.

A target for an assassin? Absurd. Wasn't it?

Frolov stuck his tortoise head out of his apartment. His face had the bruised look of a man who has been drinking all night. He blinked a lot but in a slow, heavy-lidded way. He regarded Hanson with suppressed rage and suspicion.

'What am I going to do?' he demanded.

'Do?'

'The Revolution. . . . It might never have happened.'

Hanson paused on the landing. 'They can't take the Revolution away from you.'

'Five years of my life,' Frolov said. He stumbled against the door pushing it inwards. The room beyond was littered with sheets of paper, some crumpled into untidy balls.

'Just write it as it happened.'

'But how did it happen? What makes you think historians tell the truth? What shall I do, turn Tsar Nicholas into a martyr? Make Lenin the villain?'

'Clear up this mess for a start,' Hanson said. He glanced at his watch. 'I'll give you a hand.'

Frolov stared at him wildly. 'You keep out of here. What would you know about the Revolution, an alien?' He withdrew his head and slammed the door.

The old woman on the ground floor, disturbed by the noise, opened her door and winked at Hanson. Fearing that she might beckon him inside, he stepped over a cat and walked into the cold.

Joe Palmer, who had 'something of importance' to discuss with him, was waiting at the denuded delicatessen counter of the Praga Restaurant. Palmer never invited anyone to his home; sinister reasons for his lack of hospitality had been suggested but Hanson suspected that the apartment was merely so scruffy and un-American that he was ashamed of it.

276

'Good to see you,' said Palmer, taking Hanson's arm and guiding him firmly out of the Praga into the Arbat shopping precinct. 'So what do you think of these guys?' taking a newspaper from under his arm and pointing at a story about two investigators who had been thrown out of the Party for pursuing inquiries into corruption improperly. Or too diligently, as most Muscovites claimed.

'Heavy-handed treatment,' Hanson said. 'They've made heroes of them.'

'Wouldn't surprise me if one of them didn't meet with an unfortunate accident.'

'A bullet in the head? My fate in the movie. . . .'

'We're having problems with the picture,' Palmer said with proprietorial satisfaction. 'Clashes of personality. The Mexican temptress has fallen in love with her co-star, the East German – Albert's his name but I'm changing it to Karl – and our producer, the West German widow, has threatened to withdraw her support, i.e. the cameras, if she isn't replaced. All part of the burden a director has to bear, I guess. And Penrose is determined to protect Albert from the Mex's wicked heterosexual advances.'

'Is this why you wanted to see me?'

They passed a busker staring into an empty hat and singing about riches.

'You make me think positively, Bob.'

Hanson, impressed by such a palpable lie, said nothing.

'So what am I going to do?' Palmer stroked his leathery neck and looked helpless.

'Cast Penrose as the East German's co-star instead of the Mexican?'

'I'm serious, Bob.'

'Tell Albert not to flaunt his affair with the Mexican in front of the widow.'

'And the widow?'

'Tell Albert to do what he has to do but to do it in her apartment.'

'The Mex wants him out of her apartment.'

'Tell her that if he moves out there won't be any movie.'

'The judgement of Solomon.' Palmer adjusted his fur hat which was on the large size. 'You should have been a diplomat.'

'So why did you really want to see me?'

'Never try and pull a fast one over a limey, huh? They're too. . . .'

'Treacherous?'

'If the cap fits.' Palmer gripped Hanson's arm to emphasise the joke. 'You gave me an idea the other week. You were talking about a banya, how it typified life in the Soviet Union. So why don't I shoot a sequence in one?'

'The one I go to?'

'Can you fix it?'

'I don't think you quite appreciate our status here.'

'*Our* status?'

'Mine if you prefer it. I'm part of the furnishings at the banya. A decadent shit to be tolerated but not acknowledged. What chance would I have of persuading them to let you film there?'

'How about your American buddy?'

'How do you know about him?'

They pushed their way through a queue in front of a *shashlik* stall. It was beginning to snow again, flakes as hesitant as they had been that day outside the library in Muswell Hill.

Palmer said: 'I read the newspapers. There's been a lot in them about the American trying to find his long-lost brother.'

'That doesn't make him a friend of mine.'

'Goes to the same bath-house, doesn't he? Two expats together – you're bound to be buddies.'

'We play chess.'

'Is he popular?'

'He's a lawyer,' Hanson said. 'He's acting for them.'

'Acting?' Palmer frowned incredulously.

'Helping them fight the city planners who want to pull down the banya.'

'So he could ask them. . . .'

'Why should he?'

'If you have a word in his ear.'

'You really don't understand, do you, Joe. They put up with us here because we don't do any harm. But, Christ, if you tried to infiltrate the Twilight Brigade into the holy of holies, a banya, to shoot a sequence for a movie then they would have your guts for garters.'

278

'You really believe they think that strongly?'

'It hasn't occurred to you before?'

Palmer seemed to shrink inside his coat. 'I guess it has.' He adjusted his ill-fitting hat. 'Well, you know best. Thanks for your time, Bob. I'll have a word with our two stars.' He walked away still adjusting the hat which he wore as though it were part of a disguise.

Give him his due, though, Hanson conceded, Palmer got his banya – in a derelict, onion-domed church in a wooden village to the south-east of Moscow. 'Close to a location where Eisenstein filmed shots for *Ivan the Terrible*,' he exulted.

He enlisted the full strength of the Twilight Brigade to clean the bird-droppings and detritus of abandonment from the nave of the church which he had rented from the Orthodox Church, installed tiers of benches, an oven with fire-bricks and a false, chip-board ceiling.

What part the bath-house was going to play in the unravelling of the plot was as cryptic as the plot itself. When asked to elaborate the Australian merely spread his hands. 'Ask Joe, he's got all the answers.'

But if Joe Palmer did have the answer he kept it close to his chest. 'Trust me,' he said. 'What we have is a basic structure. United States President in Russia holding talks with Soviet President. The KGB for reasons of their own want to see Soviet leader killed, allegedly by CIA. The CIA, for reasons of their own, want to see the American leader assassinated by the KGB. That's all you have to fret about – who gets killed.'

At this stage in the discussion Mayhew invariably pointed out that it would be in the interests of all the Twilight Brigade if *rapprochement* between the Soviet Union and the West was ruptured *de facto* 'because it would give us back our motives'.

And the role of the bath-house? 'Just leave the details to me,' Palmer said. 'Jesus, what atmosphere. Maybe the assassin sitting in it as steam wreathes around him. Gun in the pocket of his coat hanging in the changing-room, i.e. the vestry? Hell no, he wouldn't be that dumb.'

Hanson, who had been made assistant director, arrived for

the first day's shooting at the church, just off the Kashira road, at dawn. Mist from the river was finding its way among the wooden houses beside an estate where tsars had once sojourned and Hanson felt as if he was in old Muscovy. He skirted a frozen duck-pond and walked into the church where long ago sanctity had been left to the rats.

Palmer was already there, striding around the mock-up steam-room pencilling notes on pages of script on a clip-board. 'Hi, Bob.' He shielded his eyes against the glare from a couple of studio lights. 'So what we've got today is a little tension, part of the gradual build-up, and a little romance. Albert – Karl Ritter as I'm calling him in the credits – is the assassin. A professional hit man employed by the KGB or the CIA. Or both. He's falling for the Mex but what he doesn't know is that she's working for enlightened forces determined to prevent anything happening to either the President of the USA or the USSR. . . . At this moment in time the viewer doesn't really know who the killer is. . . .'

'And the romance?' Hanson sat on a second-tier bench and thought how incongruous it was to see mist *outside* the steam-room. A healthy-looking rat whose ancestors had probably fed on altar candles scuttered behind the fire-bricks.

'That begins to warm up in a series of exterior shots. She uses the womens' steam-room – this will have to double for it – and they meet by the pond.'

'A pond outside a bath-house?'

'A country banya, Bob. Don't let's get pedantic. They stroll along the banks of the river – let's hope the mist lifts – and stop at the cemetery. I've always liked cemeteries. You know, those opening shots at the graveside. A mobster's funeral, widow in black feigning tears, extravagant wreaths, a little rain falling. . . . Atmosphere, that's what I go for.'

The door of the church creaked open and cast and crew began to file in. Palmer segregated them while the wardrobe mistress, a Scots girl who had sought atheistic adventure outside a presbytery, handed out sheets to stars, feature players and extras who arranged themselves on the benches while a cheerful Dutchman in charge of effects applied himself to the oven and the fire-bricks.

Mayhew, Hanson thought, looked more at ease in his sheet

than the others, a Roman emperor magisterially surveying the arena of the Colosseum. Penrose looked uneasy, pugilistic face swivelling on the gentle slopes of his shoulders; the Australian, holding a script, disgruntled; the seaman, disgusted with the whole scene. The East German was lazily insular and from time to time he smiled at his own interpretation of what Palmer was saying.

Female re-enforcements arrived bringing with them the smell of mist and awakening countryside. The widow in her ravaged mink, hair more fashionably styled since the advent of the Mexican, a quiet Argentinian, a purposeful Brazilian and the Mexican.

The Mexican waved at the East German tossing errant waves of black hair the way stars do. The widow sat next to him and talked earnestly for a few moments.

Palmer held the floor. He was going to pan from one to another as the steam enveloped them. Albert – 'Karl from now on,' folding a smile – was to retire unnoticed to the changing-room, the vestry, so that when the camera re-tracked there would only be a hole in the steam where he had been sitting.

'Why does he leave?' the widow asked pleasantly.

'Because it's in the script.'

'What's in the script?' She smiled at the players. *I am the producer.*

'He has an assignation,' Palmer said wearily.

'With her?' pointing at the Mexican who was more vivacious than usual this slowly burgeoning morning.

'Who else?' Palmer appealed to the East German who spread his hands.

'Is it really necessary?'

'It's in the script.'

'Not in mine,' the Australian said.

The widow said: 'Isn't it just a little corny, this romance.'

Mayhew said: 'It isn't for real, for God's sake.' He continued to chew unidentifiable sustenance.

'People fall in love,' Penrose said sadly.

The seaman said: 'I agree – it's corny. This is an action picture, isn't it? Not *Brief Encounter*.'

'*The Third Man* was an action picture,' Palmer said. 'That

281

didn't prevent Valli walking out of Joseph Cotton's life at the end. One of the most poignant climaxes ever filmed.'

The widow, voice edged with hope, said: 'You mean she,' pointing at the Mexican, 'walks out of his life?' pointing at the East German.

'I haven't decided yet. I figure characters have to follow their destiny.'

'I think it's a good ending,' the widow said.

'I think it's lousy,' the Mexican said.

'So let's see how it works,' Palmer said checking cameras one and two. 'How's it going, Hank?' to the Dutchman who was trying to make steam.

'The bricks aren't hot enough,' the Dutchman said genially.

'Okay, so we'll test the shot without the steam.' Palmer, who hadn't found an able photographer, crouched behind No. One. 'That's great. A little steam and it will be in the can.'

The Dutchman threw water on the bricks. They hissed and steam billowed towards the false ceiling. Standing beside him, Hanson surveyed the blurred faces. One of them was blocking his exit visa – maybe. One was a spy – possibly. One was an assassin – questionably. Perhaps one of them was all three. Mayhew chewed the cud ruminatively; Penrose searched the steam for the East German; the seaman rinsed his shiny hands angrily; the Australian smiled in despair; the East German slumberously enjoyed the heat. But shouldn't any German worth his Teutonic salt be in the Fatherland at a time when its re-unification was imminent?

'Where's Albert going?' the widow demanded.

'Slipping away like I told him,' Palmer said.

'And where's the Mexican bitch?'

'I'm here,' the Mexican said, emerging from the steam.

'Shit,' Palmer said, 'the steam's clouding the lens. Okay, cut.' Chewing a fingernail, he stared at the camera.

Hanson said: 'I've got some anti-mist cloth at home. For my spectacles,' he explained.

'Okay, Bob. Bring it tomorrow. Now let's try some exterior shots. If the light's good enough.' A beam of silvery sunlight answered him through a grimy window.

Outside the mist was dispersing. Ice floes sailed ponderously on the river and families, staring warily at the aliens, gathered at their porches. A school-bus arrived panting; children, still staring, ran across the snow to it.

'I should have shot that,' Palmer said.

'We have a school-bus hijack?' the Australian asked.

'So where are our two leads?'

'Here.' The East German raised his hand. The Mexican, emerging from the church, slipped her hand beneath his other arm. 'So what do you want us to do?' she asked.

'Link arms, just the way you've done it, and walk towards the river.'

'I still think it's unnecessary,' the widow said. 'It isn't *Love Story*.'

'It isn't *The Chain-saw Massacre* either,' Palmer said.

Mayhew took a cough sweet from the pocket of his duffle-coat and popped it into his mouth. 'Any news on your front?' he asked Hanson.

'Would I be here if there was?'

'Aye, if it were bad news.'

Palmer said: 'I've just had what I figure might be a great idea. Supposing the American President really wants to meet the Russian people. . . .'

'Why would he want to do that?' Penrose asked.

'. . . what better location than a bath-house? The Soviet leader would accompany him and, hey presto, we establish them together.'

Cast and crew regarded him doubtfully.

The widow said: 'Let's try it. No harm done.'

'Anything to stop Albert walking off into the sunset with the Mexican,' the seaman whispered to Hanson.

'Sunrise,' Hanson said.

'She's right,' Palmer said. 'Can you manage that, Bob? A shot of you approaching the banya. A long-shot so that we don't realise how shitty that topcoat of yours is.'

'What about the President of the USSR?'

'He's waiting for you inside.'

'Wearing a sheet?'

'In the changing-room, you jerk.'

'Who will play him?' the seaman asked hopefully.

'I thought maybe you, Tom,' to the Australian. 'Indeterminate colouring, I guess, but we can fix that. In any case you'll be wearing a snap-brim for most of the time. The sort Petrov wears. FBI circa 1940. You too, Bob. Can you borrow a different coat tomorrow?'

After Palmer had filmed Hanson approaching the church, shooting from the doorway, they trooped through the estate, past another church with a pyramid-shaped tower, to the bank of the river. The dark water ran stolidly; ice-floes in the interminable armada shouldered each other heavily.

The East German and the Mexican walked towards the camera absorbed with each other. Whether or not this was consummate acting was not apparent.

'I think,' said the widow, as Palmer filmed them, 'that he's too young for her.'

'How old is Joan Collins, for Christ's sake?' Palmer asked.

'Joan Collins is Joan Collins.'

'You would know,' the Mexican said. 'Your generation.'

The widow laughed gaily. 'You do realise that I own the cameras?'

The East German disengaged himself and threw a stick into the river. Two ice floes ground it into splinters.

Palmer said: 'A couple more shots at the cemetery and then we're through. No physical contact,' he said to the East German.

'Not now,' Mayhew said.

Penrose stared up-river towards Moscow.

They tramped towards the cemetery by the Church of St John the Baptist which, according to the amiable Dutchman, had given the architect for St Basil's in Red Square some of his ideas.

'Just look at a grave,' Palmer said. 'Not too close together,' hastily. 'Symbolism is what we're after. Then I want you walking past the other gravestones. Death, finality. Is there going to be a killing? That's what the viewers have got to wonder.'

He filmed the East German and the Mexican leaning over the railings round a gravestone to which a photograph in a plastic covering of a middle-aged man was attached.

'And now walk out of the cemetery and up the valley towards St John the Baptist's,' Palmer said.

'Refreshments in a few minutes,' the widow called after them.

They disappeared.

'Fantastic,' Palmer exclaimed. 'Nicely timed. I held the shot for a few moments.'

On the horizon, in silhouette, the East German and the Mexican embraced, lips touching.

Michael Cooper went first to Russkovskaya Street. But Yelena Orlova had been right: there was no timber house at the number she had given him, instead a small office block where, behind frosted-glass windows, he could see clerks bent like question marks over their labours. He knocked on a few doors but no one remembered the Vysotskys or their wooden home. 'One family?' said an ageing clerk, straightening his back weighted down with the years. 'In those days they shifted whole races.'

Michael walked into nearby Sokolniki Park where tsars had once hunted with falcons and where his brother had once showed off his shooting prowess to Yelena Orlova. Apart from the exhibition site opposite the main entrance, the park, Michael imagined, was much as it had been when they strolled past its birch trees and bandstands. Although it was in Gorky Park, beneath a rowan tree, that Vasily had first kissed her, Michael fancied he could smell a bunch of violets in her hand.

Armed with Vasily's exact birth-date and the approximate date of his disappearance, Michael then took on the System. First he breached the august Lenin Library. It was not, he discovered, as accessible as New York Public Library. Could the ordinary Soviet citizen seeking to improve his mind browse there? No chance. To obtain a library card they had to prove that they had received a half-decent education. And if they got one they were only allowed to study in the general reading rooms.

To penetrate the inner sanctums they had to produce degrees of truly ambitious erudition; to gain access to its secret cells they had to have security clearance. With the help of Magda and a well-briefed Intourist official – 'Why should the Soviet Union impede a comrade from America seeking his brother?' – Michael Cooper got to the core of the library.

What he was looking for were accounts of the Great Patriotic War which might not have conformed with the official version which was won by the Soviet Union with the grudging support of the Allies who, in any case, had taken their time in opening a second front to take the strain off the Russians. In particular the Battle of Moscow and the part played in it by the Communist Battalions.

He was escorted into a study where a professorial young woman, doing her best to disguise her prettiness with a severe hair-style and a fanatic's spectacles, was trying to relate *glasnost* to the previously heretical works of Trotsky, Mao, Pasternak and Martin Cruz Smith. 'I understand,' she said in the tone of a tutorial inquisitor, 'that you want to trace your brother.' Frowning, she dared her computer to come up with anything to the contrary.

Michael sat opposite her. 'He fought with the Communist Battalions.' He handed her a slip of paper bearing his sketchy data. 'I thought you might be able to find some reference to his unit.'

Continuing her love-hate relationship with her computer, she finger-tipped the data into it, added some of her own, and waited cynically for the green and stuttering response. 'Nothing known,' she finally said with satisfaction.

'He existed,' Michael said, wishing instantly that he hadn't used the past tense.

'Of course. That doesn't mean to say that he was mentioned in any books or articles about the war. Twenty million died . . .'

Michael got the impression that she was very sure of her ground. Why else would he have been allowed into the very heart of the *Leninka*?

'I'd like to read anything you have about the Communist Battalions.'

'They weren't very big. Twelve thousand in Moscow, I think.'

'Someone counted them?'

'A rough estimate.'

'But it must be in print somewhere. You gave a very positive figure. Did someone ask you to make sure there was no mention of my brother before I came here?'

'I have more important things to consider –'

'Than my brother?'

Flustered, she took off her ascetic spectacles and blinked elaborately, teacher exasperated with a recalcitrant scholar. 'There is no trace of him,' she said.

'You've read everything that has ever been written about the Battalions?'

'There isn't that much.'

'But I can read what has been written? Books *and* newspapers published at that time?'

'You'll be wasting your time.'

'I've got plenty of that.'

'You have?' She seemed surprised and, in search of rationality, replaced her spectacles. Her grey eyes focussed lucidly.

'Have you heard differently?'

'No,' she said. 'Why should I?'

'I get the impression you know all about me.'

'Frankly, we're more interested in Trotsky here. I was told to expect you, that's all. I know what you're looking for – I read the papers.'

'But you didn't know I had my brother's birth-date did you. And his address. And the approximate period when he disappeared.'

'I knew you had fresh information,' she said, fingers stroking the keys of the computer in search of assistance.

'So I can look at anything you have on the Battalions?'

'If you'll excuse me.'

She left the room, probably to make a telephone call. When she returned she was tutorially in command once more. 'Follow me,' she said.

She led him to a small reading-room claustrophobically designed for the consumption of illicit reading matter. 'There,' pointing at two piles of books and envelopes of newspaper cuttings. 'That's all there is.'

'Tell me one thing,' he said.

'What's that, Comrade Cooper?'

'Do you keep *Lady Chatterley's Lover* here?'

'My bedside reading,' she said and the lenses of her puritanical spectacles seemed to sparkle.

When she had gone Michael settled himself at the table and retrogressed into a war fought before he had been born. He started with the newspaper cuttings in their desert-dry envelopes and heard the guns outside Moscow.

It was October, 1941, and the Germans were fifty miles west

287

of the capital. The Russian troops were outnumbered, there were no reserves available and there were gaping holes in the defences. But at least the Germans were floundering in mud and the Soviet T-34 tanks were coming into their own.

Michael opened another envelope bulging with yellowish clippings.

There still weren't enough troops to man a continuous line of defences so General Georgi Zhukov decided to protect the most important approaches to the city. The Germans attacked along these approaches, Kaluga fell to them, the fighting everywhere was savage and relentless.

On October 19th the State Defence Committee declared a state of seige. Women and children dug anti-tank trenches spiked with timber angled towards the snouts of any tanks that might penetrate the outer defences; charred flakes of paper from burned documents floated among the barrage balloons; Soviet fighters took on the German bombers in the wintering skies. And the first Communist Battalions were mobilised.

There were twenty-five such battalions comprising civil servants, scientists, writers, students, teenagers previously deemed too young to fight. . . . 12,000 volunteers within three days. *Vasily there among them.* By the end of October there were four divisions totalling 40,000. So the librarian had been wrong there.

Michael found a photograph. Among its seams and cracks a column of women and girls were on the move on snow trampled and polished by marching feet. One of them, wearing stylish shoes and smiling at the cameraman, was beautiful and Michael could have fallen in love with her. If she was twenty then she would be seventy now.

More statistics. Anti-tank squads numbering 10,000, 119 street-fighting units, a total of 450,000 citizens, mostly women, building defensive positions. . . . How different from today's splintered aspirations. That was peace for you.

He picked up another envelope. The beginning of December. Siberian reserves had arrived. Zhukov was poised to counter-attack, to save Moscow.

What had happened to November?

Michael examined the envelope. On the top right-hand corner a number written in ink that had turned the colour of rust.

Eighteen. He consulted the previous envelope. Fifteen. Two envelopes of history missing. Vasily with them?

He went back to the office where the librarian was flirting with her computer. He fanned four envelopes in front of her. Fourteen, fifteen . . . eighteen, nineteen. 'Have sixteen and seventeen been *borrowed*?'

She bent low over the keyboard. Green letters and figures trembled on the screen. 'There is no record of a withdrawal,' she said with the intransigence of a pedagogue.

'You mean they were stolen?'

'Wrongly numbered perhaps.'

'Let me put it to you this way. Would you refuse a senior member of the Party if he asked for some cuttings? Would you ring alarm bells if he took them without permission?'

'*I* would certainly report it.'

Picking up the emphasis, Michael said: 'But someone else didn't?'

'I have just returned from sick-leave.'

'So who was in charge when these envelopes were stolen?'

'I can't accept that they were stolen.'

'Maybe November never happened. Maybe Stalin never made that speech on November 7th.' Michael paced the room, turned abruptly. 'Who was in charge when you were sick?'

The librarian brightened. 'My deputy. She has been promoted. She is in charge of the principal library in Murmansk.'

'Did she take the envelopes with her?'

'That is a very serious accusation, Comrade Cooper.'

'Someone did.'

'Maybe they have been misplaced. We are in the process of putting all our records on computers.'

Round One to the System.

Michael flopped into the chair on the opposite side of her desk. 'The war records here are those that don't necessarily conform to the Soviet view of history. Is that right?'

'Some of them may have been distorted.'

'And so they contain a comprehensive record of the Battle of Moscow, official accounts *and* distortions?'

She shrugged eloquently.

'Distortions such as Stalin's order on November 13th, against Zhukov's wishes, to launch an ill-advised counter-attack. I imagine reports of that were kept well hidden while Stalin was still alive.'

'Long before my time,' she said.

'And Zhukov's popularity would have been consigned to these archives after Khrushchev sacked him as Defence Minister in 1957. That's when the historians really had to re-write the war because his role was "excessively glorified". In other words he was a threat to Khrushchev. And who emerged as the victors, the saviours of Moscow, in the re-vamped history? The Party, who else.'

'Zhukov was re-instated after Khrushchev resigned.'

'Resigned? After he was tossed out on his ear.'

'And he was awarded the Order of Lenin.'

'So his heroic exploits would no longer have any place in your files. Ironic, isn't it, that when someone is justifiably honoured he has no place here.'

'You seem to know more about Soviet history than most Soviet citizens,' she said, a reluctant note of admiration in her voice.

'And you would know more about the Battle of Moscow if you had read the clippings in those missing envelopes. Aren't you worried that they've disappeared? What will your computer say?'

'I admire your suspicious nature,' she said. 'You would make a good researcher.'

'And I'm not giving up. Tell whoever removed the envelopes that.'

'And I admire your persistence,' she said softly, glancing at the computer in case it was eavesdropping. 'Even if it's misplaced.'

'Misplaced? The brother I never knew disappears without trace. . . . Every lead I get is deliberately blocked. . . . Records are removed. . . . Do you really think it's misplaced?'

'I wish I could help you,' she said and he believed her.

Round two.

He went to an old building in Dzerzhinsky Square which had once housed the All-Russian Insurance Company and looked like an orphanage. As the headquarters of the KGB it had once been the pivot of espionage fiction but, since the purported emasculation of that intimidating body, it had lapsed into benign dotage.

He was greeted in a spacious office by an amiable officer with a Prussian hair-cut who, although wearing civilian clothes, gave the impression that he was in uniform. A hussar, Michael thought, wearing riding boots lightly dusted from some clip-clopping procession.

He raised a languid hand which embraced the room decoratively appointed for visitors. Of course he knew about Michael's pilgrimage. Who didn't. He would do his best to help but, really, what could he do? NKVD files? Why not? The secret service was an open book these days, wasn't it? He tested the recoil of his cropped hair with the flat of his hand. But the files were lodged with the militia.

Michael examined them at Petrovka. He found nothing. No more than he had expected. But at least the System knew that he was still a serious contender.

Round three.
The offices of the armed forces' newspaper, *Red Star*.

A former war correspondent named Belov was assigned to him. Thickset, with a deep and unsettling laugh, he was semi-retired and looked not unlike the late General Georgi Zhukov in advanced middle age. In his spare time Belov, who had once been a colonel in the infantry, wrote best-selling novels about the Great Patriotic War, supervised children playing *zarnitsa*, a war game, among the pine trees in Izmailovo Park and trained members of the omnipresent DOSAAF, the volunteer civil defence corps.

One of his most successful novels had been about partisans. He was also an authority on the Communist Battalions, a subject which this morning seemed farthest from his mind. 'The new freedoms are wonderful for writers,' said Belov whose latest work had been published in *Literaturnaya Gazeta*. 'Our pens can breathe – I can even write about the aid the Americans and British gave us during the war.'

On the descent to the basement where the archives were kept the universal dumbness that affects passengers in elevators encompassed them. When they emerged Michael attempted a pre-emptive strike. 'Have you ever written a novel about the Communist Battalions?'

'I wrote one about the partisans in Ukraine,' Belov said. 'Those who weren't broken by interrogation went to heaven, those who succumbed went to the other place.' He summoned a laugh from deep in his barrel chest.

'But not about the Communist Battalions?'

'My knowledge about them has been greatly exaggerated.'

They went into a vault where electronic machinery hummed and murmured in an atmosphere thick with accumulated knowledge.

'All our war records are on micro film,' Belov said.

'Can I see the original newspapers? October, 1941?'

'Why not?'

Belov led Michael to a room where newspapers hung in files, each containing six months of news. Belov found the last half of 1941. Michael placed the file, hinged with wood, on a table and flipped through the pages; he stopped at October 17th.

Behind him Belov hummed sonorously.

The main item was a progress report on the war. Strategic withdrawals, regroupings, re-alignments – the Russians' retreat was more masterly than any vulgar advance.

Beside this report one and a half columns were blank.

Michael pointed at them. 'What happened there?'

'Who knows, perhaps we won a battle.' Belov laughed irrationally. 'Maybe the censors were so surprised that they struck them out.'

'Is there any way of checking?'

'None,' Belov said.

Michael shivered.

'Are you cold, my friend?'

'Stimulated,' Michael said.

'And what has stimulated you?'

'Those.' Michael stabbed his finger at the blank spaces. 'You see I now know the exact date my brother disappeared.'

Belov laughed again but this time his laughter had lost its rich timbre.

*

The following weekend Magda took Michael to Ukraine. In Kiev they strolled along the tree-lined promenades of the Kreshchatik; descended into the Monastery of the Caves where mummies lay preserved in chilly sanctity; gazed along an avenue of moonlight joining the west bank of the Dnieper to Trukhanov Island. And Michael learned more about the ill-starred history of the republic than he might have considered necessary if his instructor had been anyone else. Did he know that Chernobyl meant 'wormwood' in Ukrainian and that, biblically, Judgement Day is presaged by a star named Wormwood that falls into the burning waters of the earth? Michael did not.

They stayed in her parents' apartment in one of the stunted blocks built in the wake of the last war when Ukraine was starved of steel and concrete. The old man and his wife, stepping from the photograph in Magda's flat in Moscow, were neat and contained and he thought how comprehensively we misjudge the elderly and patronise stoic wisdom acquired over the years.

After dinner – Chicken Kiev, what else – and two bottles of Moldavian red wine Magda's father recited the lines by Ukraine's national poet, Taras Shevchenko, which Michael had read that afternoon on a monument to him in a park opposite the university.

And in the great new family,
The family of the free,
With softly spoken, kindly word
Remember also me.

Magda translated the verse from Ukrainian and the words, and possibly the wine, moved her extravagantly. 'The new, family of the free,' she repeated. 'Soon it will come.'

Her mother said: 'Magda is a great nationalist. We never understood why she volunteered to go to Moscow.'

Michael who thought that Magda had been posted to Moscow against her will frowned at her across the table. She smiled at him inscrutably.

He asked her about the seeming contradiction the following day as she drove a black Volga borrowed from Intourist to the village of Bykovnya to the east of Kiev.

She had lied, she explained, because she didn't want her

parents to think she was in disgrace. In a court he might have pursued this reasoning. *Surely true Ukrainians like your parents would have regarded such a posting as a tribute to your nationalism?* But there was too much sharing to be enjoyed on this golden morning.

Why were they going to Bykovnya? She acted as evasively as a courier on a mystery tour, blonde hair skipping in the flow of warm air from the heating system, natural successor to the sacrificial heroines of history.

Presently they came to a village of brightly-painted timber cottages, windows framed with wooden lace, squatting beneath stems of smoke. A blue sign-post urged visitors into the pine-woods. They stopped beside a pink marble slab; Magda translated the inscription. *Here are buried 6,329 Soviet soldiers, partisans and peaceful citizens killed by the Fascist occupiers, 1941–43.*

'Bullshit,' said Joan of Arc. 'They were killed before the war by Russians on the orders of Stalin. Just as the Polish officers at Katyn were killed by Russians, not Germans.'

'Why?' Michael asked.

She shrugged. 'Because they objected to collectivisation, because they dared to speak their minds, because they were Ukrainians. . . . Investigators believe that more than 100,000 were buried here.'

Among the pine trees behind the marble slab Michael saw mounds and pits worn smooth by the years.

'No wonder so many Ukrainians welcomed the Germans,' Magda said. 'Every night lorries arrived in the forest from Korolyenko gaol and the bodies of prisoners executed there were thrown into mass graves.'

'How do you know all this?' Michael asked.

'Because my parents lived here,' Magda said. 'They saw the graves, the blood on the ground at dawn. . . .'

When they got back to the apartment her parents were waiting for them placidly in the past, present and future which are one in the lengthening years.

That day there were demonstrations in big cities all over the Soviet Union. The protesters, flexing their lungs after seventy years of enforced gestation, called for more freedom – in which to protest even more vociferously – and self-determination in their disparate republics. And such was their exuberant purpose that party-poopers all over the land broadcast appeals for calm – even the Church was recruited to preach non-violence – and troops were drafted into the cities in case it got out of hand.

In Kiev Michael and Magda joined a buoyant throng led by members of the new Ukrainian party, *Rukh*. They wanted sovereignty, they wanted their children to be taught their own language, they wanted the termination of Party privileges and the closure of Chernobyl. . . . But what they wanted most was identity and in that most reasonable aspiration they had much in common with dissenters throughout the ages.

Striding down a broad avenue on the outskirts of the city beneath blue and white banners Michael was assailed by his own question of identity. If it was clear-cut – American or Russian – what was he doing marching under the colours of Ukraine? Did he really have to compound his trauma?

Observing Magda, he was envious of her. She was in no doubt about her allegiance: she was Ukrainian from the peak of her jaunty cap to the soles of her purposeful boots. Why she had lied to her parents was less clear.

Where was she? She had disappeared somewhere in the phalanx of demonstrators. The candidates representing these people would certainly triumph in next week's local elections, Michael reflected. But only in seats where they were allowed to stand. What if the Ukrainians, 50,000,000 of them, ultimately broke from Moscow? They were all Slavs but whereas the Russian Republic needed Ukraine the reverse was open to debate.

Michael pushed his way past a bespectacled man with a paunch and an important face. 'Down with the Party hacks,' said the man in Ukrainian. Do I look like a hack in my winter clothes chosen by Barbara in Bloomingdales for winter vacations in Canada? Only a hack, or a crook, could afford anything as remotely expensive and in the minds of the warriors on the march the two were synonymous. He would have to buy a padded jacket and a rabbit-fur hat in Tsum.

He delved into the throng, away from his accuser.

'Mind where you're going,' said a tall man with a saint's face and a brigand's moustache. 'What's the hurry?' He examined Michael's sheepskin. 'Are you going to warn the militia that we're on our way?'

'They already know,' Michael said. He spoke in Russian. A mistake.

'Don't you speak Ukrainian? What are you, a spy from Moscow?' He stopped and a crowd gathered behind him.

'That's a fine coat you're wearing,' said the man with the paunch who had caught up with Michael. 'Party perks? What do you drive, *comrade*, a Volga? A Chaika perhaps?' and Michael knew that in his way this man was more dangerous than the saintly bandit.

'Neither,' Michael said.

'An apartment in Darnitsky, a dacha outside Odessa?'

'Neither.'

'Then how did you manage to buy such a fine coat?'

The crowd pressed the two inquisitors towards Michael.

The tall one said: 'Shit, let him go. We don't want trouble. A crack-down by the army, no elections – goodbye *glasnost*.'

'So who's afraid of the army?' the man with the paunch demanded. He turned and faced the crowd. 'Haven't we had enough repression?'

Everyone had.

'So why don't we throw this hack out on his ass.'

'Why don't you try?' Michael said. Such advocacy!

The man with the paunch hesitated.

Soldiers materialised between cypress trees separating waste land from the avenue. Tear-gas, rubber bullets. . . . Why was an American provoking trouble in a peaceful demo in Ukraine? An international incident. . . . Shit, thought Michael Cooper, attorney-at-law.

Why don't you tell the slob you're American?

Because I'm Russian.

A voice from the crowd: 'Go on, Dima, throw the hack on his ass.'

'Go on, Dima,' Michael said.

The tall man pointed at the troops. 'Don't play into their hands.'

'Give it to him, Dima,' shouted the voice.

Dima took off his spectacles, rubbed his eyes with his finger-tips.

Now was the moment. All he had to say was: 'I'm American.' Instead he bunched his fists.

Magda shouted at the man called Dima: 'When did *you* leave the Party?'

Blinking, he replaced his spectacles. 'What is that supposed to mean?'

'You were smart, you got out just in time.'

'Is that right, Dima?' the second interrogator asked.

'I wasn't anyone, just a member like thousands of others. . . .'

'A Volga, a Chaika, perhaps? Apartment in a smart suburb of Kiev, dacha near the Black Sea?'

'Nothing like that.'

'Throw him out on his ass,' shouted the voice in the crowd.

'I'm not Russian, I'm Ukrainian. . . .'

'On his ass.'

But he was already on his way, ducking and weaving through the crowd, and, because they were ashamed for him, they let him go.

'How did you know?' Michael asked Magda as they began to march again.

'I didn't. But I know the type. Purging his guilt. . . . I should buy yourself another coat,' she said.

'Don't disappear again,' Michael said. 'Where were you?'

'I met some old friends. Dissidents. . . . Why didn't you tell everyone you were American?'

'You wouldn't understand. For you it's clear-cut. You're Ukrainian; that's it. I envy you.'

'Don't,' she said. 'I'm a Ukrainian *and* a Soviet citizen. Never forget that – I can't.'

The demonstration passed off peacefully and when it was finished they took a train back to Moscow where, in Magda's apartment, they made love with tenderness and abandonment.

When he got back to his hotel there was a cable waiting for him. ARRIVING MOSCOW PAN-AM DIRECT FLIGHT SATURDAY MARCH 3 PLEASE MEET LOVE BARBARA.

21

Tsar Petrov. More correctly, he supposed, Tsar Viktor. Tsardom – more accurately Executive Presidency – conferred upon him by the Supreme Soviet by 306 votes to sixty-five. Hopefully to be ratified shortly by the new parliament, the Congress of People's Deputies.

As Executive President, as emperor *outside* the enfeebled Party, he would even have power to declare war. Too much power, as his enemies asserted? Answerable only to God – or Lenin! Another reformer, Alexander II, who had freed the serfs, had only been answerable to God. And look what happened to him – killed at the seventh attempt on his life.

Look what happened to the last tsar, Nicholas II, who had once confessed that he had never wanted to rule and didn't know how to anyway. Executed by the originators of my own dilemma. But at least as leader of the parliament I created – the parliament that will be asked to endorse me as President – I will be able to rule.

And what a kingdom to rule over. Sitting alone in the library of the impersonal residence, Petrov picked up a map of the Soviet Union. Then a pair of scissors.

Lithuania went first. A tiny snip. Then Estonia and Latvia. Meticulously he pared parts of the deep and contentious south but not, in truth, removing the Moslem threat. When he had finished the Russian Republic still stretched from Europe to the Pacific and Ukraine was still there beside Moldavia and Byelorussia. Georgia? Petrov gave it a half-hearted snip.

Then, pacing the library, he ran through his mind a film of the milestones on his route to tsardom.

There was only one of which he was not proud. He knelt and from the bottom shelf took a stamp album.

It wasn't much of an album, loose-leafed and cabbage-green with faded gold lettering on its spine. Countries were arranged alphabetically, stamps attached by folded hinges of gummed paper.

It had belonged to his true friend Sergei who had inherited it from an uncle who, before the Revolution, had worked for a wine and spirit export and import company, T. Denker, in St Petersburg. But joint ownership of the album had been acknowledged when, at times of aspiring debate, it had lain open between Sergei and Viktor, a symbol of unfettered communication.

It contained only a few Soviet stamps which were, in any case, commonplace, and a predominance from those countries with which T. Denker and Co. had done business, France, Spain, Germany, Great Britain, Portugal – and the USA to which they had exported vodka. When, in their early twenties, Viktor and Sergei shared a room in Moscow, when their adrenalin was a flood-tide, virtuous presidents, uncomfortably crowned monarchs and dashing explorers beckoned from its pages and sometimes winked.

The polemics of Sergei, robust of body and voice, were always stimulating; dangerous, too, when aired in the presence of students from the university who hadn't declared their political viewpoints. Stalin might be old and shrinking into his years but his vengeance was still potently administered and anyone criticising his rule was dispatched into Siberia or eternity if, that was, there was any distinction between the two. 10,000,000 were said to have been purged since he had come to power nearly thirty years earlier.

'And to think he studied to become a priest,' marvelled Sergei to a circle of admirers on the river beach, at Serebriani Bor, Silver Wood. 'The Inquisition could have done with such a priest.'

Listening to him, Petrov felt uneasy. He had known him since childhood – his father had warned him about the perils of associating with him – and he had always been the same, always provoking fate. Was it really necessary or was it flamboyant masochism? Petrov believed in much of what Sergei preached but he saw no point in self-defeatism. Reform could only be achieved through application sharpened by a little scheming – the weapons of Natural Law.

'And what has the Shining Sun of Humanity, the Father of the People, to say about the war in Korea? Not a great deal – but he is most eloquent about linguistics, the thought processes of the deaf and dumb,' said Sergei, referring to recent letters from Stalin published in *Pravda*. 'Is he perhaps considering purging all members of the Central Committee in favour of mutes?'

Stupid and unnecessary. Was Sergei in the grip of some suicidal rapture? Was he intoxicated by the attention of the girls gazing at his husky body, golden hairs running with sweat? Or was he just plain drunk? Petrov gazed at the bottles of beer stuck in the sand to be cooled by the small and mannered waves of the River Moskva.

Petrov, drowsy with beer, pickled herring and mushrooms, rested his own sturdy body on one elbow and watched a white pleasure boat pushing its way down the river. Behind him, on the strip between the beach, packed with winter-white Muscovites grilling in the sun, and the woods, ping-pong balls bounced hypnotically on sagging green tables.

'But we will not change a murderous regime by sitting on our asses and contemplating our navels.'

Petrov, surfacing from his reverie, found that Sergei and his fans were looking at him and grinning. Two couples, unnerved, perhaps, by his reckless oratory, stood up and ran whooping into the water.

'Bluster has never contributed much to intellectual revolution,' Petrov said. A couple of Sergei's fans nodded wisely and Petrov perceived sinews of authority in his own words that came as a surprise to him. 'And, of course, Lenin advocated a vanguard of intellectual revolutionaries,' he added with what he hoped was not unseemly haste.

Secretly Petrov had been entertaining heretical thoughts about Lenin. Lenin had dismissed the argument that Russia wasn't developed economically enough to sustain a Marxist revolution. Well he had been wrong, hadn't he, as every moribund five-year plan had proved. And he had advocated elite leadership which had degenerated into the despotism that now prevailed.

But without Lenin we would be nothing. 'Peace, Land, All

300

Power to the Soviet,' Petrov recited. He loved the memory of the man. But couldn't his ideals be implemented more realistically? What was so wrong with private enterprise if it gave back a man his pride?

'Nor has conformity contributed much,' said Sergei, blond curls bobbing.

But revolution, Petrov thought, needs a lot of preparation. Just like a grand master's game of chess. He said: 'Then stop conforming, Sergei, with shop-soiled rhetoric.'

A girl with wet hair and a milky skin just beginning to burn giggled and sat next to him. 'That's right, you tell him,' she said; a drop of water fell from her seal-sleek hair and ran down his back making him shiver.

They came for Sergei that night while, in the garden of a small, wooden house to the east of the city, the girl with the milky skin lay in Petrov's arms recoiling – but only marginally – when he touched her burning shoulders.

And they took away the stamp album.

It was produced at Sergei's brief trial as proof of his degenerate and capitalist sympathies. 'Why else would he collect the stamps of Britain and America?' the prosecutor asked. 'Where are the stamps of the Soviet Union?' holding aloft a page of the album to which three grubby stamps adhered like dead moths.

Petrov offered to give evidence to the effect that the album was as much his as Sergei's but he was told that it was inadmissible. When Sergei was banished to a penal camp in Siberia Petrov presented himself at the KGB headquarters at Dzerzhinsky Square. To his surprise he was admitted – into the presence of a plain-clothes officer with blood-shot eyes and thickets of hair in his ears.

Feet on his desk, he tipped himself back dangerously in his chair and said: 'Stand quite still, I've never seen a martyr before.'

'I'm not a martyr.'

'Anyone who wants to be castrated by a winter in Siberia is a martyr.' He crossed his legs on the desk. 'And for what reason? To clear your conscience?'

'The stamp album was as much mine as his.'

'But you didn't hold anti-Soviet seminars.' The officer swung his feet off the desk and picked up a typewritten sheet of paper and read from it. *'Bluster has never contributed much to intellectual revolution.'* With one finger he investigated the thicket in one of his ears. *'Of course Lenin was in favour of intellectual revolution – something like that. I'm glad you qualified your first observation; it was ambiguous.'*

So which of the students was the plant?

The officer continued reading. ' "Peace, Land, All Power to the Soviet." Stirring words, Viktor. We have peace, we have land and we are the strongest power in the world. Why should anyone want to change such an idyllic state of affairs?'

'The stamp album helped to convict Sergei. We collected the stamps together.'

The officer massaged his fatigued eyes. 'I have some advice for you, Viktor. And that's something we don't often give here. Keep clear of trouble-makers: trouble rubs off.'

'Then why wasn't I prosecuted? Is someone protecting me?' It was the first time it had occurred to him.

'It certainly seems very difficult for you to give yourself up.'

'I want to know who,' Petrov said.

'Perhaps one day you will understand.'

But he hadn't for more than fifteen years. Long after he had discovered that the girl with the sun-burned shoulders had been the plant, long after he had learned that Sergei had died of natural causes in Siberia, to wit: malnutrition and exposure.

How could he have known then that he already had a mentor who would one day become head of the secret police and subsequently leader of the Soviet Union for fifteen short months?

Petrov replaced the album, which he had claimed after Sergei's death, in the book-case. He could certainly have done more to share the complicity with Sergei. Tossed a brick through a ministerial window perhaps, so that they had to arrest him and, at his trial, claimed part ownership of the decadent postage stamps. But that wouldn't have saved Sergei and I wouldn't have been able to wage revolution in my own fashion.

Nevertheless he was not proud of the episode.

302

He picked up a video cassette lying on the table and inserted it into the recorder beneath the Japanese television. Shots of the local elections in which the reformists had won significant victories. He pressed re-wind. The demonstrations immediately before the elections. Banners and placards demanding reform.

A camera homed down on a group in Moscow whose protest appeared to be independent from the rest. Petrov leaned forward to read their banner. SAVE OUR BANYA. He frowned, shrugged and switched off the video recorder.

On the way to the Kremlin he noticed a group of women in brown uniforms walking along the pavement with a militant stride. He lowered the window of the Zil. Above the noise of the traffic he could faintly hear the jingle of medals.

The headquarters of *Pamyat*, dedicated to the restoration of a pure Russian heritage, was a bleak, incense-smelling building to the south of the city.

Tanya went there in Lazar's Moskvitch taxi to find out who had carved the Star of David on her father's scalp. And to find out why, because anti-Semitism was to her the most inscrutable of all prejudices.

They found *Pamyat*'s leader, a squat and muscular actor named Shamarin who had once played Western heavies in TV espionage serials, arranging an exhibition of Tsarist memorabilia. He wore a black shirt and he was sweating in the soupy warmth of the central heating in the hall.

'So you're Agursky's daughter.' He stood back from a trestle-table, laundered napkin bearing a crest in one hand, and examined her. 'Why does that old man make so much noise?'

'Because he's a proud old man,' Tanya said.

'Without a cause. Not even a lost one. Can anything be more frustrating?' He waved the napkin at Lazar. 'Who's this?'

'My skating partner. We're going to win the Soviet Championships.'

'Sorry,' said Shamarin. 'No chance. Wrong faith.' He spoke in staccato utterances and had the stance of a man who was about to strike an invisible opponent.

'Because I'm Jewish?'

'Nothing to do with me. The will of the people. The selection committee. They wouldn't allow it.'

'Crap,' said Lazar.

'You Jewish?'

'Armenian,' Lazar said.

'My commiserations.'

Lazar bunched a fist.

'Don't,' Tanya said. 'He's not worth it.'

'What would he do? Beat me to death with his handkerchief.'

Shamarin held up the napkin. 'This? Belonged to the Romanovs.' He indicated the imperial insignia. 'Found in Perm along with some underwear.'

'Why Perm?' Tanya asked in spite of herself.

'Because that's where the Tsarina and her daughters were taken after Nicholas and his son were executed at Ekaterinburg.'

'I thought they were all executed there.'

'You thought wrongly. They were held in the Excise Administration House. Some say they were killed there by the Jews who stole their belongings.' He flourished the napkin.

'Do you believe that?'

'They certainly went to Perm. One of my family was Perm District Prosecutor. After that. . . .' Sharmarin shrugged. 'They were probably murdered on their way back to Moscow.'

'By Jews?'

'By Bolsheviks.'

'So why mention Jews?'

'To show you the way people think.'

Lazar said: 'Why didn't the Bolsheviks execute the Tsarina at Ekaterinburg?'

'Because she was German.'

'So?'

'Supposing the Germans had won the First World War. . . .'

'Then why did the Bolsheviks kill them on the way to Moscow?'

'Because by that time the Germans were losing the war.'

Shamarin placed the napkin in a glass display case beside an ikon, a chalice and a flattering oil painting of Alexander III. 'He could bend a horseshoe with his bare hands,' Shamarin said.

Tanya stared at the wall where a poster of a Star of David

captioned DANGER hung. 'Why are you anti-Semitic?' she asked.

'I'm not. Nor is *Pamyat*. I know there's talk of a pogrom. But not by *Pamyat*. But we don't think you,' pointing at Tanya, 'are the Chosen People. Nor do we think you should flee to Israel. You are Russians!' He took a menacing step towards the invisible enemy.

'You obviously are anti-Semitic,' said Lazar who seemed to be growing in stature.

'Karl Marx was a Jew. He was also the father of communism. How did the Jews repay him? By trying to escape, that's how.'

Tanya picked up a dinner plate bearing the imperial crest. 'Who attacked my father?'

'Police?' Shamarin placed his hands on his hips defying insubstantial hordes. 'I didn't know he had been attacked.'

Tanya told him what the assailants had done.

Lazar said: 'It was barbaric.'

'I agree,' Shamarin said.

'One of your people?' Lazar took the dinner plate from Tanya.

'How should I know?'

'You could find out.'

'Why should I?'

'In the interests of your exhibition. Some of the exhibits look very fragile.' He dropped the plate which broke crisply into several pieces. 'Sorry,' he said. 'Clumsy of me.'

He took Tanya's arm and led her out of the hall beneath the Star of David.

Lying in his bath with beards of rust beneath the taps which no amount of scrubbing would remove, Hanson brooded on the failure of Lena's contact, Andrei, to identify any British spy who might have retired precipitously to Moscow. Which didn't mean to say there wasn't at least one owner of a moth-eaten cloak and a rusty dagger from Britain in the Twilight Brigade. Hanson could never quite come to terms with the passing of immediacy; how the urgency of defection had subsided into passive ritual.

He lathered himself, flesh puckered by the heat and prematurely loose with age, with a precious bar of soap. Had Andrei really refused to identify a spy or had Lena omitted to ask him?

'*So what now?*' The stranger appeared in the mirror above the washbasin.

'*Advise me. Aren't you a captain of industry, a champion of the universe?*'

'*Go to the top.*'

'*The British Ambassador?*' Hanson searched for the elusive soap beneath his legs. '*The Queen? All I will get is a formal acknowledgement.*'

'*Not if the leader of the Soviet Union has given you permission to leave.*'

'*He wouldn't give a damn.*'

'*He might if you reminded him that it was his eloquence that persuaded you to settle here. Because he realises he may have misled you.*' The stranger smiled with executive cunning. '*Because he and his wife are not novices to publicity.*'

'*And then the British would give me permission to go back because they would sound inhuman by comparison?*'

'*Worth a try, you are coming back to Russia aren't you? After the first crack of leather against willow, the first pint of bitter, the first visit to the Backs. . . .*'

Somewhere in the block a gunshot sounded.

Frolov lay on the floor of his living room amid the brain-spattered confetti of his manuscript. What was left of his inquisitive face bore an expression of mild surprise; one hand still held a heavy pistol bearing a red star and the letters CCCP on the butt. Hanson glanced at the antique typewriter on the table. He had typed a quotation by Voltaire. 'All our ancient history . . . is no more than fiction.' A cat entered the room purring and insinuated itself between Hanson's legs. He turned and saw the woman from the ground floor apartment standing at the open door. She winked at him broadly.

22

Murmansk is a stoic and secretive port of some 380,000 souls planted on the edge of the world – Murman in the Saami language means just that, according to those who will not rest until they have uprooted an origin – to the north of the Arctic Circle on a bulge of Russia shouldering Finland and the northern tip of Norway.

It is stoic because it is cold – toes warmed a little by the Gulf Stream – and, during the Polar Nights which last for sixty days, dark apart from an hour's grey dawn at lunchtime. It is secretive because armadas of the Soviet navy anchor in its ice-free waters in the Kola Gulf of the Barents Sea and, perhaps, because it has had so much to do with the British.

It was the British who urged the Russians to build an all-the-year-round port during the First World War at a time when they were both fighting the Germans. It was the British who then installed houses, nick-named 'suitcases' by the locals because their iron roofs were rounded like Russian trunks.

It was the British who first occupied Murmansk to defend it against the enemy during that war; it was the British and other allies who stayed on when the Bolsheviks suddenly became the enemy.

And it was the British and Americans who sailed there with supplies when the Russians were once again fighting the Germans in the Second World War.

Michael Cooper, calculating that he could spend two days there before returning to Moscow in time to meet his wife, departed for the edge of the world on the night train, the *Arktika*, from Moscow's Leningrad Station.

The platform was a farewell stage – sailors, soldiers, peasants, Laplanders, *apparatchiki* in expensive fur hats, embracing those

307

they were leaving behind. Women attendants at the doors of the coaches checked tickets; smoke from the *Arktika*'s samovars scented the frosted air.

Michael checked the platform to see if there was any sign of his shadow, decided there wasn't, boarded the train and entered a soft-class, two-bunk compartment. The attendant told him he had the compartment to himself but he had heard that one before.

The suburbs of Moscow drifted past the windows, then the impenetrable countryside beyond the footlights of the train took over. In the dining car he ate goulash washed down with wine he had brought with him; indeed there was little evidence of enforced abstinence on this green, night-burrowing train; after the meal passengers sang and swayed and a few wept.

Beside him sat an apologetic man in a funereal suit who nipped furtively from a hip-flask as though a censorious wife were keeping him under observation. He was preparing an article about Lapland for the Soviet magazine *Travel*. 'I'm going to look for Santa Claus,' he said. 'Or should I say Grandfather Frost? I'm sorry,' he said. 'Irreverence, a weakness of mine.' He offered the flask to Michael who poured a little of whatever it contained into his glass of tea.

The writer said: 'You're lucky – Murmansk is just coming out of the darkness. I will write my article in the summer when the sun shines at midnight.' He took a surreptitious nip from the flask. 'You are American?'

'And Russian.'

'The fishermen at Murmansk still find pieces of American Liberty ships sunk in the Patriotic War. One day in 1942 there were sixty-five air-raids. The city burned. So did the people. . . .' He stared into his tea.

'Your family?'

'My parents.'

They were silent for a while. Then Michael said: 'You must use the library a lot in Murmansk.'

'There are two. The Regional and the New.'

'There is a new librarian, I believe.'

'In the New Library. Very able, very lively. . . .'

'Lively?'

308

'Is there any reason why a librarian shouldn't be lively?' He looked alarmed at his boldness.

'Can you introduce me to her?'

'Of course.'

Michael slept fitfully, visited in his dreams by Barbara and Magda, at times indistinguishable from each other. When he awoke the dilatory light of dawn was shining through the frosted window.

As the train forged north the snow-smooth landscapes shrank. Hamlets instead of villages, solitary birch trees. As the afternoon darkness returned frozen lakes glistened with vestiges of orange light and hollows in the snow filled with mauve shadows.

Thirty-six hours after leaving Moscow he alighted at Murmansk. He booked into the Hotel Sixty-Nineth Parallel and explored the city. Trolley-buses glided along streets as wet as fish and new apartment blocks painted in pastel shades trampled wooden cottages under their concrete feet.

He met the writer outside the Puppet Theatre on Perovskoy Street; together they went to the library.

The librarian was as lively as the writer had predicted. And disarming. 'I've been expecting you,' she said.

'You have?'

'My successor at the Lenin Library told you I was here. And she told me you were very persistent.'

The representative of *Travel* excused himself and, bowing apologetically, withdrew from the librarian's office.

'Then you know what I want to know?'

'Shall we go for a walk?' She stood up, plump and pretty with reddish curls and unfathomable eyes. 'Get away from books for a while? Did you know we have more than a million volumes here?'

She put on a long, wolf-skin coat and they walked past blocks of apartments built so that their courtyards were shielded from the inquisitive winds from the interior.

'I don't know if I'll settle here,' she said. 'All they talk about is fish.'

'And the navy?'

'No one talks about that. Are you going to buy me lunch?'

'Fish?'

309

'Better to eat it than talk about it.'

They stopped beside a lake. Men and women were breaking the ice and diving and leaping into the moss-coloured water.

'It keeps them healthy,' she said. 'And kills them off.'

They went to the Panorama Restaurant which had sensational views of the city reclining in anaemic light. She ordered vodka, red caviar – and fish.

He said: 'If you knew what I wanted I'm surprised I was allowed to come.'

She smiled, showing crowded, snow-white teeth. 'You have an influential contact at Intourist.'

Just how influential, he wondered.

'In any case, I don't have to answer your questions.'

'Which are?'

'Ask them, Comrade Cooper. Ask them.'

The fish, cod served with white sauce and boiled potatoes, arrived. She ordered white wine and he said: 'I should be trying to get *you* drunk.'

'Your prerogative,' she said. 'You're paying.'

They regarded each other over brimming glasses of wine.

'All right. What happened to those envelopes?'

'Which?'

'You know which envelopes. Numbers sixteen and seventeen of the clippings relating to the Battle of Moscow kept in the inner sanctum of the Lenin Library in Moscow over which you presided until you were promoted to your present appointment.'

'Mislaid,' she said, burying a forkful of cod in white sauce.

'You can do better than that.'

'Perhaps. But why should I?'

'At least you're honest in a contradictory way. Were they removed?'

'You, Comrade Cooper, can do better than that. I don't think subtlety is your strong suit.'

'Why the cover-up?'

'About your brother? Don't be ridiculous. Why should there be?'

'Exactly. One man among the millions who disappeared and yet every inquiry I make is blocked.'

310

'You've become obsessive. No one stopped you coming here, did they?'

'But you were well briefed.'

'About missing files? Merely an example of slip-shod bureaucracy.'

'So why did the librarian at the Lenin Library bother to tell you I was on my way?'

'Purely incidental. We often talk on the phone. After all she took my job and she has a lot of queries.'

'How's the fish?' Michael asked.

'Superb. As always. Could it be anything else in Murmansk?'

'Copies of *Red Star* for the same period were censored.'

'They were sensitive times. You'e not suggesting they were censored because of your brother. . . .'

'Everyone I've approached is suffering from amnesia.'

'It *was* a long time ago.'

'Did the KGB remove those envelopes?'

'Let's have another bottle of wine.'

'You couldn't have done much about it if they had. . . .'

'The KGB aren't what they were,' she said.

'Or so they would have us believe.'

Michael stared out of the window. Mist was rolling in from the gulf. Seagulls wheeled ahead of it and he could hear them crying. He hoped the fishing fleet was safely tucked up in the harbour.

He laid down his knife and fork. 'I asked you a question.'

'The envelopes were removed by a historian. He lost them.'

'You don't expect me to believe that?'

'You don't have any alternative, do you.' She placed her elbows on the table, clasped her fingers together, rested her chin on them. 'Why don't you give up, Mikhail? You're not achieving anything. Your brother wasn't even a statistic, just a lost soul in a terrible war. You'll never trace him. I admire your obstinacy but there's no point in going any further.' She unclasped her fingers and laid one hand on his sleeve; her nails were blunt and painted shell-pink.

Michael said: 'I'm a lawyer. In New York I know by instinct when justice is being impeded. I've had that feeling ever since I started trying to trace Vasily. People do not disappear without

311

trace. Not even in Russia. Particularly not in Russia,' he corrected himself. 'This is a bureaucracy and bureaucrats cosset themselves with records because they are the justification for their existence.'

'So you won't give up?'

He shook his head.

She stared at him thoughtfully, pupils of her eyes big and as dark as wells. She glanced at her watch. 'Please excuse me,' she said, 'I have to make a 'phone call.'

When she returned she was lively once again. 'Here's to justice.' She drank her wine abruptly as though it were medicine and poured more. 'You're a very attractive man,' she said, elaborately lighting a cigarette. 'Would you like to see my apartment?'

When they got outside the fog was thick and salty. Figures drifted past like wraiths. A ship hooted; a soul lost at sea, Michael thought. She tucked her hand under the sleeve of his sheepskin coat. He sensed vaguely that they were close to the lake where the masochists had been breaking the ice to leap into the water.

A face observed him from the mist. The writer for *Travel*? Fanciful, surely. . . .

But there was nothing fanciful about the heavily-clad body that hit, caught him off balance, and propelled him forward. Nothing anonymous either: this was the man who had been playing checkers in Gorky Park. Squat, powerful, ever-watching. He had been close to Michael for too long to escape recognition.

Michael's feet slithered across grass and slush towards a wound in the ice. He struck with his elbow. Felt the momentum of the assailant's body falter.

He swallowed fog. Beneath his feet ice crunching, cracking. The bathers had been diving into the water so there was a sudden drop beneath the ice. His feet found firm ice covering a rock or a tree stump. He kicked backwards. Felt bone. A loosening of the grip, a gasping obscenity. Michael broke loose and they faced each other in the saline mist.

'Come on, comrade,' Michael said, 'I'm waiting for you,' and then, not waiting at all, no longer passive attorney waiting to be the recipient of violence, launched himself at the checkers-player. Feet skidding, he took him waist high with his shoulder. Ice split beneath them. Together they reached for firm ice. It cracked and splintered. Water jostled Michael's feet, stole up his legs. They fell, rolled to one side. Firmer ice. But Michael was beneath his attacker.

He stretched out one arm. Found an axe-head of floating ice. Struck blindly. Felt the ice strike home. Rolled clear. Clubbed again. The ice beneath him was stronger now. He crouched, looking for the checkers-player. Swiped again with his ice-axe as, blurred by mist, he came at him again. But his opponent's body had lost its combat power and his movements were slurred.

Another blow. The checkers-player fell to his knees and, as he did so, the ice parted around him. The green water was black in the dusk and the checkers-player fell into it neatly, still kneeling as though in prayer. Then he tipped forward in total supplication and disappeared.

Michael lunged after him. But there was nothing beneath his feet. His lead-heavy sheepskin was pulling him into the water and there was a blizzard in his skull. He turned and searched for the ice between him and the shore. One hand encountered the branch of a tree; he hung there for a moment, reached for it with his other hand. The branch bent, lowering him into the water. Hand over hand, he edged along its pliant length, water pouring from his treacherous coat.

When he reached the shore he called out to the librarian but there was no reply. Only the hoot of a ship somewhere in the fog-thick darkness.

Barbara arrived at Sheremetyvo airport looking as though she was embarking on a spending spree on Fifth Avenue. Matching black astrakhan coat and hat and an imperious, spending air that he knew was not quite genuine. She sometimes misread an ambience and, in the past, Michael had found this to be one of her more endearing qualities. She had once worn an evening blouse and skirt to an elaborately informal party at Sag Harbour and, subsequently, slacks to a rigidly formal function given by the same hosts. She had, of course, blamed him. What she

313

detested most was vulgarity but she was not always accomplished at identifying it.

'You look terrible,' she said as they climbed into the Volga taxi. 'Is that what being Russian does for you?'

'It's what attempted murder does for you,' he said and told her about the events in Murmansk. About the checkers-player, presumed dead, about the puzzling lack of interest displayed by the police in his fate. 'It wasn't the first time I've been attacked,' he said and told her about the incident on the Trans-Siberian.

'Jesus, Mike.' She had always called him Michael. She took off her hat. Her blonde hair tumbled around her finely-honed features that looked indulgently upon the commonplace. 'What's so special about your brother?'

'That's what I aim to find out. A guy tries to murder me and gets killed instead and no one gives a shit. When I left Murmansk they hadn't even started to drag the lake.'

Birch woods flitted past the window; wooden crosses tilted to look like battlefield fortifications, the monument to the point where the German advance on Moscow had been halted; guardian ranks of apartment blocks.

'You've got to feel Moscow,' he said, 'to understand it.'

'Defensive already?'

'It's got a sturdy soul.'

The taxi drew up outside the enormous Cosmos Hotel, designed by the French for the 1980 Olympics, on Mira Prospect.

'Is this where you're staying?' she asked.

'My hotel is downtown.'

'I thought we might be in the same place. Any reason why we aren't?'

'Because you were booked into a different one,' he said as they walked into the capacious foyer where tourists were playing fruit machines.

After she had checked in they took the elevator to the ninth floor. Room 924 was opposite a room where two women vigilantes took turns to keep an eye on the guests and pour each other tea from their samovar.

The room was adequate, airport-style, a view of a row of sparsely provisioned shops below. On the wall between two single beds was a print of birch trees in the fall.

Barbara kicked off her shoes and lay on a bed wriggling her toes. 'So what's she like?' she said.

'What's who like?'

'Your lover,' she said.

He took the metro the following morning to the VDNKh station, built for the Exhibition of Economic Achievements, and walked to the Cosmos. They drank apple juice and spooned porridge for breakfast and he took her on a troika ride round the pavilions of genuine and trumped-up Soviet enterprise. The hooves of the three horses, all greys, drummed martially on the polished snow, the jingle of bells hung like baubles on the air. She sat regally in the sleigh, a throwback from the Imperial Court at St Petersburg making a serf of the driver, but bringing with her unsolicited gifts from New York. The smell of leaves trampled in Central Park in the fall . . . chestnuts and bagels on street-corner stands . . . purposeful young men and girls with thrusting thighs on Madison . . . the vibrancy of the goddamn place in sickness and in health. . . . He thought of kosher food between Delancey and Canal . . . pasta and salami on Mulberry . . . an evicted Russian waiting on the sidewalk for him to take up his case. . . .

He said: 'Her name's Magda and she's my courier.'

'Why couldn't you tell me that last night?'

'In a hotel room?'

'I understand,' she said. 'I really do.'

'And you?'

'You and I haven't been apart all that long.' *But long enough for you.* 'And no, I won't say, "I'd like to meet her," and don't you say, "You'd like her." '

He stared at the soaring monument to Soviet cosmonauts adjoining the exhibition park and imagined the tip of the Chrysler building.

'You'd like her,' he said after a while.

'When are you coming home, Mike?'

'What's with this Mike?'

'I think of you as Mike.'

'So why didn't you ever call me Mike?'

315

'Because you were Michael, I guess. Attorney-at-law.'

'Maybe you should have called me Mike.'

'Or Mikhail?'

'No,' he said. 'Not you.'

'I've missed you.'

He was silent, listening to the punctuation of the horses' hooves and the jingling of the bells perched on the frozen air.

'Don't you believe me?' she asked.

'I believe you think you've missed me.'

'You're not in court, Mike – sorry Michael, sorry Mikhail. What's the difference?'

The horses turned, direction controlled by the one in the centre, without any persuasion from the impassive driver. Michael listened to the slither of the runners. He knew she wasn't impressed by the ambience; for her Moscow was part of a predestined scenario.

'How long are you staying?' he asked.

'Just a few days. When are you coming back?'

'When I've traced my brother.'

'Isn't it time to quit gracefully? From what you told me last night it's hopeless.'

'I would have bought that at the beginning. No more. Someone's trying to stop me so damn hard there must be some record of him. Maybe he *is* still alive. . . .'

'It could take for ever.' She glanced sideways at him. 'Or is that what you want?'

'I don't know what I want,' he said as the horses turned and made a run for home.

The next few days were complex. He took Barbara on predictable tours of Moscow – Kremlin and the Armoury, Lenin's tomb, Tretyakov Gallery, Novodevichy, the Bolshoi – and trips uncharted by Intourist to markets and dwindling streets of wooden houses and small churches kneeling amid high-rise, and sausage bars and pie stalls. All the time he was defensive, like a small-town suitor showing his bride-to-be her future home, and was irritated by her polite interest. Why should he

316

care? Was it that he was seeing Moscow through her eyes and comparing it with New York? He tried to concentrate on the Bowery and cracked streets laid bare on a Sunday morning and the dangerous caverns of the subway but each time he was distracted by the urgency of its day-time streets and the sparkle of its night-time jewellery.

Magda's attitude irritated him too. There was a lot to be said for a woman who understood her partner's dilemmas – God knows, men scoured the earth for them – but didn't such excessive forbearance suggest lack of commitment? Shouldn't she evince some disquiet that he was loose in Moscow with the woman with whom he had shared most of his adult life, a beautiful woman at that? The only indication that she was not totally happy with the arrangement was her refusal to allow him to make love to her; this did not disturb him because Barbara's proximity would have made him feel guilty. Stupid, we're getting a divorce.

What, he supposed, he resented most was the finality of decision that Barbara had transported across the Atlantic. Now or never, she seemed to say, without actually invoking memories of their courtship. Why she was resurrecting this decision he could not tell: he had truly believed that their parting was absolute.

'She is beautiful,' Magda said as they walked down Gorky Street.

'How do you know?'

'I saw her in the Cosmos,' she told him as they passed the House of the Moscow Soviet, Moscow's city hall. 'I had taken one of my groups there.'

'You recognised her just like that?'

'From your description. She looked as though she was on her way to a fashion show.'

'How could you be so sure?'

Magda stared at the sidewalk. 'Because I asked the receptionist.' She walked more quickly. 'What was your home like?'

'Placid,' he said. 'A lot of flowers in the garden.' He remembered a bed of freesias which had reminded him of miniature candelabra. 'With views of the ocean.' He smelled brine on the wind coming in from the ocean.

'I thought you lived in an apartment in Manhattan.'

317

'We had a house *and* an apartment,' he confessed. 'Just as Muscovites have an apartment *and* a dacha.'

'Some Muscovites,' she said.

They went into a big bookshop on the corner of the square containing the Aragvi restaurant. Muscovites browsed blissfully in its library quiet. Magda bought a copy of *Master and Margarita*, reasonably priced since *perestroika* had killed the black market in books.

'You must have shared a lot,' she said as they rejoined the heads-down, lunchtime crowds outside.

'We were married for a long time.'

'If your wife hadn't lost the baby you would still be together.' Statement of fact.

'Maybe.' He hadn't realised how much he had wanted a child until they had lost it. The baby, a boy, hadn't even seen the world it had struggled to enter and Michael had wondered why it had been manufactured at all. 'Everyone thought we were an ideal couple.'

'So why did you part?'

'We knew better,' Michael said, dodging a dumpling woman in black boring out of the Gastronome No. 1. 'She once gave my father a can of caviar.'

'So?'

'Caviar is one of the ultimate luxuries in America. My father was poor.'

'But it was a kind act; that was what mattered; you should have understood that.'

'Are you for the defence or the prosecution?'

'She is very insecure, your wife.'

'About as insecure as the Kremlin wall.'

'She looks so self-assured she must be insecure. We all act, you know. It's one of the first things we learn. Sad, isn't it.'

She turned abruptly and headed towards Karl Marx Prospect.

Barbara insecure? He frowned. They walked in silence for a while. Then she said: 'I think you should go back to America. They've tried to kill you once; next time they'll succeed.'

'They?'

She gave the eloquent shrug much favoured by angry women. 'Whoever.'

'I can't admit defeat.'

'Don't be trite, Comrade Cooper.'

'Why are you suddenly so mad?'

'My privilege.'

'Do you want me to go back?'

'I don't want you dead.'

Sleet was beginning to fall and they ducked their heads into it. He gave it a few moments, then said: 'If I went back would you follow me?'

'You would give up this . . . this crusade . . . if I joined you?'

'Would you?'

'Book your flight – then I'll tell you.'

But he couldn't do that; not yet.

Outside the skyscraper Intourist Hotel she kissed him and said: 'I think I could get to like your wife.'

Barbara said: 'I saw your girl-friend.'

'In a city with a population of more than 7,000,000 you saw Magda?'

'Magda . . . I guessed Lara. We saw *Dr Zhivago* in Boston. Remember?'

'How did you know it was her?' he asked patiently.

'The way she looked at me in my hotel. Then she asked the receptionist who I was. I know because I slipped him a packet of Marlboro.'

'You're learning fast,' Michael said raising his glass to her in the elegant restaurant of the re-opened Savoy Hotel on Rozhdestvenka Street.

'We're pretty damn smart on Madison Avenue. Do you always fall for blondes?'

The question sounded dangerous and he treated it evasively. 'So what do you think of this place?' He had taken her the previous evening to a co-operative restaurant, the Kolkhida, but she had been politely unenthusiastic so he had brought her to Moscow's answer to the Pierre. The walls of the restaurant were rust-red, ceiling gilded and mirrored, tables prim and covered with primrose cloths.

'It's neat,' she said.

319

Was that it? He hoped the food was good: he thought he might like to do PR for Moscow.

Caviar to start.

'That stupid thing with your father,' she said spreading the glistening black roe on a finger of toast.

'You meant well.'

She looked at him with surprise. 'You didn't think so at the time.'

'I'm getting old and wise.'

She drank vodka, neatly like a professional. 'Why don't you come back to New York with me?'

Michael experienced an eerie sensation that the talk was following a similar avenue to the conversation with Magda that morning. They both wanted him back in New York. Any moment now Barbara would tell him she could get to like Magda.

'You know why,' he said.

She sipped wine. She didn't grimace and she didn't enthuse. It was the same with Moscow. She didn't vilify it like many foreigners who measured its charm by the absence of a bathplug rather than the Fabergé eggs in the Amoury and she didn't rhapsodise. She regarded it as an extended stopover.

'You'll get yourself killed. They've tried once. . . .' *Next time they'll succeed!*

He said quickly: 'Do you know what puzzled me after the incident in Murmansk?'

She didn't.

'How sheep manage to keep dry.'

'The coat?'

'It's still dripping over the bath. My fault. I knew I had to buy a new one. Not so flashy.'

She sent back the beef because it was too tough. Insecure, Barbara?

'A lot of people will be lucky if they get beef out of a can tonight,' he told her.

'I sympathise with them. But that doesn't make my beef any more tender.' She reached for her crocodile purse. 'Dick sent you a letter.' She handed him an envelope.

'Come home, Mike, all is forgiven?'

'Read it,' she said.

320

Dear Mike,
So how is glasnost? *Not so hot, we read. Particularly if you happen to be Lithuanian. So when are you coming back? We need you! Okay, so we're handling the up-market business with our usual aplomb. Down-market things aren't quite so euphoric. We may even have to ease off in that direction.*

'So now he's resorting to threats,' Michael said.
Barbara chewed a morsel of replacement beef. 'Delicious,' she said.

Remember that family I told you about when I called at Christmas? Well, they're out on the streets. We're doing our best, Mike, we really are, but we need your touch. Blackmail?

'Pure and simple,' Michael said.

Maybe, just a touch. But don't forget we all need that down-market business because it's good for our image.

'Bullshit,' Michael said.

And your minorities need you. They really do, Mike. They always ask for you. They don't seem to trust me or the other partners. I wonder why! So hurry home. An old Ukrainian lady has just been wrongly charged with shop-lifting. She's been asking for you. Subtle, aren't I.
As ever,

'Is he persuasive?' Barbara asked, sipping red wine.
'Not persuasive enough.'
'Could you settle here?'
'It's got a lot going for it.'
'Such as?'
'A banya for one thing. A bath-house. Why don't you come along?'
'I'll pass,' Barbara said.
'Russia's got spirit. Especially now. It's founded on family, you see; no old ladies tucked out of sight in homes. Schools are good, housing is cheap – twelve roubles a month for a small

apartment – and, drugs apart, there aren't any health bills. No racist problems.'

'You could have fooled me.'

'Not in Moscow. You see,' he said, 'you mustn't judge everything by materialistic values. Take a kid, any kid. He would be just as happy with a clockwork train bought at Dietsky Mir, Children's World, as he would be with the latest computerised gadget from F.A.O. Schwarz.'

'I understand that,' she said.

'I wish you could stay longer.' *Did he?* 'See the countryside. Go cross-country skiing. You used to be a good skier,' he remembered. 'Come back to a dacha when the fields are getting lonely. Dachas smell like old toy cupboards. Light a fire and hear the pine cones spitting; drink a little fire-water and heat up a bowl of borscht. You can be at peace in a dacha, all the cruelty outside.'

'You'd really like me to stay longer?' She frowned in disbelief.

'You should see Leningrad.'

'And Kiev?'

'Why Kiev?'

'She's Ukrainian, isn't she? According to the receptionist at the Cosmos she spoke with a Ukrainian accent.'

'You still manage to astound me.' Remembering her flashes of perception, observing the familiar contradictions of her face, fragility and determination, he smiled.

'I guess I could get my visa extended.' He managed to retain the smile. 'You must have clout with Intourist. . . .'

'I'll see what I can do.'

She touched his hand. 'Don't worry – I was only kidding.' She paused while the waiter served blinys with plum jam. Then: 'You've got to come home, Mike.'

'Home?'

'New York. You could live in the apartment. I've got the florists now but I can stay with my partner.'

'Your partner?'

'A girl named Helen Kermode. And maybe we could meet up weekends.' She licked jam from her upper lip. 'You know, this isn't a blood feud. . . .'

'You seem to forget – '

322

'Nothing. But you've got to be realistic. Your brother is either dead or he doesn't want to see you.'

The second possibility hadn't occurred to Michael. 'Why the hell do you say that?'

'You told me your mission had been well publicised. If he's alive he must have heard about it. So why hasn't he been in touch?'

'Maybe he's ill. Maybe he was crippled during the war. Maybe he's lost his memory. Maybe he's a prisoner. . . .'

'Maybe he doesn't want the past resurrected.'

'I can't give up now,' he said. 'Can't you see that?'

'I went to the doctor the other day,' she said, placing her spoon carefully on her jam-smeared plate. 'He says I could still become pregnant.'

They took a taxi back to her hotel. In the foyer she kissed him on the cheek. 'I rather liked the look of your Magda,' she said. 'Maybe I could even get to like her.'

To escape from his solicitous women Michael took refuge in the banya. But tensions were running high there too. The women, exuding clandestine complacency, had called a meeting in their changing-room, a move that had been denounced by the men as a feminist plot.

The stallholder, fresh and hot from the steam-room, held high his mug of beer as though it were a torch. 'Why should we submit to their wishes? We have always conferred on neutral ground – that is the democratic way.'

There were other tensions abroad, Robert Hanson confided to Michael Cooper as they played a desultory game of chess. The Georgian carnation-seller was assiduously plotting, although what he had in mind was not apparent; the Armenian, lacking an adversary from Azerbaijan, was hectoring anyone from the south about the historic injustices suffered by his race; the Ukrainian miner, emboldened by the triumphs of *Rukh* in the elections, was patronising anyone unfortunate enough to be born outside Ukraine; the intense Lithuanian who had re-turned to Moscow with two colleagues to discuss his republic's independence with Kremlin leaders occupied a table where the stallholder customarily sat.

The stallholder stopped in front of the table. 'What do you think, comrades? You aren't regular patrons but you are free to give an opinion. That is *glasnost.*'

'We are not your comrades,' the intense Lithuanian said.

'You are Soviet citizens.' The stallholder chewed a piece of dried fish.

'We are about to regain the freedom taken away from us fifty years ago.' The Lithuanian smiled reasonably. 'That is *glasnost.*'

Further debate was cut short by the arrival of the pickpocket. 'Vilkin has betrayed us,' he said. His fingers fretted. 'Look outside.'

They gathered at the doorway. The bulldozer had moved up the street. Next to it was a truck loaded with pneumatic drills, pick-axes and sledgehammers. Half a dozen militia stood by.

The Kremlin chauffeur, still growing in stature, said: 'We must go and see what the women have to say. This is no time for sexist argument.'

'To hell with the women,' the stallholder said. 'We will fight.'

'With a belly like that?' The bodybuilder, muscles moving ominously, slapped the stallholder's stomach. 'Come, let's see what the Fighting Comrades have to offer.' He began to dress.

The women, five of them, were seated at one end of a row of tables, the laundress, at the head, flanked by the seamstress, the hairdresser, the interpreter and Tanya Agursky. The fountain splashed; the women were elaborately gracious.

The men sat down, all that was except the stallholder, and accepted glasses of tea. The laundress, wearing her uniform freshly washed at her laundrette, regarded them maternally. 'It's good to have you here,' she said. 'For the good of the banya. There was some suggestion that you wouldn't come. . . .'

The men smiled indulgently at such wayward intelligence.

She folded her arms. 'I won't waste time.' She pointed towards the street where Vilkin's task force was assembling. 'The time for words has passed. . . .'

'Then use them sparingly,' the stallholder said.

'You have a plan? Another strike with your pie stall?'

'We must fight.'

'The militia?'

'Let us hear what she has to say,' the chauffeur said.

They listened and such were her words that an inarticulate silence born of reluctant admiration settled upon them.

'We,' indicating the Fighting Comrades, 'have made an approach to the wife of the President of the Soviet Union.' The silence lengthened. 'She has agreed to see us to discuss the future of the banya.'

'She'll have to be quick,' the stallholder said. In the circumstances it was the best he could do.

Back in the mens' changing-room the atmosphere was edgy, an uneasy amalgam of hope that the banya would be saved and melancholy that it was the opposite sex who were responsible for such optimism. The stallholder was singularly affected; ignoring the Lithuanians, now treating his table as a sovereign Baltic state, he brooded savagely and there were those who feared the outcome of such concentrated deliberation.

The tricky ambience was further complicated by the arrival of a bird, a sparrow by the look of it, which flew into the changing-room as the pickpocket departed for a business appointment on the metro. It fluttered in panic in the highest corners of the ceiling before being swept back into the cold by a broom brandished aloft by the bodybuilder.

Robert Hanson explained to Michael Cooper why gloom settled so thickly in the changing-room. 'If a bird flies into a room in Russia it means death.' Whose? Michael wondered.

In his dismal apartment Leonid Lysenko, isolated from the children in the marital bedroom, cleaned his new rifle, a 7.62 mm SVD, with love and care. It was a privilege to handle such an exquisitely accurate weapon. What still worried him was whom he was expected to kill with it.

325

23

The lake lay to the north-west of the city. It wasn't as intimate as the lake on which she and Yury had skated but better proportioned for use as a rink. It was girdled on one side by silver birch; on the other fields of snow led to an infinite horizon.

Lev Grechko leaned against his red Moskvitch. Several of foreigners, Robert Hanson among them, were grouped round a camera on the shore. Tanya and Lazar waited on the ice.

Lev, beard snapping above the coils of his grey scarf, spoke into a megaphone. 'Okay, children, this is it. If I think you're good enough then we enter you for the National Championships. If you win those they can't refuse you the Olympics. If I don't think you're good enough. . . .' He lowered his beard into the scarf.

Tanya shivered as a breeze crossed the fields snuffling the snow and she noticed that her legs beneath her short white skirt – above her disgraceful old boots – were pink. Lazar, all in black, squeezed her hand and Tanya, remembering how he had stood up to the anti-Semitic thug at *Pamyat*, squeezed back.

'All right,' Lev bellowed, 'this is it.' He leaned into the Moskvitch and switched on the cassette player. A bleep telling them that the music would start in three seconds. She noticed an elderly man crouched behind the camera.

One . . . two . . . three . . . Sibelius's *Karelia Suite* issued from the red Moskvitch. Together they skated slowly down one side of the lake in the open-hold position. Faster as the music gains momentum. A power run round the perimeter, leaning forward, skates slashing the ice. . . .

Iced air in her lungs, heart thudding.

The first lift, a double overhead splits lutz. Up, up, up . . . down again, skates taking her into a curving steep back outside edge. And now, bursting from a corner of the lake, a thrown double axel. She rotates, two and a half revolutions, lands easily, and links up with Lazar.

Now the Death Spiral. The last one in the Dynamo Stadium was a fiasco. Her head actually hit the ice. . . . He holds her firmly . . . they spin, her head a centimetre or so above the ice.

The music changes to Paganini. Hasn't she read that he was supposed to be inspired by the devil? The music reaches her soul . . . . She smiles tragically at an invisible audience. . . .

The third minute of the programme. . . . As they glide into long, soft-edge movements, passing and crossing each other, she notices Lev on the shore, arms folded. She feels that he is growling.

Fourth minute. *Hello Dolly*. Daintily intricate steps . . . jigsaw patterns. . . .

Last minute. Where is Lev? She falters. Spots him leaning against the car once more. Glowering.

Karelia again. But the muscles in her legs, calf and thigh, are weakening. The music builds . . . the last lift, the sixteenth. . . . She lands imperfectly. Does it show? Everything shows when Lev is around.

Still holding Lazar's hand she skates despondently to the shore. Lev is standing there. Growling. The injustice of life overwhelms her; the breeze cools her flushed body.

Lev raises his beard from his scarf. 'You'll do,' he says.

'Great stuff,' Joe Palmer said to Robert Hanson who, having spoken to Tanya Agursky, had suggested the scene on the lake. 'I'm grateful to you, Bob, I really am. Blades of the skates slashing the ice, great symbolism for a suspense movie. Now the tricky bit.' He grimaced secretly to Hanson. 'Karl, formerly Albert, on the ice with the Mex in front of our producer.'

The widow, hands plunged into the pockets of her fur jacket, approached breezily. 'Beautiful background shots,' she said. 'Only I don't get the significance. Is any of this relevant to the plot?'

'It's an opportunity to get Karl, Albert that is, and the girl into an off-beat setting. You know, there is supposed to be a feeling developing between them. Just in the script, that is,' he added, thereby, Hanson felt, unnecessarily complicating the issue.

'Isn't Albert supposed to be an assassin? I mean do we really want a romantic killer?'

'That's one of the principal story-lines. A guy falling in love . . . something he never thought possible. . . . Now he doesn't want to kill anymore. . . . But his paymaster threatens him . . . . If he doesn't carry out this last contract they'll tell the girl he's a murderer. . . .'

They were joined by Michael Cooper who had come with Hanson, Penrose, Hanson's deputy victim, the Australian scriptwriter and his deputy, Mayhew. Everyone concerned with the movie, Hanson thought, was now taking it more seriously than normal expatriate life. It *was* more stimulating. Palmer was Alfred Hitchcock, the Australian was William Goldman, Mayhew was Goldman's *eminence grise*, the Mexican was an enchantress, I am the President of the United States, Penrose is Vice-President, Albert is an assassin. . . . .

The widow said: 'Can the Mexican skate?'

The Australian, improvising on a plot that had long ago escaped his jurisdiction, said: 'That's the beauty of it – Karl teaches her to skate. Isn't that right, Joe?'

'On the button,' Palmer said.

'All you seem to be missing,' Michael Cooper said, 'are the two stars.'

Hanson saw them coming through the birch trees. There was about them a togetherness which he envied in the young couples strolling in Gorky Park. Judging by the expression of fierce indulgence on the widow's face she had sensed it too.

The East German, who was wearing a hunting jacket, smiled lazily. 'Sorry we're late, you know how it is.' *You know what we've been about.*

The Mexican, blue-black hair streaming in the breeze, squeezed his arm. 'Rehearsing,' she said.

'We used to call it something quite different,' Mayhew said.

'Okay,' Palmer said, 'on with your skates. Are you any good, Karl?'

'He's very good,' the Mexican said. She wore pale blue ski-pants which emphasised her buttocks.

The East German skated languidly like an uncommitted ice-hockey player; the Mexican tottered beside him, grabbing him enthusiastically whenever she was about to fall.

Penrose said: 'Over-acting. Can't you do something about that, Joe?'

'She's just fine,' Palmer said. 'Naturally vivacious, is all.' He aimed the camera at them.

The seaman approached. 'So you'll be off soon,' he said to Hanson.

'This year, next year, sometime, never.'

'Sooner rather than later?' He took off his peaked cap and rubbed his baldness with his hand.

'If you say so.'

'You're a cagey bastard.'

'Or a caged bastard? Like all of us?'

The Mexican slipped, fell. The East German, fair hair falling silkily across his forehead, gathered her up. She clung to him for a moment, then they skated across the ice scarred by slashes from Lazar and Tanya's skates.

'Okay,' Palmer called. 'That wraps it up. But as we're here I want a few shots of you, Bob. Also Karl lurking in the birch trees with his rifle.'

The East German, who still hesitated when addressed as Karl, fetched his replica of a rifle from the widow's BMW.

'You first,' Palmer said to Hanson. 'You're leaving the leader of the Soviet Union's dacha. There are security goons around, of course, but they aren't on camera. You want a little time to think . . . a proposition put by your rival President. Will you lose face by accepting it? Is it a diplomatic double-cross? Your doubts are contrasted by the tranquillity of the snow.' Palmer was becoming excited. 'A silhouette. But is it you or the President of the Soviet Union? Americans wanting you good and dead, Russians wanting their man likewise.'

They trooped round the lake to a bush as round as a cabbage beside a hollow in the snow.

The widow said: 'This is more like it, for God's sake.'

'Sure it is,' Palmer said, pulling at the ears of his fur hat. 'Okay, Bob. All you've got to do is walk, looking like you're torn apart by decisions, i.e. look like you always do.' He laughed absent-mindedly and set up his camera. 'Okay, I'm shooting. . . .'

Feeling foolish, Hanson circumvented the bush and walked round the brim of the hollow, concentrating on the wording of his plea to Petrov for an exit visa.

Palmer congratulated him. 'What they used to call "method". Didn't know you had it in you. . . .'

'Is that all?'

'For the moment. Now we've got to shoot Karl while the light's good enough.'

The East German removed one hand from the Mexican's buttocks. 'Ready when you are, Joe.'

'Among the birch trees,' Palmer told him. 'Shafts of light coming through the branches . . . one of them on your face. . . . You feel the spotlight and move away. . . . Can you manage that?'

'Anyone can manage that,' the East German said gently.

As he shrank into the wood Palmer followed with his camera. 'There, hold it,' he shouted.

The East German stopped and lay down obligingly in a corridor of sunlight.

Palmer aimed his camera, then told him to move into the shade. 'Now aim your rifle at Bob.'

'I can't see him,' the East German said mildly.

'No matter. Aim it at someone. Anyone.'

Albert aimed the rifle at Michael Cooper framed on the skyline, sun beginning to settle behind him, and pulled the trigger.

'Fantastic,' Palmer said. 'A real pro.'

The East German rose, dusting snow and dead leaves from his jacket.

The widow got to him before the Mexican. She held up both hands. 'I almost forgot – great news.' She turned to the Mexican. 'I've persuaded your husband to be co-producer. Isn't that wonderful?' She looked at her expectantly.

Hanson crashed his Zhiguli near the Bolshevik sweet factory on Leningradsky Prospect. Although, as he subsequently admitted, he was driving too fast he was distracted by the stranger who had appeared in the driving mirror.

'So you're going to do what I advised. . . .'

'Petition the President? There's nothing else I can do.'

'You should have consulted me long ago.'

'I didn't know you existed.'

'I've always existed,' his features in urbane repose, a lifetime of achievement behind him.

'I'm glad I didn't know.'

'Why? Because you might not have embarked upon your great adventure? Might now be chairman of Rotary, second home in the Dordogne, Caribbean cruises on luxury banana boats, coffers augmented by a little inside knowledge in the City. . . .'

'I had Weinreb instead of you.'

'Poor Weinreb. A classic victim of circumstance. If Hitler hadn't come to power. If his brother hadn't fought for the Nazis, he might now be burgomaster of Nuremberg. Instead he died of a surfeit of plonk and pasta.'

'He was very brave.' Remembering how Weinreb had flung himself in front of the tongue-lolling schoolmaster as he raised the metal-edged ruler for another strike. Hanson took his right hand from the steering wheel to massage the ball of the thumb of his left hand and it was at that moment that the Zhiguli went out of control.

It veered first left and then, as Hanson over-reacted, to the right, brushing against an aged Volga that was overtaking him. The Volga lurched to one side and stopped. Hanson braked but the tyres skidded on a patch of ice and the Zhiguli swung round so that it was facing the opposite direction. He turned it round once more and parked at the side of the road. The driver of the Volga, a large and sterterous man wearing a lived-in suit, lumbered across the street. 'Just what the hell did you think you were doing?' he demanded, clenching and unclenching one incongruously dimpled fist.

Hanson held up both hands. 'I'm sorry.'

The other driver, unused to the acceptance of blame, rubbed his pendulous throat with his little knuckles. Further debate was terminated by the arrival of two traffic cops on motorcycles.

Hands on hips, they surveyed the scene appreciatively.

Finally one of them turned to the driver of the Volga. 'Been to a party, comrade?'

The driver crumpled. 'So I had a couple of nips.'

'You know that under Soviet law it is an offence to drive after consuming any alcohol?'

'Take me away. Lock me up. Let my wife and children starve.'

Hanson climbed out of the Zhiguli. 'It was my fault,' he said.

'And who are you, comrade?' And when Hanson told him: 'On your way. You haven't been drinking.'

'But – '

'I said on your way.' He guided Hanson back to the Zhiguli and, with an air of anticipation, turned his attention to the driver of the Volga.

Hanson parked the Zhiguli outside the apartment house, made his way along the path of the apologetic garden and climbed the stairs past the door of the late Comrade Frolov. How should he make his approach to Petrov?

The problem was taken out of his hands as the old-fashioned bell stopped stuttering, as the door opened and Lena stood there, uncharacteristically agitated. 'A special messenger called,' she said. She wetted her lips. 'From the Kremlin. You have an audience tomorrow. With the President.'

24

Petrov was weary of winter. He wanted the sun to melt its grimy shell, to hear the music of the thaw.

At 8.30 a.m., after he had been working at his desk for one and a half hours, he left his office in the building of the Council of Ministers to take the air, to see if it contained any messages from spring.

Hands behind his back, he walked past Napoleon's cannons outside the mustard walls of the Arsenal. Guards followed with stoic resignation.

He crossed the main thoroughfare leading from Trinity Tower through which tourists would stream later in the day and made his way down the street, closed to the public, beside the incongruously named Palace of Amusements where Stalin had once lived.

He stopped at the Secret Garden at the apex of the Kremlin's triangle. Here at least he could smell the river.

The guards hovered nervously as though he might escape through the secret tunnel said to pass under the walls. He smiled: perhaps one day he would.

But of spring there was no word. Ahead meetings with Lenitsky, Kirov and Razin. And Robert Hanson. He brightened a little and made his way back to his office.

First Kirov. Heavyweight spectacles perched on his fragile cheekbones. Burdened with dire prophecies – the latest plot to assassinate Petrov, a whisper that a marksman had been approached.

'Then find him,' Petrov said tracing the patterns of the inlaid wood on his desk with one stubby finger.

'It would help if you stuck to your schedules.'

'You sometimes sound as if *you* would like to have me assassinated. After all you have the apparatus behind you to have anyone disposed of.'

The old schemer rose stiffly. 'Why should I bother? There are so many other candidates. . . .'

Next Razin, *darling of the underdog*, his features those of an ageing but unmarked prize-fighter.

Petrov regarded him enviously across the desk. To have the comon touch. . . .

Razin said: 'You've guessed why I've come?'

'To discuss the Presidency of the Russian Republic?' There had been an article in the *Moscow News* that morning stating that his election was a foregone conclusion.

'Executive Presidency of it.' Razin smiled plumply. 'A nice touch?'

'I admire your nerve.'

'Perhaps one day Executive Presidency of the Soviet Union?'

Perhaps one day they will be one and the same thing, Petrov thought.

Next Lenitsky. Martyr. Crucified on the cross of a failed tenet of Marxist–Leninism.

Petrov paced the panelled office. 'So what is it, Lithuania?'

'Whatever happens you mustn't let them break away unconstitutionally. Others would follow. It would be the end of everything.' He stroked one cheek as though trying to erase the furrows of disillusion.

'If they declare independence' – which they will, Petrov thought – 'I will bargain from a position of power. That is the only way to negotiate.'

'Send in the tanks?'

'But no bloodshed. Not like Azerbaijan.'

'You should have sent them in a long time ago,' Lenitsky said. 'To Poland, Hungary, the German Democratic Republic. . . .'

'Isn't it a contradiction, tanks to enforce ideals?'

Next Robert Hanson.

*

334

Hanson was a shock. Since Kirov had found him in the banya, he had composed him in his mind, etched the strong lines he expected to see. Instead he was confronted by a face that had draped loose flesh around the bones of conviction; eyes that looked backward, shoulders that had the slope of defeat. Was I responsible? Petrov asked himself.

A girl of inscrutable demeanour served tea and anaemic biscuits. They bit into them simultaneously and regarded each other warily.

Tsar Petrov, searching for words, said: 'My invitation' – *order* – 'must have come as a great surprise.'

It had, Hanson agreed without looking surprised at all. He gave the impression of a man who had abdicated the aptitude to be concerned by anything except predestination. Or escape?

Petrov picked up a word-processed resumé of his file and read aloud extracts emphasising authoritative but superficial details. Towards the end he improvised. 'I understand you want to leave the Soviet Union.'

'I was going to petition you,' Muscovite accent so perfect that the image of the young Hanson began to assemble vividly.

'Did I persuade you to settle in the Soviet Union?'

'You, Comrade President.'

'And you're angry with me?'

'Not because you persuaded me: I loved you for that.'

'Why then?'

'Because you betrayed me.'

Petrov picked up another biscuit and bit snappily into it. Grey light illumined the office from the implacable day outside. It seemed illogically important to Petrov to justify himself to this jaded Englishman.

'Because I have given the Soviet people freedom of choice?'

'Because you've admitted the sermon you preached to me was fraudulent.'

'I thought I believed it at the time.'

'Thought? You took away twenty years of my life.'

'I didn't realise it was impracticable.'

'Nearly thirty years of Stalin and you thought communism was practicable?'

'I wasn't thinking of Stalinism: I was thinking of equality.'

'Aren't *you* a dictator?'

335

'Do dictators favour free elections?'

Hanson stared at him hopelessly. 'You persuaded me to leave a way of life; now you're trying to create that same way of life.'

'What I want to create,' Petrov told Hanson and himself, 'is equality given a cutting edge by initiative. Is that contradictory?'

'Impracticable,' Hanson said.

'Why don't you stay and see if I can make it work?'

'I want to go back to Britain first.'

'Why?'

'To see if I was right all those years ago.'

'It matters where you were born?'

'Only circumstance matters,' Hanson said. 'Don't you understand that?'

'I had a goat, a kid, called Misha once. Misha changed the face of the Soviet Union, possibly the world.'

'Some goat,' Hanson said.

One of the cream phones on the desk, part of the exclusive *vertushka* system, rang. Petrov answered it. A reminder of a Politburo meeting in ten minutes.

Replacing the receiver, Petrov said: 'Will you come back?'

'This is my home.'

'You have a politician's gift for not answering a question. But I accept it.'

'Accept it?' Hanson buttoned the jacket of his check suit that must have been fashionably cut a quarter of a century ago. 'What do you mean, accept it?'

'I have a proposition.' And, almost shyly, Petrov explained that he wanted Hanson to assess the popular view of Tsar Viktor Petrov. What better place than a banya?

'You mean you don't know? What about the demonstration in Red Square yesterday? They didn't seem mad about the Party – or you for that matter.'

'A chant is infectious. If it wasn't for me they wouldn't have been able to demonstrate. I want to know what people really think. And you can find out.'

'Oh I can find out all right,' Hanson said.

'I want you to report to me privately at my dacha.'

'You'll have to send a Zil – my car's off the road.'

'You shall have a Zil.'

'And then?'

'You will get your exit visa.'

'Supposing the British won't have me?'

'They'll have you,' Petrov said. 'The British ambassador is a most reasonable man.'

'I get the visa even if the patrons of the banya vote against you?'

'Even if they want to lynch me.'

The cream phone rang again. Five minutes.

'You'll have to excuse me,' Petrov said. 'I have to meet some people whose views I value rather less than those of the patrons of the banya.'

In their bolt-hole apartment not far from the Tass building Viktor Petrov and his wife watched television. A programme live on Channel One from Moscow's Yaroslavsky railway station about the old and elegant Eastern Express that had been wheeled out of retirement to make a journey from Paris to Hong Kong via Berlin, Warsaw, Moscow, Novosibirsk, Irkutsk, Harbin and Beijing.

Viktor, arm round Natalia's shoulders, watched enthralled as the dark blue wagon-lits lettered in bronze regally drew to a halt at the platform. Candle-lit tables, gold silk curtains . . . a conductor, red bag slung over his shoulder, peaked cap perched meticulously on his head, strode past the restaurant car. . . .

Petrov touched his wife's cheek; she knew how he loved trains. Anything from Cherepanov's 1834 steam engine to the Class E locomotives of his childhood and the electrified serpents that now nosed across Siberia.

Petrov nodded at the screen. 'That has just been hauled through Byelorussia by an old P-36.'

'Fascinating,' Natalia said and pressed his hand against her cheek. He wished he could spend more time with her, the prerogative of most sixty-year-old husbands. Resignation, retirement? Soon, perhaps, but first he had to know what the people scavaging in denuded stores really thought about him.

Natalia leaned forward abruptly and pointed at the television. 'Look.' The reception committee on the platform were looking too – at a sturdy figure with a drum-belly parting their ranks

337

with a pie stall. The cameras swung away from the dignitaries, from the conductor and his aristocratic coaches to favour the vendor and stall. On the front of the stall hung what looked like a folded white sheet bearing the words SAVE OUR BANYA.

Where had he seen that before? Natalia jumped to her feet and began to talk rapidly and not altogether coherently. Something about a deputation of women she had agreed to meet. She paused. 'Viktor Petrov, man of the people? I have this great idea,' she said.

To assess the patrons' view of their President Hanson enlisted an accomplice, Michael Cooper, and made his move at a meeting of both sexes, held in the men's changing-room, to debate the stallholder's television appearance and subsequent imprisonment in Petrovka police headquarters.

Michael made the running. 'It's difficult to see how they can hold him for long,' he told the joint committee sitting at the trestle table in the well of the unheated chamber. 'What crime has he committed?'

'The crime of stupidity,' the laundress said.

'Trespass perhaps? I understand he knew one of the railway officials who let him onto the platform.'

'I wonder what the bribe was,' the laundress said, addressing patrons sitting shoulder to shoulder on the tiers of benches. 'One of his pies? I can think of only one bribe that would have less effect – two of his pies.'

'And, perhaps, incitement,' Michael said. 'He's already on militia records after the episode in Red Square.'

'We had it all worked out,' the laundress said. 'Didn't we?' to the seamstress. 'An audience with the President's wife and the banya would have been saved. Instead this big fool makes an even bigger fool of himself and turns our campaign into a farce. Will she see us now?'

Hanson struck. 'Why don't we go to the President himself?'

'Because we want to speak woman to woman.'

Hanson glanced at Michael Cooper who responded intelligently. 'The President is surely the person to see. The creator of *glasnost*. Is this freedom, the arbitrary demolition of the banya?'

No, they growled from the benches.

Hanson said: 'Let's have a vote.' The patrons regarded him uneasily, this long-serving interloper who until now had closeted his opinions with his treachery. 'First, do we believe in the President?'

Silence. A drop of condensation from the ceiling splashed on the table.

The seamstress said: 'Of course we do.'

Michael Cooper made a witness of her. 'How can you speak for everyone? Has *perestroika* brought you more food, more fuel, a better standard of living?'

'All *perestroika* has brought,' the Ukrainian miner said, 'is hardship.'

'You see,' Michael said to the seamstress, 'you do not speak for everyone.'

Hanson, whose voice had acquired an uncharacteristic resonance, said: '*Perestroika* may have brought hardship but that doesn't mean its author hasn't done his best for us, does it?'

'I think he's a good man,' the pickpocket ventured.

'No one asked for your opinion,' the bodybuilder said.

The pickpocket regarded him thoughtfully, hands unmoving in his lap.

Said the Kremlin driver: 'He has given us the right to speak our minds. When did we last have that, if ever?'

Said the Lithuanian: 'He hasn't given my people any rights.'

'Wrong,' said the chauffeur in the tone of muted triumph he had acquired since the confrontation with Vilkin. 'He has given you the right to decide your own destiny.'

'And if we choose to split with Moscow?'

'Then it will have to be done constitutionally.' The chauffeur's shoulder blades moved beneath his jacket.

Michael turned to the laundress. 'And your opinion of your Executive President?'

'Good for business.' No one laughed. 'I think he is . . . sincere.'

'Let's put it to the vote,' Hanson said. 'Then we can decide who the delegation should see. Perhaps the President *and* his wife.' He smiled deviously at the women members of the committee.

Michael raised his hands to quieten non-existent protest. 'Do you realise that if it wasn't for the President we wouldn't even be able to have a vote?' He lowered his hands. 'So what is the motion?'

Hanson said: 'That this meeting trusts the President. Those in favour raise their hands.'

After the vote Hanson called the telephone number Petrov had given him from a call box down the street. How apt, he thought, if the Kremlin chauffeur had to drive him to the President's dacha.

25

The pickpocket broke his word the following morning. He had sworn that he would never steal from those who patronised the banya but adversity can make a cracked bell out of the soundest of oaths. Police were waging a relentless campaign against pickpockets on the metro and he was finding it increasingly difficult to support his wife, son and ailing father. Who better to supplement his diminished earnings than the bodybuilder who had belittled him in front of a mass meeting of patrons?

He waited until the early shift was taking the steam, dispatched the aged attendant to buy a jug of beer and turned his attention to the bodybuilder's black leather jacket suspended from a wire hanger. What he hoped to find was hard currency – the bodybuilder seemed to have no difficulty in buying meat for his dogs – or some commodity that he could sell for such currency.

Hands writhing, he approached the jacket as though it clothed the bodybuilder. A thoroughly professional foray, none of the furtiveness that betrays the amateur. Hand into one pocket. Empty. A second approach from the other side of the rack. He removed the wallet – as the bodybuilder and Michael Cooper emerged from the steam-room.

Despite the sudden sharp pain in his chest, the pickpocket still behaved professionally. Wallet spirited into a pocket of his own imitation leather jacket, distancing himself from the hangers with an imperceptible lengthening of his stride. The bodybuilder, as usual, scarcely acknowledged his presence.

Out through the door as the bewildered attendant returned with the beer, into the street. What now? If the bodybuilder missed his wallet he would immediately suspect him. The pickpocket imagined the play of the bodybuilder's muscles as he moved in for the kill. If he doesn't immediately miss it then I might be able to leave it somewhere in the changing-room; then find it and earn his undying gratitude! At the moment there was only one course of action open: to leg it as fast as possible away from the banya.

He made his way to Petrovsky Boulevard, found an empty bench and flipped through the wallet, frowning like a man who has lost a prize-winning certificate for his lottery bond. Internal passport containing the dark blue *propiska* stamp, assorted ID, registration numbers for his dogs, telephone numbers of butchers – what did they receive in exchange for meat? – health club membership, photograph of a girl staring at the camera with such resentment that she was almost cross-eyed and a silver crucifix. No money, nothing incriminating, nothing to sell. Not yet. The pickpocket's trained fingers squeezed the plastic envelope containing the passport. Thicker than it should have been. The pickpocket's breathing quickened.

He eased the passport from the plastic. Stared for a few moments at what lay beneath. Then walked rapidly to a telephone kiosk on the boulevard and called the banya. Was the bodybuilder there? No, said the attendant, he had left fifteen minutes earlier. With the American.

The pickpocket hurried back to the banya. There he cornered the Kremlin chauffeur. Where had the bodybuilder and Michael Cooper gone? To the wolf-dog compound, the chauffeur told him. Why was he so anxious to know?

'Because,' said the pickpocket, 'the American may be in great danger.'

'Are you sure?' Michael asked as the Volga skidded round a corner on the outskirts of the city.

'Quite sure,' the bodybuilder said. 'The old man kept another bag in the gun-room. There were letters in it, green with mould, gnawed by rats, but decipherable in places. Two of them were signed *Vasily*. . . .'

'Did you read them?'

'Bits here and there. I'm sure you'll find plenty of clues.'

Snow flew at the windscreen. Excitement fraught with imponderables settled upon Michael.

The Volga headed into the snow covered countryside.

Michael said: 'Supposing I get picked up by the police. The compound is outside the limit.' It hadn't occurred to him before.

'You won't get picked up. Not with my registration. Just try and look like a Russian.'

'I don't?'

'You look like an American.'

'Is that so bad?'

'Not so bad. Everyone envies Americans. We even did in the days when we were supposed to despise you.'

'Are you envious?'

'Not me. I am. . . .' He frowned, searching for the word. 'Fulfilled?'

A police car approached from the opposite direction. Michael did his best to look Russian. The police car zipped past, driver as cavalier in his attitude to the perilous road surface as the bodybuilder.

The snow began to fall more heavily.

The Kremlin chauffeur drove, the Ukrainian miner who owned the punished Zhiguli beside him, pickpocket in the back. The chauffeur occasionally compared the little car with the majestic Zils and Chaikas to which he was accustomed but he drove with great panache, cutting up more staidly handled vehicles and making swashbuckling left turns long before the blue and white signs authorising them.

As the suburbs thinned the miner turned to the pickpocket. 'Are you quite sure?'

'That the American's in danger? I don't know for sure. But there have been two attempts on his life.'

'Both a long way from Moscow.'

The chauffeur, shooting a red light, spoke magisterially. 'Consider the evidence. He,' indicating the pickpocket, 'found a folded sheet of paper on which were written details of the American's movements – his journeys to Siberia and Murmansk – his hotel room and the telephone number and address of the

Intourist girl. Beneath that, beneath his internal passport, his KGB card.'

'So he's the informer,' the miner said. 'There's always one, isn't there. I never liked the bastard. . . .'

'But why should anyone want to kill the American?' the pickpocket ventured.

'Perhaps,' suggested the chauffeur, 'his brother wants him dead.' He spoke with the tentative authority of one who will recall a statement as fact if his supposition proves to be true.

'Why would he want to do that?' the miner demanded but the chauffeur was through dispensing wisdom.

'Do you think we'll get there in time?' the pickpocket asked.

Without answering the chauffeur took to the centre of the road as though he were at the wheel of a Kremlin limousine.

Michael heard the wolf-dogs barking a kilometre or so from the compound. As the Volga slewed onto the vacant ground outside they hurled themselves at the chain-link fencing and Sasha, the Carpathian wolfhound, jumped higher than any of them.

The bodybuilder took the leather cane from the backseat and unlocked the gate. The wolf-dogs came at him, hesitated, paused slavering. All except Sasha who advanced cautiously. The bodybuilder cracked him across the muzzle, then across the back. Sasha subsided.

'They're starving,' Michael said. 'Aren't you going to feed them?'

'They can wait. If I feed them as soon as I arrive they don't appreciate me.'

He led the way to the hut where they had sheltered from the blizzard, took an unlabelled bottle of vodka and placed it on the table beside a single glass.

'Aren't you going to drink?'

'You're the one who's going to need a drink.' The bodybuilder reached into a gunny bag and produced a long-barrelled pistol. Resting one elbow on the arm of his cane chair, he aimed it at Michael. 'I want to tell you a story,' he said. 'Setting Moscow. Date, October 16th, 1941.'

344

It was not a story of communal heroism. Nor was it a tale of cowardice. More an account of public bewilderment that found an outlet in humanity's instinct for survival.

It began on the morning of the sixteenth with the publication of an official communiqué: *During the night of October 14th–15th the position on the Western Front became worse. The German-Fascist troops hurled against our troops large quantities of tanks and motorised infantry, and in one sector broke through our defences.*

Although they knew that diplomats and Party officials had been evacuated, although they were busy digging trenches inside and outside the city, this was the first time that the people of Moscow had been told categorically that their lives were in peril.

Tens of thousands fled. While untrained Siberians were thrown into battle, while amateur soldiers hurled home-made petrol bombs at tanks, while pilots, resorting to suicide, rammed German aircraft in mid-air, refugees streamed eastwards by road and rail.

Railway stations were beseiged; roads were jammed with official limousines, trucks, horse-drawn carts and pedestrians. Public transport inside the city seized up, shops were looted, the police vanished from the streets.

Among those who witnessed this unseemly behaviour was a young member of the Communist Battalions poised uneasily between adolescence and manhood. His name was Vasily Vysotsky.

He was a crack shot and, as such, had been allowed to leave his bench at a munitions factory and fight with the civilian volunteers. He was courting a girl named Yelena Orlova whose father was a photographer and he was intensely patriotic.

On the day of the great exodus Vasily and a few hundred young members of the Communist Battalions were ordered to plug a gap in the Soviet lines in the Volokolamsk sector eighty kilometres north-west of Moscow.

There they came under intense fire. Untrained and uneducated in the manner of dying with fortitude, and having observed their elders in Moscow practising the art of survival (this was Michael Cooper's interpretaion of what the bodybuilder told him) they turned and ran – into the guns of NKVD troops strategically positioned to deter deserters.

Fourteen were killed. The bodybuilder took a document from the gunny bag and tossed it on the table. Michael picked it up. It was Vasily's death certificate.

A terrible satisfaction settled upon Michael. A crusade fulfilled with the discovery of a crucifixion.

Silence strummed in his ears. Outside the hut the wolf-dogs cried; water dripped from icicles at the window.

The bodybuilder brandished the pistol. 'So, you see, your brother was a coward. A pity you refused to give up the search for someone of such little worth. A pity you have to die too.'

'He wasn't a coward,' Michael said. 'He was young, that was his crime. He followed the example of his elders. . . .'

'He didn't matter,' the bodybuilder said. 'That was all. You do.'

'Why?' Knowledge of his brother's premature death had made Michael curiously fatalistic.

'Do you think the Kremlin wants details of October 16th broadcast all over the world? The Battle of Moscow was supposed to be a heroic defence.'

'Historians know about the panic that day. They also know that it was a minor transgression compared with the overall heroism of the Soviet people.' But it did explain the blank spaces in *Red Star* on the 17th, Michael thought.

'Does the general public know?'

'It doesn't matter,' Michael said. 'All that mattered was the final outcome of the war. Okay, so you're going to kill me. Why?'

The bodybuilder stared at the barrel of the pistol as though it were smoking.

He said: 'I believe you have an expression – opening up a can of worms.'

'We make a habit of opening them,' Michael said.

He wondered if there was any point in lunging for the pistol. In bad movies perhaps but not in life.

'The worms in the can you have insisted on opening are very . . . poisonous.' With his free hand he smoothed his dark, oiled hair. 'You see the NKVD officer who ordered his men to shoot those young members of the Communist Battalions is now a highly respected member of the Kremlin hierarchy.'

'KGB, successors to the NKVD?'

'It doesn't matter what he is.'

'If you're going to kill me it matters.'

'What matters is that his involvement must not be revealed. Bad news, NKVD slaughtering patriotic young Russians. Especially as it is about to be revealed that it *was* the NKVD who massacred the Poles at Katyn. Who wants another scandal? Russians murdered by Russians?' He waved his pistol despairingly.

'Politburo?'

'Let's just say a member of the Old Guard who doesn't want corpses exhumed. Leave it at that. You shouldn't have tried to dig one up,' the bodybuilder said pleasantly. 'You should have realised you were digging your own grave.'

'Get it over with then,' Michael said, deciding to make a fight of it.

'Your wife has returned to America?'

'Yesterday.'

'That's fortunate; that only leaves Magda.'

'What do you know about Magda?'

'I know everything about Magda,' the bodybuilder said. 'Now let's go outside. The dogs are very hungry. One shot between the eyes and they will feed off your body and no one will ever know how you really died. Make a fight of it here and I will wound you and they will smell your blood and feed off you while you're still alive.

The miner said: 'I can hear the dogs.' He reached into the glove compartment of the Zhiguli and took out a pistol.

The chauffeur made a slithering turn round a sharp-angled bend and aimed the little car towards the compound.

The pickpocket knitted his fingers together and kept them tightly clasped.

*

347

The bodybuilder led Michael out of the hut at gun-point. The wolf-dogs, jowels dripping with saliva, Sasha at their head, watched them.

'Beautiful animals,' the bodybuilder said.

'Haven't you forgotten something?'

'The last sacrament?'

'Your cane.'

Sasha leaped as the bodybuilder glanced at his hand grasping the pistol instead of the cane. The rest of the pack followed, snapping, biting, ripping.

The bodybuilder fell under their weight and lay in the snow staring at Michael as they began to devour his cultivated muscles.

Michael took the pistol from his outstretched hand, aimed the barrel at his head and pulled the trigger. The wolf-dogs paused for a moment, then continued their long-overdue feed.

Still holding the pistol, Michael walked to the gate as the Zhiguli skidded to a halt and the patrons of the banya piled out.

He stood at the window of Magda's apartment staring at the illuminated Ostanko TV tower.

'So it's over,' he said.

Standing behind him, she slipped an arm round his waist. 'You can stay longer. . . .'

'No point.' He turned. 'Were you involved?'

'What's sad,' she said, 'is that you have to ask.'

'Were you?'

She shook her head slowly and wearily.

'Will you come to New York?'

'Perhaps one day – when I've sorted out the future of Ukraine.'

'Not *the* Ukraine.' He bent and kissed her. 'I'll show you around; I'm a good courier.'

He let himself out of the apartment. In the street he looked up and saw her silhouetted in the window. She waved once, then the light went out and she was lost. As though she had never been there, he thought.

26

March 8th. Women's Day. All over the Soviet Union women were venerated. Speeches were made in their honour in the Kremlin; articles were published in the Press promising them equality with men; their menfolk cooked indigestible meals, washed the dishes and gave them bunches of mimosa and carnations bought at extortionate prices from Georgian flower sellers. On this day the lot of women was much as Lenin had envisaged it; on the other 364 days of the year it wasn't so cosy.

The Fighting Comrades wore carnations on the breasts of their brown uniforms but at the banya the atmosphere was less harmonious than it was elsewhere in the land. A tracked vehicle bearing aloft an immense steel ball suspended on a chain had arrived and with it Vilkin.

Watched by patrons of both sexes, the laundress folded her arms across her bosom, endangering the white carnation given to her by her husband whose feats of sloth and intemperance were legendary in the womens' changing-room. 'You can't touch the banya,' she told Vilkin. 'We have been granted an audience with the wife of the Executive President of the Soviet Union.'

Vilkin patted his penny-black moustache with one finger; the gesture of someone who knows a thing or two. 'You applied for an audience; you have not been granted one. I have the written authority of the Minister of Planning to demolish the banya.' He produced a document from the inside pocket of his Kremlin-style overcoat.

The Kremlin chauffeur, authority only marginally impaired by the terrible scene at the wolf-dog compound, beckoned Vilkin to one side. 'The son of that surveyor you mentioned. . . . Has he now got a job in your department?'

'He's working in Leningrad. There has been no question of favours.' *As if I would have allowed such partiality.*

'Didn't you say on that cassette, "Have you ever had your feet in wet concrete, comrade?" '

'I told the Minister about that. He thought it a most appropriate fate. A great sense of humour, the minister.'

They were joined by the laundress. 'So you're going down in history as a mass murderer?' she said to Vilkin.

'I don't understand,' said Vilkin who manifestly did.

'Knock the walls down and everyone inside will be crushed to death.'

'But I am very concerned about everyone's safety: there will be no one inside the banya.' He pointed at uniformed militia barring the doors to the two changing-rooms.

A mini-bus stopped outside the banya and a squad of demolition workers wearing hard hats climbed out. The operators of the ball and chain and the bulldozer climbed into their seats.

The black Zil drove up as Vilkin picked up a hailer to order them to begin their work of destruction. From the back climbed Viktor Petrov and his wife. Vilkin lowered the hailer.

'So this is the famous banya,' Petrov said. He wore a topcoat similar to Vilkin's and his FBI hat. 'May we go inside?'

'Of course, Comrade President.' Vilkin dismissed the militia, the interlopers.

A convoy of automobiles drew up disgorging reporters and cameramen from Press, TV and radio. Cameras whirred. Vilkin blinked at them. The laundress thrust her medals towards them. The chauffeur inclined his head in the manner of a man whose covert strategies have come predictably to fruititon.

A few patrons glanced knowingly at Natalia Petrov. It was, after all, Women's Day, and her flair for recognising good publicity had not passed unnoticed.

The chauffeur bowed, permitting himself an urbane smile. 'Which changing-room would you prefer, Comrade President?'

Natalia Petrov replied. 'On this day of days? What do you think?'

The chauffeur gave his smile a little more licence: that had been his feeling too.

The seamstress switched on the fountain; the hairdresser attended to the samovar; the dressmaker and Tanya Agursky arranged the chairs. The media crowded in.

Petrov said: 'So where is the owner of the pie stall?'

The chauffeur left this one to someone else.

'He's in police custody,' Michael Cooper said.

'So you're the American I've been reading about. . . . Have you traced your brother?'

'He's dead, Comrade President.'

'I'm sorry.' And looked as though he genuinely was. 'Will you go back to America?'

'I have to go back.'

Petrov studied the patrons, all still standing. He raised one hand. 'Good to see you, Comrade Hanson.'

The others looked puzzled.

Finally Petrov and his wife sat down.

'A cause such as yours,' said Petrov, taking off his hat and placing it among the microphones and recorders on the table, 'must surely have a committee. Maybe two,' knowingly. 'Why don't you all sit down. And you, Comrade Vilkin.'

The hairdresser served tea.

Natalia sipped hers, indicated that it was to her liking and addressed the women. 'I am touched that you asked to see me. I think we should now hear your reasons for wanting the banya preserved. And then the views of the men?' She looked questioningly at her husband who nodded benevolently.

The laundress spoke forcibly about heritage and history. Hadn't Lenin once used these very baths?

The chauffeur echoed her views adding, with the intimacy of one who might once have driven the President: 'The banya is a forum of debate; here we debate *perestroika*.'

Petrov, theatrically raising one eyebrow, said: 'I used to patronise a banya. . . .' He turned to Vilkin. 'Your views, comrade?'

Vilkin was at his most reasonable. He had, sadly, inherited many decisions made during the inflexible, pre-*glasnost* era. He agreed most fervently with the speakers' views and hoped that this would be the opportunity to illustrate that *perestroika* could undo the knots tied by the intractable bureaucrats of old.

Petrov placed his stubby hands on either side of his hat.

351

'Then there is nothing more to be said. I will see the minister later today. You may continue to take the steam – and debate *perestroika*.' He looked quizzically at the chauffeur.

Prolonged applause. The cameras whirred and panned.

The laundress cleared her throat, directed her words at the President's wife. As it was Women's Day, adjusting her carnation, there were a couple more points she would like to make. She explained the ban imposed on her at GUM.

Natalia thought that could be negotiated. The other point?

The laundress told her about Tanya Agursky and the intransigence of the Olympic Selection Committee.

'Where is she?' Natalia Petrov scanned the crowd. Tanya was pushed to the forefront. 'Are you good enough to represent your country?'

Tanya said she thought she might be.

'So why can't you train with the other contestants?'

The laundress answered for Tanya. 'Because she's Jewish.'

Petrov stood up. 'Is this true?'

Tanya told him about her father.

Petrov had heard of him, he said. He paused, pointed one finger at the cameras. 'I never want to hear any suggestion of anti-Semitism in this country of ours. Is that understood? There is only one criterion and that is merit,' he said to the invisible Olympic Selection Committee.

Another outburst of clapping.

Tanya, lips trembling, said: 'Forgive me, but what about my father?'

'Tell him to apply for his emigration papers to Israel tomorrow.'

Natalia Petrov said to the chauffeur: 'I'm sure you have another request.'

Said her husband: 'You needn't bother – the pieman will be free by this afternoon. Is there anything else?'

The chauffeur hesitated professionally. 'Would the President honour us by taking the steam here one day?'

The President would.

Outside a banner that comprehensively covered the wall of the banya had miraculously appeared. It proclaimed REPRIEVED BY VIKTOR PETROV. As the bulldozer and the vehicle carrying the ball and chain trundled away, as the hard-hatted demolition workers piled into their mini-bus, the photographers focussed their cameras on the banner rippling in the breeze.

Said Vilkin, nodding at Petrov: 'A true man of the people.'

The laundress looked at Vilkin speculatively. She had, she said, obtained a dozen bars of perfumed soap manufactured in Helsinki. Would he be interested?

Dinner at the Agurskys was a spirited occasion because Petrov's exercise in PR had been on television, prime time, including the invitation to Tanya's father to apply for his exit visa the following day.

'Clever,' he said, swallowing chopped liver. 'An astute politician, no one can deny that.'

'With an astute wife,' Tanya's mother said.

'So I don't have an astute wife? Even now I know what you're thinking. . . .'

Tanya said: 'What is she thinking?'

'That I've lost my platform.'

'She's right. You're free to go to Israel. What you've always wanted.'

He applied himself to his liver. When he lowered his head Tanya could see the healing angles of the Star of David on his bald patch.

He said: 'Thousands of Russian Jews are leaving for the Promised Land. So many that Israel will soon be Russian. . . .'

His astute wife said: 'So you don't want to go anymore?'

'I am a campaigner,' he said. 'What would I be without a campaign?'

'We're staying?'

'We have to fight. We Jews always have to fight.'

'So what are we fighting now?' his wife asked patiently.

'*Pamyat*, of course. Anti-Semitism. One day,' he said, embracing the whole world with his eloquent hands, 'we will win.' He applied himself to his liver.

His wife, sighing with exasperated devotion, said to Tanya: 'But you lead your own life. Soon you will be famous, an Olympic star. You and Yury will conquer the world. . . .'

353

Tanya, briefly glimpsing a past that was recklessly detaching itself from the present, said: 'Lazar and me.'

Napkins to their lips, the Agurskys regarded each other with inscrutable familiarity.

In Leonid Lysenko's apartment the children were playing up and his wife was laying the table with controlled fury. Who could blame her? The neighbours, employing some undisclosed brand of *blat*, had obtained an apartment in a new block. Worse, the block could be seen from the window of their own cell; no doubt the departing neighbours would wave to them from time to time.

The coveted telephone rang. A well remembered voice. 'Pushkin Embankment, by the landing-stage in half an hour.'

Standing up, Lysenko said he would have to forego lunch.

'All the more for us,' his wife said, dealing three plates.

Lysenko caught the metro to Gorky Park and made his way to the landing-stage from which ferry boats sailed in summer. The man with the crumpled features was staring across the numbed river.

He said: 'Have you made up your mind?'

'You've brought the money?'

He took an envelope from the pocket of his expensive coat with the astrakhan collar. 'Dollars.'

Lysenko took the envelope. 'Who do I have to kill?' When he knew he stood still for a moment listening to the ice creaking on the river.

Then he said: 'When?'

'Today.' And he told him where and how.

'One more question,' Lysenko said. 'Why?'

'Because he has betrayed us.' He turned and walked along the embankment in the direction of Krimsky Bridge, sealskin boots slipping a little on the scallops of hard snow.

Not far away, beside an empty bandstand in Gorky Park which abuts the embankment, two men embarked on a conversation that was not dissimilar.

'Empty parks were always favourite settings for espionage,' Mayhew said, popping a stale-looking toffee into his mouth. 'In the days, that is, when it was a respectable profession.'

The East German looked at him curiously. 'What do you want?' Despite the cold he was hatless and a breeze tripping in from the river blew his fair hair across his untroubled forehead.

'A deal, lad.'

'I'm not in a position to do any deals.' The East German spoke English with a pleasant accent. 'I have nothing to offer.'

'Nothing to hide?' They walked ruminatively, heads down, towards the hibernating ferris wheel. 'I understand you want to return to East Germany. To your family, your girlfriend.'

'What gave you that idea?'

'I hear things, lad. I hear things.' He unrolled another toffee wrapped in shiny mauve paper. 'I have certain connections.'

'You're involved with the KGB?' The East German stopped and stared incredulous at Mayhew. 'You were a *real* defector?'

'I had my moments. Trade mission to Soviet Union . . . privy to classified information . . . . What the buggers overlooked were my contacts at the Foreign Office. . . .'

'Middle-man?'

'In a manner of speaking. But I knew the game would be up one day so I decided to get out in time. Settle at the fount of my convictions. How about that? You see I believed, I really did. Which is why we're going to do a deal, you and I.'

'I don't see what sort of deal we could possibly do.' The East German stared at the cabins of the ferris wheel lodged in the sky.

'You were a member of the *Stasi*, the German Democratic Republic secret police. Don't bother to deny it.' He held up one hand and released the mauve toffee paper which fluttered away like an out-of-season butterfly. 'I know lad. I *know*. And you came to Moscow for consultations with your true lords and masters – and to wait and see which way the wind blew in your country. Well now you know – the *Stasi* are marked men.'

The East German regarded Mayhew thoughtfully, his expression no longer untroubled. 'So?'

'Not many people in East Germany know what you were up to so you can go back, marry your girl, and make your name –

movie star, perhaps? – in a united and prosperous Germany. Unless. . . . '

'What sort of deal had you in mind?'

'I wasn't the only one who truly believed, you know. To hell with democracy, we thought. Left wing, right wing, it didn't matter a damn – materialism ruled. So with Stalin long dead we decamped to Russia where something called 'ideals' was once forged.'

'What's the deal?' the East German asked impatiently.

'But those ideals were flawed, weren't they. Stood no chance against human nature. And now the buggers are reverting to what we fled from. Pitiful, isn't it.'

'If you say so.'

'And Robert Hanson is going to get his visa to return to Britain. I happen to know. . . . '

'. . . .You hear things.'

'And he will tell the world what a pathetic bunch we are. Ostracised by our own kind, barely tolerated by our hosts, feeding off ourselves. . . . You know Robert Hanson?'

'Of course. I'm supposed to kill him.'

Mayhew held his arm. 'See to it, lad.' He unwrapped another toffee and together they watched the paper, blue this time, flutter towards the ferris wheel. 'And get yourself a real gun.'

The Zil, as augustly funereal as a hearse, drew up outside the apartment house at 3 p.m. Observing it from the window, Hanson turned to Lena. 'How do you like being married to a VIP?'

Lena, whose life had not prepared her for such pretension, spread her hands helplessly. 'After this you will really be able to go home?'

'This is home.'

'You mean that?'

Discovering to his surprise that he might, Hanson held her shoulders, feeling their sharp angles, and kissed her. Then, smiling, he put on his movie hat, J. Edgar Hoover vintage, and walked out of the apartment.

The Zil, a phlegmatic colleague of the Kremlin chauffeur at the wheel, proceeded majestically towards Petrov's dacha. As it left the suburbs behind the stranger made a transient appearance in one of the wing mirrors.

Hanson regarded him quizzically. *'So how's this for style?'*

'To the manor born.'

'If only I had known to which manor.'

The stranger tapped his patrician nose and vanished.

The driver parked the Zil next to an identical model in Petrov's drive. Petrov ushered Hanson into his study where snacks had been laid out beside frosted bottles of vodka and Narzan mineral water.

They each drank a shot of vodka, doused it with Narzan and ate gherkins and dark bread.

'So what did you think about the banya?' Petrov asked.

'Superb public relations,' Hanson said.

'My wife's idea. What is more important is the way the people who use the banya felt before Women's Day.'

Hanson spread red caviar on a finger of toast.

'Well?'

Hanson licked caviar from his lips. 'Twenty-four votes against,' he said.

'And for?'

'Twenty-four,' Hanson said.

The assassin nestled in a copse of birch trees thirty miles from the intersection where the approach road to Petrov's dacha joined the main highway to Moscow. Dusk would soon be settling but the sky was clear and the target would be precisely silhouetted in the back of the Zil. With luck the interior light might even be switched on. A bird took off from the summit of the birch trees showering him with snow. He dabbed some from the barrel of the rifle and adjusted his wool mask. His motorcycle lay hidden beside the highway.

In another birch wood, in Sokolniki Park, Joe Palmer, shooting the last takes of *Thriller* on location, fumed happily about the unreliability of his cast. Here he was poised for the climax in

which either the President of the USSR or the USA was assassinated – you could hear the audience debating which had died as
the credits rolled – and neither the assassin, the East German,
nor the American President, Robert Hanson, was present.

'Wouldn't you know it,' he agonised, spreading wide his
arms to his dutiful team. 'Never give anyone a break if you value
your front teeth. You,' to Penrose, 'take over from Hanson.' He
tossed him a snap-brimmed hat with a black band. 'And you,'
to the seaman, 'lie down over there,' pointing at a hollow
beneath the birches, 'and look like you want to kill someone.'
He tossed him the replica of the Dragunov SVD, a peaked cap
and a face mask.

'Where is Albert?' the West German widow asked.

'Search me,' Joe Palmer said.

'Where's the Mex?'

'I'm here,' said the Mexican clinging onto the arm of the
assistant producer, her husband.

'Okay,' Palmer said, 'let's move it.' He dispatched Penrose
to a stretch of snowy pasture where he would be silhouetted
against the sky; arranged the seaman behind his fake rifle. 'I'm
going to shoot this a little out of focus,' he told the seaman, 'so
no one realises you're a stand-in. It's been done a million
times. . . .' The seaman peered through the telescopic sight
and stroked the trigger with one finger.

Petrov and Hanson stood between the two Zils in the drive.
They shook hands, a tight grip, then walked to their respective
limousines.

It was perfect. A light in the back of the Zil, hat still firmly
clamped on his head. He got him nicely centred in the sight,
stayed with him for fifty metres or so, held his breath, pulled
the trigger with gentle persuasion.

*

358

The body of Robert Hanson lay in a red-draped, open coffin in Donskoi Monastery prior to cremation. And the Twilight Brigade were there in force as they always were at times of depletion.

What occupied them as much as the mourning was the debate about the manner of his death which had been as enigmatic as his life. A self-inflicted gunshot wound, according to police. Had his application to return to Britain finally been turned down?

The demeanour of his widow also aroused comment. Fatalistic calm rather than grief. But who could tell? Hanson had always been unfathomable, never quite one of the gang, and she might have acquired some of his characteristics.

Such a pity that he had never been able to go home.

Mayhew, sucking a peppermint, took the East German aside. 'Well done,' he whispered. 'We couldn't let him go back. . . .'

The East German stared at Mayhew. 'But I didn't shoot him,' he said. 'I was waiting further down the highway.'

Frowning, they returned to the coffin and stared down at Hanson's alabaster features. 'Odd,' remarked Mayhew. 'He looks different.' He peered closer. 'The authoritative nose, the mouth, the style of his hair. . . . Why, he looks positively smug.'

Mayhew crunched his peppermint.

From his seat in the New York-bound jet Michael Cooper gazed down at Moscow and tried hopelessly to pick out the banya. Then the jet pierced the cloud-base and Moscow was gone. Lowering his head, he placed his hands to his face; faintly he smelled eucalyptus.

Far below, Viktor Petrov donned a sheet and strode into the steam-room. He stayed for a few moments on the bottom tier, then climbed to the top where the heat was at its most intense. He would, he decided, stay there as long as he could bear it.